SHADOWS OF CARCOSA

Tales of Cosmic Horror

Selected by

D. THIN

NEW YORK REVIEW BOOKS

nyrb

New York

THIS IS A NEW YORK REVIEW BOOK
PUBLISHED BY THE NEW YORK REVIEW OF BOOKS
207 East 32nd Street, New York, NY 10016
www.nyrb.com

D. Thin would like to thank Richard Buchsbaum, Michael Dirda, John Gray, Stephen King, Fred Murphy, Geoffrey O'Brien, and Richard Price for assistance in making this selection.

Library of Congress Cataloging-in-Publication Data
Shadows of Carcosa : tales of cosmic horror / selected by D. Thin.
pages cm. — (New York Review Books Classics)
Original title: The Colour out of space: tales of cosmic horror
ISBN 978-1-59017-943-7 (paperback)
1. Horror tales, American. 2. Horror tales, English. I. Thin, D. (Douglas) editor.
PS648.H6C655 2015
813'.0873808—dc23

ISBN 978-1-59017-943-7
Available as an electronic book; ISBN 978-1-59017-873-7

Book design by Lizzie Scott
Printed in the United States of America on acid-free paper.
10 9 8 7 6 5

CONTENTS

EDGAR ALLAN POE

MS. FOUND IN A BOTTLE

Qui n'a plus qu'un moment à vivre
N'a plus rien à dissimuler.

QUINAULT—*ATYS*

OF MY COUNTRY and of my family I have little to say. Ill usage and length of years have driven me from the one, and estranged me from the other. Hereditary wealth afforded me an education of no common order, and a contemplative turn of mind enabled me to methodize the stores which early study very diligently garnered up. —Beyond all things, the study of the German moralists gave me great delight; not from any ill-advised admiration of their eloquent madness, but from the ease with which my habits of rigid thought enabled me to detect their falsities. I have often been reproached with the aridity of my genius; a deficiency of imagination has been imputed to me as a crime; and the Pyrrhonism of my opinions has at all times rendered me notorious. Indeed, a strong relish for physical philosophy has, I fear, tinctured my mind with a very common error of this age—I mean the habit of referring occurrences, even the least susceptible of such reference, to the principles of that science. Upon the whole, no person could be less liable than myself to be led away from the severe precincts of truth by the *ignes fatui* of superstition. I have thought proper to premise thus much, lest the incredible tale I have to tell should be considered rather the raving of a crude imagination, than the positive experience of a mind to which the reveries of fancy have been a dead letter and a nullity.

After many years spent in foreign travel, I sailed in the year 18—, from the port of Batavia, in the rich and populous island of Java, on a voyage to the Archipelago of the Sunda islands. I went as passenger—having no other inducement than a kind of nervous restlessness which haunted me as a fiend.

Our vessel was a beautiful ship of about four hundred tons, copper-fastened, and built at Bombay of Malabar teak. She was freighted with cotton-wool and oil, from the Lachadive islands. We had also on board coir, jaggeree, ghee, cocoa-nuts, and a few cases of opium. The stowage was clumsily done, and the vessel consequently crank.

We got under way with a mere breath of wind, and for many days stood along the eastern coast of Java, without any other incident to beguile the monotony of our course than the occasional meeting with some of the small grabs of the Archipelago to which we were bound.

One evening, leaning over the taffrail, I observed a very singular, isolated cloud, to the N.W. It was remarkable, as well for its colour, as from its being the first we had seen since our departure from Batavia. I watched it attentively until sunset, when it spread all at once to the eastward and westward, girting in the horizon with a narrow strip of vapor, and looking like a long line of low beach. My notice was soon afterwards attracted by the dusky-red appearance of the moon, and the peculiar character of the sea. The latter was undergoing a rapid change, and the water seemed more than usually transparent. Although I could distinctly see the bottom, yet, heaving the lead, I found the ship in fifteen fathoms. The air now became intolerably hot, and was loaded with spiral exhalations similar to those arising from heated iron. As night came on, every breath of wind died away, and a more entire calm it is impossible to conceive. The flame of a candle burned upon the poop without the least perceptible motion, and a long hair, held between the finger and thumb, hung without the possibility of detecting a vibration. However, as the captain said he could perceive no indication of danger, and as we were drifting in bodily to shore, he ordered the sails to be furled, and the anchor let go. No watch was set, and the crew, consisting principally of Malays, stretched themselves deliberately upon deck. I went below—not without a full presentiment of evil. Indeed, every appearance warranted me in apprehending a Simoom. I told the captain my fears; but he paid no attention to what I said, and left me without deigning to give a reply. My uneasiness, however, prevented me from sleeping, and about midnight I went upon deck. —As I placed my foot upon the upper step of the companion-ladder, I was startled by a loud, humming noise, like that occasioned by the rapid revolution of a mill-wheel, and before I could ascertain its meaning, I found the ship quivering to its centre. In the next instant, a wilderness of foam hurled us upon our beam-ends, and, rushing over us fore and aft, swept the entire decks from stem to stern.

The extreme fury of the blast proved, in a great measure, the salvation of the ship. Although completely water-logged, yet, as her masts had gone by the board, she rose, after a minute, heavily from the sea, and, staggering awhile beneath the immense pressure of the tempest, finally righted.

By what miracle I escaped destruction, it is impossible to say. Stunned by the shock of the water, I found myself, upon recovery, jammed in between the stern-post and rudder. With great difficulty I gained my feet, and looking dizzily around, was, at first, struck with the idea of our being among breakers; so terrific, beyond the wildest imagination, was the whirlpool of mountainous and foaming ocean within which we were engulfed. After a while, I heard the voice of an old Swede, who had shipped with us at the moment of our leaving port. I hallooed to him with all my strength, and presently he came reeling aft. We soon discovered that we were the sole survivors of the accident. All on deck, with the exception of ourselves, had been swept overboard;—the captain and mates must have perished as they slept, for the cabins were deluged with water. Without assistance, we could expect to do little for the security of the ship, and our exertions were at first paralyzed by the momentary expectation of going down. Our cable had, of course, parted like pack-thread, at the first breath of the hurricane, or we should have been instantaneously overwhelmed. We scudded with frightful velocity before the sea, and the water made clear breaches over us. The frame-work of our stern was shattered excessively, and, in almost every respect, we had received considerable injury; but to our extreme joy we found the pumps unchoked, and that we had made no great shifting of our ballast. The main fury of the blast had already blown over, and we apprehended little danger from the violence of the wind; but we looked forward to its total cessation with dismay; well believing, that, in our shattered condition, we should inevitably perish in the tremendous swell which would ensue. But this very just apprehension seemed by no means likely to be soon verified. For five entire days and nights—during which our only subsistence was a small quantity of jaggeree, procured with great difficulty from the forecastle—the hulk flew at a rate defying computation, before rapidly succeeding flaws of wind, which without equalling the first violence of the Simoom, were still more terrific than any tempest I had before encountered. Our course for the first four days was, with trifling variations, S. E. and by S.; and we must have run down the coast of New Holland— On the fifth day the cold became extreme, although the wind had hauled round a point more to the northward. —The sun arose with a sickly yellow lustre, and clambered a very few degrees above the horizon—emitting no decisive light. —There were no clouds apparent, yet the wind was upon the increase, and blew with a fitful and unsteady fury. About noon, as nearly as we could guess, our attention was again arrested by the appearance of the sun. It gave out no light, properly so called, but a dull and sullen glow without reflection, as if all its rays were polarized. Just before sinking within the turgid sea, its central fires suddenly went out, as if hurriedly extinguished by some unaccountable power. It was a dim, silver-like rim, alone, as it rushed down the unfathomable ocean.

We waited in vain for the arrival of the sixth day—that day to me has not arrived—to the Swede, never did arrive. Thenceforward we were enshrouded in pitchy darkness, so that we could not have seen an object at twenty paces from the ship. Eternal night continued to envelop us, all unrelieved by the phosphoric sea-brilliancy to which we had been accustomed in the tropics. We observed too, that, although the tempest continued to rage with unabated violence, there was no longer to be discovered the usual appearance of surf, or foam, which had hitherto attended us. All around were horror, and thick gloom, and a black sweltering desert of ebony. —Superstitious terror crept by degrees into the spirit of the old Swede, and my own soul was wrapped up in silent wonder. We neglected all care of the ship, as worse than useless, and securing ourselves, as well as possible, to the stump of the mizen-mast, looked out bitterly into the world of ocean. We had no means of calculating time, nor could we form any guess of our situation. We were, however, well aware of having made farther to the southward than any previous navigators, and felt great amazement at not meeting with the usual impediments of ice. In the meantime every moment threatened to be our last—every mountainous billow hurried to overwhelm us. The swell surpassed anything I had imagined possible, and that we were not instantly buried is a miracle. My companion spoke of the lightness of our cargo, and reminded me of the excellent qualities of our ship; but I could not help feeling the utter hopelessness of hope itself, and prepared myself gloomily for that death which I thought nothing could defer beyond an hour, as, with every knot of way the ship made, the swelling of the black stupendous seas became more dismally appalling. At times we gasped for breath at an elevation beyond the albatross—at times became dizzy with the velocity of our descent into some watery hell, where the air grew stagnant, and no sound disturbed the slumbers of the kraken.

We were at the bottom of one of these abysses, when a quick scream from my companion broke fearfully upon the night. "See! see!" cried he, shrieking in my ears, "Almighty God! see! see!" As he spoke, I became aware of a dull, sullen glare of red light which streamed down the sides of the vast chasm where we lay, and threw a fitful brilliancy upon our deck. Casting my eyes upwards, I beheld a spectacle which froze the current of my blood. At a terrific height directly above us, and upon the very verge of the precipitous descent, hovered a gigantic ship of, perhaps, four thousand tons. Although upreared upon the summit of a wave, more than a hundred times her own altitude, her apparent size still exceeded that of any ship of the line or East India-man in existence. Her huge hull was of a deep dingy black, unrelieved by any of the customary carvings of a ship. A single row of brass cannon protruded from her open ports, and dashed from their polished surfaces the fires of innumerable battle-lanterns, which swung to and fro about her rigging. But what mainly inspired us with horror and astonishment, was that she bore up under a press of sail in the very teeth of that supernatural sea, and of that ungovernable hurricane. When we first discovered her, her bows were alone to be seen, as she rose slowly from the dim and horrible gulf beyond her. For a moment of intense terror she paused upon the giddy pinnacle, as if in contemplation of her own sublimity, then trembled and tottered, and—came down.

At this instant, I know not what sudden self-possession came over my spirit. Staggering as far aft as I could, I awaited fearlessly the ruin that was to overwhelm. Our own vessel was at length ceasing from her struggles, and sinking with her head to the sea. The shock of the descending mass struck her, consequently, in that portion of her frame which was already under water, and the inevitable result was to hurl me, with irresistible violence, upon the rigging of the stranger.

As I fell, the ship hove in stays, and went about; and to the confusion ensuing I attributed my escape from the notice of the crew. With little difficulty I made my way unperceived to the main hatchway, which was partially open, and soon found an opportunity of secreting myself in the hold. Why I did so I can hardly tell. An indefinite sense of awe, which at first sight of the navigators of the ship had taken hold of my mind, was perhaps the principle of my concealment. I was unwilling to trust myself with a race of people who had offered, to the cursory glance I had taken, so many points of vague novelty, doubt, and apprehension. I therefore thought proper to contrive a hiding-place in the hold. This I did by removing a small portion of the shifting-boards, in such a manner as to afford me a convenient retreat between the huge timbers of the ship.

I had scarcely completed my work, when a footstep in the hold forced me to make use of it. A man passed by my place of concealment with a feeble and unsteady gait. I could not see his face, but had an opportunity of observing his general appearance. There was about it an evidence of great age and infirmity. His knees tottered beneath a load of years, and his entire frame quivered under the burthen. He muttered to himself, in a low broken tone, some words of a language which I could not understand, and groped in a corner among a pile of singular-looking instruments, and decayed charts of navigation. His manner was a wild mixture of the peevishness of second childhood, and the solemn dignity of a God. He at length went on deck, and I saw him no more.

⋆

A feeling, for which I have no name, has taken possession of my soul—a sensation which will admit of no analysis, to which the lessons of by-gone times are inadequate, and for which I fear futurity itself will offer me no key. To a mind constituted like my own, the latter consideration is an evil. I shall never—I know that I shall never—be satisfied with regard to the nature of my conceptions. Yet it is not wonderful that these conceptions are indefinite, since they have their origin in sources so utterly novel. A new sense—a new entity is added to my soul.

⋆

It is long since I first trod the deck of this terrible ship, and the rays of my destiny are, I think, gathering to a focus. Incomprehensible men! Wrapped up in meditations of a kind which I cannot divine, they pass me by unnoticed. Concealment is utter folly on my part, for the people *will not* see. It was but just now that I passed directly before the eyes of the mate—it was no long while ago that I ventured into the captain's own private cabin, and took thence the materials with which I write, and have written. I shall from time to time continue this journal. It is true that I may not find an opportunity of transmitting it to the world, but I will not fail to make the endeavour. At the last moment I will enclose the MS. in a bottle, and cast it within the sea.

⋆

An incident has occurred which has given me new room for meditation. Are such things the operation of ungoverned Chance? I had ventured upon deck and thrown myself down, without attracting any notice, among a pile of ratlin-stuff and old sails, in the bottom of the yawl. While musing upon the singularity of my fate, I unwittingly daubed with a tar-brush the edges of a neatly-folded studding-sail which lay near me on a barrel. The studding-sail is now bent upon the ship, and the thoughtless touches of the brush are spread out into the word DISCOVERY. * * *

I have made many observations lately upon the structure of the vessel. Although well armed, she is not, I think, a ship of war. Her rigging, build, and general equipment, all negative a supposition of this kind. What she *is not*, I can easily perceive—what she *is* I fear it is impossible to say. I know not how it is, but in scrutinizing her strange model and singular cast of spars, her huge size and overgrown suits of canvass, her severely simple bow and antiquated stern, there will occasionally flash across my mind a sensation of familiar things, and there is always mixed up with such indistinct shadows of recollection, an unaccountable memory of old foreign chronicles and ages long ago. * * *

I have been looking at the timbers of the ship. She is built of a material to which I am a stranger. There is a peculiar character about the wood which strikes me as rendering it unfit for the purpose to which it has been applied. I mean its extreme *porousness*, considered independently of the worm-eaten condition which is a consequence of navigation in these seas, and apart from the rottenness attendant upon age. It will appear perhaps an observation somewhat over-curious, but this wood would have every characteristic of Spanish oak, if Spanish oak were distended by any unnatural means.

In reading the above sentence a curious apothegm of an old weather-beaten Dutch navigator comes full upon my recollection. "It is as sure," he was wont to say, when any doubt was entertained of his veracity, "as sure as there is a sea where the ship itself will grow in bulk like the living body of the seaman." * * *

About an hour ago, I made bold to thrust myself among a group of the crew. They paid me no manner of attention, and, although I stood in the very midst of them all, seemed utterly unconscious of my presence. Like the one I had at first seen in the hold, they all bore about them the marks of a hoary old age. Their knees trembled with infirmity; their shoulders were bent double with decrepitude; their shrivelled skins rattled in the wind; their voices were low, tremulous and broken; their eyes glistened with the rheum of years; and their gray hairs streamed terribly in the tempest. Around them on every part of the deck, lay scattered mathematical instruments of the most quaint and obsolete construction. * * *

I mentioned some time ago the bending of a studding-sail. From that period the ship, being thrown dead off the wind, has continued her terrific course due south, with every rag of canvass packed upon her, from her trucks to her lower studding-sail booms, and rolling every moment her top-gallant yard-arms into the most appalling hell of water which it can enter into the mind of man to imagine. I have just left the deck, where I find it impossible to maintain a footing, although the crew seem to experience little inconvenience. It appears to me a miracle of miracles that our enormous bulk is not swallowed up at once and forever. We are surely doomed to hover continually upon the brink of Eternity, without taking a final plunge into the abyss. From billows a thousand times more stupendous than any I have ever seen, we glide away with the facility of the arrowy sea-gull; and the colossal waters rear their heads above us like demons of the deep, but like demons confined to simple threats and forbidden to destroy. I am led to attribute these frequent escapes to the only natural cause which can account for such effect. —I must suppose the ship to be within the influence of some strong current, or impetuous under-tow. * * *

I have seen the captain face to face, and in his own cabin—but, as I expected, he paid me no attention. Although in his appearance there is, to a casual observer, nothing which might bespeak him more or less than man—still a feeling of irrepressible reverence and awe mingled with the sensation of wonder with which I regarded him. In stature he is nearly my own height; that is, about five feet eight inches. He is of a well-knit and compact frame of body, neither robust nor remarkably otherwise. But it is the singularity of the expression which reigns upon the face—it is the intense, the wonderful, the thrilling evidence of old age, so utter, so extreme, which excites within my spirit a sense—a sentiment ineffable. His forehead, although little wrinkled, seems to bear upon it the stamp of a myriad of years. —His gray hairs are records of the past, and his grayer eyes are Sybils of the future. The cabin floor was thickly strewn with strange, iron-clasped folios, and mouldering instruments of science, and obsolete long-forgotten charts. His head was bowed down upon his hands, and he pored, with a fiery unquiet eye, over a paper which I took to be a commission, and which, at all events, bore the signature of a monarch. He muttered to himself, as did the first seaman whom I saw in the hold, some low peevish syllables of a foreign tongue, and although the speaker was close at my elbow, his voice seemed to reach my ears from the distance of a mile. * * *

The ship and all in it are imbued with the spirit of Eld. The crew glide to and fro like the ghosts of buried centuries; their eyes have an eager and uneasy meaning; and when their fingers fall athwart my path in the wild glare of the battle-lanterns, I feel as I have never felt before, although I have been all my life a dealer in antiquities, and have imbibed the shadows of fallen columns at Balbec, and Tadmor, and Persepolis, until my very soul has become a ruin. * * *

When I look around me I feel ashamed of my former apprehensions. If I trembled at the blast which has hitherto attended us, shall I not stand aghast at a warring of wind and ocean, to convey any idea of which the words tornado and simoom are trivial and ineffective? All in the immediate vicinity of the ship is the blackness of eternal night, and a chaos of foamless water; but, about a league on either side of us, may be seen, indistinctly and at intervals, stupendous ramparts of ice, towering away into the desolate sky, and looking like the walls of the universe. * * *

As I imagined, the ship proves to be in a current; if that appellation can properly be given to a tide which, howling and shrieking by the white ice, thunders on to the southward with a velocity like the headlong dashing of a cataract. * * *

To conceive the horror of my sensations is, I presume, utterly impossible; yet a curiosity to penetrate the mysteries of these awful regions, predominates even over my despair, and will reconcile me to the most hideous aspect of death. It is evident that we are hurrying onwards to some exciting knowledge—some never-to-be-imparted secret, whose attainment is destruction. Perhaps this current leads us to the southern pole itself. It must be confessed that a supposition apparently so wild has every probability in its favor. * * *

The crew pace the deck with unquiet and tremulous step; but there is upon their countenances an expression more of the eagerness of hope than of the apathy of despair.

In the meantime the wind is still in our poop, and, as we carry a crowd of canvass, the ship is at times lifted bodily from out the sea— Oh, horror upon horror! the ice opens suddenly to the right, and to the left, and we are whirling dizzily, in immense concentric circles, round and round the borders of a gigantic amphitheatre, the summit of whose walls is lost in the darkness and the distance. But little time will be left me to ponder upon my destiny—the circles rapidly grow small—we are plunging madly within the grasp of the whirlpool—and amid a roaring, and bellowing, and thundering of ocean and of tempest, the ship is quivering, oh God! and—going down.

*

NOTE. —The "MS. Found in a Bottle," was originally published in 1831, and it was not until many years afterwards that I became acquainted with the maps of Mercator, in which the ocean is represented as rushing, by four mouths, into the (northern) Polar Gulf, to be absorbed into the bowels of the earth; the Pole itself being represented by a black rock, towering to a prodigious height.

BRAM STOKER

THE SQUAW

NUREMBERG at the time was not so much exploited as it has been since then. Irving had not been playing *Faust*, and the very name of the old town was hardly known to the great bulk of the travelling public. My wife and I being in the second week of our honeymoon, naturally wanted someone else to join our party, so that when the cheery stranger, Elias P. Hutcheson, hailing from Isthmian City, Bleeding Gulch, Maple Tree County, Neb., turned up at the station at Frankfurt, and casually remarked that he was going on to see the most all-fired old Methuselah of a town in Yurrup, and that he guessed that so much travelling alone was enough to send an intelligent, active citizen into the melancholy ward of a daft house, we took the pretty broad hint and suggested that we should join forces. We found, on comparing notes afterwards, that we had each intended to speak with some diffidence or hesitation so as not to appear too eager, such not being a good compliment to the success of our married life; but the effect was entirely marred by our both beginning to speak at the same instant—stopping simultaneously and then going on together again. Anyhow, no matter how, it was done; and Elias P. Hutcheson became one of our party. Straightway Amelia and I found the pleasant benefit; instead of quarrelling, as we had been doing, we found that the restraining influence of a third party was such that we now took every opportunity of spooning in odd corners. Amelia declares that ever since she has, as the result of that experience, advised all her friends to take a friend on the honeymoon. Well, we "did"

Nuremberg together, and much enjoyed the racy remarks of our transatlantic friend, who, from his quaint speech and his wonderful stock of adventures, might have stepped out of a novel. We kept for the last object of interest in the city to be visited the Burg, and on the day appointed for the visit strolled round the outer wall of the city by the eastern side.

The Burg is seated on a rock dominating the town, and an immensely deep fosse guards it on the northern side. Nuremberg has been happy in that it was never sacked; had it been it would certainly not be so spick and span perfect as it is at present. The ditch has not been used for centuries, and now its base is spread with tea-gardens and orchards, of which some of the trees are of quite respectable growth. As we wandered round the wall, dawdling in the hot July sunshine, we often paused to admire the views spread before us, and in especial the great plain covered with towns and villages and bounded with a blue line of hills, like a landscape of Claude Lorrain. From this we always turned with new delight to the city itself, with its myriad of quaint old gables and acre-wide red roofs dotted with dormer windows, tier upon tier. A little to our right rose the towers of the Burg, and nearer still, standing grim, the torture tower, which was, and is, perhaps, the most interesting place in the city. For centuries the tradition of the Iron Virgin of Nuremberg has been handed down as an instance of the horrors of cruelty of which man is capable; we had long looked forward to seeing it; and here at last was its home.

In one of our pauses we leaned over the wall of the moat and looked down. The garden seemed quite fifty or sixty feet below us, and the sun pouring into it with an intense, moveless heat like that of an oven. Beyond rose the grey grim wall seemingly of endless height, and losing itself right and left in the angles of bastion and counterscarp. Trees and bushes crowned the wall, and above again towered the lofty houses on whose massive beauty time has only set the hand of approval. The sun was hot and we were lazy; time was our own, and we lingered, leaning on the wall. Just below us was a pretty sight—a great black cat lying stretched in the sun, whilst round her gambolled prettily a tiny black kitten. The mother would wave her tail for the kitten to play with, or would raise her feet and push away the little one as an encouragement to further play. They were just at the foot of the wall, and Elias P. Hutcheson, in order to help the play, stooped and took from the walk a moderate sized pebble.

"See!" he said, "I will drop it near the kitten, and they will both wonder where it came from."

"Oh, be careful," said my wife; "you might hit the dear little thing!"

"Not me, ma'am," said Elias P. "Why, I'm as tender as a Maine cherry tree. Lor, bless ye, I wouldn't hurt the poor pooty little critter more'n I'd scalp a baby. An' you may bet your variegated socks on that! See, I'll drop it fur away on the outside so's not to go near her!" Thus saying, he leaned over and held his arm out at full length and dropped the stone. It may be that there is some attractive force which draws lesser matters to greater; or more probably that the wall was not plumb but sloped to its base—we not noticing the inclination from above; but the stone fell with a sickening thud that came up to us through the hot air, right on the kitten's head, and shattered out its little brains then and there. The black cat cast a swift upward glance, and we saw her eyes like green fire fixed an instant on Elias P. Hutcheson; and then her attention was given to the kitten, which lay still with just a quiver of her tiny limbs, whilst a thin red stream trickled from a gaping wound. With a muffled cry, such as a human being might give, she bent over the kitten, licking its wound and moaning. Suddenly she seemed to realize that it was dead, and again threw her eyes up at us. I shall never forget the sight, for she looked the perfect incarnation of hate. Her green eyes blazed with lurid fire, and the white, sharp teeth seemed to almost shine through the blood which dabbled her mouth and whiskers. She gnashed her teeth, and her claws stood out stark and at full length on every paw. Then she made a wild rush up the wall as if to reach us, but when the momentum ended fell back, and further added to her horrible appearance for she fell on the kitten, and rose with her black fur smeared with its brains and blood. Amelia turned quite faint, and I had to lift her back from the wall. There was a seat close by in shade of a spreading plane tree, and here I placed her whilst she composed herself. Then I went back to Hutcheson, who stood without moving, looking down on the angry cat below.

As I joined him, he said: "Wall, I guess that air the savagest beast I ever see—'cept once when an Apache squaw had an edge on a half-breed what they nicknamed 'Splinters' 'cos of the way he fixed up her papoose which he stole on a raid just to show that he appreciated the way they had given his mother the fire torture. She got that kinder look so set on her face that it jest seemed to grow there. She followed Splinters more'n three year till at last the braves got him and handed him over to her. They did say that no man, white or Injun, had ever been so long a-dying under the tortures of the Apaches. The only time I ever see her smile was when I wiped her out. I kem on the camp just in time to see Splinters pass in his checks, and he wasn't sorry to go either. He was a hard citizen, and though I never could shake with him after that papoose business—for it was bitter bad, and he should have been a white man, for he looked like one—I see he had got paid out in full. Durn me, but I took a piece of his hide from one of his skinnin' posts an' had it made into a pocket-book. It's here now!" and he slapped the breast pocket of his coat.

Whilst he was speaking the cat was continuing her frantic efforts to get up the wall. She would take a run back and then charge up, sometimes reaching an incredible height. She did not seem to mind the heavy fall which she got each time but started with renewed vigour; and at every tumble her appearance became more horrible. Hutcheson was a kind-hearted man—my wife and I had both noticed little acts of kindness to animals as well as to persons—and he seemed concerned at the state of fury to which the cat had wrought herself.

"Wall, now!" he said, "I du declare that that poor critter seems quite desperate. There! there! poor thing, it was all an accident—though that won't bring back your little one to you. Say! I wouldn't have had such a thing happen for a thousand! Just shows what a clumsy fool of a man can do when he tries to play! Seems I'm too darned slipperhanded to even play with a cat. Say Colonel!" it was a pleasant way he had to bestow titles freely—"I hope your wife don't hold no grudge against me on account of this unpleasantness? Why, I wouldn't have had it occur on no account."

He came over to Amelia and apologized profusely, and she with her usual kindness of heart hastened to assure him that she quite understood that it was an accident. Then we all went again to the wall and looked over.

The cat missing Hutcheson's face had drawn back across the moat, and was sitting on her haunches as though ready to spring. Indeed, the very instant she saw him she did spring, and with a blind unreasoning fury, which would have been grotesque, only that it was so frightfully real. She did not try to run up the wall, but simply launched herself at him as though hate and fury could lend her wings to pass straight through the great distance between them. Amelia, womanlike, got quite concerned, and said to Elias P. in a warning voice: "Oh! you must be very careful. That animal would try to kill you if she were here; her eyes look like positive murder."

He laughed out jovially. "Excuse me, ma'am," he said, "but I can't help laughin'. Fancy a man that has fought grizzlies an' Injuns bein' careful of bein' murdered by a cat!"

When the cat heard him laugh, her whole demeanour

seemed to change. She no longer tried to jump or run up the wall, but went quietly over, and sitting again beside the dead kitten began to lick and fondle it as though it were alive.

"See!" said I, "the effect of a really strong man. Even that animal in the midst of her fury recognizes the voice of a master, and bows to him!"

"Like a squaw!" was the only comment of Elias P. Hutcheson, as we moved on our way round the city fosse. Every now and then we looked over the wall and each time saw the cat following us. At first she had kept going back to the dead kitten, and then as the distance grew greater took it in her mouth and so followed. After a while, however, she abandoned this, for we saw her following all alone; she had evidently hidden the body somewhere. Amelia's alarm grew at the cat's persistence, and more than once she repeated her warning; but the American always laughed with amusement, till finally, seeing that she was beginning to be worried, he said: "I say, ma'am, you needn't be skeered over that cat. I go heeled, I du!" Here he slapped his pistol pocket at the back of his lumbar region. "Why sooner'n have you worried, I'll shoot the critter, right here, an' risk the police interferin' with a citizen of the United States for carryin' arms contrary to reg'lations!" As he spoke he looked over the wall, but the cat, on seeing him, retreated, with a growl, into a bed of tall flowers, and was hidden. He went on: "Blest if that ar critter ain't got more sense of what's good for her than most Christians. I guess we've seen the last of her! You bet, she'll go back now to that busted kitten and have a private funeral of it, all to herself!"

Amelia did not like to say more, lest he might, in mistaken kindness to her, fulfil his threat of shooting the cat: and so we went on and crossed the little wooden bridge leading to the gateway whence ran the steep paved roadway between the Burg and the pentagonal torture tower. As we crossed the bridge we saw the cat again down below us. When she saw us her fury seemed to return, and she made frantic efforts to get up the steep wall. Hutcheson laughed as he looked down at her, and said: "Good-bye, old girl. Sorry I injured your feelin's, but you'll get over it in time! So long!" And then we passed through the long, dim archway and came to the gate of the Burg.

When we came out again after our survey of this most beautiful old place which not even the well-intentioned efforts of the Gothic restorers of forty years ago have been able to spoil—though their restoration was then glaring white—we seemed to have quite forgotten the unpleasant episode of the morning. The old lime tree and its great trunk gnarled with the passing of nearly nine centuries, the deep well cut through the heart of the rock by those captives of old, and the lovely view from the city wall whence we heard, spread over almost a full quarter of an hour, the multitudinous chimes of the city, had all helped to wipe out from our minds the incident of the slain kitten.

We were the only visitors who had entered the torture tower that morning—so at least said the old custodian—and as we had the place all to ourselves were able to make a minute and more satisfactory survey than would have otherwise been possible. The custodian, looking to us as the sole source of his gains for the day, was willing to meet our wishes in any way. The torture tower is truly a grim place, even now when many thousands of visitors have sent a stream of life, and the joy that follows life, into the place; but at the time I mention it wore its grimmest and most gruesome aspect. The dust of ages seemed to have settled on it, and the darkness and the horror of its memories to have become sentient in a way that would have satisfied the pantheistic souls of Philo or Spinoza. The lower chamber where we entered was seemingly, in its normal state, filled with incarnate darkness; even the hot sunlight streaming in through the door seemed to be lost in the vast thickness of the walls, and only showed the masonry rough as when the builder's scaffolding had come down, but coated with dust and marked here and there with patches of dark stain which, if walls could speak, could have given their own dread memories of fear and pain. We were glad to pass up the dusty wooden staircase, the custodian leaving the outer door open to light us somewhat on our way; for to our eyes the one long-wick'd, evil-smelling candle stuck in a sconce on the wall gave an inadequate light. When we came up through the open trap in the corner of the chamber overhead, Amelia held on to me so tightly that I could actually feel her heart beat. I must say for my own part that I was not surprised at her fear, for this room was even more gruesome than that below. Here there was certainly more light, but only just sufficient to realize the horrible surroundings of the place. The builders of the tower had evidently intended that only they who should gain the top should have any of the joys of light and prospect. There, as we had noticed from below, were ranges of windows, albeit of medieval smallness, but elsewhere in the tower were only a very few narrow slits such as were habitual in places of medieval defence. A few of these only lit the chamber, and these so high up in the wall that from no part could the sky be seen through the thickness of the walls. In racks, and leaning in disorder against the walls, were a number of headsmen's swords, great double-handed weapons with broad blade and keen edge. Hard by were several blocks whereon the necks of the victims had lain, with here and there deep notches where the steel had bitten through the guard of flesh and shored into the wood. Round the chamber, placed in all sorts of irregular ways, were many implements of torture which made one's heart ache to see—chairs full of spikes which gave instant and excruciating pain; chairs and couches with dull knobs whose torture was seemingly less, but which, though slower, were equally efficacious; racks, belts, boots, gloves, collars, all made for compressing at will; steel baskets in which the head could be slowly crushed into a pulp if necessary; watchmen's hooks with long handle and knife that cut at resistance—this a speciality of the old Nuremberg police system; and many, many other devices for man's injury to man. Amelia grew quite pale with the horror of the things, but fortunately did not faint, for being a little overcome she sat down on a torture chair, but jumped up again with a shriek, all tendency to faint gone. We both pretended that it was the injury done to her dress by the dust of the chair, and the rusty spikes which had upset her, and Mr. Hutcheson acquiesced in accepting the explanation with a kind-hearted laugh.

But the central object in the whole of this chamber of horrors was the engine known as the Iron Virgin, which stood near the centre of the room. It was a rudely shaped figure of a woman, something of the bell order, or, to make a closer comparison, of the figure of Mrs. Noah in the children's Ark, but without that slimness of waist and perfect *rondeur* of hip which marks the aesthetic type of the Noah family. One would hardly have recognized it as intended for a human figure at all had not the founder shaped on the forehead a rude semblance of a woman's face. The machine was coated with rust without, and covered with dust; a rope was fastened to a ring in the front of the figure, about where the waist should have been, and was drawn through a pulley, fastened on the wooden pillar which sustained the flooring above. The custodian pulling this rope showed that a section of the front was hinged like a door at one side; we then saw that the engine was of considerable thickness, leaving just room enough inside for a man to be placed. The door was of equal thickness and of great weight, for it took the custodian all his strength, aided though he was by the contrivance of the pulley, to open it. This weight was partly due to the fact that the door was of manifest purpose hung so as to throw its weight downwards, so that it might shut of its own accord when the strain was released. The inside was honeycombed with rust—nay more, the rust alone that comes through time would hardly have eaten so deep into the iron walls; the rust of the cruel stains was deep indeed! It was only, however, when we came to look at the inside of the door that the diabolical intention was manifest to the full. Here were several long spikes, square and massive, broad at the base and sharp at the points, placed in such a position that when the door should close the upper ones would pierce the eyes of the victim, and the lower ones his heart and vitals. The sight was too much for poor Amelia, and this time she fainted dead off, and I had to carry her down the stairs, and place her on a bench outside till she recovered. That she felt it to the quick was afterwards shown by the fact that my eldest son bears to this day a rude birthmark on his breast, which has, by family consent, been accepted as representing the Nuremberg Virgin.

When we got back to the chamber we found Hutcheson still opposite the Iron Virgin; he had been evidently philosophizing, and now gave us the benefit of his thought in the shape of a sort of exordium.

"Wall, I guess I've been learnin' somethin' here while madam has been gettin' over her faint. 'Pears to me that we're a long way behind the times on our side of the big drink. We uster think out on the plains that the Injun could give us points in tryin' to make a man oncomfortable; but I guess your old medieval law-and-order party could raise him every time. Splinters was pretty good in his bluff on the squaw, but this here young miss held a straight flush all high on him. The points of them spikes air sharp enough still, though even the edges air eaten out by what uster be on them. It'd be a good thing for our Indian section to get some specimens of this here play-toy to send round to the reservations jest to knock the stuffin' out of the bucks, and the squaws too, by showing them as how old civilization lays over them at their best. Guess but I'll get in that box a minute jest to see how it feels!"

"Oh no! no!" said Amelia. "It is too terrible!"

"Guess, ma'am, nothin's too terrible to the explorin' mind. I've been in some queer places in my time. Spent a night inside a dead horse while a prairie fire swept over me in Montana territory—an' another time slept inside a dead buffler when the Comanches was on the war-path an' I didn't keer to leave my kyard on them. I've been two days in a caved-in tunnel in the Billy Broncho gold mine in New Mexico, an' was one of the four shut up for three parts of a day in the caisson what slid over on her side when we was settin' the foundations of the Buffalo Bridge. I've not funked an odd experience yet, an' I don't propose to begin now!"

We saw that he was set on the experiment, so I said: "Well, hurry up, old man, and get through it quick."

"All right, General," said he, "but I calculate we ain't quite ready yet. The gentlemen, my predecessors, what stood in that thar canister, didn't volunteer for the office—not much! And I guess there was some ornamental tyin' up before the big stroke was made. I want to go into this thing fair and square, so I must get fixed up proper first. I dare say this old galoot can rise some string and tie me up accordin' to sample?"

This was said interrogatively to the old custodian, but the latter, who understood the drift of his speech, though perhaps not appreciating to the full the niceties of dialect and imagery, shook his head. His protest was, however, only formal and made to be overcome. The American thrust a gold piece into his hand, saying, "Take it, pard! it's your pot; and don't be skeer'd. This ain't no necktie party that you're asked to assist in!" He produced some thin frayed rope and proceeded to bind our companion with sufficient strictness for the purpose. When the upper part of his body was bound, Hutcheson said: "Hold on a moment, Judge. Guess I'm too heavy for you to tote into the canister. You jest let me walk in, and then you can wash up regardin' my legs!"

Whilst speaking he had backed himself into the opening

which was just enough to hold him. It was a close fit and no mistake. Amelia looked on with fear in her eyes, but she evidently did not like to say anything. Then the custodian completed his task by tying the American's feet together so that he was now absolutely helpless and fixed in his voluntary prison. He seemed to really enjoy it, and the incipient smile which was habitual to his face blossomed into actuality as he said: "Guess this here Eve was made out of the rib of a dwarf! There ain't much room for a full-grown citizen of the United States to hustle. We uster make our coffins more roomier in Idaho territory. Now, Judge, you jest begin to let this door down, slow, on to me. I want to feel the same pleasure as the other jays had when those spikes began to move toward their eyes!"

"Oh no! no! no!" broke in Amelia hysterically. "It is too terrible! I can't bear to see it!—I can't! I can't!"

But the American was obdurate. "Say, Colonel," said he, "Why not take Madame for a little promenade? I wouldn't hurt her feelin's for the world; but now that I am here, havin' kem eight thousand miles, wouldn't it be too hard to give up the very experience I've been pinin' an' pantin' fur? A man can't get to feel like canned goods every time! Me and the Judge here'll fix up this thing in no time, an' then you'll come back, an' we'll all laugh together!"

Once more the resolution that is born of curiosity triumphed, and Amelia stayed holding tight to my arm and shivering whilst the custodian began to slacken slowly inch by inch the rope that held back the iron door. Hutcheson's face was positively radiant as his eyes followed the first movement of the spikes.

"Wall!" he said, "I guess I've not had enjoyment like this since I left Noo York. Bar a scrap with a French sailor at Wapping—an' that warn't much of a picnic neither—I've not had a show fur real pleasure in this dod-rotted continent, where there ain't no b'ars nor no Injuns, an' wheer nary man goes heeled. Slow there, Judge! Don't you rush this business! I want a show for my money this game—I du!"

The custodian must have had in him some of the blood of his predecessors in that ghastly tower, for he worked the engine with a deliberate and excruciating slowness which after five minutes, in which the outer edge of the door had not moved half as many inches, began to overcome Amelia. I saw her lips whiten, and felt her hold upon my arm relax. I looked around an instant for a place whereon to lay her, and when I looked at her again found that her eye had become fixed on the side of the Virgin. Following its direction I saw the black cat crouching out of sight. Her green eyes shone like danger lamps in the gloom of the place, and their colour was heightened by the blood which still smeared her coat and reddened her mouth. I cried out: "The cat! look out for the cat!" for even then she sprang out before the engine. At this moment she looked like a triumphant demon. Her eyes blazed with ferocity, her hair bristled out till she seemed twice her normal size, and her tail lashed about as does a tiger's when the quarry is before it.

Elias P. Hutcheson when he saw her was amused, and his eyes positively sparkled with fun as he said: "Darned if the squaw hain't got on all her war-paint! Jest give her a shove off if she comes any of her tricks on me, for I'm so fixed everlastingly by the boss, that durn my skin if I can keep my eyes from her if she wants them! Easy there, Judge! don't you slack that ar rope or I'm euchred!"

At this moment Amelia completed her faint, and I had to clutch hold of her round the waist or she would have fallen to the floor. Whilst attending to her I saw the black cat crouching for a spring, and jumped up to turn the creature out.

But at that instant, with a sort of hellish scream, she hurled herself, not as we expected at Hutcheson, but straight at the face of the custodian. Her claws seemed to be tearing wildly as one sees in the Chinese drawings of the dragon rampant, and as I looked I saw one of them light on the poor man's eye, and actually tear through it and down his cheek, leaving a wide band of red where the blood seemed to spurt from every vein.

With a yell of sheer terror which came quicker than even his sense of pain, the man leaped back, dropping as he did so the rope which held back the iron door. I jumped for it, but was too late, for the cord ran like lightning through the pulley-block, and the heavy mass fell forward from its own weight.

As the door closed I caught a glimpse of our poor companion's face. He seemed frozen with terror. His eyes stared with a horrible anguish as if dazed, and no sound came from his lips.

And then the spikes did their work. Happily the end was quick, for when I wrenched open the door they had pierced so deep that they had locked in the bones of the skull through which they had crushed, and actually tore him—it—out of his iron prison till, bound as he was, he fell at full length with a sickly thud upon the floor, the face turning upwards as he fell.

I rushed to my wife, lifted her up and carried her out, for I feared for her very reason if she should wake from her faint to such a scene. I laid her on the bench outside and ran back. Leaning against the wooden column was the custodian moaning in pain whilst he held his reddening handkerchief to his eyes. And sitting on the head of the poor American was the cat, purring loudly as she licked the blood which trickled through the gashed sockets of his eyes.

I think no one will call me cruel because I seized one of the old executioners' swords and shore her in two as she sat.

AMBROSE BIERCE

MOXON'S MASTER

"ARE YOU serious?—do you really believe that a machine thinks?"

I got no immediate reply; Moxon was apparently intent upon the coals in the grate, touching them deftly here and there with the fire-poker till they signified a sense of his attention by a brighter glow. For several weeks I had been observing in him a growing habit of delay in answering even the most trivial of commonplace questions. His air, however, was that of preoccupation rather than deliberation: one might have said that he had "something on his mind."

Presently he said:

"What is a 'machine'? The word has been variously defined. Here is one definition from a popular dictionary: 'Any instrument or organization by which power is applied and made effective, or a desired effect produced.' Well, then, is not a man a machine? And you will admit that he thinks—or thinks he thinks."

"If you do not wish to answer my question," I said, rather testily, "why not say so?—all that you say is mere evasion. You know well enough that when I say 'machine' I do not mean a man, but something that man has made and controls."

"When it does not control him," he said, rising abruptly and looking out of a window, whence nothing was visible in the blackness of a stormy night. A moment later he turned about and with a smile said: "I beg your pardon; I had no thought of evasion. I considered the dictionary man's unconscious testimony suggestive and worth something in the discussion. I can give your question a direct answer easily enough: I do believe that a machine thinks about the work that it is doing."

That was direct enough, certainly. It was not altogether pleasing, for it tended to confirm a sad suspicion that Moxon's devotion to study and work in his machine-shop had not been good for him. I knew, for one thing, that he suffered from insomnia, and that is no light affliction. Had it affected his mind? His reply to my question seemed to me then evidence that it had; perhaps I should think differently about it now. I was younger then, and among the blessings that are not denied to youth is ignorance. Incited by that great stimulant to controversy, I said:

"And what, pray, does it think with—in the absence of a brain?"

The reply, coming with less than his customary delay, took his favorite form of counter-interrogation:

"With what does a plant think—in the absence of a brain?"

"Ah, plants also belong to the philosopher class! I should be pleased to know some of their conclusions; you may omit the premises."

"Perhaps," he replied, apparently unaffected by my foolish irony, "you may be able to infer their convictions from their acts. I will spare you the familiar examples of the sensitive mimosa, the several insectivorous flowers and those whose stamens bend down and shake their pollen upon the entering bee in order that he may fertilize their distant mates. But observe this. In an open spot in my garden I planted a climbing vine. When it was barely above the surface I set a stake into the soil a yard away. The vine at once made for it, but as it was about to reach it after several days I removed it a few feet. The vine at once altered its course, making an acute angle, and again made for the stake. This manœuvre was repeated several times but finally, as if discouraged, the vine abandoned the pursuit and ignoring further attempts to divert it traveled to a small tree, further away, which it climbed.

"Roots of the eucalyptus will prolong themselves incredibly in search of moisture. A well-known horticulturist relates that one entered an old drain pipe and followed it until it came to a break, where a section of the pipe had been removed to make way for a stone wall that had been built across its course. The root left the drain and followed the wall until it found an opening where a stone had fallen out. It crept through and following the other side of the wall back to the drain, entered the unexplored part and resumed its journey."

"And all this?"

"Can you miss the significance of it? It shows the consciousness of plants. It proves that they think."

"Even if it did—what then? We were speaking, not of plants, but of machines. They may be composed partly of wood—wood that has no longer vitality—or wholly of metal. Is thought an attribute also of the mineral kingdom?"

"How else do you explain the phenomena, for example, of crystallization?"

"I do not explain them."

"Because you cannot without affirming what you wish to deny, namely, intelligent cooperation among the constituent elements of the crystals. When soldiers form lines, or hollow squares, you call it reason. When wild geese in flight take the form of a letter V you say instinct. When the homogeneous atoms of a mineral, moving freely in solution arrange themselves into shapes mathematically perfect, or particles of frozen moisture into the symmetrical and beautiful forms of snowflakes, you have nothing to say. You have not even invented a name to conceal your heroic unreason."

Moxon was speaking with unusual animation and earnestness. As he paused I heard in an adjoining room known to me as his "machine-shop," which no one but himself was permitted to enter, a singular thumping sound, as of some one pounding upon a table with an open hand. Moxon heard it at the same moment and, visibly agitated, rose and hurriedly passed into the room whence it came. I thought it odd that any one else should be in there, and my interest in my friend—with doubtless a touch of unwarrantable curiosity—led me to listen intently, though, I am happy to say, not at the keyhole. There were confused sounds, as of a struggle or scuffle; the floor shook. I distinctly heard hard breathing and a hoarse whisper which said "Damn you!" Then all was silent, and presently Moxon reappeared and said, with a rather sorry smile:

"Pardon me for leaving you so abruptly. I have a machine in there that lost its temper and cut up rough."

Fixing my eyes steadily upon his left cheek which was traversed by four parallel excoriations showing blood, I said:

"How would it do to trim its nails?"

I could have spared myself the jest; he gave it no attention, but seated himself in the chair that he had left and resumed the interrupted monologue as if nothing had occurred:

"Doubtless you do not hold with those (I need not name them to a man of your reading) who have taught that all matter is sentient, that every atom is a living, feeling, conscious being. *I* do. There is no such thing as dead, inert matter; it is all alive; all instinct with force, actual and potential; all sensitive to the same forces in its environment and susceptible to the contagion of higher and subtler ones residing in such superior organisms as it may be brought into relation with, as those of man when he is fashioning it into an instrument of his will. It absorbs something of his intelligence and purpose—more of them in proportion to the complexity of the resulting machine and that of its work.

"Do you happen to recall Herbert Spencer's definition of 'Life'? I read it thirty years ago. He may have altered it afterward, for anything I know, but in all that time I have been unable to think of a single word that could profitably be changed or added or removed. It seems to me not only the best definition, but the only possible one.

"'Life,' he says, 'is a definite combination of heterogeneous changes, both simultaneous and successive, in correspondence with external coexistences and sequences.'"

"That defines the phenomenon," I said, "but gives no hint of its cause."

"That," he replied, 'is all that any definition can do. As Mill points out, we know nothing of cause except as an antecedent—nothing of effect except as a consequent. Of certain phenomena, one never occurs without another, which is dissimilar: the first in point of time we call cause, the second, effect. One who had many times seen a rabbit pursued by a dog, and had never seen rabbits and dogs otherwise, would think the rabbit the cause of the dog.

"But I fear," he added, laughing naturally enough, "that my rabbit is leading me a long way from the track of my legitimate quarry: I'm indulging in the pleasure of the chase for its own sake. What I want you to observe is that in Herbert Spencer's definition of 'life' the activity of a machine is included—there is nothing in the definition that is not applicable to it. According to this sharpest of observers and deepest of thinkers, if a man during his period of activity is alive, so is a machine when in operation. As an inventor and constructor of machines I know that to be true."

Moxon was silent for a long time, gazing absently into the fire. It was growing late and I thought it time to be going, but somehow I did not like the notion of leaving him in that isolated house, all alone except for the presence of some person of whose nature my conjectures could go no further than that it was unfriendly, perhaps malign. Leaning toward him and looking earnestly into his eyes while making a motion with my hand through the door of his workshop, I said:

"Moxon, whom have you in there?"

Somewhat to my surprise he laughed lightly and answered without hesitation:

"Nobody; the incident that you have in mind was caused by my folly in leaving a machine in action with nothing to act upon, while I undertook the interminable task of enlightening your understanding. Do you happen to know that Consciousness is the creature of Rhythm?"

"O bother them both!" I replied, rising and laying hold of my overcoat. "I'm going to wish you good night; and I'll add the hope that the machine which you inadvertently left in action will have her gloves on the next time you think it needful to stop her."

Without waiting to observe the effect of my shot I left the house.

Rain was falling, and the darkness was intense. In the sky beyond the crest of a hill toward which I groped my way along precarious plank sidewalks and across miry, unpaved streets I could see the faint glow of the city's lights, but behind me nothing was visible but a single window of Moxon's house. It glowed with what seemed to me a mysterious and fateful meaning. I knew it was an uncurtained aperture in my friend's "machine-shop," and I had little doubt that he had resumed the studies interrupted by his duties as my instructor in mechanical consciousness and the fatherhood of Rhythm. Odd, and in some degree humorous, as his convictions seemed to me at that time, I could not wholly divest myself of the feeling that they had some tragic relation to his life and character—perhaps to his destiny—although I no longer entertained the notion that they were the vagaries of a disordered mind. Whatever might be thought of his views, his exposition of them was too logical for that. Over and over, his last words came back to me: "Consciousness is the creature of Rhythm." Bald and terse as the statement was, I now found it infinitely alluring. At each recurrence it broadened in meaning and deepened in suggestion. Why, here, (I thought) is something upon which to found a philosophy. If consciousness is the product of rhythm all things *are* conscious, for all have motion, and all motion is rhythmic. I wondered if Moxon knew the significance and breadth of his thought—the scope of this momentous generalization, or had he arrived at his philosophic faith by the tortuous and uncertain road of observation?

That faith was then new to me, and all Moxon's expounding had failed to make me a convert; but now it seemed as if a great light shone about me, like that which fell upon Saul of Tarsus; and out there in the storm and darkness and solitude I experienced what Lewes calls "The endless variety and excitement of philosophic thought." I exulted in a new sense of knowledge, a new pride of reason. My feet seemed hardly to touch the earth; it was as if I were uplifted and borne through the air by invisible wings.

Yielding to an impulse to seek further light from him whom I now recognized as my master and guide, I had unconsciously turned about, and almost before I was aware of having done so found myself again at Moxon's door. I was drenched with rain, but felt no discomfort. Unable in my excitement to find the doorbell I instinctively tried the knob. It turned and, entering, I mounted the stairs to the room that I had so recently left. All was dark and silent; Moxon, as I had supposed, was in the adjoining room—the "machine-shop." Groping along the wall until I found the communicating door I knocked loudly several times, but got no response, which I attributed to the uproar outside, for the wind was blowing a gale and dashing the rain against the thin walls in sheets. The drumming upon the shingle roof spanning the unceiled room was loud and incessant.

I had never been invited into the machine-shop—had, indeed, been denied admittance, as had all others, with one exception, a skilled metal worker, of whom no one knew anything except that his name was Haley and his habit silence. But in my spiritual exaltation, discretion and civility were alike forgotten and I opened the door. What I saw took all philosophical speculation out of me in short order.

Moxon sat facing me at the farther side of a small table upon which a single candle made all the light that was in the room. Opposite him, his back toward me, sat another person. On the table between the two was a chess-board; the men were playing. I knew little of chess, but as only a few pieces were on the board it was obvious that the game was near its close. Moxon was intensely interested—not so much, it seemed to me, in the game as in his antagonist, upon whom he had fixed so intent a look that, standing though I did directly in the line of his vision, I was altogether unobserved. His face was ghastly white, and his eyes glittered like diamonds. Of his antagonist I had only a back view, but that was sufficient; I should not have cared to see his face.

He was apparently not more than five feet in height, with proportions suggesting those of a gorilla—a tremendous breadth of shoulders, thick, short neck and broad, squat head, which had a tangled growth of black hair and was topped with a crimson fez. A tunic of the same color, belted tightly to the waist, reached the seat—apparently a box—upon which he sat; his legs and feet were not seen. His left forearm appeared to rest in his lap; he moved his pieces with his right hand, which seemed disproportionately long.

I had shrunk back and now stood a little to one side of the doorway and in shadow. If Moxon had looked farther than the face of his opponent he could have observed nothing now, except that the door was open. Something forbade me either to enter or to retire, a feeling—I know not how it came—that I was in the presence of an imminent tragedy and might serve my friend by remaining. With a scarcely conscious rebellion against the indelicacy of the act I remained.

The play was rapid. Moxon hardly glanced at the board before making his moves, and to my unskilled eye seemed to move the piece most convenient to his hand, his motions in doing so being quick, nervous and lacking in precision. The response of his antagonist, while equally prompt in the inception, was made with a slow, uniform, mechanical and, I thought, somewhat theatrical movement of the arm, that was a sore trial to my patience. There was something unearthly about it all, and I caught myself shuddering. But I was wet and cold.

Two or three times after moving a piece the stranger slightly inclined his head, and each time I observed that Moxon shifted his king. All at once the thought came to me that the man was dumb. And then that he was a machine—an automaton chess-player! Then I remembered that Moxon had once spoken to me of having invented such a piece of mechanism, though I did not understand that it had actually been constructed. Was all his talk about the consciousness and intelligence of machines merely a prelude to eventual exhibition of this device—only a trick to intensify the effect of its mechanical action upon me in my ignorance of its secret?

A fine end, this, of all my intellectual transports—my "endless variety and excitement of philosophic thought"! I was about to retire in disgust when something occurred to hold my curiosity. I observed a shrug of the thing's great shoulders, as if it were irritated: and so natural was this—so entirely human—that in my new view of the matter it startled me. Nor was that all, for a moment later it struck the table sharply with its clenched hand. At that gesture Moxon seemed even more startled than I: he pushed his chair a little backward, as in alarm.

Presently Moxon, whose play it was, raised his hand high above the board, pounced upon one of his pieces like a sparrow-hawk and with the exclamation "checkmate!" rose quickly to his feet and stepped behind his chair. The automaton sat motionless.

The wind had now gone down, but I heard, at lessening intervals and progressively louder, the rumble and roll of thunder. In the pauses between I now became conscious of a low humming or buzzing which, like the thunder, grew momentarily louder and more distinct. It seemed to come from the body of the automaton, and was unmistakably a whirring of wheels. It gave me the impression of a disordered mechanism which had escaped the repressive and regulating action of some controlling part—an effect such as might be expected if a pawl should be jostled from the teeth of a ratchet-wheel. But before I had time for much conjecture as to its nature my attention was taken by the strange motions of the automaton itself. A slight but continuous convulsion appeared to have possession of it. In body and head it shook like a man with palsy or an ague chill, and the motion augmented every moment until the entire figure was in violent agitation. Suddenly it sprang to its feet and with a movement almost too quick for the eye to follow shot forward across table and chair, with both arms thrust forth to their full length—the posture and lunge of a diver. Moxon tried to throw himself backward out of reach, but he was too late: I saw the horrible thing's hands close upon his throat, his own clutch its wrists. Then the table was overturned, the candle thrown to the floor and extinguished, and all was black dark. But the noise of the struggle was dreadfully distinct, and most terrible of all were the raucous, squawking sounds made by the strangled man's efforts to breathe. Guided by the infernal hubbub, I sprang to the rescue of my friend, but had hardly taken a stride in the darkness when the whole room blazed with a blinding white light that burned into my brain and heart and memory a vivid picture of the combatants on the floor, Moxon underneath, his throat still in the clutch of those iron hands, his head forced backward, his eyes protruding, his mouth wide open and his tongue thrust out; and—horrible contrast!—upon the painted face of his assassin an expression of tranquil and profound thought, as in the solution of a problem in chess! This I observed, then all was blackness and silence.

Three days later I recovered consciousness in a hospital. As the memory of that tragic night slowly evolved in my ailing brain I recognized in my attendant Moxon's confidential workman, Haley. Responding to a look he approached, smiling.

"Tell me about it," I managed to say, faintly—"all about it."

"Certainly," he said; "you were carried unconscious from a burning house—Moxon's. Nobody knows how you came to be there. You may have to do a little explaining. The origin of the fire is a bit mysterious, too. My own notion is that the house was struck by lightning."

"And Moxon?"

"Buried yesterday—what was left of him."

Apparently this reticent person could unfold himself on occasion. When imparting shocking intelligence to the sick he was affable enough. After some moments of the keenest mental suffering I ventured to ask another question:

"Who rescued me?"

"Well, if that interests you—I did."

"Thank you, Mr. Haley, and may God bless you for it. Did you rescue, also, that charming product of your skill, the automaton chess-player that murdered its inventor?"

The man was silent a long time, looking away from me. Presently he turned and gravely said:

"Do you know that?"

"I do," I replied; "I saw it done."

That was many years ago. If asked to-day I should answer less confidently.

AMBROSE BIERCE

THE DAMNED THING

1.
ONE DOES NOT ALWAYS EAT WHAT IS ON THE TABLE

By the light of a tallow candle which had been placed on one end of a rough table a man was reading something written in a book. It was an old account book, greatly worn; and the writing was not, apparently, very legible, for the man sometimes held the page close to the flame of the candle to get a stronger light on it. The shadow of the book would then throw into obscurity a half of the room, darkening a number of faces and figures; for besides the reader, eight other men were present. Seven of them sat against the rough log walls, silent, motionless, and the room being small, not very far from the table. By extending an arm any one of them could have touched the eighth man, who lay on the table, face upward, partly covered by a sheet, his arms at his sides. He was dead.

The man with the book was not reading aloud, and no one spoke; all seemed to be waiting for something to occur; the dead man only was without expectation. From the blank darkness outside came in, through the aperture that served for a window, all the ever unfamiliar noises of night in the wilderness—the long nameless note of a distant coyote; the stilly pulsing thrill of tireless insects in trees; strange cries of night birds, so different from those of the birds of day; the drone of great blundering beetles, and all that mysterious chorus of small sounds that seem always to have been but half heard when they have suddenly ceased, as if conscious of an indiscretion. But nothing of all this was noted in that company; its members were not overmuch addicted to idle interest in matters of no practical importance; that was obvious in every line of their rugged faces—obvious even in the dim light of the single candle. They were evidently men of the vicinity—farmers and woodsmen.

The person reading was a trifle different; one would have said of him that he was of the world, worldly, albeit there was that in his attire which attested a certain fellowship with the organisms of his environment. His coat would hardly have passed muster in San Francisco; his foot-gear was not of urban origin, and the hat that lay by him on the floor (he was the only one uncovered) was such that if one had considered it as an article of mere personal adornment he would have missed its meaning. In countenance the man was rather prepossessing, with just a hint of sternness; though that he may have assumed or cultivated, as appropriate to one in authority. For he was a coroner. It was by virtue of his office that he had possession of the book in which he was reading; it had been found among the dead man's effects—in his cabin, where the inquest was now taking place.

When the coroner had finished reading he put the book into his breast pocket. At that moment the door was pushed open and a young man entered. He, clearly, was not of mountain birth and breeding: he was clad as those who dwell in cities. His clothing was dusty, however, as from travel. He had, in fact, been riding hard to attend the inquest.

The coroner nodded; no one else greeted him.

"We have waited for you," said the coroner. "It is necessary to have done with this business to-night."

The young man smiled. "I am sorry to have kept you," he said. "I went away, not to evade your summons, but to post to my newspaper an account of what I suppose I am called back to relate."

The coroner smiled.

"The account that you posted to your newspaper," he said, "differs, probably, from that which you will give here under oath."

"That," replied the other, rather hotly and with a visible flush, "is as you please. I used manifold paper and have a copy of what I sent. It was not written as news, for it is incredible, but as fiction. It may go as a part of my testimony under oath."

"But you say it is incredible."

"That is nothing to you, sir, if I also swear that it is true."

The coroner was silent for a time, his eyes upon the floor. The men about the sides of the cabin talked in whispers, but seldom withdrew their gaze from the face of the corpse. Presently the coroner lifted his eyes and said: "We will resume the inquest."

The men removed their hats. The witness was sworn.

"What is your name?" the coroner asked.

"William Harker."

"Age?"

"Twenty-seven."

"You knew the deceased, Hugh Morgan?"

"Yes."

"You were with him when he died?"

"Near him."

"How did that happen—your presence, I mean?"

"I was visiting him at this place to shoot and fish. A part of my purpose, however, was to study him and his odd, solitary way of life. He seemed a good model for a character in fiction. I sometimes write stories."

"I sometimes read them."

"Thank you."

"Stories in general—not yours."

Some of the jurors laughed. Against a sombre background humor shows high lights. Soldiers in the intervals of battle laugh easily, and a jest in the death chamber conquers by surprise.

"Relate the circumstances of this man's death," said the coroner. "You may use any notes or memoranda that you please."

The witness understood. Pulling a manuscript from his breast pocket he held it near the candle and turning the leaves until he found the passage that he wanted began to read.

2.
WHAT MAY HAPPEN IN A FIELD OF WILD OATS

"...The sun had hardly risen when we left the house. We were looking for quail, each with a shotgun, but we had only one dog. Morgan said that our best ground was beyond a certain ridge that he pointed out, and we crossed it by a trail through the *chaparral*. On the other side was comparatively level ground, thickly covered with wild oats. As we emerged from the *chaparral* Morgan was but a few yards in advance. Suddenly we heard, at a little distance to our right and partly in front, a noise as of some animal thrashing about in the bushes, which we could see were violently agitated.

"'We've started a deer,' I said. 'I wish we had brought a rifle.'

"Morgan, who had stopped and was intently watching the agitated *chaparral*, said nothing, but had cocked both barrels of his gun and was holding it in readiness to aim. I thought him a trifle excited, which surprised me, for he had a reputation for exceptional coolness, even in moments of sudden and imminent peril.

"'O, come,' I said. 'You are not going to fill up a deer with quail-shot, are you?'

"Still he did not reply; but catching a sight of his face as he turned it slightly toward me I was struck by the intensity of his look. Then I understood that we had serious business in hand and my first conjecture was that we had 'jumped' a grizzly. I advanced to Morgan's side, cocking my piece as I moved.

"The bushes were now quiet and the sounds had ceased, but Morgan was as attentive to the place as before.

"'What is it? What the devil is it?' I asked.

"'That Damned Thing!' he replied, without turning his head. His voice was husky and unnatural. He trembled visibly.

"I was about to speak further, when I observed the wild oats near the place of the disturbance moving in the most inexplicable way. I can hardly describe it. It seemed as if stirred by a streak of wind, which not only bent it, but pressed it down—crushed it so that it did not rise; and this movement was slowly prolonging itself directly toward us.

"Nothing that I had ever seen had affected me so strangely as this unfamiliar and unaccountable phenomenon, yet I am unable to recall any sense of fear. I remember—and tell it here because, singularly enough, I recollected it then—that once in looking carelessly out of an open window I momentarily mistook a small tree close at hand for one of a group of larger trees at a little distance away. It looked the same size as the others, but being more distinctly and sharply defined in mass and detail seemed out of harmony with them. It was a mere falsification of the law of aërial perspective, but it startled, almost terrified me. We so rely upon the orderly operation of familiar natural laws that any seeming suspension of them is noted as a menace to our safety, a warning of unthinkable calamity. So now the apparently causeless movement of the herbage and the slow, undeviating approach of the line of disturbance were distinctly disquieting. My companion appeared actually frightened, and I could hardly credit my senses when I saw him suddenly throw his gun to his shoulder and fire both barrels at the agitated grain! Before the smoke of the discharge had cleared away I heard a loud savage cry—a scream like that of a wild animal—and flinging his gun upon the ground Morgan sprang away and ran swiftly from the spot. At the same instant I was thrown violently to the ground by the impact of something unseen in the smoke—some soft, heavy substance that seemed thrown against me with great force.

"Before I could get upon my feet and recover my gun, which seemed to have been struck from my hands, I heard Morgan crying out as if in mortal agony, and mingling with his cries were such hoarse, savage sounds as one hears from fighting dogs. Inexpressibly terrified, I struggled to my feet and looked in the direction of Morgan's retreat; and may Heaven in mercy spare me from another sight like that! At a distance of less than thirty yards was my friend, down upon one knee, his head thrown back at a frightful angle, hatless, his long hair in disorder and his whole body in violent movement from side to side, backward and forward. His right arm was lifted and seemed to lack the hand—at least, I could see none. The other arm was invisible. At times, as my memory now reports this extraordinary scene, I could discern but a part of his body; it was as if he had been partly blotted out—I cannot otherwise express it—then a shifting of his position would bring it all into view again.

"All this must have occurred within a few seconds, yet in that time Morgan assumed all the postures of a determined wrestler vanquished by superior weight and strength. I saw nothing but him, and him not always distinctly. During the entire incident his shouts and curses were heard, as if through an enveloping uproar of such sounds of rage and fury as I had never heard from the throat of man or brute!

"For a moment only I stood irresolute, then throwing down my gun I ran forward to my friend's assistance. I had a vague belief that he was suffering from a fit, or some form of convulsion. Before I could reach his side he was down and quiet. All sounds had ceased, but with a feeling of such terror as even these awful events had not inspired I now saw again the mysterious movement of the wild oats, prolonging itself from the trampled area about the prostrate man toward the edge of a wood. It was only when it had reached the wood that I was able to withdraw my eyes and look at my companion. He was dead."

3.
A MAN THOUGH NAKED MAY BE IN RAGS

The coroner rose from his seat and stood beside the dead man. Lifting an edge of the sheet he pulled it away, exposing the entire body, altogether naked and showing in the candle-light a claylike yellow. It had, however, broad maculations of bluish black, obviously caused by extravasated blood from contusions. The chest and sides looked as if they had been beaten with a bludgeon. There were dreadful lacerations; the skin was torn in strips and shreds.

The coroner moved round to the end of the table and undid a silk handkerchief which had been passed under the chin and knotted on the top of the head. When the handkerchief was drawn away it exposed what had been the throat. Some of the jurors who had risen to get a better view repented their curiosity and turned away their faces. Witness Harker went to the open window and leaned out across the sill, faint and sick. Dropping the handkerchief upon the dead man's neck the coroner stepped to an angle of the room and from a pile of clothing produced one garment after another, each of which he held up a moment for inspection. All were torn, and stiff with blood. The jurors did not make a closer inspection. They seemed rather uninterested. They had, in truth, seen all this before; the only thing that was new to them being Harker's testimony.

"Gentlemen," the coroner said, "we have no more evidence, I think. Your duty has been already explained to you; if there is nothing you wish to ask you may go outside and consider your verdict."

The foreman rose—a tall, bearded man of sixty, coarsely clad.

"I should like to ask one question, Mr. Coroner," he said. "What asylum did this yer last witness escape from?"

"Mr. Harker," said the coroner, gravely and tranquilly, "from what asylum did you last escape?"

Harker flushed crimson again, but said nothing, and the seven jurors rose and solemnly filed out of the cabin.

"If you have done insulting me, sir," said Harker, as soon as he and the officer were left alone with the dead man, "I suppose I am at liberty to go?"

"Yes."

Harker started to leave, but paused, with his hand on the door latch. The habit of his profession was strong in him—stronger than his sense of personal dignity. He turned about and said:

"The book that you have there—I recognize it as Morgan's diary. You seemed greatly interested in it; you read in it while I was testifying. May I see it? The public would like——"

"The book will cut no figure in this matter," replied the official, slipping it into his coat pocket; "all the entries in it were made before the writer's death."

As Harker passed out of the house the jury reëntered and stood about the table, on which the now covered corpse showed under the sheet with sharp definition. The foreman seated himself near the candle, produced from his breast pocket a pencil and scrap of paper and wrote rather laboriously the following verdict, which with various degrees of effort all signed:

"We, the jury, do find that the remains come to their death at the hands of a mountain lion, but some of us thinks, all the same, they had fits."

4.
AN EXPLANATION FROM THE TOMB

In the diary of the late Hugh Morgan are certain interesting entries having, possibly, a scientific value as suggestions. At the inquest upon his body the book was not put in evidence; possibly the coroner thought it not worth while to confuse the jury. The date of the first of the entries mentioned cannot be ascertained; the upper part of the leaf is torn away; the part of the entry remaining follows:

". . . would run in a half-circle, keeping his head turned always toward the centre, and again he would stand still, barking furiously. At last he ran away into the brush as fast as he could go. I thought at first that he had gone mad, but on returning to the house found no other alteration in his manner than what was obviously due to fear of punishment.

"Can a dog see with his nose? Do odors impress some cerebral centre with images of the thing that emitted them? . . .

"Sept. 2.—Looking at the stars last night as they rose above the crest of the ridge east of the house, I observed them successively disappear—from left to right. Each was eclipsed but an instant, and only a few at the same time, but along the entire length of the ridge all that were within a degree or two of the crest were blotted out. It was as if something had passed along between me and them; but I could not see it, and the stars were not thick enough to define its outline. Ugh! I don't like this." . . .

Several weeks' entries are missing, three leaves being torn from the book.

"Sept. 27.—It has been about here again—I find evidences of its presence every day. I watched again all last night in the same cover, gun in hand, double-charged with buckshot. In the morning the fresh footprints were there, as before. Yet I would have sworn that I did not sleep—indeed, I hardly sleep at all. It is terrible, insupportable! If these amazing experiences are real I shall go mad; if they are fanciful I am mad already.

"Oct. 3.—I shall not go—it shall not drive me away. No, this is *my* house, *my* land. God hates a coward....

"Oct. 5.—I can stand it no longer; I have invited Harker to pass a few weeks with me—he has a level head. I can judge from his manner if he thinks me mad.

"Oct. 7.—I have the solution of the mystery; it came to me last night—suddenly, as by revelation. How simple—how terribly simple!

"There are sounds that we cannot hear. At either end of the scale are notes that stir no chord of that imperfect instrument, the human ear. They are too high or too grave. I have observed a flock of blackbirds occupying an entire tree-top—the tops of several trees—and all in full song. Suddenly—in a moment—at absolutely the same instant—all spring into the air and fly away. How? They could not all see one another—whole tree-tops intervened. At no point could a leader have been visible to all. There must have been a signal of warning or command, high and shrill above the din, but by me unheard. I have observed, too, the same simultaneous flight when all were silent, among not only blackbirds, but other birds—quail, for example, widely separated by bushes—even on opposite sides of a hill.

"It is known to seamen that a school of whales basking or sporting on the surface of the ocean, miles apart, with the convexity of the earth between, will sometimes dive at the same instant—all gone out of sight in a moment. The signal has been sounded—too grave for the ear of the sailor at the masthead and his comrades on the deck—who nevertheless feel its vibrations in the ship as the stones of a cathedral are stirred by the bass of the organ.

"As with sounds, so with colors. At each end of the solar spectrum the chemist can detect the presence of what are known as 'actinic' rays. They represent colors—integral colors in the composition of light—which we are unable to discern. The human eye is an imperfect instrument; its range is but a few octaves of the real 'chromatic scale.' I am not mad; there are colors that we cannot see.

"And, God help me! the Damned Thing is of such a color!"

AMBROSE BIERCE

AN INHABITANT OF CARCOSA

> FOR THERE be divers sorts of death—some wherein the body remaineth; and in some it vanisheth quite away with the spirit. This commonly occurreth only in solitude (such is God's will) and, none seeing the end, we say the man is lost, or gone on a long journey—which indeed he hath; but sometimes it hath happened in sight of many, as abundant testimony showeth. In one kind of death the spirit also dieth, and this it hath been known to do while yet the body was in vigor for many years. Sometimes, as is veritably attested, it dieth with the body, but after a season is raised up again in that place where the body did decay.

Pondering these words of Hali (whom God rest) and questioning their full meaning, as one who, having an intimation, yet doubts if there be not something behind, other than that which he has discerned, I noted not whither I had strayed until a sudden chill wind striking my face revived in me a sense of my surroundings. I observed with astonishment that everything seemed unfamiliar. On every side of me stretched a bleak and desolate expanse of plain, covered with a tall overgrowth of sere grass, which rustled and whistled in the autumn wind with heaven knows what mysterious and disquieting suggestion. Protruded at long intervals above it, stood strangely shaped and somber-colored rocks, which seemed to have an understanding with one another and to exchange looks of uncomfortable significance, as if they had reared their heads to watch the issue of some foreseen event. A few blasted trees here and there appeared as leaders in this malevolent conspiracy of silent expectation.

The day, I thought, must be far advanced, though the sun was invisible; and although sensible that the air was raw and chill my consciousness of that fact was rather mental than physical—I had no feeling of discomfort. Over all the dismal landscape a canopy of low, lead-colored clouds hung like a visible curse. In all this there were a menace and a portent—a hint of evil, an intimation of doom. Bird, beast, or insect there was none. The wind sighed in the bare branches of the dead trees and the gray grass bent to whisper its dread secret to the earth; but no other sound nor motion broke the awful repose of that dismal place.

I observed in the herbage a number of weather-worn stones, evidently shaped with tools. They were broken, covered with moss and half sunken in the earth. Some lay prostrate, some leaned at various angles, none was vertical. They were obviously headstones of graves, though the graves themselves no longer existed as either mounds or depressions; the years had leveled all. Scattered here and there, more massive blocks showed where some pompous tomb or ambitious monument had once flung its feeble defiance at oblivion. So old seemed these relics, these vestiges of vanity and memorials of affection and piety, so battered and worn and stained—so neglected, deserted, forgotten the place, that I could not help thinking myself the discoverer of the burial-ground of a prehistoric race of men whose very name was long extinct.

Filled with these reflections, I was for some time heedless of the sequence of my own experiences, but soon I thought, "How came I hither?" A moment's reflection seemed to make this all clear and explain at the same time, though in a disquieting way, the singular character with which my fancy had invested all that I saw or heard. I was ill. I remembered now that I had been prostrated by a sudden fever, and that my family had told me that in my periods of delirium I had constantly cried out for liberty and air, and had been held in bed to prevent my escape out-of-doors. Now I had eluded the vigilance of my attendants and had wandered hither to—to where? I could not conjecture. Clearly I was at a considerable distance from the city where I dwelt—the ancient and famous city of Carcosa.

No signs of human life were anywhere visible nor audible; no rising smoke, no watchdog's bark, no lowing of cattle, no shouts of children at play—nothing but that dismal burial-place, with its air of mystery and dread, due to my own disordered brain. Was I not becoming again delirious, there beyond human aid? Was it not indeed *all* an illusion of my madness? I called aloud the names of my wives and sons, reached out my hands in search of theirs, even as I walked among the crumbling stones and in the withered grass.

A noise behind me caused me to turn about. A wild animal—a lynx—was approaching. The thought came to me: If I break down here in the desert—if the fever return and I fail, this beast will be at my throat. I sprang toward it, shouting. It trotted tranquilly by within a hand's breadth of me and disappeared behind a rock.

A moment later a man's head appeared to rise out of the ground a short distance away. He was ascending the farther slope of a low hill whose crest was hardly to be distinguished from the general level. His whole figure soon came into view against the background of gray cloud. He was half naked, half clad in skins. His hair was unkempt, his beard long and ragged. In one hand he carried a bow and arrow; the other held a blazing torch with a long trail of black smoke. He walked slowly and with caution, as if he feared falling into some open grave concealed by the tall grass. This strange apparition surprised but did not alarm, and taking such a course as to intercept him I met him almost face to face, accosting him with the familiar salutation, "God keep you."

He gave no heed, nor did he arrest his pace.

"Good stranger," I continued, "I am ill and lost. Direct me, I beseech you, to Carcosa."

The man broke into a barbarous chant in an unknown tongue, passing on and away.

An owl on the branch of a decayed tree hooted dismally and was answered by another in the distance. Looking upward, I saw through a sudden rift in the clouds Aldebaran and the Hyades! In all this there was a hint of night—the lynx, the man with the torch, the owl. Yet I saw—I saw even the stars in absence of the darkness. I saw, but was apparently not seen nor heard. Under what awful spell did I exist?

I seated myself at the root of a great tree, seriously to consider what it were best to do. That I was mad I could no longer doubt, yet recognized a ground of doubt in the conviction. Of fever I had no trace. I had, withal, a sense of exhilaration and vigor altogether unknown to me—a feeling of mental and physical exaltation. My senses seemed all alert; I could feel the air as a ponderous substance; I could hear the silence.

A great root of the giant tree against whose trunk I leaned as I sat held inclosed in its grasp a slab of stone, a part of which protruded into a recess formed by another root. The stone was thus partly protected from the weather, though greatly decomposed. Its edges were worn round, its corners eaten away, its surface deeply furrowed and scaled. Glittering particles of mica were visible in the earth about it—vestiges of its decomposition. This stone had apparently marked the grave out of which the tree had sprung ages ago. The tree's exacting roots had robbed the grave and made the stone a prisoner.

A sudden wind pushed some dry leaves and twigs from the uppermost face of the stone; I saw the low-relief letters of an inscription and bent to read it. God in Heaven! *my* name in full!—the date of *my* birth!—the date of *my* death!

A level shaft of light illuminated the whole side of the tree as I sprang to my feet in terror. The sun was rising in the rosy east. I stood between the tree and his broad red disk—no shadow darkened the trunk!

A chorus of howling wolves saluted the dawn. I saw them sitting on their haunches, singly and in groups, on the summits of irregular mounds and tumuli filling a half of my desert prospect and extending to the horizon. And then I knew that these were ruins of the ancient and famous city of Carcosa.

Such are the facts imparted to the medium Bayrolles by the spirit Hoseib Alar Robardin.

R. W. CHAMBERS

THE REPAIRER OF REPUTATIONS

Ne raillons pas les fous; leur folie dur plus longtemps que la notre.... Voilà toute la différence.

1.

TOWARD the end of the year 1920 the Government of the United States had practically completed the programme, adopted during the last months of President Winthrop's administration. The country was apparently tranquil. Everybody knows how the Tariff and Labor questions were settled. The war with Germany, incident on that country's seizure of the Samoan Islands, had left no visible scars upon the republic, and the temporary occupation of Norfolk by the invading army had been forgotten in the joy over repeated naval victories and the subsequent ridiculous plight of General Von Gartenlaube's forces in the State of New Jersey. The Cuban and Hawaiian investments had paid one hundred per cent. and the territory of Samoa was well worth its cost as a coaling station. The country was in a superb state of defence. Every coast city had been well supplied with land fortifications; the army under the parental eye of the General Staff, organized according to the Prussian system, had been increased to 300,000 men with a territorial reserve of a million; and six magnificent squadrons of cruisers and battleships patrolled the six stations of the navigable seas, leaving a steam reserve amply fitted to control home waters. The gentlemen from the West had at last been constrained to acknowledge that a college for the training of diplomats was as necessary as law schools are for the training of barristers; consequently we were no longer represented abroad by incompetent patriots. The nation was prosperous. Chicago, for a moment paralyzed after a second great fire, had risen from its ruins, white and imperial, and more beautiful than the white city which had been built for its plaything in 1893. Everywhere good architecture was replacing bad, and even in New York, a sudden craving for decency had swept away a great portion of the existing horrors. Streets had been widened, properly paved and lighted, trees had been planted, squares laid out, elevated structures demolished and underground roads built to replace them. The new government buildings and barracks were fine bits of architecture, and the long system of stone quays which completely surrounded the island had been turned into parks which proved a godsend to the population. The subsidizing of the state theatre and state opera brought its own reward. The United States National Academy of Design was much like European institutions of the same kind. Nobody envied the Secretary of Fine Arts, either his cabinet position or his portfolio. The Secretary of Forestry and Game Preservation had a much easier time, thanks to the new system of National Mounted Police. We had profited well by the latest treaties with France and England; the exclusion of foreign-born Jews as a measure of national self-preservation, the settlement of the new independent Negro state of Suanee, the checking of immigration, the new laws concerning naturalization, and the gradual centralization of power in the executive all contributed to national calm and prosperity. When the Government solved the Indian problem and squadrons of Indian cavalry scouts in native costume were substituted for the pitiable organizations tacked on to the tail of skeletonized regiments by a former Secretary of War, the nation drew a long sigh of relief. When, after the colossal Congress of Religions, bigotry and intolerance were laid in their graves and kindness and charity began to draw warring sects together, many thought the millennium had arrived, at least in the new world, which after all is a world by itself.

But self-preservation is the first law, and the United States had to look on in helpless sorrow as Germany, Italy, Spain and Belgium writhed in the throes of Anarchy, while Russia, watching from the Caucasus, stooped and bound them one by one.

In the city of New York the summer of 1899 was signalized by the dismantling of the Elevated Railroads. The summer of 1900 will live in the memories of New York people for many a cycle; the Dodge Statue was removed in that year. In the following winter began that agitation for the repeal of the laws prohibiting suicide which bore its final fruit in the month of April, 1920, when the first Government Lethal Chamber was opened on Washington Square.

I had walked down that day from Dr. Archer's house on Madison Avenue, where I had been as a mere formality. Ever since that fall from my horse, four years before, I had been troubled at times with pains in the back of my head and neck, but now for months they had been absent, and the doctor sent me away that day saying there was nothing more to be cured in me. It was hardly worth his fee to be told that; I knew it myself. Still I did not begrudge him the money. What I minded was the mistake which he made at first. When they picked me up from the pavement where I lay unconscious, and somebody had mercifully sent a bullet through my horse's head, I was carried to Doctor Archer, and he, pronouncing my brain affected, placed me in his private asylum where I was obliged to endure treatment for insanity. At last he decided that I was well, and I, knowing that my mind had always been as sound as his, if not sounder, "paid my tuition" as he jokingly called it, and left. I told him, smiling, that I would get even with him for his mistake, and he laughed heartily, and asked me to call once in a while. I did so, hoping for a chance to even up accounts, but he gave me none, and I told him I would wait.

The fall from my horse had fortunately left no evil results; on the contrary it had changed my whole character for the better. From a lazy young man about town, I had become active, energetic, temperate, and above all—oh, above all else—ambitious. There was only one thing which troubled me. I laughed at my own uneasiness, and yet it troubled me.

During my convalescence I had bought and read for the first time, "The King in Yellow." I remembered after finishing the first act that it occurred to me that I had better stop. I started up and flung the book into the fireplace; the volume struck the barred grate and fell open on the hearth in the firelight. If I had not caught a glimpse of the opening words in the second act I should never have finished it, but as I stooped to pick it up, my eyes became riveted to the open page, and with a cry of terror, or perhaps it was of joy so poignant that I suffered in every nerve, I snatched the thing out of the coals and crept to my bedroom, where I read it and reread it, and wept and laughed and trembled with a horror which at times assails me yet. This is the thing that troubles me, for I cannot forget Carcosa where black stars hang in the heavens; where the shadows of men's thoughts lengthen in the afternoon, when the twin suns sink into the Lake of Hali; and my mind will bear forever the memory of the Pallid Mask. I pray God will curse the writer, as the writer has cursed the world with this beautiful, stupendous creation, terrible in its simplicity, irresistible in its truth—a world which now trembles before the King in Yellow. When the French Government seized the translated copies which had just arrived in Paris, London, of course, became eager to read it. It is well known how the book spread like an infectious disease, from city to city, from continent to continent, barred out here, confiscated there, denounced by press and pulpit, censured even by the most advanced of literary anarchists. No definite principles had been violated in those wicked pages, no doctrine promulgated, no convictions outraged. It could not be judged by any known standard, yet, although it was acknowledged that the supreme note of art had been struck in "The King in Yellow," all felt that human nature could not bear the strain, nor thrive on words in which the essence of purest poison lurked. The very banality and innocence of the first act only allowed the blow to fall afterward with more awful effect.

It was, I remember, the 13th day of April, 1920, that the first Government Lethal Chamber was established on the south side of Washington Square, between Wooster Street and South Fifth Avenue. The block which had formerly consisted of a lot of shabby old buildings, used as cafés and restaurants for foreigners, had been acquired by the Government in the winter of 1898. The French and Italian cafés were torn down; the whole block was enclosed by a gilded iron railing, and converted into a lovely garden with lawns, flowers and fountains. In the centre of the garden stood a small, white building, severely classical in architecture, and surrounded by thickets of flowers. Six Ionic columns supported the roof, and the single door was of bronze. A splendid marble group of "The Fates" stood before the door, the work of a young American sculptor, Boris Yvain, who had died in Paris when only twenty-three years old.

The inauguration ceremonies were in progress as I crossed University Place and entered the square. I threaded my way through the silent throng of spectators, but was stopped at Fourth Street by a cordon of police. A regiment of United States lancers were drawn up in a hollow square around the Lethal Chamber. On a raised tribune facing Washington Park stood the Governor of New York, and behind him were grouped the Mayor of New York and Brooklyn, the Inspector-General of Police, the Commandant of the state troops, Colonel Livingston, military aide to the President of the United States, General Blount, commanding at Governor's Island,

Major-General Hamilton, commanding the garrison of New York and Brooklyn, Admiral Buffby of the fleet in the North River, Surgeon-General Lanceford, the staff of the National Free Hospital, Senators Wyse and Franklin of New York, and the Commissioner of Public Works. The tribune was surrounded by a squadron of hussars of the National Guard.

The Governor was finishing his reply to the short speech of the Surgeon-General. I heard him say: "The laws prohibiting suicide and providing punishment for any attempt at self-destruction have been repealed. The Government has seen fit to acknowledge the right of man to end an existence which may have become intolerable to him, through physical suffering or mental despair. It is believed that the community will be benefited by the removal of such people from their midst. Since the passage of this law, the number of suicides in the United States has not increased. Now that the Government has determined to establish a Lethal Chamber in every city, town and village in the country, it remains to be seen whether or not that class of human creatures from whose desponding ranks new victims of self-destruction fall daily will accept the relief thus provided." He paused, and turned to the white Lethal Chamber. The silence in the street was absolute. "There a painless death awaits him who can no longer bear the sorrows of this life. If death is welcome let him seek it there." Then quickly turning to the military aide of the President's household, he said, "I declare the Lethal Chamber open," and again facing the vast crowd he cried in a clear voice: "Citizens of New York and of the United States of America, through me the Government declares the Lethal Chamber to be open."

The solemn hush was broken by a sharp cry of command, the squadron of hussars filed after the Governor's carriage, the lancers wheeled and formed along Fifth Avenue to wait for the commandant of the garrison, and the mounted police followed them. I left the crowd to gape and stare at the white marble Death Chamber, and, crossing South Fifth Avenue, walked along the western side of that thoroughfare to Bleecker Street. Then I turned to the right and stopped before a dingy shop which bore the sign,

HAWBERK, ARMORER

I glanced in at the doorway and Hawberk busy in his little shop at the end of the hall. He looked up, and catching sight of me cried in his deep, hearty voice, "Come in, Mr. Castaigne!" Constance, his daughter, rose to meet me as I crossed the threshold, and held out her pretty hand, but I saw the blush of disappointment on her cheeks, knew that it was another Castaigne she had expected, my cousin Louis. I smiled at her confusion and complimented her on the banner which she was embroidering from a colored plate. Old Hawberk sat riveting the worn greaves of some ancient suit of armor, and the ting! ting! ting! of his little hammer sounded pleasantly in the quaint shop. Presently he dropped his hammer, and fussed about for a moment with a tiny wrench. The soft clash of the mail sent a thrill of pleasure through me. I loved to hear the music of steel brushing against steel, the mellow shock of the mallet on thigh pieces, and the jingle of chain armor. That was the only reason I went to see Hawberk. He had never interested me personally, nor did Constance, except for the fact of her being in love with Louis. This did occupy my attention, and sometimes even kept me awake at night. But I knew in my heart that all would come right, and that I should arrange their future as I expected to arrange that of my kind doctor, John Archer. However, I should never have troubled myself about visiting them just then, had it not been, as I say, that the music of the tinkling hammer had for me this strong fascination. I would sit for hours, listening and listening, and when a stray sunbeam struck the inlaid steel, the sensation it gave me was almost too keen to endure.

My eyes would become fixed, dilating with a pleasure that stretched every nerve almost to breaking, until some movement of the old armorer cut off the ray of sunlight, then, still thrilling secretly, I leaned back and listened again to the sound of the polishing rag, swish! swish! rubbing rust from the rivets.

Constance worked with the embroidery over her knees, now and then pausing to examine more closely the pattern in the colored plate from the Metropolitan Museum.

"Who is this for?" I asked.

Hawberk explained, that in addition to the treasures of armor in the Metropolitan Museum of which he had been appointed armorer, he also had charge of several collections belonging to rich amateurs. This was the missing greave of a famous suit which a client of his had traced to a little shop in Paris on the Quai d'Orsay. He, Hawberk, had negotiated for and secured the greave, and now the suit was complete. He laid down his hammer and read me the history of the suit, traced since 1450 from owner to owner until it was acquired by Thomas Stainbridge. When his superb collection was sold, this client of Hawberk's bought the suit, and since then the search for the missing greave had been pushed until it was, almost by accident, located in Paris.

"Did you continue the search so persistently without any certainty of the greave being still in existence?" I demanded.

"Of course," he replied coolly.

Then for the first time I took a personal interest in Hawberk.

"It was worth something to you," I ventured.

"No," he replied, laughing, "my pleasure in finding it was my reward."

"Have you no ambition to be rich?" I asked smiling.

"My one ambition is to be the best armorer in the world," he answered gravely.

Constance asked me if I had seen the ceremonies at the

Lethal Chamber. She herself had noticed cavalry passing up Broadway that morning, and had wished to see the inauguration, but her father wanted the banner finished, and she had stayed at his request.

"Did you see your cousin, Mr. Castaigne, there?" she asked with the slightest tremor of her soft eyelashes.

"No," I replied carelessly. "Louis' regiment is manoeuvring out in Westchester County." I rose and picked up my hat and cane.

"Are you going upstairs to see the lunatic again?" laughed old Hawberk. If Hawberk knew how I loathe that word "lunatic," he would never use it in my presence. It rouses certain feelings within me which I do not care to explain. However, I answered him quietly: "I think I shall drop in and see Mr. Wilde for a moment or two."

"Poor fellow," said Constance, with a shake of her head, "it must be hard to live alone year after year, poor, crippled and almost demented. It is very good of you, Mr. Castaigne, to visit him as often as you do."

"I think he is vicious," observed Hawberk, beginning again with his hammer. I listened to the golden tinkle on the greave plates; when he had finished I replied:

"No, he is not vicious, nor is he in the least demented. His mind is a wonder chamber, from which he can extract treasures that you and I would give years of our lives to acquire."

Hawberk laughed.

I continued a little impatiently: "He knows history as no one else could know it. Nothing, however trivial, escapes his search, and his memory is so absolute, so precise in details, that were it known in New York that such a man existed the people could not honor him enough."

"Nonsense," muttered Hawberk, searching on the floor for a fallen rivet.

"Is it nonsense," I asked, managing to suppress what I felt, "is it nonsense when he says that the tassets and cuissards of the enamelled suit of armor commonly known as the 'Prince's Emblazoned' can be found among a mass of rusty theatrical properties, broken stoves and ragpicker's refuse in a garret in Pell Street?"

Hawberk's hammer fell to the ground, but he picked it up and asked, with a great deal of calm, how I knew that the tassets and left cuissard were missing from the "Prince's Emblazoned."

"I did not know until Mr. Wilde mentioned it to me the other day. He said they were in the garret of 998 Pell Street."

"Nonsense," he cried, but I noticed his hand trembling under his leathern apron.

"Is this nonsense too?" I asked pleasantly. "Is it nonsense when Mr. Wilde continually speaks of you as the Marquis of Avonshire and of Miss Constance—"

I did not finish, for Constance had started to her feet with terror written on every feature. Hawberk looked at me and slowly smoothed his leathern apron. "That is impossible," he observed, "Mr. Wilde may know a great many things—"

"About armor, for instance, and the 'Prince's Emblazoned,'" I interposed, smiling.

"Yes," he continued, slowly, "about armor also—maybe—but he is wrong in regard to the Marquis of Avonshire, who, as you know, killed his wife's traducer years ago, and went to Australia where he did not long survive his wife."

"Mr. Wilde is wrong," murmured Constance. Her lips were blanched but her voice was sweet and calm.

"Let us agree, if you please, that in this one circumstance Mr. Wilde is wrong," I said.

2.

I climbed the three dilapidated flights of stairs, which I had so often climbed before, and knocked at a small door at the end of the corridor. Mr. Wilde opened the door and I walked in.

When he had double-locked the door and pushed a heavy chest against it, he came and sat down beside me, peering up into my face with his little light-colored eyes. Half a dozen new scratches covered his nose and cheeks, and the silver wires which supported his artificial ears had become displaced. I thought I had never seen him so hideously fascinating. He had no ears. The artificial ones, which now stood out at an angle from the fine wire, were his one weakness. They were made of wax and painted a shell pink, but the rest of his face was yellow. He might better have revelled in the luxury of some artificial fingers for his left hand, which was absolutely fingerless, but it seemed to cause him no inconvenience, and he was satisfied with his wax ears. He was very small, scarcely higher than a child of ten, but his arms were magnificently developed, and his thighs as thick as any athlete's. Still, the most remarkable thing about Mr. Wilde was that a man of his marvelous intelligence and knowledge should have such a head. It was flat and pointed, like the heads of many of those unfortunates whom people imprison in asylums for the weak-minded. Many called him insane but I knew him to be as sane as I was.

I do not deny that he was eccentric; the mania he had for keeping that cat and teasing her until she flew at his face like a demon, was certainly eccentric. I never could understand why he kept the creature, nor what pleasure he found in shutting himself up in his room with the surly, vicious beast. I remembered once, glancing up from the manuscript I was studying by the light of some tallow dips, and seeing Mr. Wilde squatting motionless on his high chair, his eyes fairly blazing with excitement, while the cat, which had risen from her place before the stove, came creeping across the floor right at him. Before I could move she flattened her belly to the ground, crouched, trembled, and sprang into his face. Howling and foaming they rolled over and over the floor, scratching and clawing, until the cat screamed and fled under the cabinet, and Mr. Wilde turned over on his back, his limbs contracting and curling up like the legs of a dying spider. He *was* eccentric.

Mr. Wilde had climbed into his high chair, and, after studying my face, picked up a dog's-eared ledger and opened it.

"Henry B. Matthews," he read, "bookkeeper with Whysot Whysot and Company, dealers in church ornaments. Called April 3d. Reputation damaged on the race-track. Known as a welcher. Reputation to be repaired by August 1st. Retainer Five Dollars." He turned the page and ran his fingerless knuckles down the closely-written columns.

"P. Greene Dusenberry, Minister of the Gospel, Fairbeach, New Jersey. Reputation damaged in the Bowery. To be repaired as soon as possible. Retainer $100."

He coughed and added, "Called, April 6th."

"Then you are not in need of money, Mr. Wilde," I inquired.

"Listen," he coughed again.

"Mrs. C. Hamilton Chester, of Chester Park, New York City. Called April 7th. Reputation damaged at Dieppe, France. To be repaired by October 1st. Retainer $500.

"Note—C. Hamilton Chester, Captain, U.S.S. *Avalanche* ordered home from South Sea Squadron October 1st."

"Well," I said, "the profession of a Repairer of Reputations is lucrative."

His colorless eyes sought mine. "I only wanted to demonstrate that I was correct. You said it was impossible to succeed as a Repairer of Reputations; that even if I did succeed in certain cases it would cost me more than I would gain by it. To-day I have five hundred men in my employ, who are poorly paid, but who pursue the work with an enthusiasm which possibly may be born of fear. These men enter every shade and grade of society; some even are pillars of the most exclusive social temples; others are the prop and pride of the financial world; still others, hold undisputed sway among the

'Fancy and the Talent.' I choose them at my leisure from those who reply to my advertisements. It is easy enough, they are all cowards. I could treble the number in twenty days if I wished. So you see, those who have in their keeping the reputations of their fellow-citizens, *I* have in my pay."

"They may turn on you," I suggested.

He rubbed his thumb over his cropped ears, and adjusted the wax substitutes. "I think not," he murmured thoughtfully, "I seldom have to apply the whip, and then only once. Besides, they like their wages."

"How do you apply the whip?" I demanded.

His face for a moment was awful to look upon. His eyes dwindled to a pair of green sparks.

"I invite them to come and have a little chat with me," he said in a soft voice.

A knock at the door interrupted him, and his face resumed its amiable expression.

"Who is it?" he inquired.

"Mr. Steylette," was the answer.

"Come to-morrow," replied Mr. Wilde.

"Impossible," began the other, but was silenced by a sort of bark from Mr. Wilde.

"Come to-morrow," he repeated.

We heard somebody move away from the door and turn the corner by the stairway.

"Who is that?" I asked.

"Arnold Steylette, Owner and Editor in Chief of the great New York daily."

He drummed on the ledger with his fingerless hand adding: "I pay him very badly, but he thinks it a good bargain."

"Arnold Steylette!" I repeated amazed.

"Yes," said Mr. Wilde with a self-satisfied cough.

The cat, which had entered the room as he spoke, hesitated, looked up at him and snarled. He climbed down from the chair and squatting on the floor, took the creature into his arms and caressed her. The cat ceased snarling and presently began a loud purring which seemed to increase in timbre as he stroked her.

"Where are the notes?" I asked. He pointed to the table, and for the hundredth time I picked up the bundle of manuscript entitled

THE IMPERIAL DYNASTY OF AMERICA

One by one I studied the well-worn pages, worn only by my own handling, and although I knew all by heart, from the beginning, "When from Carcosa, the Hyades, Hastur, and Aldebaran," to "Castaigne, Louis de Calvados, born December 19th, 1877," I read it with an eager rapt attention, pausing to repeat parts of it aloud, and dwelling especially on "Hildred de Calvados, only son of Hildred Castaigne and Edythe Landes Castaigne, first in success," etc., etc.

When I finished, Mr. Wilde nodded and coughed.

"Speaking of your legitimate ambition," he said, "how do Constance and Louis get along?"

"She loves him," I replied simply.

The cat on his knee suddenly turned and struck at his eyes, and he flung her off and climbed on to the chair opposite me.

"And Doctor Archer! But that's a matter you can settle any time you wish," he added.

"Yes," I replied, "Doctor Archer can wait, but it is time I saw my cousin Louis."

"It is time," he repeated. Then he took another ledger from the table and ran over the leaves rapidly.

"We are now in communication with ten thousand men," he muttered. "We can count on one hundred thousand within the first twenty-eight hours, and in forty-eight hours the state will rise *en masse*. The country follows the state, and the portion that will not, I mean California and the Northwest, might better never have been inhabited. I shall not send them the Yellow Sign."

The blood rushed to my head, but I only answered, "A new broom sweeps clean."

"The ambition of Caesar and of Napoleon pales before that which could not rest until it had seized the minds of men and controlled even their unborn thoughts," said Mr. Wilde.

"You are speaking of the King in Yellow," I groaned with a shudder.

"He is a king whom emperors have served."

"I am content to serve him," I replied.

Mr. Wilde sat rubbing his ears with his crippled hand. "Perhaps Constance does not love him," he suggested.

I started to reply, but a sudden burst of military music from the street below drowned my voice. The twentieth dragoon regiment, formerly in garrison at Mount St. Vincent, was returning from the manoeuvres in Westchester County, to its new barracks on East Washington Square. It was my cousin's regiment. They were a fine lot of fellows, in their pale-blue, tight-fitting jackets, jaunty busbys and white riding breeches with the double yellow stripe, into which their limbs seemed molded. Every other squadron was armed with lances, from the metal points of which fluttered yellow and white pennons. The band passed, playing the regimental march, then came the colonel and staff, the horses crowding and trampling, while their heads bobbed in unison, and the pennons fluttered from their lance points. The troopers, who rode with the beautiful English seat, looked brown as berries from their bloodless campaign among the farms of Westchester, and the music of their sabres against the stirrups, and the jingle of spurs and carbines was delightful to me. I saw Louis riding with his squadron. He was as handsome an officer as I have ever seen. Mr. Wilde, who had mounted a chair by the window, saw him too, but said nothing. Louis turned and looked straight at Hawberk's shop as he passed, and I could see the flush on his brown cheeks. I think Constance must have been at the window. When the last troopers had clattered by, and the last pennons vanished into South Fifth Avenue, Mr. Wilde clambered out of his chair and dragged the chest away from the door.

"Yes," he said, "it is time that you saw your cousin Louis."

He unlocked the door and I picked up my hat and stick and stepped into the corridor. The stairs were dark. Groping about, I set my foot on something soft, which snarled and spit, and I aimed a murderous blow at the cat, but my cane shivered to splinters against the balustrade, and the beast scurried back into Mr. Wilde's room.

Passing Hawberk's door again I saw him still at work on the armor, but I did not stop, and stepping out into Bleecker Street, I followed it to Wooster, skirted the grounds of the Lethal Chamber, and crossing Washington Park went straight to my rooms in the Benedick. Here I lunched comfortably, read the *Herald* and the *Meteor*, and finally went to the steel safe in my bedroom and set the time combination. The three and three-quarter minutes which it is necessary to wait, while the time lock is opening, are to me golden moments. From the instant I set the combination to the moment when I grasp the knobs and swing back the solid steel doors, I live in an ecstasy of expectation. Those moments must be like the moments passed in Paradise. I know what I am to find at the end of the time limit. I know what the massive safe holds secure for me, for me alone, and the exquisite pleasure of waiting is hardly enhanced when the safe opens and I lift, from its velvet crown, a diadem of purest gold, blazing with diamonds. I do this every day, and yet the joy of waiting and at last touching the diadem, only seems to increase as the days pass. It is a diadem fit for a King among kings, an Emperor among emperors. The King in Yellow might scorn it, but it shall be worn by his royal servant.

I held it in my arms until the alarm on the safe rang

harshly, and then tenderly, proudly, I replaced it and shut the steel doors. I walked slowly back into my study, which faces Washington Square, and leaned on the windowsill. The afternoon sun poured into my windows, and a gentle breeze stirred the branches of the elms and maples in the park, now covered with buds and tender foliage. A flock of pigeons circled about the tower of the Memorial Church; sometimes alighting on the purple tiled roof, sometimes wheeling downward to the lotos fountain in front of the marble arch. The gardeners were busy with the flower beds around the fountain, and the freshly-turned earth smelled sweet and spicy. A lawn mower, drawn by a fat white horse, clinked across the green sward, and watering carts poured showers of spray over the asphalt drives. Around the statue of Peter Stuyvesant, which in 1897 had replaced the monstrosity supposed to represent Garibaldi, children played in the spring sunshine, and nurse girls wheeled elaborate baby-carriages with a reckless disregard for the pasty-faced occupants, which could probably be explained by the presence of half a dozen trim dragoon troopers languidly lolling on the benches. Through the trees, the Washington Memorial Arch glistened like silver in the sunshine, and beyond, on the eastern extremity of the square the gray stone barracks of the dragoons, and the white granite artillery stables were alive with color and motion.

I looked at the Lethal Chamber on the corner of the square opposite. A few curious people still lingered about the gilded iron railing, but inside the grounds the paths were deserted. I watched the fountains ripple and sparkle; the sparrows had already found this new bathing nook, and the basins were crowded with the dusty-feathered little things. Two or three white peacocks picked their way across the lawns, and a drab-colored pigeon sat so motionless on the arm of one of the Fates, that it seemed to be a part of the sculptured stone.

As I was turning carelessly away, a slight commotion in

the group of curious loiterers around the gates attracted my attention. A young man had entered, and was advancing with nervous strides along the gravel path which leads to the bronze doors of the Lethal Chamber. He paused a moment before the Fates, and as he raised his head to those three mysterious faces, the pigeon rose from its sculptured perch, circled about for a moment and wheeled to the east. The young man pressed his hands to his face, and then with an undefinable gesture sprang up the marble steps, the bronze doors closed behind him, and half an hour later the loiterers slouched away, and the frightened pigeon returned to its perch in the arms of Fate.

I put on my hat and went out into the park for a little walk before dinner. As I crossed the central driveway a group of officers passed, and one of them called out, "Hello, Hildred," and came back to shake hands with me. It was my cousin Louis, who stood smiling and tapping his spurred heels with his riding-whip.

"Just back from Westchester," he said; "been doing the bucolic; milk and curds, you know, dairy-maids in sunbonnets, who say 'haeow' and 'I don't think' when you tell them they are pretty. I'm nearly dead for a square meal at Delmonico's. What's the news?"

"There is none," I replied pleasantly. "I saw your regiment coming in this morning."

"Did you? I didn't see you. Where were you?"

"In Mr. Wilde's window."

"Oh hell!" he began impatiently, "that man is stark mad! I don't understand why you—"

He saw how annoyed I felt by this outburst, and begged my pardon.

"Really, old chap," he said, "I don't mean to run down a man you like, but for the life of me I can't see what the deuce you find in common with Mr. Wilde. He's not well-bred, to put it generously; he's hideously deformed; his head is the head of a criminally insane person. You know yourself he's been in an asylum—"

"So have I," I interrupted calmly.

Louis looked startled and confused for a moment, but recovered and slapped me heartily on the shoulder.

"You were completely cured," he began, but I stopped him again.

"I suppose you mean that I was simply acknowledged never to have been insane."

"Of course that—that's what I meant," he laughed.

I disliked his laugh because I knew it was forced, but I nodded gaily and asked him where he was going. Louis looked after his brother officers who had now almost reached Broadway.

"We had intended to sample a Brunswick cocktail, but to tell you the truth I was anxious for an excuse to go and see Hawberk instead. Come along, I'll make you my excuse."

We found old Hawberk, neatly attired in a fresh spring suit, standing at the door of his shop and sniffing the air.

"I had just decided to take Constance for a little stroll before dinner," he replied to the impetuous volley of questions from Louis. "We thought of walking on the park terrace along the North River."

At that moment Constance appeared and grew pale and rosy by turns as Louis bent over her small gloved fingers. I tried to excuse myself, alleging an engagement up-town, but Louis and Constance would not listen, and I saw I was expected to remain and engage old Hawberk's attention. After all it would be just as well if I kept my eye on Louis, I thought, and when they hailed a Spring Street horsecar, I got in after them and took my seat beside the armorer.

The beautiful line of parks and granite terraces overlooking the wharves along the North River, which were built in 1910 and finished in the autumn of 1917, had become one of the most popular promenades in the metropolis. They extended from the battery to 190th Street, overlooking the noble river and affording a fine view of the Jersey shore and the Highlands opposite. Cafés and restaurants were scattered here and there among the trees, and twice a week military bands from the garrison played in the kiosques on the parapets.

We sat down in the sunshine on the bench at the foot of the equestrian statue of General Sheridan. Constance tipped her sunshade to shield her eyes, and she and Louis began a murmuring conversation which was impossible to catch. Old Hawberk, leaning on his ivory-headed cane, lighted an excellent cigar, the mate to which I politely refused, and smiled at vacancy. The sun hung low above the Staten Island woods, and the bay was dyed with golden hues reflected from the sun-warmed sails of the shipping in the harbor.

Brigs, schooners, yachts, clumsy ferry-boats, their decks swarming with people, railroad transports carrying lines of brown, blue and white freight cars, stately sound steamers, *declassé* tramp steamers, coasters, dredgers, scows, and everywhere pervading the entire bay impudent little tugs puffing and whistling officiously;—these were the crafts which churned the sunlit waters as far as the eye could reach. In calm contrast to the hurry of sailing vessel and steamer a silent fleet of white warships lay motionless in midstream.

Constance's merry laugh aroused me from my reverie.

"What *are* you staring at?" she inquired.

"Nothing—the fleet," I smiled.

Then Louis told us what the vessels were, pointing out each by its relative position to the old Red Fort on Governor's Island.

"That little cigar-shaped thing is a torpedo boat," he explained; "there are four more lying close together. They are the *Tarpon*, the *Falcon*, the *Sea Fox* and the *Octopus*. The gun-boats just above are the *Princeton*, the *Champlain*, the *Still Water* and the *Erie*. Next to them lie the cruisers *Farragut* and *Los Angeles*, and above them the battleships *California* and *Dakota*, and the *Washington* which is the flag-ship. Those two squatty-looking chunks of metal which are anchored there off Castle William are the double-turreted monitors *Terrible* and *Magnificent*; behind them lies the ram, *Osceola*."

Constance looked at him with deep approval in her beautiful eyes. "What loads of things you know for a soldier," she said, and we all joined in the laugh which followed.

Presently Louis rose with a nod to us and offered his arm to Constance, and they strolled away along the river wall. Hawberk watched them for a moment and then turned to me.

"Mr. Wilde was right," he said. "I have found the missing tassets and left cuissard of the 'Prince's Emblazoned,' in a vile old junk garret in Pell Street."

"998?" I inquired, with a smile.

"Yes."

"Mr. Wilde is a very intelligent man," I observed.

"I want to give him the credit of this most important discovery," continued Hawberk. "And I intend it shall be known that he is entitled to the fame of it."

"He won't thank you for that," I answered sharply; "please say nothing about it."

"Do you know what it is worth?" said Hawberk.

"No, fifty dollars, perhaps."

"It is valued at five hundred, but the owner of the 'Prince's Emblazoned' will give two thousand dollars to the person who completes his suit; that reward also belongs to Mr. Wilde."

"He doesn't want it! He refuses it!" I answered angrily. "What do you know about Mr. Wilde? He doesn't need the money. He is rich—or will be—richer than any living man except myself. What will we care for money then—what will we care, he and I, when—when—"

"When what?" demanded Hawberk, astonished.

"You will see," I replied, on my guard again.

He looked at me narrowly, much as Doctor Archer used to, and I knew he thought I was mentally unsound. Perhaps it was fortunate for him that he did not use the word lunatic just then.

"No," I replied to his unspoken thought, "I am not mentally

weak; my mind is as healthy as Mr. Wilde's. I do not care to explain just yet what I have on hand, but it is an investment which will pay more than mere gold, silver and precious stones. It will secure the happiness and prosperity of a continent—yes, a hemisphere!"

"Oh," said Hawberk.

"And eventually," I continued more quietly, "it will secure the happiness of the whole world."

"And incidentally your own happiness and prosperity as well as Mr. Wilde's?"

"Exactly," I smiled. But I could have throttled him for taking that tone.

He looked at me in silence for a while and then said very gently, "Why don't you give up your books and studies, Mr. Castaigne, and take a tramp among the mountains somewhere or other? You used to be fond of fishing. Take a cast or two at the trout in the Rangeleys."

"I don't care for fishing any more," I answered, without a shade of annoyance in my voice.

"You used to be fond of everything," he continued; "athletics, yachting, shooting, riding—"

"I have never cared to ride since my fall," I said quietly.

"Ah, yes, your fall," he repeated, looking away from me.

I thought this nonsense had gone far enough, so I turned the conversation back to Mr. Wilde; but he was scanning my face again in a manner highly offensive to me.

"Mr. Wilde," he repeated, "do you know what he did this afternoon? He came down stairs and nailed a sign over the hall door next to mine; it read:

MR. WILDE,
REPAIRER OF REPUTATIONS,
3d Bell.

Do you know what a Repairer of Reputations can be?"

"I do," I replied, suppressing the rage within.

"Oh," he said again.

Louis and Constance came strolling by and stopped to ask if we would join them. Hawberk looked at his watch. At the same moment a puff of smoke shot from the casemates of Castle William, and the boom of the sunset gun rolled across the water and was re-echoed from the Highlands opposite. The flag came running down from the flag-pole, the bugles sounded on the white decks of the warships, and the first electric light sparkled out from the Jersey shore.

As I turned into the city with Hawberk I heard Constance murmur something to Louis which I did not understand; but Louis whispered, "My darling," in reply; and again, walking ahead with Hawberk through the square I heard a murmur of "sweetheart," and "my own Constance," and I knew the time had nearly arrived when I should speak of important matters with my cousin Louis.

3.

One morning early in May I stood before the steel safe in my bedroom, trying on the golden jewelled crown. The diamonds flashed fire as I turned to the mirror, and the heavy beaten gold burned like a halo about my head. I remembered Camilla's agonized scream and the awful words echoing through the streets of Carcosa. They were the last lines in the first act, and I dared not think of what followed—dared not, even in the spring sunshine, there in my own room, surrounded with familiar objects, reassured by the bustle from the street and the voices of the servants in the hallway outside. For those poisoned words had dropped slowly into my heart, as death-sweat drops upon a bed-sheet and is absorbed. Trembling, I put the diadem from my head and wiped my forehead, but I thought of Hastur and of my own rightful ambition, and I remembered Mr. Wilde as I had last left him, his face all torn and bloody from the claws of that devil's creature, and what he said—ah, what he said! The alarm bell in the safe began to whirr harshly, and I knew my time was up; but I would not heed it, and replacing the flashing circlet upon my head I turned defiantly to the mirror. I stood for a long time absorbed in the changing expression of my own eyes. The mirror reflected a face which was like my own, but whiter, and so thin that I hardly recognized it. And all the time I kept repeating between my clenched teeth, "The day has come! the day has come!" while the alarm in the safe whirred and clamored, and the diamonds sparked and flamed above my brow. I heard a door open but did not heed it. It was only when I saw two faces in the mirror;—it was only when another face rose over my shoulder, and two other eyes met mine. I wheeled like a flash and seized a long knife from the dressing-table, and my cousin sprang back very pale, crying: "Hildred! for God's sake!" then as my hand fell, he said: "It is I, Louis, don't you know me?" I stood silent. I could not have spoken for my life. He walked up to me and took the knife from my hand.

"What is all this?" he inquired, in a gentle voice. "Are you ill?"

"No," I replied. But I doubt if he heard me.

"Come, come, old fellow," he cried, "take off that brass crown and toddle into the study. Are you going to a masquerade? What's all this theatrical tinsel anyway?"

I was glad he thought the crown was made of brass and paste, yet I didn't like him any the better for thinking so. I let him take it from my hand, knowing it was best to humor him. He tossed the splendid diadem in the air, and catching it, turned to me smiling.

"It's dear at fifty cents," he said. "What's it for?"

I did not answer, but took the circlet from his hands, and placing it in the safe shut the massive steel door. The alarm ceased its infernal din at once. He watched me curiously, but did not seem to notice the sudden ceasing of the alarm. He did, however, speak of the safe as a biscuit box. Fearing lest he might examine the combination I led the way into the study. Louis threw himself on the sofa and flicked at flies with his eternal riding-whip. He wore his fatigue uniform with the braided jacket and jaunty cap, and I noticed that his riding-boots were all splashed with red mud.

"Where have you been?" I inquired.

"Jumping mud creeks in Jersey," he said. "I haven't had time to change yet; I was rather in a hurry to see you. Haven't you got a glass of something? I'm dead tired; been in the saddle twenty-four hours."

I gave him some brandy from my medicinal store, which he drank with a grimace.

"Damned bad stuff," he observed. "I'll give you an address where they sell brandy that is brandy."

"It's good enough for my needs," I said indifferently. "I used it to rub my chest with." He stared and flicked at another fly.

"See here, old fellow," he began, "I've got something to suggest to you. It's four years now that you've shut yourself up in here like an owl, never going anywhere, never taking any healthy exercise, never doing a damned thing but poring over those books up there on the mantelpiece."

He glanced along the row of shelves. "Napoleon, Napoleon, Napoleon!" he read. "For heaven sake, have you nothing but Napoleons there?"

"I wish they were bound in gold," I said. "But wait, yes, there is another book, 'The King in Yellow.'" I looked him steadily in the eye.

"Have you never read it?" I asked.

"I? No, thank God! I don't want to be driven crazy."

I saw he regretted his speech as soon as he had uttered it.

There is only one word which I loathe more than I do lunatic and that word is crazy. But I controlled myself and asked him why he thought "The King in Yellow" dangerous.

"Oh, I don't know," he said, hastily. "I only remember the excitement it created and the denunciations from pulpit and press. I believe the author shot himself after bringing forth this monstrosity, didn't he?"

"I understand he is still alive," I answered.

"That's probably true," he muttered; "bullets couldn't kill a fiend like that."

"It is a book of great truths," I said.

"Yes," he replied, "Of 'truths' which send men frantic and blast their lives. I don't care if the thing is, as they say, the very supreme essence of art. It's a crime to have written it and I for one shall never open its pages."

"Is that what you have come to tell me?" I asked.

"No," he said, "I came to tell you that I am going to be married."

I believe for a moment my heart ceased to beat, but kept my eyes on his face.

"Yes," he continued, smiling happily, "married to the sweetest girl on earth."

"Constance Hawberk," I said mechanically.

"How did you know?" he cried, astonished. "I didn't know it myself until that evening last April, when we strolled down to the embankment before dinner."

"When is it to be?" I asked.

"It was to have been next September, but an hour ago a despatch came ordering our regiment to the Presidio, San Francisco. We leave at noon to-morrow. To-morrow," he repeated. "Just think, Hildred, to-morrow I shall be the happiest fellow that ever drew breath in this jolly world, for Constance will go with me."

I offered him my hand in congratulation, and he seized and shook it like the good-natured fool he was—or pretended to be.

"I am going to get my squadron as a wedding present," he rattled on. "Captain and Mrs. Louis Castaigne, eh, Hildred?"

Then he told me where it was to be and who were to be there, and made me promise to come and be best man. I set my teeth and listened to his boyish chatter without showing what I felt, but—

I was getting to the limit of my endurance, and when he jumped up, and, switching his spurs till they jingled, said he must go, I did not detain him.

"There's one thing I want to ask of you," I said quietly.

"Out with it, it's promised," he laughed.

"I want you to meet me for a quarter of an hour's talk to-night."

"Of course, if you wish," he said, somewhat puzzled. "Where?"

"Anywhere, in the park there."

"What time, Hildred?"

"Midnight."

"What in the name of—" he began, but checked himself and laughingly assented. I watched him go down the stairs and hurry away, his sabre banging at every stride. He turned into Bleecker Street, and I knew he was going to see Constance. I gave him ten minutes to disappear and then followed in his footsteps, taking with me the jewelled crown and the silken robe embroidered with the Yellow Sign. When I turned into Bleecker Street, and entered the doorway which bore the sign,

MR. WILDE,
REPAIRER OF REPUTATIONS,
3d Bell,

I saw old Hawberk moving about in his shop, and imagined I heard Constance's voice in the parlor; but I avoided them both and hurried up the trembling stairways to Mr. Wilde's apartment. I knocked, and entered without ceremony. Mr. Wilde lay groaning on the floor, his face covered with blood, his clothes torn to shreds. Drops of blood were scattered about over the carpet, which had also been ripped and frayed in the evidently recent struggle.

"It's that cursed cat," he said, ceasing his groans, and turning his colorless eyes to me; "she attacked me while I was asleep. I believe she will kill me yet."

This was too much, so I went into the kitchen and seizing a hatchet from the pantry, started to find the infernal beast and settle her then and there. My search was fruitless, and after a while I gave it up and came back to find Mr. Wilde squatting on his high chair by the table. He had washed his face and changed his clothes. The great furrows which the cat's claws had ploughed up in his face he had filled with collodion, and a rag hid the wound in his throat. I told him I should kill the cat when I came across her, but he only shook his head and turned to the open ledger before him. He read name after name of the people who had come to him in regard to their reputation, and the sums he had amassed were startling.

"I put the screws on now and then," he explained.

"One day or other some of these people will assassinate you," I insisted.

"Do you think so?" he said, rubbing his mutilated ears.

It was useless to argue with him, so I took down the manuscript entitled Imperial Dynasty of America, for the last time I should ever take it down in Mr. Wilde's study. I read it through, thrilling and trembling with pleasure. When I had finished Mr. Wilde took the manuscript and, turning to the dark passage which leads from his study to his bed-chamber, called out in a loud voice, "Vance." Then for the first time, I noticed a man crouching there in the shadow. How I had overlooked him during my search for the cat, I cannot imagine.

"Vance, come in," cried Mr. Wilde.

The figure rose and crept toward us, and I shall never forget the face that he raised to mine, as the light from the window illuminated it.

"Vance, this is Mr. Castaigne," said Mr. Wilde. Before he had finished speaking, the man threw himself on the ground before the table, crying and gasping, "Oh, God! Oh, my God! Help me! Forgive me—Oh, Mr. Castaigne, keep that man away. You cannot, you cannot mean it! You are different—save me! I am broken down—I was in a madhouse and now—when all was coming right—when I had forgotten the King—the King in Yellow and—but I shall go mad again—I shall go mad—"

His voice died into a choking rattle, for Mr. Wilde had leapt on him and his right hand encircled the man's throat. When Vance fell in a heap on the floor, Mr. Wilde clambered nimbly into his chair again, and rubbing his mangled ears with the stump of his hand, turned to me and asked me for the ledger. I reached it down from the shelf and he opened it. After a moment's searching among the beautifully written pages, he coughed complacently, and pointed to the name Vance.

"Vance," he read aloud, "Osgood Oswald Vance." At the sound of his name, the man on the floor raised his head and turned a convulsed face to Mr. Wilde. His eyes were injected with blood, his lips tumefied. "Called April 28th," continued Mr. Wilde. "Occupation, cashier in the Seaforth National Bank; has served a term of forgery at Sing Sing, from whence he was transferred to the Asylum for the Criminal Insane. Pardoned by the Governor of New York, and discharged from the Asylum, January 19, 1918. Reputation damaged at Sheepshead Bay. Rumors that he lives beyond his income. Reputation to be repaired at once. Retainer $1,500.

"Note—has embezzled sums amounting to $30,000 since March 20th, 1919, excellent family, and secured present position through uncle's influence. Father, President of Seaforth Bank."

I looked at the man on the floor.

"Get up, Vance," said Mr. Wilde in a gentle voice. Vance rose as if hypnotized. "He will do as we suggest now," observed Mr. Wilde, and opening the manuscript, he read the entire history of the Imperial Dynasty of America. Then in a kind and soothing murmur he ran over the important points with Vance, who stood like one stunned. His eyes were so blank and vacant that I imagined he had become half-witted, and remarked it to Mr. Wilde who replied that it was of no consequence anyway. Very patiently we pointed out to Vance what his share in the affair would be, and he seemed to understand after a while. Mr. Wilde explained the manuscript, using several volumes on heraldry to substantiate the result of his researches. He mentioned the establishment of the Dynasty in Carcosa, the lake which connected Hastur, Aldebaran and the mystery of the Hyades. He spoke of Cassilda and Camilla, and sounded the cloudy depths of Demhe, and the lake of Hali. "The scalloped tatters of the King in Yellow must hide Yhtill forever," he muttered, but I do not believe Vance heard him. Then by degrees he led Vance along the ramifications of the Imperial family, to Uoht and Thale, from Naotalba and Phantom of Truth, to Aldones, and then tossing aside his manuscript and notes, he began the wonderful story of the Last King. Fascinated and thrilled I watched him. He threw up his head, his long arms were stretched out in a magnificent gesture of pride and power, and his eyes blazed deep in their sockets like two emeralds. Vance listened stupefied. As for me, when at last Mr. Wilde had finished, and pointing to me, cried, "The cousin of the King!" my head swam with excitement.

Controlling myself with a superhuman effort, I explained to Vance why I alone was worthy of the crown and why my cousin must be exiled or die. I made him understand that my cousin must never marry, even after renouncing all his claims, and how that least of all he should marry the daughter of the Marquis of Avonshire and bring England into the question. I showed him a list of thousands of names which Mr. Wilde had drawn up; every man whose name was there had received the Yellow Sign which no living human being dared disregard. The city, the state, the whole land, were ready to rise and tremble before the Pallid Mask.

The time had come, the people should know the son of Hastur, and the whole world bow to the Black Stars which hang in the sky over Carcosa.

Vance leaned on the table, his head buried in his hands. Mr. Wilde drew a rough sketch on the margin of yesterday's *Herald* with a bit of lead pencil. It was a plan of Hawberk's rooms. Then he wrote out the order and affixed the seal, and shaking like a palsied man I signed my first writ of execution with my name Hildred-Rex.

Mr. Wilde clambered to the floor and unlocking the cabinet, took a long square box from the first shelf. This he brought to the table and opened. A new knife lay in the tissue paper inside and I picked it up and handed it to Vance, along with the order and the plan of Hawberk's apartment. Then Mr. Wilde told Vance he could go; and he went, shambling like an outcast of the slums.

I sat for a while watching the daylight fade behind the square tower of the Judson Memorial Church, and finally, gathering up the manuscript and notes, took my hat and started for the door.

Mr. Wilde watched me in silence. When I had stepped into the hall I looked back. Mr. Wilde's small eyes were still fixed on me. Behind him, the shadows gathered in the fading light. Then I closed the door behind me and went out into the darkening streets.

I had eaten nothing since breakfast, but I was not hungry. A wretched half-starved creature, who stood looking across the street at the Lethal Chamber, noticed me and came up to tell me a tale of misery. I gave him money, I don't know why, and he went away without thanking me. An hour later another outcast approached and whined his story. I had a blank bit of paper in my pocket, on which was traced the Yellow Sign and I handed it to him. He looked at it stupidly for a moment and then with an uncertain glance at me, folded it with what seemed to me exaggerated care and placed it in his bosom.

The electric lights were sparkling among the trees, and the new moon shone in the sky above the Lethal Chamber. It was tiresome waiting in the square; I wandered from the Marble Arch to the artillery stables, and back again to the lotos fountain. The flowers and grass exhaled a fragrance which troubled me. The jet of the fountain played in the moonlight, and the musical splash of falling drops reminded me of the tinkle of chained mail in Hawberk's shop. But it was not so fascinating, and the dull sparkle of the moonlight on the water brought no such sensations of exquisite pleasure, as when the sunshine played over the polished steel of a corselet on Hawberk's knee. I watched the bats darting and turning above the water plants in the fountain basin, but their rapid, jerky flight set my nerves on edge, and I went away again to walk aimlessly to and fro among the trees.

The artillery stables were dark, but in the cavalry barracks the officer's windows were brilliantly lighted, and the sallyport was constantly filled with troopers in fatigue, carrying straw and harness and baskets filled with tin dishes.

Twice the mounted sentry at the gates was changed, while I wandered up and down the asphalt walk. I looked at my watch. It was nearly time. The lights in the barracks went out one by one, the barred gate was closed, and every minute or two an officer passed in through the side wicket, leaving a rattle of accoutrements and a jingle of spurs on the night air. The square had become very silent. The last homeless loiterer had been driven away by the gray-coated park policemen, the car tracks along Wooster Street were deserted, and the only sound which broke the stillness was the stamping of the sentry's horse and the ring of his sabre against the saddle pommel. In the barracks, the officer's quarters were still lighted, and military servants passed and repassed before the bay windows. Twelve o'clock sounded from the new spire of St. Francis Xavier, and at the last stroke of the sad-toned bell a figure passed through the wicket beside the portcullis, returned the salute of the sentry, and crossing the street entered the square and advanced toward the Benedick apartment house.

"Louis," I called.

The man pivoted on his spurred heels and came straight toward me.

"Is that you, Hildred?"

"Yes, you are on time."

I took his offered hand, and we strolled toward the Lethal Chamber.

He rattled on about his wedding and the graces of Constance, and their future prospects, calling my attention to his captain's shoulder-straps, and the triple gold arabesque on his sleeve and fatigue cap. I believe I listened as much to the music of his spurs and sabre as I did to his boyish babble, and at last we stood under the elms on the Fourth Street corner of the square opposite the Lethal Chamber. Then he laughed and asked me what I wanted with him. I motioned him to a seat on a bench under the electric light, and sat down beside him. He looked at me curiously, with that same searching glance which I hate and fear so in doctors. I felt the insult of his look, but he did not know it, and I carefully concealed my feelings.

"Well, old chap," he inquired, "what can I do for you?"

I drew from my pocket the manuscript and notes of the Imperial Dynasty of America, and looking him in the eye said:

"I will tell you. On your word as a soldier, promise me to read this manuscript from beginning to end, without asking me a question. Promise me to read these notes in the same way, and promise me to listen to what I have to tell later."

"I promise, if you wish it," he said pleasantly. "Give me the paper, Hildred."

He began to read, raising his eyebrows with a puzzled whimsical air, which made me tremble with suppressed anger. As he advanced, his eyebrows contracted, and his lips seemed to form the word, "rubbish."

Then he looked slightly bored, but apparently for my sake read, with an attempt at interest, which presently ceased to be an effort. He started when in the closely-written pages he came to his own name, and when he came to mine he lowered the paper, and looked sharply at me for a moment. But he kept his word, and resumed his reading, and I let the half-formed question die on his lips unanswered. When he came to the end and read the signature of Mr. Wilde, he folded the paper carefully and returned it to me. I handed him the notes, and he settled back, pushing his fatigue cap up to his forehead, with a boyish gesture, which I remembered so well in school. I watched his face as he read, and when he finished I took the notes with the manuscript, and placed them in my pocket. Then I unfolded a scroll marked with the Yellow Sign. He saw the sign, but he did not seem to recognize it, and I called his attention to it somewhat sharply.

"Well," he said, "I see it. What is it?"

"It is the Yellow Sign," I said, angrily.

"Oh, that's it, is it?" said Louis, in that flattering voice, which Doctor Archer used to employ with me, and would probably have employed again, had I not settled his affair for him.

I kept my rage down and answered as steadily as possible, "Listen, you have engaged your word?"

"I am listening, old chap," he replied soothingly.

I began to speak very calmly.

"Dr. Archer, having by some means become possessed of the secret of the Imperial Succession, attempted to deprive me of my right, alleging that because of a fall from my horse four years ago, I had become mentally deficient. He presumed to place me under restraint in his own house in hopes of either driving me insane or poisoning me. I have not forgotten it. I visited him last night and the interview was final."

Louis turned quite pale, but did not move. I resumed triumphantly, "There are yet three people to be interviewed in the interests of Mr. Wilde and myself. They are my cousin Louis, Mr. Hawberk, and his daughter Constance."

Louis sprang to his feet and I arose also, and flung the paper marked with the Yellow Sign to the ground.

"Oh, I don't need that to tell you what I have to say," I cried with a laugh of triumph. "You must renounce the crown to me, do you hear, to *me*."

Louis looked at me with a startled air, but recovering himself said kindly, "Of course I renounce the—what is it I must renounce?"

"The crown," I said angrily.

"Of course," he answered, "I renounce it. Come, old chap, I'll walk back to your rooms with you."

"Don't try any of your doctor's tricks on me," I cried, trembling with fury. "Don't act as if you think I am insane."

"What nonsense," he replied. "Come, it's getting late, Hildred."

"No," I shouted, "you must listen. You cannot marry, I forbid it. Do you hear? I forbid it. You shall renounce the crown, and in reward I grant you exile, but if you refuse you shall die."

He tried to calm me but I was roused at last, and drawing my long knife barred his way.

Then I told him how they would find Dr. Archer in the

cellar with his throat open, and I laughed in his face when I thought of Vance and his knife, and the order signed by me.

"Ah, you are the King," I cried, "but I shall be King. Who are you to keep me from Empire over all the habitable earth! I was born the cousin of a king, but I shall be King!"

Louis stood white and rigid before me. Suddenly a man came running up Fourth Street, entered the gate of the Lethal Temple, traversed the path to the bronze doors at full speed, and plunged into the death chamber with the cry of one demented, and I laughed until I wept tears, for I had recognized Vance, and knew that Hawberk and his daughter were no longer in my way.

"Go," I cried to Louis, "you have ceased to be a menace. You will never marry Constance now, and if you marry anyone else in your exile, I will visit you as I did my doctor last night. Mr. Wilde takes charge of you to-morrow." Then I turned and darted into South Fifth Avenue, and with a cry of terror Louis dropped his belt and sabre and followed me like the wind. I heard him close behind me at the corner of Bleecker Street, and I dashed into the doorway under Hawberk's sign. He cried, "Halt, or I fire!" but when he saw that I flew up the stairs leaving Hawberk's shop below, he left me and I heard him hammering and shouting at their door as though it was possible to arouse the dead.

Mr. Wilde's door was open, and I entered crying, "It is done, it is done! Let the nations rise and look upon their King!" but I could not find Mr. Wilde, so I went to the cabinet and took the splendid diadem from its case. Then I drew on the white silk robe, embroidered with the Yellow Sign, and placed the crown upon my head. At last I was King, King by my right in Hastur, King because I knew the mystery of the Hyades, and my mind had sounded the depths of the Lake of Hali. I was King! The first gray pencillings of dawn would raise a tempest which would shake two hemispheres. Then as I stood, my every nerve pitched to the highest tension, faint with the joy and splendor of my thought, without, in the dark passage, a man groaned.

I seized the tallow dip and sprang to the door. The cat passed me like a demon, and the tallow dip went out, but my long knife flew swifter than she, and I heard her screech, and I knew that my knife had found her. For a moment I listened to her tumbling and thumping about in the darkness, and then when her frenzy ceased, I lighted a lamp and raised it over my head. Mr. Wilde lay on the floor with his throat torn open. At first I thought he was dead, but as I looked, a green sparkle came into his sunken eyes, his mutilated hand trembled, and then a spasm stretched his mouth from ear to ear. For a moment my terror and despair gave place to hope, but as I bent over him his eyeballs rolled clean around in his head, and he died. Then while I stood, transfixed with rage and despair, seeing my crown, my empire, every hope and every ambition, my very life, lying prostrate there with the dead master, *they* came, seized me from behind, and bound me until my veins stood out like cords, and my voice failed with paroxysms of my frenzied screams. But I still raged, bleeding and infuriated among them, and more than one policeman felt my sharp teeth. Then when I could no longer move they came nearer; I saw old Hawberk, and behind him my cousin Louis' ghastly face, and farther away, in the corner, a woman, Constance, weeping softly.

"Ah! I see it now!" I shrieked. "You have seized the throne and the empire. Woe! woe to you who are crowned with the crown of the King in Yellow!"

[EDITOR'S NOTE: Mr. Castaigne died yesterday in the Asylum for the Criminal Insane.]

M. P. SHIEL

THE HOUSE OF SOUNDS

E caddi come l'uom cui sonno piglia.

—*DANTE*

A GOOD many years ago, when a young man, a student in Paris, I knew the great Carot, and witnessed by his side many of those cases of mind-malady, in the analysis of which he was such a master. I remember one little maid of the Marais who, until the age of nine, did not differ from her playmates; but one night, lying abed she whispered into her mother's ear: "Mama, can you not hear *the sound of the world*?" It appears that her geography had just taught her that our globe reels with an enormous velocity on an orbit about the sun; and this *sound of the world* of hers was merely a murmur in the ear, heard in the silence of night. Within six months she was as mad as a March-hare.

I mentioned the case to my friend, Haco Harfager, then occupying with me an old mansion in St. Germain, shut in by a wall and jungle of shrubbery. He listened with singular interest, and during a good while sat wrapped in gloom.

Another case which I gave made a great impression upon my friend: A young man, a toy-maker of St. Antoine, suffering from consumption—but sober, industrious—returning one gloaming to his garret, happened to purchase one of those factious journals which circulate by lamplight over the Boulevards. This simple act was the beginning of his doom. He had never been a reader: knew little of the reel and turmoil of the world. But the next night he purchased another journal. Soon he acquired a knowledge of politics, the huge movements, the tumult of life. And this interest grew absorbing. Till late into the night, every night, he lay poring over the roar of action, the printed passion. He would awake sick, but brisk in spirit—and bought a morning paper. And the more his teeth gnashed, the less they ate. He grew negligent, irregular at work, turning on his bed through the day. Rags overtook him. As the grand interest grew upon his frail soul so every lesser interest failed in him. There came a day when he no more cared for his own life; and another day when he tore the hairs from his head.

As to this man the great Carot said to me:

"Really, one does not know whether to chuckle or to weep over such a business. Observe, for one thing, how diversely men are made! There are minds precisely so sensitive as a thread of melted lead: *every* breath will fret and trouble them: and how about the hurricane? For such this scheme of things is clearly no fit habitation, but a Machine of Death, a baleful Immense. *Too* cruel to some is the rushing shriek of Being—they *cannot* stand the world. Let each look well to his own little shred of existence, I say, and leave the monstrous Automaton alone! Here in this poor toy-maker you have a case of the ear: it is only the neurosis, Oxyecoia. Grand was that Greek myth of 'the Harpies'—by *them* was this creature snatched away—or say, caught by a limb in the wheels of the universe, and so perished. It is quite a ravishing exit—translation in a chariot of flame! Only remember that the member first seized was *the pinna* he bent *ear* to the howl of the world, and ended by himself howling. Between chaos and our shoes swings, I assure you, the thinnest film! I knew a man who had this aural peculiarity: that every sound brought him some knowledge of the matter causing the sound: a rod for instance, of mixed copper and tin striking upon a rod of mixed iron and lead, conveyed to him not merely the proportion of each metal in each rod, but some knowledge of the essential meaning and spirit, as it were, of copper, of tin, of iron and of lead. Him also did the Harpies snatch aloft!"

I have mentioned that I related some of these cases to my friend, Harfager: and I was astonished at the obvious pains which he gave himself to hide his interest, his gaping nostrils . . .

From first days when we happened to attend the same seminary in Stockholm an intimacy had sprung up between us. But it was not an intimacy accompanied by the ordinary signs of friendship. Harfager was the shyest, most isolated, of beings. Though our joint housekeeping (brought about by a chance meeting at a midnight *séance*) had now lasted some months, I knew nothing of his plans. Through the day we read together, he rapt back into the past, I engrossed with the present; late at night we reclined on sofas within the vast cave of a hearth-place *Louis Onze*, and smoked over the dying fire in silence. Occasionally a *soirée* or lecture might draw me from the house; except once, I never understood that Harfager left it. On that occasion I was hurrying through the Rue St. Honoré, where a rush of traffic rattles over the old pavers retained there, when I came upon him. In this tumult he stood in a listening attitude; and for a moment did not know me.

Even as a boy I had seen in my friend the genuine patrician—not that his personality gave any impression of loftiness or opulence: on the contrary. He did, however, suggest an incalculable *ancientness*; and I have known no nobleman who so bore in his expression the assurance of the essential Prince, whose pale blossom is of yesterday, and will perish tomorrow, but whose root shoots through the ages. This much I knew of Harfager; also that on one or other of his islands north of Zetland lived his mother and an aunt; that he was somewhat deaf; but liable to a thousand torments or delights at certain sounds, the whine of a door, the note of a bird. . . .

He was somewhat under the middle height; and inclined to portliness. His nose rose highly aquiline from that sort of brow called "the musical"—that is, with temples which incline *outward* to the cheek-bones, making breadth for the base of the brain; while the direction of the heavy-lidded eyes and of the eyebrows was a downward *droop* from the nose of their outer ends. He wore a thin chin-beard. But the feature of his face were the ears, which were nearly circular, very small and flat, without that outer curve called "the helix." I came to understand that this had long been a trait of his race. Over the whole wan face of my friend was engraved an air of woeful inability, utter gravity of sorrow: one said "Sardanapalus," frail last of the race of Nimrod.

After a year I found it necessary to mention to Harfager my intention of leaving Paris, as we reclined one night in our nooks within the fireplace. He replied to my tidings with a polite "Indeed!" and continued to gloat over the grate: but after an hour turned to me and observed: "Well, it seems to be a hard world."

Truisms uttered in just such a tone of discovery I occasionally heard from him; but his earnest gaze, his despondency now, astonished me.

"Apropos of what?" I asked.

"My friend, do not leave me!" He spread his arms.

I learned that he was the object of a devilish malice; that he was the prey of a horrible temptation. That a lure, a becking hand, a lurking lust, which it was the effort of his life to escape (and to which he was especially liable in solitude) perpetually enticed him; and that so it had been almost from the day when, at the age of five, he had been sent by his father from his desolate home in the ocean.

And whose was this malice?

He told me his mother's and aunt's.

And what was this temptation?

He said it was the temptation to go back—to hurry with the very frenzy of hunger—back to that home.

I demanded with what motives, and in what way, the

malice of his mother and aunt manifested itself. He answered that there was, he fancied, no definite motive, but only a fated malevolence; and that the respect in which it manifested itself was the prayers and commands with which they plagued him to go again to the hold of his ancestors.

All this I could not understand, and said so. In what consisted this magnetism, and this peril, of his home? To this Harfager did not reply, but rising from his seat, disappeared behind the hearth-curtains, and left the apartment. When he returned, it was with a quarto tome bound in hide, which proved to be Hugh Gascoigne's *Chronicle of Norse Families* in English black-letter. The passage to which he pointed I read as follows:

"Now of these two brothers the older, Harold, being of seemly personage and prowess, did go a pilgrimage into Danemark, wherefrom he repaired again home to Hjaltland (Zetland), and with him fetched the amiable Thronda for his wife, who was a daughter of the sank (blood) royal of Danemark. And his younger brother, Sweyn, that was sad and debonair, but far surpassed the other in cunning, received him with all good cheer.

"But eftsoons (soon after) fell Sweyn sick for all his love that he had of Thronda, his brother's wife. And while the worthy Harold ministered about the bed where Sweyn lay sick, lo, Sweyn fastened on him a violent stroke with a sword, and with no longer tarrying enclosed his hands in bonds, and cast him in the bottom of a deep hold. And because Harold would not deprive himself of the governance of Thronda his wife, Sweyn cut off both his ear(s), and put out one of his eyes, and after divers such torments was ready to slay him. But on a day the valiant Harold, breaking his bonds, and embracing his adversary, did by the sleight of wrestling overthrow him, and escaped. Notwithstanding, he faltered when he came to the Somburg Head, not far from the Castle, and, albeit that he was swift-foot, could no farther run, by reason that he was faint with the long plagues of his brother. And whilst he there lay in a swoon, did Sweyn come upon him, and when he had stricken him with a dart, cast him from Somburg Head into the sea.

"Not long hereafterward did the lady Thronda (though she knew not the manner of her lord's death, nor, verily, if he was dead or alive) receive Sweyn into favour, and with great gaudying and blowing of beamous (trumpets) did become his wife. And right soon they two went thence to sojourn in far parts.

"Now, it befell that Sweyn was minded by a dream to have built a great mansion in Hjaltland for the home-coming of the lady Thronda; wherefore he called to him a cunning Master-workman, and sent him to England to gather men for the building of this lusty House, while he himself remained with his lady at Rome. Then came this Architect to London, but passing thence to Hjaltland was drowned, he and his feers (mates), all and some.

"And after two years, which was the time assigned, Sweyn Harfager sent a letter to Hjaltland to understand how his great House did: for he knew not of the drowning of the Architect: and soon after he received answer that the House *did well*, and was building on the Isle of Rayba. But that was not the Isle where Sweyn had appointed the building to be: and he was afeard, and near fell down dead for dread, because, in the letter, he saw before him the manner of writing of his brother Harold. And he said in this form: 'Surely Harold is alive, else be this letter writ with ghostly hand.' And he was wo many days, seeing that this was a deadly stroke.

"Thereafter he took himself back to Hjaltland to know how the matter was, and there the old Castle on Somburg Head was break down to the earth. Then Sweyn was wode-wroth, and cried: 'Jhesu mercy, where is all the great house of my fathers gone? alas! this wicked day of destiny!' And one of the people told him that a host of workmen from far parts had break it down. And he said: 'Who hath bid them?' but that could none answer. Then he said again: 'nis (is not) my brother Harold alive? for I have behold his writing': and that, too, could none answer. So he went to Rayba, and saw there a great House stand, and when he looked on it, he said: 'This, sooth, was y-built by my brother Harold, be he dead or be he on-live.' And there he dwelt, and his lady, and his sons' sons until now: for that the House is ruthless and without pity; wherefore 'tis said that upon all who dwell there falleth a wicked madness and a lecherous anguish; and that by way of the ears do they drinck the cup of the furie of the earless Harold, till the time of the House be ended."

After I had read the narrative half-aloud, I smiled, saying: "This, Harfager, is very tolerable romance on the part of the good Gascoigne, but has the look of indifferent history."

"It is, nevertheless, *history*," he replied.

"You believe that?"

"The house stands solidly on Rayba."

"But you believe that mediaeval ghosts superintended the building of their family mansions?"

"Gascoigne nowhere says that," he answered: "for to be 'stricken with a darte,' is not necessarily to die; nor, if he did say it, have I any knowledge on the subject."

"And what, Harfager, is the nature of that 'wicked madness,' that 'lecherous anguish,' of which Gascoigne speaks?"

"Do you ask me?"—he spread his arms—"what do I know? I know nothing! I was banished from the place at the age of five. Yet the cry of it still rings in my mind. And have I not *told* you of anguishes—even in myself—of inherited longing and loathing. . . ."

Anyway, I *had* to go to Heidelberg just then: so I said I would compromise by making my absence short, and rejoin him in a few weeks. I took his moody silence to mean assent; and soon afterwards left him.

But I was detained: and when I got back to our old house found it empty. Harfager was gone.

It was only after twelve years that a letter was forwarded me—a rather wild letter, an awfully long one—in the writing of my friend. It was dated at Rayba. From the writing I understood that it had been dashed off *with furious haste*, so that I was the more astonished at the very trivial nature of the contents. On the first half page he spoke of our old friendship, and asked if I would see his mother, who was dying; the rest of the epistle consisted of an analysis of his mother's family-tree, the apparent aim being to show that she was a genuine Harfager, and a distant cousin of his father. He then went on to comment on the great prolificness of his race, stating that since the fourteenth century over *four millions* of its members had lived; three only of them, he believed, being now left. This settled, the letter ended.

Influenced by this, I travelled northward; reached Caithness; passed the stormy Orkneys; reached Lerwick; and from Unst, the most bleak and northerly of the Zetlands, contrived, by dint of bribes, to pit the weather-worthiness of a lug-sailed "sixern" (identical with the "langschips" of the Vikings) against a flowing sea and an ugly sky. The trip, I was told, was at such a season of some risk. It was the sombre December of those seas; and the weather, they said, although never cold, is seldom other than tempestuous. A mist now lay over the billows, enclosing our boat in a dome of doleful gloaming; and there was a ghostly something in the look of the silent sea and brooding sky which produced upon my nerves the mood of a journey out of nature, a cruise beyond the world. Occasionally, however, we ran past one of those "skerries," or sea-stacks, whose craggy sea-walls, disintegrated by the struggles of the Gulf Stream with the North Sea, had a look of awful ruin and havoc. But I only noticed three of these: for before the dun day had well run half its course, sudden darkness was upon us; and with it one of those storms of which the winter of this semi-Arctic sea is one succession. During the haggard glimpses of the following day the rain did not stop; but before darkness had quite fallen, my skipper (who talked continuously to a mate of seal-maidens, and water-horses, and *grülies*), paused to point me out a mound of gloomier grey on the weather-bow, which, he said, should be Rayba.

Rayba, he said, was the centre of quite a nest of those *rösts* (eddies) and cross-currents which the tidal wave hurls with complicated swirlings among all the islands: but at Rayba they ran with more than usual angriness, owing to the row of sea-crags which garrisoned the land around; approach was therefore at all times difficult, and at night foolhardy. With a running sea, however, we came sufficiently close to see the mane of foam which railed round the coast-wall. Its shock, according to the captain, had often more than all the efficiency of artillery, tossing tons of rock to heights of six hundred feet upon the island.

When the sun next pried above the horizon, we had closely approached the coast; and it was then that for the first time the impression of some spinning motion of the island (due probably to the swirling movements of the water) was produced upon me. We affected a landing at a *voe*, or sea-arm, on the west coast—the east, though the point of my aim, was out of the question on account of the swell. Here I found in two *skeoes* (or sheds), thatched with feal, five or six seamen, who gained a livelihood by trading for the groceries of the great house on the east: and, taking one of them for a guide, I began the climb of the island.

Now, during the night in the boat, I had been aware of a booming in the ears for which even the roar of the sea round the coast seemed insufficient to account; and this now, as we went on, became immensely augmented—and with it, once more, that conviction within me of *spinning* motions. Rayba I found to be a land of precipices of granite and flaggy gneiss; at about the centre, however, we came upon a table-land, sloping from west to east, and covered by a lot of lochs, which sullenly flowed into one another. I could see no shore eastward to this chain of waters, and by dint of shouting to my leader, and bending ear to his shoutings, I came to know that there *was* no such shore—I say *shout*, for nothing less could have sounded through the steady bellowing as of ten thousand bisons that now resounded on every side. A certain trembling, too, of the earth became distinct. In vain, meantime, did the eye in its dreary survey seek a tree or shrub—for no kind of vegetation, save peat, could brave for a day the perennial tempest of this benighted island. Darkness, half an hour after noon, commenced to fall upon us: and it was soon afterwards that my guide, pointing down a defile near the east coast, hurriedly started back upon the way he had come. I bawled a question after him, as he went: but at this point the voice of mortals had ceased to be in the least audible.

Down this defile, with a sinking of the heart, and a singular sickness of giddiness, I passed; and, on reaching its end, emerged upon a ledge of rock which shuddered to the immediate onsets of the sea—though all this part of the island was, besides, in the grip of an ague not due to the great guns of the sea. Hugging a crag of cliff for steadiness from the gusts, I gazed forth upon a scene not less eerily dismal than some drear district of the dreams of Dante. Three "skerries," flanked by stacks as fantastic and twisted as a witch's finger, and giving a home to hosts of osprey and scart, seal and walrus, lay at some fathoms distance; and from its rush among them, the sea in blanched, tumultuous, but inaudible wrath, like an army with banners, ranted toward the land. Letting go my crag, I staggered some distance to the left: and now all at once an amphitheatre opened before me, and there broke upon my view a panorama of such appalling majesty as had never entered my heart to fancy.

"An amphitheatre," I said: but it was rather the form of a Norman door that I saw. Fancy such a door, half a mile wide, flat on the ground, the rounded part farthest from the sea; and all round it let a wall of rock tower perpendicular forty yards: and now down this rounded door-shape, and *over its whole extent*, let a roaring ocean roll its tonnage in hoary fury—and the stupor with which I looked, and then the shrinking, and then the instinct of flight, will find comprehension.

This was the disemboguement of the lochs of Rayba.

And within the curve of this Norman cataract, robed in the world of its smokes and far-excursive surfs, stood a fabric of brass.

The last beam of the day had now nearly passed; but I could still see through the mist which bleakly nimbused it as in tears, that the building was low in proportion to the hugeness of its circumference; that it was roofed with a dome; and that round it ran two rows of Norman windows, the upper smaller than the lower. Certain indications led me to infer that the house had been founded upon a bed of rock which lay, circular and detached, within the curve of the cataract; but this nowhere emerged above the flood: for the whole floor which I had before me dashed one reeking deep river to the beachless sea—passage to the mansion being made possible by a massive causeway-bridge, with arches, all bearded with seaweed.

Descending from my ledge, I passed along it, now drenched in spray; and, as I came nearer, could see that the house, too, was to half its height more thickly bearded than an old hull with barnacles and every variety of bright seaweed; also—what was very surprising—that from many spots near the top of the brazen wall ponderous chains, dropping beards, reached out in rays: so that the fabric had the aspect of a many-anchored ark. But without pausing to look closely, I pushed forward, and rushing through the smooth waterfall which poured all round from the roof, by one of its many porches I entered the dwelling.

Darkness now was around me—and sound. I seemed to stand in the centre of some yelling planet, the row resembling the resounding of many thousands of cannon, punctuated by strange crashing and breaking uproars. And a sadness descended on me; I was near to tears. "Here," I said, "is the place of weeping; not elsewhere is the vale of sighing." However, I passed forward through a succession of halls, and was wondering where to go next, when a hideous figure, with a lamp in his hand, stamped towards me. I shrank from him! It seemed the skeleton of a lank man wrapped in a winding-sheet, till the light of one tiny eye, and a film of skin over a portion of the face reassured one. Of ears he showed no sign. His name, I afterwards learned, was Aith; and his appearance was explained by his pretence (true or false), that he had once suffered *burning*, almost to the cinder-stage, but had somehow recovered. With an expression of malice, and agitated gestures, he led the way to a chamber on the upper stage, where, having struck light to a taper, he made signs toward a spread table, and left me.

For a long time I sat in solitude, conscious of the shaking of the mansion, though every sense was swallowed up and confounded in the one impression of sound. Water, water, was the world—a nightmare on my breast, a desire to gasp for breath, a tingling on my nerves, a sense of being infinitely drowned and buried in boundless deluges; and when the feeling of giddiness, too, increased, I sprang up and paced—but suddenly stopped, angry, I scarce knew why, with myself. I had, in fact, caught myself walking with a certain *hurry*, not usual with me, not natural to me. So I forced myself to stand and take note of the hall. It was large, and damp with mists, so that its tattered, but rich, furniture looked lost in it, its centre occupied by a tomb bearing the name of a Harfager of the fourteenth century, and its walls old panels of oak. Having drearily seen these things, I waited on with an intolerable consciousness of solitude; but a little after midnight the tapestry parted, and Harfager with a rapid stalk walked in.

In twelve years my friend had grown old. He showed, it is

true, a tendency to portliness: yet, to a knowing eye he was in reality tabid, ill-nourished. And his neck stuck forward from his chest; and the lower part of his back had quite a forward bend of age; and his hair floated about his face and shoulders in a wildness of awful whiteness, while a white chin-beard hung to his chest. His dress was a robe of bauge, which, as he went, waved aflaunt from his bare and hairy shins; and he was shod in those soft slippers called *rivlins.*

To my astonishment, he spoke. When I passionately shouted that I could gather no fragment of sound from his moving mouth, he clapped both his palms to his ears, and then anew besieged mine: but again without result: and now, with an angry throw of the hand, he caught up his taper, and walked from the apartment.

There was something strikingly unnatural in his manner—something which reminded me of the skeleton, Aith: an excess of zeal, a fever, a rage, a *loudness*, an eagerness of gait, a great extravagance of gesture. His hand constantly dashed wiffs of hair from a face which, though of the saffron of death, had red eyes—thick-lidded eyes, fixed in a downward and sideward gaze. When he came back to me, it was with a leaf of ivory, and a piece of graphite, hanging from the cord tied round his garment; and he rapidly wrote a petition that, if not too tired, I would take part with him in the funeral of his mother.

I shouted assent.

Once more he clapped his palms to his ears; then wrote: "Do not shout: no whisper in any part of the building is inaudible to me."

I remembered that in early life he had been slightly *deaf.*

We passed together through many apartments, he shading the taper with his hand—a necessary action, for, as I quickly discovered, in no nook of the quivering building was the air in a state of rest, but was for ever commoved by a curious agitation, a faint windiness, like an echo of tempests, which communicated a universal nervousness to the curtains. Everywhere I met the same past grandeur, present raggedness and decay. In many of the rooms were tombs; one was a museum thronged with bronzes, but broken, grown with fungoids, dripping with moisture—it was as if the mansion, in ardour of travail, sweated; and a miasma of decomposition tainted all the air.

I followed Harfager through the maze of his way with some difficulty, for he went headlong—only once stopping, when with a face ungainly wild over the glare of the light, he tossed up his fingers, and gave out a single word: from the form of his lips I guessed the word *"Hark!"*

Presently we entered a very long chamber, in which, on chairs beside a bed, lay a coffin flanked by a file of candles. The coffin was very deep, and had this singularity—that the foot-piece was absent, so that the soles of the corpse could be seen as we approached. I saw, too, three upright rods secured to a side of the coffin, each rod fitted at its top with a little silver bell of the sort called *morrice*, pendent from a flexible spring. And at the head of the bed, Aith, with an air of irascibility, was stamping to and fro within a narrow area.

Harfager deposited the taper upon a stone table, and stood poring with a crazy intentness over the body. I, too, stood and looked at death so grim and rigorous as I think I never saw. The coffin looked angrily full of tangled grey locks, the lady being of great age, bony and hook-nosed; and her face shook with solemn constancy to the quivering of the building. I noticed that over the body had been fixed three bridges, like the bridge of a violin, their sides fitting into grooves in the coffin's sides, and their tops of a shape to fit the slope of the two coffin-lids when closed. One of these bridges passed over the knees of the dead lady; another bridged her stomach; the third her neck. In each of them was a hole, and across each of the three holes passed a string from the morrice-bell above it—the three holes being thus divided by the three tight strings into six semi-circles. Before I could guess the significance of all this, Harfager closed the folding coffin-lids, which had little holes for the passage of the three strings. He then turned the key in the lock, and uttered a word which I took to be "come."

Aith now took hold of the handle at the coffin's head; and out of the dark parts of the hall a lady in black walked forward. She was tall, pallid, of imposing aspect; and from the curvature of her nose, and her circular ears, I guessed her the lady Swertha, aunt of Harfager. Her eyes were quite red—if with crying I could not tell.

Harfager and I taking each a handle near the coffin-foot, and the lady bearing before us one of the black candlesticks, the obsequies began. When I got to the doorway, I noticed in a corner there two more coffins, engraved with the names Harfarger and his aunt. Thence we wound our way down a wide stairway winding to a lower floor; and descending thence still lower by narrow brass steps, came to a portal of metal, where the lady, depositing the candlestick, left us.

The chamber of death into which we now bore the body had for its outer wall the brazen outer wall of the whole house at a spot where this closely approached the cataract, and was no doubt profoundly drowned in the world of surge without: so that the earthquake there was urgent. On every side the place was piled with coffins, ranged high and wide upon shelves; and the huge rush and scampering which ensued on our entrance proved it the paradise of troops of rats. As it was inconceivable that these could have eaten a way through sixteen brazen feet—for even the floor here was brazen—I assumed that some fruitful pair must have found in the house, on its building, an ark from the waters. Even this guess, though, seemed wild; and Harfager afterwards confided to me his suspicion that they had for some reason been *placed* there by the original builder.

We deposited our load upon a stone bench in the centre;

whereupon Aith made haste to be away. Harfager then repeatedly walked from end to end of the place, scrutinising with many a stoop and peer and upward stretch, the shelves and their props. Could he, I was led to wonder, have any doubts as to their soundness? Damp, in fact, and decay pervaded everything. A bit of timber which I touched crumbled to dust under my thumb.

He presently beckoned to me, and, with yet one halt and "*Hark!*" from him, we passed through the house to my chamber; where, left alone, I paced about, agitated with a vague anger; then tumbled to an agony of slumber.

In the far interior of the mansion even the bleared day of this land of bleakness never rose upon our gloom; but I was able to regulate my gettings-up by a clock which stood in my chamber; or I was called by Harfager, with whom in a short time I renewed more than all our former friendship. That I should say *more* is curious: but so it *was*: and this was proved by the fact that we grew to take, and to excuse, freedoms of speech and of manner which, as two persons of more than usual reserve, we had once never dreamed of permitting to ourselves in respect of each other. Once, for example, in our pacings of aimless haste down passages that vanished in shadow and length of perspective remoteness, he wrote that my step was very slow. I replied that it was just such a step as suited my then mood. He wrote: "You have developed a tendency to *fret*." I was very offended, and said: "Certainly, there are more fingers than one in the world which *that* ring will fit!"

Another day he was no less than rude to me for seeking to reveal to him the secret of the unhuman keenness of his hearing—and of mine! For I, too, to my dismay, began, as time passed, to catch hints of shouted sounds. The cause might be found, I asserted, in a fervour of the auditory nerve, which, if the cataract were absent, the roar of the ocean, and the row of the perpetual tempest round us, might by themselves be sufficient to bring about; his own ear-interior, I said, must be inflamed to an exquisite pitch of fever; and I named the disease to him as the "Paracusis Wilisü." When he frowned dissent, I, quite undeterred, proceeded to relate the case (that had occurred within my own experience) of a very deaf lady who could hear the drop of a pin in a railway-train;* and now he made me the reply: "Of ignorant people I am accustomed to consider the mere scientist the most ignorant!"

But I, for my part, regarded it as merely far-fetched that he should pretend to be in the dark as to the morbid state of his hearing! He himself, indeed, confessed to me his own, Aith's, and the lady Swertha's proneness to paroxysms of *vertigo.* I was startled! for I had myself shortly previously been roused out of sleep by feelings of reeling and nausea, and an assurance that the room furiously flew round with me. The impression passed away, and I attributed it, perhaps hastily, to some disturbance in the nerve-endings of "the labyrinth," or inner ear. In Harfager, however, the conviction of whirling motions in the house, in the world, got to so horrible a degree of certainty, that its effects sometimes resembled those of lunacy or energumenal possession. Never, he said, was the sensation of giddiness altogether dead in him; seldom the sensation that he gazed with stretched-out arms over the brink of abysms which wooed his half-consenting foot. Once, as we walked, he was hurled as by unearthly powers to the ground, and there for an hour sprawled, bathed in sweat, with distraught bedazzlement and amaze in his stare, which watched the racing walls. He was constantly racked, moreover, with the consciousness of sounds so peculiar in their character, that I could account for them on no other supposition than that of a *tinnitus* infinitely sick. Through the roar there

*Such cases are known to many medical men. The concussion on the deaf nerve is the cause of the acquired sensitiveness; nor is there any limit to that sensitiveness when the tumult is immensely augmented.

sometimes visited him, he told me, the lullaby of some bird, from the burden of whose song he had the consciousness that she derived from a very remote country, was of the whiteness of foam, and crested with a comb of mauve. Or else he knew of accumulated human tones, distant, yet articulate, busily contending in volubility, and in the end melting into a medley of musical movements. Or, anon, he was shocked by an infinite and imminent crashing, like the monstrous racket of the crackling of a cosmos of crockery round his ears. He told me, moreover, that he could frequently see, rather than hear, the particoloured wheels of a mazy sphere-music deep, deep within the black dark of the cataract's roar. These impressions, which I protested *must* be merely entotic had sometimes a pleasing effect upon him, and he would stand long to listen with a lifted hand to their seduction: others again inflamed him to a mad anger. I guessed that they were the cause of those "*Harks!*" that at intervals of about an hour did not fail to break from him. But in this I was wrong: and it was with a thrill of dismay that I soon came to know the truth.

For, as we were once passing by an iron door on the lower floor, he stopped, and for some minutes stood listening with a leer most keen and cunning. Presently the cry "*Hark!*" escaped him; and he then turned to me and wrote on the tablet: "Did you not hear?" I had heard nothing but the roar; and he howled into my ear in sounds now audible to me as an echo caught far off in dreams: "You shall see."

He took up the candlestick; produced from the pocket of his robe a key; unlocked the iron door; and we passed into a room very loftily domed in proportion to its area, and empty, save that a pair of steps lay against its wall, and that in the centre of its marble floor was a pool, like a Roman "impluvium," only round like the room—a pool evidently profound in depth, full of a thick and inky fluid. I was very perturbed by its present aspect, for as the candle burned upon its surface, I observed that this had been quite recently *disturbed*, in a style for which the shivering of the house could not account, since *ripples* of slime were now rounding out from its middle to its brink. When I glanced at Harfager for explanation, he gave me a signal to wait; and now for about an hour, with his hands behind his back, paced the chamber; but then paused, and we two stood together by the pool's margin, gazing into the water. Suddenly his clutch tightened on my arm, and I saw, with a touch of horror, a tiny ball, probably of lead, but daubed blood-red by some chemical, fall from the roof, and sink into the middle of the pool. It hissed on contact with the water a whiff of mist.

"In the name of all that is sinister," I whispered, "what thing is this?"

Again he made me a busy and confident signal to wait, moved the ladder-steps toward the pool, handed me the taper. When I had mounted, holding high the light, I saw hanging out of the fogs in the dome a globe of old copper, lengthened into balloon-shape by a neck, at the end of which I could spy a tiny hole. Painted over the globe was barely visible in red print-letters:

"HARFAGER-HOUS: 1389–188."

I was down quicker than I went up!

"But the meaning?" I panted.

"Did you see the writing?"

"Yes. The meaning?"

He wrote: "By comparing Gascoigne with Thrunster, I find that the house was *built* about 1389."

"But the last figures?"

"After the last 8," he replied, "there is another figure not quite obliterated by a tarnish-spot."

"What figure?" I asked.

"It cannot be read, but may be surmised. As the year 1888 is now all but passed, it can only be the figure 9."

"Oh, you are depraved in mind!" I cried, very irritated: "you assume—you *state*—in a manner which no mind trained to base its conclusions on facts can bear with patience."

"And you are irrational," he wrote. "You know, I suppose, the formula of Archimedes by which, the diameter of a globe being known, its volume also is known? Now, the diameter of that globe in the dome I know to be four and a half feet; and the diameter of the leaden balls about the third of an inch. Supposing, then, that 1389 was the year in which the globe was full of balls, you may readily calculate that not many fellows of the four million and odd which have since dropped at the rate of one an hour are now left within. The fall of the balls *cannot* persist another year. The figure 9 is therefore forced upon us."

"But you assume, Harfager!" I cried: "Oh, believe me, my friend, this is the very wantonness of wickedness! By what algebra of despair do you know that each ball represents one of the scions of your house, or that the last date was intended to correspond with the stoppage of the horologe. And, even if so, what is the significance of it? It can have no *significance*!"

"Do you want to madden me?" he shouted. Then furiously writing; "I swear that I know nothing of its significance! But it is not evident to you that the thing is a big hour-glass, intended to count the hours, not of a day, but of a cycle; and of a cycle of five hundred years?"

"But the whole contrivance," I passionately cried, "is a baleful phantasm of our brains! How is the fall of the balls regulated? Ah, my friend, you wander—your mind is debauched in this brawl of waters."

"I have not ascertained," he replied, "by what internal works, or clammy medium, or spiral coil, dependent probably for its action upon the liberation of the mansion, the balls are retarded in their fall: that was a matter well within the skill of the mediaeval mechanic, the inventor of the clock; but this at least is clear, that one element of their retardation is the smallness of the aperture through which they have to pass; that this element, by known laws of statics, will cease to operate when no more than three balls remain; and that, consequently, the last three will fall at almost the same instant."

"In Heaven's name!" I exclaimed, careless now what folly I poured out, "but your mother is dead, Harfager! Do you deny that there remain but you and the Lady Swertha?"

A glance of disdain was all the answer he then gave me as to this.

But he confessed to me a day later that the leaden drops were a constant sorrow to his ears; that from hour to hour his life was a keen waiting for their fall; that even from his brief sleeps he infallibly started awake at each descent; that in whatever region of the mansion he chanced to be, they found him out with a crashing *loudness*; and that each crash tweaked him with a twinge of anguish within the ear. I was therefore shocked at his declaration that these droppings had now become as the life of life to him; had acquired an entwining so close with the tone of his mind, that their ceasing might even mean for him the reeling of Reason: at which confession he sobbed, with his face buried, as he leant upon a column. When this paroxysm was past, I asked him if it was out of the question that he should once for all cast off the fascination of the horologe, and escape with me from the place. He wrote in mysterious reply: "A *three*-fold cord is not easily broken." I started, asking—"How three-fold?" He wrote with a bitter smile: "To be in love with pain—to pine after aching—is not that a wicked madness?" I stood astonished that he had unconsciously quoted Gascoigne! "a wicked madness!" "a lecherous anguish!" "You have seen my aunt's face," he proceeded; "your eyes were dim if you did not see in it an impious calm, the glee of a blasphemous patience, a grin behind her daring smile." He then spoke of a prospect at the terror of which his whole soul trembled, yet which sometimes laughed in his heart in the form of a *hope*. It was the prospect of any considerable increase in the volume of sound about his ears. At *that*, he said, the brain must totter. On the night of my arrival the noise of my boots, and, since then, my voice occasionally raised, had produced acute pain in him. To such an ear, I understood him to say, the luxury of torture involved in a large sound-increase around was an allurement from which no human virtue could turn: and when I said that I could not even conceive such an increase, much less the means by which it could be effected, he brought out from the archives of the mansion some annals kept by the heads of his family. From these it appeared that the tempests that ever lacerated the latitude of Rayba did not fail to give place, at intervals of some years, to one mammoth madness, one Samson among the merry men, and Sirius among the suns. At such periods the rains descended—and the floods came—even as in the first world-deluge; those *rösts*, or eddies, which ever encircled Rayba, spurning then the bands of lateral space, burst aloft into a whirl of water-spouts, to dance about the little land, upon which, converging, some of them discharged their waters: and the locks which flowed to the cataract thus redoubled their volume, and crashed with redoubled roar. Harfager said it was miraculous that for eighteen years no such grand event had transacted itself at Rayba.

"And what," I asked, "in addition to the dropping balls, and the prospect of an increase of sound, is the third strand of that '*three-fold cord*' of which you have spoken."

For answer he led me to a circular hall which, he said, he had ascertained to be the centre of the circular mansion. It was a very large hall—so large as I think I never saw—so large that the amount of wall lighted at one time by the candle seemed nearly flat: and nearly the whole of its area, from floor to roof, was occupied by a column of brass, the space between the wall and column being only such as to admit of a stretched-out arm.

"This column," Harfager wrote, "goes up to the dome and

passes beyond it; it goes down to the lower floor, and passes through that; it goes down thence to the brazen flooring of the vaults and *passes through that* into the bedrock. Under each floor it spreads out, helping to support the floor. What is the precise quality of the impression which I have made upon your mind by this description?"

"I do not know," I answered, turning from him: "ask me none of your enigmas, Harfager: I feel a giddiness. . . ."

"But answer me," he said: "consider *the strangeness* of that brazen lowest floor, which I have discovered to be some six feet thick, and whose under-surface, I have reason to think, is somewhat *above* the bedrock; remember that the fabric is at no point *fastened* to the column; think of the *chains* which ray out from the outer wall, apparently *anchoring* the house to the ground. Tell me, what impression have I *now* made?"

"And is it for *this* you wait?" I cried. "Yet there may have been no malevolent intention! You jump at conclusions! Any fixed building in such a land and spot as this would at any time be liable to be broken up by some sovereign tempest! What if it was the intention of the builder that in such a case the chains should break, and the building, by yielding, be saved?"

"You have no lack of charity at least," he replied; and we then went back to the book we were reading together.

He had not wholly lost the old habit of study, although he could no longer get himself to *sit* to read; so with a volume (often tossed down) he would stamp about within the region of the lamplight; or I, unconscious of my voice, might read to him. By a whim of his mood the few books which now lay within the limits of his patience had all for their motive something of the *picaresque*, or the foppishly speculative: Quevedo's "Tacaño"; or the system of Tycho Brahe; above all, George Hakewill's "Power and Providence of God." One day, however, as I read, he interrupted me with the sentence, apropos of nothing: "What I cannot understand is that you, a scientist, should believe that life ceases with the ceasing of breathing"—and from that moment the tone of our reading changed. For he led me to the crypts of the library in the lowest part of the building, and hour after hour, with a *furore* of triumph overwhelmed me with books proving the length of life after "death." What, he asked, was my opinion of Baron Verulam's account of the dead man who was heard to utter words of prayer? or of the bounding bowels of the dead convict? On my expressing unbelief, he seemed surprised, and reminded me of the writhing of dead cobras, of the long beating of a frog's heart after "death." "She is not dead," he quoted, "but *sleepeth.*" The idea of Bacon and Paracelsus that the principle of life resides in a spirit or fluid was proof to him that such fluid could not, from its very nature, undergo any *sudden* annihilation, while the organs which it pervades remain. When I asked what limit he, then, set to the persistence of "life" in the "dead," he answered that when decay had so far advanced that the nerves could no longer be called nerves, or when the brain had been disconnected at the neck from the body, as by rats gnawing, then the king of terrors was king verily. With an indiscretion strange to me before my residence at Rayba, I now blurted out the question whether in all this he could be referring to his mother? For a while he stood thoughtful, then wrote: "Even if I had not had reason to believe that my own and Swertha's life in some way hung upon the final cessations of hers, I should still have taken precautions to ascertain the march of the destroyer on her frame: as it is, I shall not lack even the exactest information." He then explained that the rats which ran riot in the place of death would in time do their full work upon her; but would be unable to reach to the region of the throat without first gnawing their way through the three strings stretched across the holes of the bridges within the coffin, and thus, one by one, liberating the three morrisco-bells to tinklings.

The winter solstice had gone, another year began. I was sleeping a deep sleep by night when Harfager came into my chamber, and shook me. His face was ghastly in the taper's glare. A change within a short time had taken place upon him. He was hardly the same. He was like some poor wight into whose surprised eyes in the night have pried the eyes of Affright.

He said that he was aware of strainings and creakings, which gave him the feeling of being suspended in airy spaces by a thread which must break to his weight; and he begged me, for God's sake, to accompany him to the coffins. We passed together through the house, he craven, haggard, his gait now laggard, into the chamber of the dead, where he stole to and fro examining the shelves. Out of the footless coffin of the dowager trembling on its bench I saw a water-rat crawl; and as Harfager passed beneath one of the shortest of the shelves which bore one coffin, it suddenly dropped from a height to dust at his feet. He screamed the cry of a frightened creature; tottered to my support; and I bore him back to the upper parts of the palace.

He sat, with his face buried, in a corner of a small chamber, doddering, overtaken, as it were, with the extremity of age, no longer marking with his "*Hark!*" the fall of the leaden drops. To my remonstrances he responded only with the moan, "so soon!" Whenever I looked for him, I found him there, his manhood now collapsed in an ague. I do not think that during this time he slept.

On the second night, as I was approaching him, he sprang suddenly upright with the outcry: "The first bell is tinkling!"

And he had scarcely screamed it when, from some long way off, a faint wail, which at its origin must have been a fierce shriek, reached my now feverish ears. Harfager, for his part, clapped his palms to his ears, and dashed from his place, I following in hot chase through the black breadth of the mansion: till we came to a chamber containing a candelabrum, and arrased in faded red. On the floor in swoon lay the lady Swertha, her dark-grey hair in disarray wrapping her like an angry sea; tufts of it scattered, torn from the roots; and on her throat prints of strangling fingers. We bore her to her bed in an alcove; and, having discovered some tincture in a cabinet, I administered it between her fixed teeth. In her rapt countenance I saw that death was not; and, as I found something appalling in her aspect, shortly afterwards left her to Harfager.

When I next saw him his manner had undergone a kind of change which I can only describe as gruesome. It resembled the officious self-importance seen in a person of weak intellect who spurs himself with the thought, "to business! the time is short!" while his walk sickened me with a hint of *ataxie locomotrice.* When I asked him as to his aunt, as to the meaning of the marks of violence on her body, bending ear to his deep and unctuous tones, I could hear: "An attempt has been made upon her life by the skeleton, Aith."

He seemed not to share my astonishment at this thing! nor could give me any clear answer as to his reason for retaining such a servant, or as to the origin of Aith's service. Aith, he told me, had been admitted into the palace during the period of his own absence in youth, and he knew little of him beyond the fact that he was extraordinarily strong. *Whence* he had come, or how, no person except the lady Swertha was aware: and she, it seems, feared, or at least persistently flinched from admitting him into the mystery. He added that, as a matter of fact, the lady, from the day of his coming back to Rayba, had with some object imposed upon herself a dumbness on all subjects, which he had never once known her to break through, except by an occasional note.

With an ataxic strenuousness, with the airs of a drunken man constraining himself to ordered action, Harfager now set himself to the doing of a host of trivial things: he collected chronicles and arranged them in order of date; he docketed or ticketed packets of documents; he insisted upon my assistance in turning the faces of paintings to the wall. He was, however, now constantly stopped by bursts of vertigo, six times in a single hour being hurled to the ground, while blood frequently guttered from his ears. He complained to me in a tone of piteous wail of the wooing of a silver *piccolo* that continually seduced him. As he bent, sweating, over his momentous nothings, his hands fluttered like aspen. I noted the movements of his whimpering lips, the rheum of his sunken eyes: sudden doting had come upon his youth.

On a day he threw it utterly off, and was young anew. He entered my room; roused me from dreams; I observed the lunacy of bliss in his eyes, heard his hiss in my ear:

"Up! *The storm*!"

Ah! I had known it—in the nightmare of the night. I felt it in the air of the room. It had come. I saw it lurid by the lamplight on the hell of Harfager's face.

A glee burst at once into birth within me, as I sprang from my couch, glancing at the clock: it was eight—in the morning. Harfager, with the naked stalk of some maniac prophet, had already taken himself away; and I started out after him. A deepening was clearly felt in the quivering of the edifice; anon for a second it stopped still, as if, breathlessly, to listen; its air was troubled with a vague gustiness. Occasionally there came to me as it were the noising of some far-off lamentation and voice in Ramah, but whether this was in my ear or the screaming of the gale I could not tell; or again I could hear one clear chord of an organ's vaunt. About noon I spied Harfager, lamp in hand, running along a corridor, with naked soles. As we met he looked at me, but hardly with recognition, and passed by; stopped, however, and ran back to howl into my ear the question: "Would you *see*?" He then beckoned before me, and I followed to a very small opening in the outer wall, closed with a slab of brass. As he lifted the latch, the slab dashed inward with instant impetuosity and tossed him a long way, while the breath of the tempest, braying through the brazen tube with a brutal bravura, caught and pinned me upon a corner of a wall, and all down the corridor a long crashing racket of crowds of pictures and couches followed. I nevertheless managed to push my way on the belly to the opening. Hence the sea should have been visible; but my senses were met by nothing but a vision of tumbled tenebrousness, and a general impression of the letter O. The sun of Rayba had gone out. In a moment of opportunity our two forces got the shutter shut again.

"Come!"—he had obtained a fresh glimmer, and beckoned before me—"let's go see how the dead fare in the great desolation": and we ran, but had hardly got to the middle of the stairway, when I was thrilled by the consciousness of some great shock, the bass of a dull thud, which nothing save the thumping to the floor of the whole lump of the coffins could have caused. I looked for Harfager, and for a moment only saw his heels skedaddling, panic-hounded, his ears stopped, his mouth round! Then, indeed, fear reached me—a tremor in the audacity of my heart, a thought that now at any rate I must desert him in his extremity, and work out my own salvation. Yet it was with hesitancy that I turned to search for him for the last farewell—a hesitancy which I felt to be not unselfish, but selfish, and unhealthy. I rambled through the night, seeking light, and having happened upon a lamp, proceeded to seek for Harfager. Several hours went by in this way, during which I could not doubt from the state of the air in the house that the violence about me was being wildly heightened. Sounds as of screams—unreal, like the shriekings of demons—now reached my ears. As the time of night came on, I began to detect in the greatly augmented baritone of the cataract a fresh character—a shrillness—the whistle of a rapture—a malice—the menace of a rabies blind and deaf. It must have been at about the hour of six that I found Harfager. He sat in an obscure room, with his brow bowed down, his hands on his knees, his face covered with hair, and with blood from the ears. The right sleeve of his robe had been rent away in some renewed attempt, I imagined, to manage a window; and the rather crushed arm hung lank from the shoulder. For some time I stood and eyed him mouthing his mumblings; but now that I had found him uttered nothing as to my departure. Presently he looked sharply up with the call *"Hark!"*—then with impatience, "Hark! Hark!"—then with a shout, "The second bell!" And *again*, in immediate sequence upon his shout, there sounded a wail, vague yet real, through the house. Harfager at the instant dropped reeling with giddiness; but I, snatching up a lamp, dashed out, shivering but eager. For some while the wild wailing went on (either actually, or by reflex action of my ear); and as I ran for the lady's apartment, I saw opposite to it the open door of an armoury, into which I passed, caught up a battle-axe, and was now about to dart in to her aid, when Aith, with a blazing eye, shied out of her chamber. I cast up my axe, and, shouting, dashed forward to down him: but by some chance the lamp fell from me, and before I knew anything more, the axe sprang from my grasp, and I was cast far backward by some most grim vigour. There was, however, enough light shining out of the chamber to show that the skeleton had darted into a door of the armoury, so I instantly slammed and locked the door near me by which I had procured the axe, and hurrying to the other, secured it, too. Aith was thus a prisoner. I then entered the lady's chamber. She lay over the bed in the alcove, and to my bent ear grossly croaked the ruckle of death. A glance at her mangled throat convincing me that her last moments were come, I settled her on the bed, curtained her within the loosened festoons of the hangings of black, and turned from the cursedness of her aspect. On an *escritoire* near I noticed a note, intended apparently for Harfager: "I mean to defy, and fly; not from fear, but for the delight of the defiance itself. *Can* you come?"

Taking a flame from the candelabrum, I left her to her loneliness, and throes of her death.

I had passed some way backward when I was startled by a queer sound—a crash—resembling the crash of a tamboureen; and as I could hear it pretty clearly, and from a distance, this meant some prodigious energy. In two minutes it again broke out; and thenceforth at regular intervals—with an effect of pain upon me; and the conviction grew gradually within me that Aith had unhung two of the old brass shields from their pegs, and holding them by their handles, and dashing them viciously together, thus expressed the frenzy that had now overtaken him. When I found my way back to Harfager, very anguish was now stamping in him about the chamber; he shook his head like a tormented horse, brushing and barring from his hearing each crash of the brass shields. "Ah, when—when——" he hoarsely groaned into my ear, "will that ruckle cease in her throat? I will myself, I tell you—*with my own hand*—oh God . . . " Since the morning his auditory fever (as indeed my own also) appeared to have increased in steady proportion with the roaring and screeching chaos round; and the death-struggle in the lady's throat bitterly filled for him the intervals of the grisly cymbaling of Aith. He presently sent twinkling fingers into the air, and, with his arms cast out, darted into the darkness.

And again I sought him, and long again in vain. As the hours passed, and the day deepened toward its baleful midnight, the cry of the now redoubled cataract, mixed with the mass and majesty of the now climatic tempest, took on too intentional a *shriek* to be longer tolerable to any reason. My own mind escaped my sway, and went its way: for here in the hot-bed of fever I was fevered. I wandered from chamber to chamber, precipitate, dizzy on the upbuoyance of a joy. "As a man upon whom sleep seizes," so I had fallen. Even yet, as I passed near the region of the armoury, the rapturous shields of Aith did not fail to smash faintly upon my ear.

Harfager I did not see, for he, too, was doubtless roaming a hurtling Ahasuerus round the world of the house. However, at about midnight, observing light shining from a door on the lower stage, I entered and saw him there—the chamber of the dropping horologe. He sat hugging himself on the ladder-steps, gazing at the gloomy pool. The final lights of the riot of the day seemed dying in his eyes; and he gave me no glance as I ran in. His hands, his bare arm, were all washed with new-shed blood; but of this, too, he looked unconscious; his mouth was hanging open to his pantings. As I eyed him, he suddenly leapt high, smiting his hands with the yell, "The last bell tinkling!" and ran out raving. He therefore did not see (though he may have understood by hearing) the thing which, with cowering awe, I now saw: for a ball slipped from the horologe with a hiss and mist of smoke into the pool; and while the clock once ticked another: and while the clock yet ticked, another! and the smoke of the first had not perfectly thinned, when the smoke of the third, mixing with it, floated toward the dome. Understanding that the sands of the mansion were run, I, too, throwing up my arm, rushed from the spot; but was suddenly stopped in my flight by the sense of some stupendous destiny emptying its vials upon the edifice; and was made aware by a crackling racket, like musketry, above, and the downpour of a world of waters, that some waterspout, in the waltz and whirl, had hurled its broken summit upon us, and burst through the dome. At that moment I beheld Harfager running toward me, his hands buried in his hair; and, as he raced past, I caught him, crying: "Harfager, save yourself! the very fountains, Harfager—by the grand God, man"—I hissed it into his inmost ear—"*the very fountains of the Great Deep . . . !*" He glared at me, and went on his way, while I, whisking myself into a room, closed the door. Here for some time with weak knees I waited; but the eagerness of my frenzy pressed me, and I again stepped out, to find the corridors everywhere thigh-deep with water; while rags of the storm, bragging through the hole in the dome, were now blustering about the house. My light was at once puffed out; but I was surprised by the presence of *another* light—most ghostly, gloomy, bluish—mild, yet wild—which now gloated everywhere through the house. I was standing in wonder at this when a gust of auguster passion galloped up the mansion; and, with it, I was made aware of the *snap* of something somewhere. There was a minute's infinite waiting—and then—quick—ever quicker—came the throb, snap, pop, in spacious succession, of the anchoring chains of the mansion before the hurried shoulder of the hurricane. And *again* a second of breathless stillness—and then—deliberately—its hour came—the house moved. My flesh worked like the flesh of worms which squirm. Slowly moved, and stopped—then there was a sweep—and a swirl—and a pause! then a swirl—and a sweep—and a pause! then steady labour on the brazen axis as the labourer tramps by the harrow; then a heightening of zest—then intensity—then the final light liveliness of flight. And now once again, as, staggering and plunging, I spun, the notion of escape for a moment came to me, but this time I shook an impious fist. "No, but, God, no, no," I gasped, "I will no more go from here: here let me waltzing pass in this carnival of the vortices, anarchy of the thunders!" —and I ran staggering. But memory gropes in a greyer gloaming as to all that followed. I struggled up the stairway, now flowing a river, and for a good while ran staggering and plunging, full of wild rantings, about, amid the downfall of roofs, and the ruins of walls. The air was thick with splashes, the whole roof now, save three rafters, having been snatched by the wind away; and in the blush of that bluish moonshine the tapestries were flapping and trailing wildly out after the flying place, like the streaming hair of some ranting fakir stung reeling by the tarantulas of distraction. At one point, where the largest of the porticoes protruded, the mansion began at every revolution to bump with grum shudderings against some obstruction: it bumped, and while the lips said one-two-three it three times bumped again. It was the maenadism of mass! Swift—still swifter—in an ague of flurry it raced, every portico a sail to the gale, racking its great frame to fragments. I, running by the door of a room littered with the ruins of a wall, saw through that livid moonlight Harfager sitting on a tomb—a drum by him, upon which, with a club in his bloody fist, he feebly, but persistingly, beat. The speed of the leaning house had now attained the *sleeping* stage, that last pitch of the spinning-top; and now all at once Harfager dashed away the mat of hair which wrapped his face, sprang, stretched his arms, and began to spin—giddily—in the same direction as the mansion—nor less sleep-embathed, with lifted hair, with quivering cheeks.... From such a sight I shied with retching; and staggering, plunging, presently found myself on the lower floor opposite a porch, where an outer door chancing to crash before me, the breath of the tempest smote freshly upon me. On this an impulse, partly of madness, more of sanity, spurred in my soul; and I spurted out of the doorway, to be whirled far out into the limbo without.

The river at once rushed me deep-drenched toward the sea—though even there, in that depth of whirlpool, a shrill din, like the splitting of a world, reached my ears. It had hardly passed when my body butted in its course upon one of the arches, cushioned with seaweed, of the not all demolished causeway. Nor had I utterly lost consciousness. A clutch freed my head from the drench; and in the end I heaved myself to the level of the summit. Hence to the ledge of rock by which I had come, the bridge being intact, I rowed myself on my face under the thumps of the wind, and under a rushing of rain, like a shimmering of silk through the air. Noticing the same wild shining about me which had blushed through the broken dome into the mansion, I glanced backward—and saw that the dwelling of the Harfagers was a memory of the past; then upward—and the whole north heaven, to the zenith, shone one ocean of variegated glories—the *aurora borealis*, which was being fairly brushed and flustered by the gale. At the augustness of which sight, I was touched to a gush of tears. And with them the dream broke! the infatuation passed! a palm seemed to skin back from my brain the films and media of delusion; and on my knees I threw my hands to heaven in thankfulness for the marvel of my rescue from all the temptation, the tribulation, and the breakage, of Rayba.

ARTHUR MACHEN

THE WHITE PEOPLE

PROLOGUE

"Sorcery and sanctity," said Ambrose, "these are the only realities. Each is an ecstasy, a withdrawal from the common life."

Cotgrave listened, interested. He had been brought by a friend to this mouldering house in a northern suburb, through an old garden to the room where Ambrose the recluse dozed and dreamed over his books.

"Yes," he went on, "magic is justified of her children. There are many, I think, who eat dry crusts and drink water, with a joy infinitely sharper than anything within the experience of the 'practical' epicure."

"You are speaking of the saints?"

"Yes, and of the sinners, too. I think you are falling into the very general error of confining the spiritual world to the supremely good; but the supremely wicked, necessarily, have their portion in it. The merely carnal, sensual man can no more be a great sinner than he can be a great saint. Most of us are just indifferent, mixed-up creatures; we muddle through the world without realizing the meaning and the inner sense of things, and, consequently, our wickedness and our goodness are alike second-rate, unimportant."

"And you think the great sinner, then, will be an ascetic, as well as the great saint?"

"Great people of all kinds forsake the imperfect copies and go to the perfect originals. I have no doubt but that many of the very highest among the saints have never done a 'good action' (using the words in their ordinary sense). And, on the other hand, there have been those who have sounded the very depths of sin, who all their lives have never done an 'ill deed.' "

He went out of the room for a moment, and Cotgrave, in high delight, turned to his friend and thanked him for the introduction.

"He's grand," he said. "I never saw that kind of lunatic before."

Ambrose returned with more whisky and helped the two men in a liberal manner. He abused the teetotal sect with ferocity, as he handed the seltzer, and pouring out a glass of water for himself, was about to resume his monologue, when Cotgrave broke in—

"I can't stand it, you know," he said, "your paradoxes are too monstrous. A man may be a great sinner and yet never do anything sinful! Come!"

"You're quite wrong," said Ambrose. "I never make paradoxes; I wish I could. I merely said that a man may have an exquisite taste in Romanée Conti, and yet never have even smelt four ale. That's all, and it's more like a truism than a paradox, isn't it? Your surprise at my remark is due to the fact that you haven't realized what sin is. Oh, yes, there is a sort of connexion between Sin with the capital letter, and actions which are commonly called sinful: with murder, theft, adultery, and so forth. Much the same connexion that there is between the A, B, C and fine literature. But I believe that the misconception—it is all but universal—arises in great measure from our looking at the matter through social spectacles. We think that a man who does evil to *us* and to his neighbours must be very evil. So he is, from a social standpoint; but can't you realize that Evil in its essence is a lonely thing, a passion of the solitary, individual soul? Really, the average murderer, *qua* murderer, is not by any means a sinner in the true sense of the word. He is simply a wild beast that we have to get rid of to save our own necks from his knife. I should class him rather with tigers than with sinners."

"It seems a little strange."

"I think not. The murderer murders not from positive qualities, but from negative ones; he lacks something which non-murderers possess. Evil, of course, is wholly positive—only it is on the wrong side. You may believe me that sin in its proper sense is very rare; it is probable that there have been far fewer sinners than saints. Yes, your standpoint is all very well for practical, social purposes; we are naturally inclined to think that a person who is very disagreeable to us must be a very great sinner! It is very disagreeable to have one's pocket picked, and we pronounce the thief to be a very great sinner. In truth, he is merely an undeveloped man. He cannot be a saint, of course; but he may be, and often is, an infinitely better creature than thousands who have never broken a single commandment. He is a great nuisance to *us*, I admit, and we very properly lock him up if we catch him; but between his troublesome and unsocial action and evil—Oh, the connexion is of the weakest."

It was getting very late. The man who had brought Cotgrave had probably heard all this before, since he assisted with a bland and judicious smile, but Cotgrave began to think that his "lunatic" was turning into a sage.

"Do you know," he said, "you interest me immensely? You think, then, that we do not understand the real nature of evil?"

"No, I don't think we do. We over-estimate it and we under-estimate it. We take the very numerous infractions of our social 'bye-laws'—the very necessary and very proper regulations which keep the human company together—and we get frightened at the prevalence of 'sin' and 'evil.' But this is really nonsense. Take theft, for example. Have you any *horror* at the thought of Robin Hood, of the Highland caterans of the seventeenth century, of the moss-troopers, of the company promoters of our day?

"Then, on the other hand, we underrate evil. We attach such an enormous importance to the 'sin' of meddling with our pockets (and our wives) that we have quite forgotten the awfulness of real sin."

"And what is sin?" said Cotgrave.

"I think I must reply to your question by another. What would your feelings be, seriously, if your cat or your dog began to talk to you, and to dispute with you in human accents? You would be overwhelmed with horror. I am sure of it. And if the roses in your garden sang a weird song, you would go mad. And suppose the stones in the road began to swell and grow before your eyes, and if the pebble that you noticed at night had shot out stony blossoms in the morning?

"Well, these examples may give you some notion of what sin really is."

"Look here," said the third man, hitherto placid, "you two seem pretty well wound up. But I'm going home. I've missed my tram, and I shall have to walk."

Ambrose and Cotgrave seemed to settle down more profoundly when the other had gone out into the early misty morning and the pale light of the lamps.

"You astonish me," said Cotgrave. "I had never thought of that. If that is really so, one must turn everything upside down. Then the essence of sin really is—"

"In the taking of heaven by storm, it seems to me," said Ambrose. "It appears to me that it is simply an attempt to penetrate into another and higher sphere in a forbidden manner. You can understand why it is so rare. There are few, indeed, who wish to penetrate into other spheres, higher or lower, in ways allowed or forbidden. Men, in the mass, are amply content with life as they find it. Therefore there are few saints, and sinners (in the proper sense) are fewer still, and men of genius, who partake sometimes of each character are rare also. Yes; on the whole, it is, perhaps, harder to be a great sinner than a great saint."

"There is something profoundly unnatural about sin? Is that what you mean?"

"Exactly. Holiness requires as great, or almost as great, an effort; but holiness works on lines that *were* natural once; it is an effort to recover the ecstasy that was before the Fall. But sin is an effort to gain the ecstasy and the knowledge that pertain alone to angels, and in making this effort man becomes a demon. I told you that the mere murderer is not *therefore* a sinner; that is true, but the sinner is sometimes a murderer. Gilles de Rais is an instance. So you see that while the good and the evil are unnatural to man as he now is—to man the social, civilized being—evil is unnatural in a much deeper sense than good. The saint endeavours to recover a gift which he has lost; the sinner tries to obtain something which was never his. In brief, he repeats the Fall."

"But are you a Catholic?" said Cotgrave.

"Yes; I am a member of the persecuted Anglican Church."

"Then, how about those texts which seem to reckon as sin that which you would set down as a mere trivial dereliction?"

"Yes; but in one place the word 'sorcerers' comes in the same sentence, doesn't it? That seems to me to give the key-note. Consider: can you imagine for a moment that a false statement which saves an innocent man's life is a sin? No; very good, then, it is not the mere liar who is excluded by those words; it is, above all, the 'sorcerers' who use the material life, who use the failings incidental to material life as instruments to obtain their infinitely wicked ends. And let me tell you this: our higher senses are so blunted, we are so drenched with materialism, that we should probably fail to recognize real wickedness if we encountered it."

"But shouldn't we experience a certain horror—a terror such as you hinted we would experience if a rose tree sang—in the mere presence of an evil man?"

"We should if we were natural: children and women feel this horror you speak of, even animals experience it. But with most of us convention and civilization and education have blinded and deafened and obscured the natural reason. No, sometimes we may recognize evil by its hatred of the good—one doesn't need much penetration to guess at the influence which dictated, quite unconsciously, the 'Blackwood' review of Keats—but this is purely incidental; and, as a rule, I suspect that the Hierarchs of Tophet pass quite unnoticed, or, perhaps, in certain cases, as good but mistaken men."

"But you used the word 'unconscious' just now, of Keats' reviewers. Is wickedness ever unconscious?"

"Always. It must be so. It is like holiness and genius in this as in other points; it is a certain rapture or ecstasy of the soul; a transcendent effort to surpass the ordinary bounds. So, surpassing these, it surpasses also the understanding, the faculty that takes note of that which comes before it. No, a man may be infinitely and horribly wicked and never suspect it. But I tell you, evil in this, its certain and true sense, is rare, and I think it is growing rarer."

"I am trying to get hold of it all," said Cotgrave. "From what you say, I gather that the true evil differs generically from that which we call evil?"

"Quite so. There is, no doubt, an analogy between the two; a resemblance such as enables us to use, quite legitimately, such terms as the 'foot of the mountain' and the 'leg of the table.' And, sometimes, of course, the two speak, as it were, in the same language. The rough miner, or 'puddler,' the untrained, undeveloped 'tiger-man,' heated by a quart or two above his usual measure, comes home and kicks his irritating and injudicious wife to death. He is a murderer. And Gilles de Rais was a murderer. But you see the gulf that separates the two? The 'word,' if I may so speak, is accidentally the same in each case, but the 'meaning' is utterly different. It is flagrant 'Hobson Jobson' to confuse the two, or rather, it is as if one supposed that Juggernaut and the Argonauts had something to do etymologically with one another. And no doubt the same weak likeness, or analogy, runs between all the 'social' sins and the real spiritual sins, and in some cases, perhaps, the lesser may be 'schoolmaster' to lead one on to the greater—from the shadow to the reality. If you are anything of a theologian, you will see the importance of all this."

"I am sorry to say," remarked Cotgrave, "that I have devoted very little of my time to theology. Indeed, I have often wondered on what grounds theologians have claimed the title of Science of Sciences for their favourite study; since the 'theological' books I have looked into have always seemed to me to be concerned with feeble and obvious pieties, or with the kings of Israel and Judah. I do not care to hear about those kings."

Ambrose grinned.

"We must try to avoid theological discussion," he said. "I perceive that you would be a bitter disputant. But perhaps the 'dates of the kings' have as much to do with theology as the hobnails of the murderous puddler with evil."

"Then, to return to our main subject, you think that sin is an esoteric, occult thing?"

"Yes. It is the infernal miracle as holiness is the supernal. Now and then it is raised to such a pitch that we entirely fail to suspect its existence; it is like the note of the great pedal pipes of the organ, which is so deep that we cannot hear it. In other cases it may lead to the lunatic asylum, or to still stranger issues. But you must never confuse it with mere social misdoing. Remember how the Apostle, speaking of the 'other side,' distinguishes between 'charitable' actions and charity. And as one may give all one's goods to the poor, and yet lack charity; so, remember, one may avoid every crime and yet be a sinner."

"Your psychology is very strange to me," said Cotgrave, "but I confess I like it, and I suppose that one might fairly deduce from your premisses the conclusion that the real sinner might very possibly strike the observer as a harmless personage enough?"

"Certainly; because the true evil has nothing to do with social life or social laws, or if it has, only incidentally and accidentally. It is a lonely passion of the soul—or a passion of the lonely soul—whichever you like. If, by chance, we understand it, and grasp its full significance, then, indeed, it will fill us with horror and with awe. But this emotion is widely distinguished from the fear and the disgust with which we regard the ordinary criminal, since this latter is largely or entirely founded on the regard which we have for our own skins or purses. We hate a murderer, because we know that we should hate to be murdered, or to have any one that we like murdered. So, on the 'other side,' we venerate the saints, but we don't 'like' them as we like our friends. Can you persuade yourself that you would have 'enjoyed' St. Paul's company? Do you think that you and I would have 'got on' with Sir Galahad?

"So with the sinners, as with the saints. If you met a very evil man, and recognized his evil; he would, no doubt, fill you with horror and awe; but there is no reason why you should 'dislike' him. On the contrary, it is quite possible that if you could succeed in putting the sin out of your mind you might find the sinner capital company, and in a little while you might have to reason yourself back into horror. Still, how awful it is. If the roses and the lilies suddenly sang on this coming morning; if the furniture began to move in procession, as in De Maupassant's tale!"

"I am glad you have come back to that comparison," said Cotgrave, "because I wanted to ask you what it is that corresponds in humanity to these imaginary feats of inanimate things. In a word—what is sin? You have given me, I know, an abstract definition, but I should like a concrete example."

"I told you it was very rare," said Ambrose, who appeared willing to avoid the giving of a direct answer. "The materialism of the age, which has done a good deal to suppress sanctity, has done perhaps more to suppress evil. We find the earth so very comfortable that we have no inclination either for ascents or descents. It would seem as if the scholar who decided to 'specialize' in Tophet, would be reduced to purely antiquarian researches. No palæontologist could show you a *live* pterodactyl."

"And yet you, I think, have 'specialized,' and I believe that your researches have descended to our modern times."

"You are really interested, I see. Well, I confess that I have dabbled a little, and if you like I can show you something that bears on the very curious subject we have been discussing."

Ambrose took a candle and went away to a far, dim corner of the room. Cotgrave saw him open a venerable bureau that stood there, and from some secret recess he drew out a parcel, and came back to the window where they had been sitting.

Ambrose undid a wrapping of paper, and produced a green book.

"You will take care of it?" he said. "Don't leave it lying about. It is one of the choicer pieces in my collection, and I should be very sorry if it were lost."

He fondled the faded binding.

"I knew the girl who wrote this," he said. "When you read it, you will see how it illustrates the talk we have had tonight. There is a sequel, too, but I won't talk of that."

"There was an odd article in one of the reviews some months ago," he began again, with the air of a man who changes the subject. "It was written by a doctor—Dr. Coryn, I think, was the name. He says that a lady, watching her little girl playing at the drawing-room window, suddenly saw the heavy sash give way and fall on the child's fingers. The lady fainted, I think, but at any rate the doctor was summoned, and when he had dressed the child's wounded and maimed fingers he was summoned to the mother. She was groaning with pain, and it was found that three fingers of her hand, corresponding with those that had been injured on the child's hand, were swollen and inflamed, and later, in the doctor's language, purulent sloughing set in."

Ambrose still handled delicately the green volume.

"Well, here it is," he said at last, parting with difficulty, it seemed, from his treasure.

"You will bring it back as soon as you have read it," he said, as they went out into the hall, into the old garden, faint with the odour of white lilies.

There was a broad red band in the east as Cotgrave turned to go, and from the high ground where he stood he saw that awful spectacle of London in a dream.

THE GREEN BOOK

The morocco binding of the book was faded, and the colour had grown faint, but there were no stains nor bruises nor marks of usage. The book looked as if it had been bought "on a visit to London" some seventy or eighty years ago, and had somehow been forgotten and suffered to lie away out of sight. There was an old, delicate, lingering odour about it, such an odour as sometimes haunts an ancient piece of furniture for a century or more. The end-papers, inside the binding, were oddly decorated with coloured patterns and faded gold. It looked small, but the paper was fine, and there were many leaves, closely covered with minute, painfully formed characters.

I found this book (the manuscript began) in a drawer in the old bureau that stands on the landing. It was a very rainy day and I could not go out, so in the afternoon I got a candle and rummaged in the bureau. Nearly all the drawers were full of old dresses, but one of the small ones looked empty, and I found this book hidden right at the back. I wanted a book like this, so I took it to write in. It is full of secrets. I have a great many other books of secrets I have written, hidden in a safe place, and I am going to write here many of the old secrets and some new ones; but there are some I shall not put down at all. I must not write down the real names of the days and months which I found out a year ago, nor the way to make the Aklo letters, or the Chian language, or the great beautiful Circles, nor the Mao Games, nor the chief songs. I may write something about all these things but not the way to do them, for peculiar reasons. And I must not say who the Nymphs are, or the Dôls, or Jeelo, or what voolas mean. All these are most secret secrets, and I am glad when I remember what they are, and how many wonderful languages I know, but there are some things that I call the secrets of the secrets of the secrets that I dare not think of unless I am quite alone, and then I shut my eyes, and put my hands over them and whisper the word, and the Alala comes. I only do this at night in my room or in certain woods that I know, but I must not describe them, as they are secret woods. Then there are the Ceremonies, which are all of them important, but some are more delightful than others—there are the White Ceremonies, and the Green Ceremonies, and the Scarlet Ceremonies. The Scarlet Ceremonies are the best, but there is only one place where they can be performed properly, though there is a very nice imitation which I have done in other places. Besides these, I have the dances, and the Comedy, and I have done the Comedy sometimes when the others were looking, and they didn't understand anything about it. I was very little when I first knew about these things.

When I was very small, and mother was alive, I can remember remembering things before that, only it has all got confused. But I remember when I was five or six I heard them talking about me when they thought I was not noticing. They were saying how queer I was a year or two before, and how nurse had called my mother to come and listen to me talking all to myself, and I was saying words that nobody could understand. I was speaking the Xu language, but I only remember a very few of the words, as it was about the little white faces that used to look at me when I was lying in my cradle. They used to talk to me, and I learnt their language and talked to them in it about some great white place where they lived, where the trees and the grass were all white, and there were white hills as high up as the moon, and a cold wind. I have often dreamed of it afterwards, but the faces went away when I was very little. But a wonderful thing happened when I was about five. My nurse was carrying me on her shoulder; there was a field of yellow corn, and we went through it, it was very hot. Then we came to a path through a wood, and a tall man came after us, and went with us till we came to a place where there was a deep pool, and it was very dark and shady. Nurse put me down on the soft moss under a tree, and she said: "She can't get to the pond now." So they left me there, and I sat quite still and watched, and out of the water and out of the wood came two wonderful white people, and they began to play and dance and sing. They were a kind of creamy white like the old ivory figure in the drawing-room; one was a beautiful lady with kind dark eyes, and a grave face, and long black hair, and she smiled such a strange sad smile at the other, who laughed and came to her. They played together, and danced round and round the pool, and they sang a song till I fell asleep. Nurse woke me up when she came back, and she was looking something like the lady had looked, so I told her all about it, and asked her why she looked like that. At first she cried, and then she looked very frightened, and turned quite pale. She put me down on the grass and stared at me, and I could see she was shaking all over. Then she said I had been dreaming, but I knew I hadn't. Then she made me promise not to say a word about it to anybody, and if I did I should be thrown into the black pit. I was not frightened at all, though nurse was, and I never forgot about it, because when I shut my eyes and it was quite quiet, and I was all alone, I could see them again, very faint and far away, but very splendid; and little bits of the song they sang came into my head, but I couldn't sing it.

I was thirteen, nearly fourteen, when I had a very singular adventure, so strange that the day on which it happened is always called the White Day. My mother had been dead for more than a year, and in the morning I had lessons, but they let me go out for walks in the afternoon. And this afternoon I walked a new way, and a little brook led me into a new country, but I tore my frock getting through many bushes, and beneath the low branches of trees, and up thorny thickets on the hills, and by dark woods full of creeping thorns. And it was a long, long way. It seemed as if I was going on for ever and ever, and I had to creep by a place like a tunnel where a brook must have been, but all the water had dried up, and the floor was rocky, and the bushes had grown overhead till they met, so that it was quite dark. And I went on and on through that dark place; it was a long, long way. And I came to a hill that I never saw before. I was in a dismal thicket full of black twisted boughs that tore me as I went through them, and I cried out because I was smarting all over, and then I found that I was climbing, and I went up and up a long way, till at last the thicket stopped and I came out crying just under the top of a big bare place, where there were ugly grey stones lying all about on the grass, and here and there a little twisted, stunted tree came out from under a stone, like a snake. And I went up, right to the top, a long way. I never saw such big ugly stones before; they came out of the earth some of them, and some looked as if they had been rolled to where they were, and they went on and on as far as I could see, a long, long way. I looked out from them and saw the country, but it was strange. It was winter time, and there were black terrible woods hanging from the hills all round; it was like seeing a large room hung with black curtains, and the shape of the trees seemed quite different from any I had ever seen before. I was afraid. Then beyond the woods there were other hills round in a great ring, but I had never seen any of them; it all looked black, and everything had a voor over it. It was all so still and silent, and the sky was heavy and grey and sad, like a wicked voorish dome in Deep Dendo. I went on into the dreadful rocks. There were hundreds and hundreds of them. Some were like horrid-grinning men; I could see their faces as if they would jump at me out of the stone, and catch hold of me, and drag me with them back into the rock, so that I should always be there. And there were other rocks that were like animals, creeping, horrible animals, putting out their tongues, and others were like words that I could not say, and others like dead people lying on the grass. I went on among them, though they frightened me, and my heart was full of wicked songs that they put into it; and I wanted to make faces and twist myself about in the way they did, and I went on and on a long way till at last I liked the rocks, and they didn't frighten me any more. I sang the songs I thought of; songs full of words that must not be spoken or written down. Then I made faces like the faces on the rocks, and I twisted myself about like the twisted ones, and I lay down flat on the ground like the dead ones, and I went up to one that was grinning, and put my arms round him and hugged him. And so I went on and on through the rocks till I came to a round mound in the middle of them. It was higher than a mound, it was nearly as high as our house, and it was like a great basin turned upside down, all smooth and round and green, with one stone, like a post, sticking up at the top. I climbed up the sides, but they were so steep I had to stop or I should have rolled all the way down again, and I should have knocked against the stones at the bottom, and perhaps been killed. But I wanted to get up to the very top of the big round mound, so I lay down flat on my face, and took hold of the grass with my hands and drew myself up, bit by bit, till I was at the top. Then I sat down on the stone in the middle, and looked all round about. I felt I had come such a long, long way, just as if I were a hundred miles from home, or in some other country, or in one of the strange places I had read about in the *Tales of the Genie* and the *Arabian Nights*, or as if I had gone across the sea, far away, for years and I had found another world that nobody had ever seen or heard of before, or as if I had somehow flown through the sky and fallen on one of the stars I had read about where everything is dead and cold and grey, and there is no air, and the wind doesn't blow. I sat on the stone and looked all round and down and round about me. It was just as if I was sitting on a tower in the middle of a great empty town, because I could see nothing all around but the grey rocks on the ground. I couldn't make out their shapes any more, but I could see them on and on for a long way, and I looked at them, and they seemed as if they had been arranged into patterns, and shapes, and figures. I knew they couldn't be, because I had seen a lot of them coming right out of the earth, joined to the deep rocks below, so I looked again, but still I saw nothing but circles, and small circles inside big ones, and pyramids, and domes, and spires, and they seemed all to go round and round the place where I was sitting, and the more I looked, the more I saw great big rings of rocks, getting bigger and bigger, and I stared so long that it felt as if they were all moving and turning, like a great wheel, and I was turning, too, in the middle. I got quite dizzy and queer in the head, and everything began to be hazy and not clear, and I saw little sparks of blue light, and the stones looked as if they were springing and dancing and twisting as they went round and round and round. I was frightened again, and I cried out loud, and jumped up from the stone I was sitting on, and fell down. When I got up I was so glad they all looked still, and I sat down on the top and slid down the mound, and went on again. I danced as I went in the peculiar way the rocks had danced when I got giddy, and I was so glad I could do it quite well, and I danced and danced along, and sang extraordinary songs that came into my head. At last I came to the edge of that great flat hill, and there were no more rocks, and the way went again through a dark thicket in a hollow. It was just as bad as the other one I went through climbing up, but I didn't mind this one, because I was so glad I had seen those singular dances and could imitate them. I went down, creeping through the bushes, and a tall nettle stung me on my leg, and made me burn, but I didn't mind it, and I tingled with the boughs and the thorns, but I only laughed and sang. Then I got out of the thicket into a close valley, a little secret place like a dark passage that nobody ever knows of, because it was so narrow and deep and the woods were so thick round it. There is a steep bank with trees hanging over it, and there the ferns keep green all through the winter, when they are dead and brown upon the hill, and the ferns there have a sweet, rich smell like what oozes out of fir trees. There was a little stream of water running down this valley, so small that I could easily step across it. I drank the water with my hand, and it tasted like bright, yellow wine, and it sparkled and bubbled as it ran down over beautiful red and yellow stones, so that it seemed alive and all colours at once. I drank it, and I drank more with my hand, but I couldn't drink enough, so I lay down and bent my head and sucked the water up with my lips. It tasted much better, drinking it that way, and a ripple would come up to my mouth and give me a kiss, and I laughed, and drank again, and pretended there was a nymph, like the one in the old picture at home, who lived in the water and was kissing me. So I bent low down to the water, and put my lips softly to it, and whispered to the nymph that I would come again. I felt sure it would not be common water, I was so glad when I got up and went on; and I danced again and went up and up the valley, under hanging hills. And when I came to the top, the ground rose up in front of me, tall and steep as a wall, and there was nothing but the green wall and the sky. I thought of "for ever and for ever, world without end, Amen"; and I thought I must have really found the end of the world, because it was like the end of everything, as if there could be nothing at all beyond, except the kingdom of Voor, where the light goes when it is put out, and the water goes when the sun takes it away. I began to think of all the long, long way I had journeyed, how I had found a brook and followed it, and followed it on, and gone through bushes and thorny thickets, and dark woods full of creeping thorns. Then I had crept up a tunnel under trees, and climbed a thicket, and seen all the grey rocks, and sat in the middle of them when they turned round, and then I had gone on through the grey rocks and come down the hill through the stinging thicket and up the dark valley, all a long, long way. I wondered how I should get home again, if I could ever find the way, and if my home was there any more, or if it were turned and everybody in it into grey rocks, as in the *Arabian Nights*. So I sat down on the grass and thought what I should do next. I was tired, and my feet were hot with walking, and as I looked about I saw there was a wonderful well just under the high, steep wall of grass. All the ground round it was covered with bright, green, dripping moss; there was every kind of moss there, moss like beautiful little ferns, and like palms and fir trees, and it was all green as jewellery, and drops of water hung on it like diamonds. And in the middle was the great well, deep and shining and beautiful, so clear it looked as if I could touch the red sand at the bottom, but it was far below. I stood by it and looked in, as if I were looking in a glass. At the bottom of the well, in the middle of it, the red grains of sand were moving and stirring all the time, and I saw how the water bubbled up, but at the top it was quite smooth, and full and brimming. It was a great well, large like a bath, and with the shining, glittering green moss about it, it looked like a great white jewel, with green jewels all round. My feet were so hot and tired that I took off my boots and stockings, and let my feet down into the water, and the water was soft and cold, and when I got up I wasn't tired any more, and I felt I must go on, farther and farther, and see what was on the other side of the wall. I climbed up it very slowly, going sideways all the time, and when I got to the top and looked over, I was in the queerest country I had seen, stranger even than the hill of the grey rocks. It looked as if earth-children had been playing there with their spades, as it was all hills and hollows, and castles and walls made of earth and covered with grass. There were two mounds like big bee-hives, round and great and solemn, and then hollow basins, and then a steep mounting wall like the ones I saw once by the seaside where the big guns and the soldiers were. I nearly fell into one of the round hollows, it went away from under my feet so suddenly, and I ran fast down the side and stood at the bottom and looked up. It was strange and solemn to look up. There was nothing but the grey, heavy sky and the sides of the hollow; everything else had gone away, and the hollow was the whole world, and I thought that at night it must be full of ghosts and moving shadows and pale things when the moon shone down to the bottom at the dead of the night, and the wind wailed up above. It was so strange and solemn and lonely, like a hollow temple of dead heathen gods. It reminded me of a tale my nurse had told me when I was quite little; it was the same nurse that took me into the wood where I saw the beautiful white people. And I remembered how nurse had told me the story one winter night, when the wind was beating the trees against the wall, and crying and moaning in the nursery chimney. She said there was, somewhere or other, a hollow pit, just like the one I was standing in, everybody was afraid to go into it or near it, it was such a bad place. But once upon a time there was a poor girl who said she would go into the hollow pit, and everybody tried to stop her, but she would go. And she went down into the pit and came back laughing, and said there was nothing there at all, except green grass and red stones, and white stones and yellow flowers. And soon after people saw she had most beautiful emerald earrings, and they asked how she got them, as she and her mother were quite poor. But she laughed, and said her earrings were not made of emeralds at all, but only of green grass. Then, one day, she wore on her breast the reddest ruby that any one had ever seen, and it was as big as a hen's egg, and glowed and sparkled like a hot burning coal of fire. And they asked how she got it, as she and her mother were quite poor. But she laughed, and said it was not a ruby at all, but only a red stone. Then one day she wore round her neck the loveliest necklace that any one had ever seen, much finer than the queen's finest, and it was made of great bright diamonds, hundreds of them, and they shone like all the stars on a night in June. So they asked her how she got it, as she and her mother were quite poor. But she laughed, and said they were not diamonds at all, but only white stones. And one day she went to the court, and she wore on her head a crown of pure angel-gold, so nurse said, and it shone like the sun, and it was much more splendid than the crown the king was wearing himself, and in her ears she wore the emeralds, and the big ruby was the brooch on her breast, and the great diamond necklace was sparkling on her neck. And the king and queen thought she was some great princess from a long way off, and got down from their thrones and went to meet her, but somebody told the king and queen who she was, and that she was quite poor. So the king asked why she wore a gold crown, and how she got it, as she and her mother were so poor. And she laughed, and said it wasn't a gold crown at all, but only some yellow flowers she had put in her hair. And the king thought it was very strange, and said she should stay at the court, and they would see what would happen next. And she was so lovely that everybody said that her eyes were greener than the emeralds, that her lips were redder than the ruby, that her skin was whiter than the diamonds, and that her hair was brighter than the golden crown. So the king's son said he would marry her, and the king said he might. And the bishop married them, and there was a great supper, and afterwards the king's son went to his wife's room. But just when he had his hand on the door, he saw a tall, black man, with a dreadful face, standing in front of the door, and a voice said—

Venture not upon your life,
This is mine own wedded wife.

Then the king's son fell down on the ground in a fit. And they came and tried to get into the room, but they couldn't, and they hacked at the door with hatchets, but the wood had turned hard as iron, and at last everybody ran away, they were so frightened at the screaming and laughing and shrieking and crying that came out of the room. But next day they went in, and found there was nothing in the room but thick black smoke, because the black man had come and taken her away. And on the bed there were two knots of faded grass and a red stone, and some white stones, and some faded yellow flowers. I remembered this tale of nurse's while I was standing at the bottom of the deep hollow; it was so strange and solitary there, and I felt afraid. I could not see any stones or flowers, but I was afraid of bringing them away without knowing, and I thought I would do a charm that came into my head to keep the black man away. So I stood right in the very middle of the hollow, and I made sure that I had none of those things on me, and then I walked round the place, and touched my eyes, and my lips, and my hair in a peculiar manner, and whispered some queer words that nurse taught me to keep bad things away. Then I felt safe and climbed up out of the hollow, and went on through all those mounds and hollows and walls, till I came to the end, which was high above all the rest, and I could see that all the different shapes of the earth were arranged in patterns, something like the grey rocks, only the pattern was different. It was getting late, and the air was indistinct, but it looked from where I was standing something like two great figures of people lying on the grass. And I went on, and at last I found a certain wood, which is too secret to be described, and nobody knows of the passage into it, which I found out in a very curious manner, by seeing some little animal run into the wood through it. So I went in after the animal by a very narrow dark way, under thorns and bushes, and it was almost dark when I came to a kind of open place in the middle. And there I saw the most wonderful sight I have ever seen, but it was only for a minute, as I ran away directly, and crept out of the wood by the passage I had come by, and ran and ran as fast as ever I could, because I was afraid, what I had seen was so wonderful and so strange and beautiful. But I wanted to get home and think of it, and I did not know what might not happen if I stayed by the wood. I was hot all over and trembling, and my heart was beating, and strange cries that I could not help came from me as I ran from the wood. I was glad that a great white moon came up from over a round hill and showed me the way, so I went back through the mounds and hollows and down the close valley, and up through the thicket over the place of the grey rocks, and so at last I got home again. My father was busy in his study, and the servants had not told about my not coming home, though they were frightened, and wondered what they ought to do, so I told them I had lost my way, but I did not let them find out the real way I had been. I went to bed and lay awake all through the night, thinking of what I had seen. When I came out of the narrow way, and it looked all shining, though the air was dark, it seemed so certain, and all the way home I was quite sure that I had seen it, and I wanted to be alone in my room, and be glad over it all to myself, and shut my eyes and pretend it was there, and do all the things I would have done if I had not been so afraid. But when I shut my eyes the sight would not come, and I began to think about my adventures all over again, and I remembered how dusky and queer it was at the end, and I was afraid it must be all a mistake, because it seemed impossible it could happen. It seemed like one of nurse's tales, which I didn't really believe in, though I was frightened at the bottom of the hollow; and the stories she told me when I was little came back into my head, and I wondered whether it was really there what I thought I had seen, or whether any of her tales could have happened a long time ago. It was so queer; I lay awake there in my room at the back of the house, and the moon was shining on the other side towards the river, so the bright light did not fall upon the wall. And the house was quite still. I had heard my father come upstairs, and just after the clock struck twelve, and after the house was still and empty, as if there was nobody alive in it. And though it was all dark and indistinct in my room, a pale glimmering kind of light shone in through the white blind, and once I got up and looked out, and there was a great black shadow of the house covering the garden, looking like a prison where men are hanged; and then beyond it was all white; and the wood shone white with black gulfs between the trees. It was still and clear, and there were no clouds in the sky. I wanted to think of what I had seen but I couldn't, and I began to think of all the tales that nurse had told me so long ago that I thought I had forgotten, but they all came back, and mixed up with the thickets and the grey rocks and the hollows in the earth and the secret wood, till I hardly knew what was new and what was old, or whether it was not all dreaming. And then I remembered that hot summer afternoon, so long ago, when nurse left me by myself in the shade, and the white people came out of the water and out of the wood, and played, and danced, and sang, and I began to fancy that nurse told me about something like it before I saw them, only I couldn't recollect exactly what she told me. Then I wondered whether she had been the white lady, as I remembered she was just as white and beautiful, and had the same dark eyes and black hair; and sometimes she smiled and looked like the lady had looked, when she was telling me some of her stories, beginning with "Once on a time," or "In the time of the fairies." But I thought she couldn't be the lady, as she seemed to have gone a different way into the wood, and I didn't think the man who came after us could be the other, or I couldn't have seen that wonderful secret in the secret wood. I thought of the moon: but it was afterwards when I was in the middle of the wild land, where the earth was made into the shape of great figures, and it was all walls, and mysterious hollows, and smooth round mounds, that I saw the great white moon come up over a round hill. I was wondering about all these things, till at last I got quite frightened, because I was afraid something had happened to me, and I remembered nurse's tale of the poor girl who went into the hollow pit, and was carried away at last by the black man. I knew I had gone into a hollow pit too, and perhaps it was the same, and I had done something dreadful. So I did the charm over again, and touched my eyes and my lips and my hair in a peculiar manner, and said the old words from the fairy language, so that I might be sure I had not been carried away. I tried again to see the secret wood, and to creep up the passage and see what I had seen there, but somehow I couldn't, and I kept on thinking of nurse's stories. There was one I remembered about a young man who once upon a time went hunting, and all the day he and his hounds hunted everywhere, and they crossed the rivers and went into all the woods, and went round the marshes, but they couldn't find anything at all, and they hunted all day till the sun sank down and began to set behind the mountain. And the young man was angry because he couldn't find anything, and he was going to turn back, when just as the sun touched the mountain, he saw come out of a brake in front of him a beautiful white stag. And he cheered to his hounds, but they whined and would not follow, and he cheered to his horse, but it shivered and stood stock still, and the young man jumped off the horse and left the hounds and began to follow the white stag all alone. And soon it was quite dark, and the sky was black, without a single star shining in it, and the stag went away into the darkness. And though the man had brought his gun with him he never shot at the stag, because he wanted to catch it, and he was afraid he would lose it in the night. But he never lost it once, though the sky was so black and the air was so dark, and the stag went on and on till the young man didn't know a bit where he was. And they went through enormous woods where the air was full of whispers and a pale, dead light came out from the rotten trunks that were lying on the ground, and just as the man thought he had lost the stag, he would see it all white and shining in front of him, and he would run fast to catch it, but the stag always ran faster, so he did not catch it. And they went through the enormous woods, and they swam across rivers, and they waded through black marshes where the ground bubbled, and the air was full of will-o'-the-wisps, and the stag fled away down into rocky narrow valleys, where the air was like the smell of a vault, and the man went after it. And they went over the great mountains, and the man heard the wind come down from the sky, and the stag went on and the man went after. At last the sun rose and the young man found he was in a country that he had never seen before; it was a beautiful valley with a bright stream running through it, and a great, big round hill in the middle. And the stag went down the valley, towards the hill, and it seemed to be getting tired and went slower and slower, and though the man was tired, too, he began to run faster, and he was sure he would catch the stag at last. But just as they got to the bottom of the hill, and the man stretched out his hand to catch the stag, it vanished into the earth, and the man began to cry; he was so sorry that he had lost it after all his long hunting. But as he was crying he saw there was a door in the hill, just in front of him, and he went in, and it was quite dark, but he went on, as he thought he would find the white stag. And all of a sudden it got light, and there was the sky, and the sun shining, and birds singing in the trees, and there was a beautiful fountain. And by the fountain a lovely lady was sitting, who was the queen of the fairies, and she told the man that she had changed herself into a stag to bring him there because she loved him so much. Then she brought out a great gold cup, covered with jewels, from her fairy palace, and she offered him wine in the cup to drink. And he drank, and the more he drank the more he longed to drink, because the wine was enchanted. So he kissed the lovely lady, and she became his wife, and he stayed all that day and all that night in the hill where she lived, and when he woke he found he was lying on the ground, close to where he had seen the stag first, and his horse was there and his hounds were there waiting, and he looked up, and the sun sank behind the mountain. And he went home and lived a long time, but he would never kiss any other lady because he had kissed the queen of the fairies, and he would never drink common wine any more, because he had drunk enchanted wine. And sometimes nurse told me tales that she had heard from her great-grandmother, who was very old, and lived in a cottage on the mountain all alone, and most of these tales were about a hill where people used to meet at night long ago, and they used to play all sorts of strange games and do queer things that nurse told me of, but I couldn't understand, and now, she said, everybody but her great-grandmother had forgotten all about it, and nobody knew where the hill was, not even her great-grandmother. But she told me one very strange story about the hill, and I trembled when I remembered it. She said that people always went there in summer, when it was very hot, and they had to dance a good deal. It would be all dark at first, and there were trees there, which made it much darker, and people would come, one by one, from all directions, by a secret path which nobody else knew, and two persons would keep the gate, and every one as they came up had to give a very curious sign, which nurse showed me as well as she could, but she said she couldn't show me properly. And all kinds of people would come; there would be gentle folks and village folks, and some old people and boys and girls, and quite small children, who sat and watched. And it would all be dark as they came in, except in one corner where some one was burning something that smelt strong and sweet, and made them laugh, and there one would see a glaring of coals, and the smoke mounting up red. So they would all come in, and when the last had come there was no door any more, so that no one else could get in, even if they knew there was anything beyond. And once a gentleman who was a stranger and had ridden a long way, lost his path at night, and his horse took him into the very middle of the wild country, where everything was upside down, and there were dreadful marshes and great stones everywhere, and holes underfoot, and the trees looked like gibbet-posts, because they had great black arms that stretched out across the way. And this strange gentleman was very frightened, and his horse began to shiver all over, and at last it stopped and wouldn't go any farther, and the gentleman got down and tried to lead the horse, but it wouldn't move, and it was all covered with a sweat, like death. So the gentleman went on all alone, going farther and farther into the wild country, till at last he came to a dark place, where he heard shouting and singing and crying, like nothing he had ever heard before. It all sounded quite close to him, but he couldn't get in, and so he began to call, and while he was calling, something came behind him, and in a minute his mouth and arms and legs were all bound up, and he fell into a swoon. And when he came to himself, he was lying by the roadside, just where he had first lost his way, under a blasted oak with a black trunk, and his horse was tied beside him. So he rode on to the town and told the people there what had happened, and some of them were amazed; but others knew. So when once everybody had come, there was no door at all for anybody else to pass in by. And when they were all inside, round in a ring, touching each other, some one began to sing in the darkness, and some one else would make a noise like thunder with a thing they had on purpose, and on still nights people would hear the thundering noise far, far away beyond the wild land, and some of them, who thought they knew what it was, used to make a sign on their breasts when they woke up in their beds at dead of night and heard that terrible deep noise, like thunder on the mountains. And the noise and the singing would go on and on for a long time, and the people who were in a ring swayed a little to and fro; and the song was in an old, old language that nobody knows now, and the tune was queer. Nurse said her great-grandmother had known some one who remembered a little of it, when she was quite a little girl, and nurse tried to sing some of it to me, and it was so strange a tune that I turned all cold and my flesh crept as if I had put my hand on something dead. Sometimes it was a man that sang and sometimes it was a woman, and sometimes the one who sang it did it so well that two or three of the people who were there fell to the ground shrieking and tearing with their hands. The singing went on, and the people in the ring kept swaying to and fro for a long time, and at last the moon would rise over a place they called the Tole Deol, and came up and showed them swinging and swaying from side to side, with the sweet thick smoke curling up from the burning coals, and floating in circles all around them. Then they had their supper. A boy and a girl brought it to them; the boy carried a great cup of wine, and the girl carried a cake of bread, and they passed the bread and the wine round and round, but they tasted quite different from common bread and common wine, and changed everybody that tasted them. Then they all rose up and danced, and secret things were brought out of some hiding place, and they played extraordinary games, and danced round and round and round in the moonlight, and sometimes people would suddenly disappear and never be heard of afterwards, and nobody knew what had happened to them. And they drank more of that curious wine, and they made images and worshipped them, and nurse showed me how the images were made one day when we were out for a walk, and we passed by a place where there was a lot of wet clay. So nurse asked me if I would like to know what those things were like that they made on the hill, and I said yes. Then she asked me if I would promise never to tell a living soul a word about it, and if I did I was to be thrown into the black pit with the dead people, and I said I wouldn't tell anybody, and she said the same thing again and again, and I promised. So she took my wooden spade and dug a big lump of clay and put it in my tin bucket, and told me to say if any one met us that I was going to make pies when I went home. Then we went on a little way till we came to a little brake growing right down into the road, and nurse stopped, and looked up the road and down it, and then peeped through the hedge into the field on the other side, and then she said "Quick!" and we ran into the brake, and crept in and out among the bushes till we had gone a good way from the road. Then we sat down under a bush, and I wanted so much to know what nurse was going to make with the clay, but before she would begin she made me promise again not to say a word about it, and she went again and peeped through the bushes on every side, though the lane was so small and deep that hardly anybody ever went there. So we sat down, and nurse took the clay out of the bucket, and began to knead it with her hands, and do queer things with it, and turn it about. And she hid it under a big dock-leaf for a minute or two and then she brought it out again, and then she stood up and sat down, and walked round the clay in a peculiar manner, and all the time she was softly singing a sort of rhyme, and her face got very red. Then she sat down again, and took the clay in her hands and began to shape it into a doll, but not like the dolls I have at home, and she made the queerest doll I had ever seen, all out of the wet clay, and hid it under a bush to get dry and hard, and all the time she was making it she was singing these rhymes to herself, and her face got redder and redder. So we left the doll there, hidden away in the bushes where nobody would ever find it. And a few days later we went the same walk, and when we came to that narrow, dark part of the lane where the brake runs down to the bank, nurse made me promise all over again, and she looked about, just as she had done before, and we crept into the bushes till we got to the green place where the little clay man was hidden. I remember it all so well, though I was only eight, and it is eight years ago now as I am writing it down, but the sky was a deep violet blue, and in the middle of the brake where we were sitting there was a great elder tree covered with blossoms, and on the other side there was a clump of meadowsweet, and when I think of that day the smell of the meadowsweet and elder blossom seems to fill the room, and if I shut my eyes I can see the glaring sky, with little clouds very white floating across it, and nurse who went away long ago sitting opposite me and looking like the beautiful white lady in the wood. So we sat down and nurse took out the clay doll from the secret place where she had hidden it, and she said we must "pay our respects," and she would show me what to do, and I must watch her all the time. So she did all sorts of queer things with the little clay man, and I noticed she was all streaming with perspiration, though we had walked so slowly, and then she told me to "pay my respects," and I did everything she did because I liked her, and it was such an odd game. And she said that if one loved very much, the clay man was very good, if one did certain things with it, and if one hated very much, it was just as good, only one had to do different things, and we played with it a long time, and pretended all sorts of things. Nurse said her great-grandmother had told her all about these images, but what we did was no harm at all, only a game. But she told me a story about these images that frightened me very much, and that was what I remembered that night when I was lying awake in my room in the pale, empty darkness, thinking of what I had seen and the secret wood. Nurse said there was once a young lady of the high gentry, who lived in a great castle. And she was so beautiful that all the gentlemen wanted to marry her, because she was the loveliest lady that anybody had ever seen, and she was kind to everybody, and everybody thought she was very good. But though she was polite to all the gentlemen who wished to marry her, she put them off, and said she couldn't make up her mind, and she wasn't sure she wanted to marry anybody at all. And her father, who was a very great lord, was angry, though he was so fond of her, and he asked her why she wouldn't choose a bachelor out of all the handsome young men who came to the castle. But she only said she didn't love any of them very much, and she must wait, and if they pestered her, she said she would go and be a nun in a nunnery. So all the gentlemen said they would go away and wait for a year and a day, and when a year and a day were gone, they would come back again and ask her to say which one she would marry. So the day was appointed and they all went away; and the lady had promised that in a year and a day it would be her wedding day with one of them. But the truth was, that she was the queen of the people who danced on the hill on summer nights, and on the proper nights she would lock the door of her room, and she and her maid would steal out of the castle by a secret passage that only they knew of, and go away up to the hill in the wild land. And she knew more of the secret things than any one else, and more than any one knew before or after, because she would not tell anybody the most secret secrets. She knew how to do all the awful things, how to destroy young men, and how to put a curse on people, and other things that I could not understand. And her real name was the Lady Avelin, but the dancing people called her Cassap, which meant somebody very wise, in the old language. And she was whiter than any of them and taller, and her eyes shone in the dark like burning rubies; and she could sing songs that none of the others could sing, and when she sang they all fell down on their faces and worshipped her. And she could do what they called the shib-show, which was a very wonderful enchantment. She would tell the great lord, her father, that she wanted to go into the woods to gather flowers, so he let her go, and she and her maid went into the woods where nobody came, and the maid would keep watch. Then the lady would lie down under the trees and begin to sing a particular song, and she stretched out her arms, and from every part of the wood great serpents would come, hissing and gliding in and out among the trees, and shooting out their forked tongues as they crawled up to the lady. And they all came to her, and twisted round her, round her body, and her arms, and her neck, till she was covered with writhing serpents, and there was only her head to be seen. And she whispered to them, and she sang to them, and they writhed round and round, faster and faster, till she told them to go. And they all went away directly, back to their holes, and on the lady's breast there would be a most curious, beautiful stone, shaped something like an egg, and coloured dark blue and yellow, and red, and green, marked like a serpent's scales. It was called a glame stone, and with it one could do all sorts of wonderful things, and nurse said her great-grandmother had seen a glame stone with her own eyes, and it was for all the world shiny and scaly like a snake. And the lady could do a lot of other things as well, but she was quite fixed that she would not be married. And there were a great many gentlemen who wanted to marry her, but there were five of them who were chief, and their names were Sir Simon, Sir John, Sir Oliver, Sir Richard, and Sir Rowland. All the others believed she spoke the truth, and that she would choose one of them to be her man when a year and a day was done; it was only Sir Simon, who was very crafty, who thought she was deceiving them all, and he vowed he would watch and try if he could find out anything. And though he was very wise he was very young, and he had a smooth, soft face like a girl's, and he pretended, as the rest did, that he would not come to the castle for a year and a day, and he said he was going away beyond the sea to foreign parts. But he really only went a very little way, and came back dressed like a servant girl, and so he got a place in the castle to wash the dishes. And he waited and watched, and he listened and said nothing, and he hid in dark places, and woke up at night and looked out, and he heard things and he saw things that he thought were very strange. And he was so sly that he told the girl that waited on the lady that he was really a young man, and that he had dressed up as a girl because he loved her so very much and wanted to be in the same house with her, and the girl was so pleased that she told him many things, and he was more than ever certain that the Lady Avelin was deceiving him and the others. And he was so clever, and told the servant so many lies, that one night he managed to hide in the Lady's Avelin's room behind the curtains. And he stayed quite still and never moved, and at last the lady came. And she bent down under the bed, and raised up a stone, and there was a hollow place underneath, and out of it she took a waxen image, just like the clay one that I and nurse had made in the brake. And all the time her eyes were burning like rubies. And she took the little wax doll up in her arms and held it to her breast, and she whispered and she murmured, and she took it up and she laid it down again, and she held it high, and she held it low, and she laid it down again. And she said, "Happy is he that begat the bishop, that ordered the clerk, that married the man, that had the wife, that fashioned the hive, that harboured the bee, that gathered the wax that my own true love was made of." And she brought out of an aumbry a great golden bowl, and she brought out of a closet a great jar of wine, and she poured some of the wine into the bowl, and she laid her mannikin very gently in the wine, and washed it in the wine all over. Then she went to a cupboard and took a small round cake and laid it on the image's mouth, and then she bore it softly and covered it up. And Sir Simon, who was watching all the time, though he was terribly frightened, saw the lady bend down and stretch out her arms and whisper and sing, and then Sir Simon saw beside her a handsome young man, who kissed her on the lips. And they drank wine out of the golden bowl together, and they ate the cake together. But when the sun rose there was only the little wax doll, and the lady hid it again under the bed in the hollow place. So Sir Simon knew quite well what the lady was, and he waited and he watched, till the time she had said was nearly over, and in a week the year and a day would be done. And one night, when he was watching behind the curtains in her room, he saw her making more wax dolls. And she made five, and hid them away. And the next night she took one out, and held it up, and filled the golden bowl with water, and took the doll by the neck and held it under the water. Then she said—

Sir Dickon, Sir Dickon, your day is done,
You shall be drowned in the water wan.

And the next day news came to the castle that Sir Richard had been drowned at the ford. And at night she took another doll and tied a violet cord round its neck and hung it up on a nail. Then she said—

Sir Rowland, your life has ended its span,
High on a tree I see you hang.

And the next day news came to the castle that Sir Rowland had been hanged by robbers in the wood. And at night she took another doll, and drove her bodkin right into its heart. Then she said—

> Sir Noll, Sir Noll, so cease your life,
> Your heart piercèd with the knife.

And the next day news came to the castle that Sir Oliver had fought in a tavern, and a stranger had stabbed him to the heart. And at night she took another doll, and held it to a fire of charcoal till it was melted. Then she said—

> Sir John, return, and turn to clay,
> In fire of fever you waste away.

And the next day news came to the castle that Sir John had died in a burning fever. So then Sir Simon went out of the castle and mounted his horse and rode away to the bishop and told him everything. And the bishop sent his men, and they took the Lady Avelin, and everything she had done was found out. So on the day after the year and a day, when she was to have been married, they carried her through the town in her smock, and they tied her to a great stake in the market-place, and burned her alive before the bishop with her wax image hung round her neck. And people said the wax man screamed in the burning of the flames. And I thought of this story again and again as I was lying awake in my bed, and I seemed to see the Lady Avelin in the market-place, with the yellow flames eating up her beautiful white body. And I thought of it so much that I seemed to get into the story myself, and I fancied I was the lady, and that they were coming to take me to be burnt with fire, with all the people in the town looking at me. And I wondered whether she cared, after all the strange things she had done, and whether it hurt very much to be burned at the stake. I tried again and again to forget nurse's stories, and to remember the secret I had seen that afternoon, and what was in the secret wood, but I could only see the dark and a glimmering in the dark, and then it went away, and I only saw myself running, and then a great moon came up white over a dark round hill. Then all the old stories came back again, and the queer rhymes that nurse used to sing to me; and there was one beginning "Halsy cumsy Helen musty," that she used to sing very softly when she wanted me to go to sleep. And I began to sing it to myself inside of my head, and I went to sleep.

The next morning I was very tired and sleepy, and could hardly do my lessons, and I was very glad when they were over and I had had my dinner, as I wanted to go out and be alone. It was a warm day, and I went to a nice turfy hill by the river, and sat down on my mother's old shawl that I had brought with me on purpose. The sky was grey, like the day before, but there was a kind of white gleam behind it, and from where I was sitting I could look down on the town, and it was all still and quiet and white, like a picture. I remembered that it was on that hill that nurse taught me to play an old game called "Troy Town," in which one had to dance, and wind in and out on a pattern in the grass, and then when one had danced and turned long enough the other person asks you questions, and you can't help answering whether you want to or not, and whatever you are told to do you feel you have to do it. Nurse said there used to be a lot of games like that that some people knew of, and there was one by which people could be turned into anything you liked, and an old man her great-grandmother had seen had known a girl who had been turned into a large snake. And there was another very ancient game of dancing and winding and turning, by which you could take a person out of himself and hide him away as long as you liked, and his body went walking about quite empty, without any sense in it. But I came to that hill because I wanted to think of what had happened the day before, and of the secret of the wood. From the place where I was sitting I could see beyond the town, into the opening I had found, where a little brook had led me into an unknown country. And I pretended I was following the brook over again, and I went all the way in my mind, and at last I found the wood, and crept into it under the bushes, and then in the dusk I saw something that made me feel as if I were filled with fire, as if I wanted to dance and sing and fly up into the air, because I was changed and wonderful. But what I saw was not changed at all, and had not grown old, and I wondered again and again how such things could happen, and whether nurse's stories were really true, because in the daytime in the open air everything seemed quite different from what it was at night, when I was frightened, and thought I was to be burned alive. I once told my father one of her little tales, which was about a ghost, and asked him if it was true, and he told me it was not true at all, and that only common, ignorant people believed in such rubbish. He was very angry with nurse for telling me the story, and scolded her, and after that I promised her I would never whisper a word of what she told me, and if I did I should be bitten by the great black snake that lived in the pool in the wood. And all alone on the hill I wondered what was true. I had seen something very amazing and very lovely, and I knew a story, and if I had really seen it, and not made it up out of the dark, and the black bough, and the bright shining that was mounting up to the sky from over the great round hill, but had really seen it in truth, then there were all kinds of wonderful and lovely and terrible things to think of, so I longed and trembled, and I burned and got cold. And I looked down on the town, so quiet and still, like a little white picture, and I thought over and over if it could be true. I was a long time before I could make up my mind to anything; there was such a strange fluttering at my heart that seemed to whisper to me all the time that I had not made it up out of my head, and yet it seemed quite impossible, and I knew my father and everybody would say it was dreadful rubbish. I never dreamed of telling him or anybody else a word about it, because I knew it would be of no use, and I should only get laughed at or scolded, so for a long time I was very quiet, and went about thinking and wondering; and at night I used to dream of amazing things, and sometimes I woke up in the early morning and held out my arms with a cry. And I was frightened, too, because there were dangers, and some awful thing would happen to me, unless I took great care, if the story were true. These old tales were always in my head, night and morning, and I went over them and told them to myself over and over again, and went for walks in the places where nurse had told them to me; and when I sat in the nursery by the fire in the evenings I used to fancy nurse was sitting in the other chair, and telling me some wonderful story in a low voice, for fear anybody should be listening. But she used to like best to tell me about things when we were right out in the country, far from the house, because she said she was telling me such secrets, and walls have ears. And if it was something more than ever secret, we had to hide in brakes or woods; and I used to think it was such fun creeping along a hedge, and going very softly, and then we would get behind the bushes or run into the wood all of a sudden, when we were sure that none was watching us; so we knew that we had our secrets quite all to ourselves, and nobody else at all knew anything about them. Now and then, when we had hidden ourselves as I have described, she used to show me all sorts of odd things. One day, I remember, we were in a hazel brake, overlooking the brook, and we were so snug and warm, as though it was April; the sun was quite hot, and the leaves were just coming out. Nurse said she would show me something funny that would make me laugh, and then she showed me, as she said, how one could turn a whole house upside down, without anybody being able to find out, and the pots and pans would jump about, and the china would be broken, and the chairs would tumble over of themselves. I tried it one day in the kitchen, and I found I could do it quite well, and a whole row of plates on the dresser fell off it, and cook's little work-table tilted up and turned right over "before her eyes," as she said, but she was so frightened and turned so white that I didn't do it again, as I liked her. And afterwards, in the hazel copse, when she had shown me how to make things tumble about, she showed me how to make rapping noises, and I learnt how to do that, too. Then she taught me rhymes to say on certain occasions, and peculiar marks to make on other occasions, and other things that her great-grandmother had taught her when she was a little girl herself. And these were all the things I was thinking about in those days after the strange walk when I thought I had seen a great secret, and I wished nurse were there for me to ask her about it, but she had gone away more than two years before, and nobody seemed to know what had become of her, or where she had gone. But I shall always remember those days if I live to be quite old, because all the time I felt so strange, wondering and doubting, and feeling quite sure at one time, and making up my mind, and then I would feel quite sure that such things couldn't happen really, and it began all over again. But I took great care not to do certain things that might be very dangerous. So I waited and wondered for a long time, and though I was not sure at all, I never dared to try to find out. But one day I became sure that all that nurse said was quite true, and I was all alone when I found it out. I trembled all over with joy and terror, and as fast as I could I ran into one of the old brakes where we used to go—it was the one by the lane, where nurse made the little clay man—and I ran into it, and I crept into it; and when I came to the place where the elder was, I covered up my face with my hands and lay down flat on the grass, and I stayed there for two hours without moving, whispering to myself delicious, terrible things, and saying some words over and over again. It was all true and wonderful and splendid, and when I remembered the story I knew and thought of what I had really seen, I got hot and I got cold, and the air seemed full of scent, and flowers, and singing. And first I wanted to make a little clay man, like the one nurse had made so long ago, and I had to invent plans and stratagems, and to look about, and to think of things beforehand, because nobody must dream on anything that I was doing or going to do, and I was too old to carry clay about in a tin bucket. At last I thought of a plan, and I brought the wet clay to the brake, and did everything that nurse had done, only I made a much finer image than the one she had made; and when it was finished I did everything that I could imagine and much more than she did, because it was the likeness of something far better. And a few days later, when I had done my lessons early, I went for the second time by the way of the little brook that had led me into a strange country. And I followed the brook, and went through the bushes, and beneath the low branches of trees, and up thorny thickets on the hill, and by dark woods full of creeping thorns, a long, long way. Then I crept through the dark tunnel where the brook had been and the ground was stony, till at last I came to the thicket that climbed up the hill, and though the leaves were coming out upon the trees, everything looked almost as black as it was on the first day that I went there. And the thicket was just the same, and I went up slowly till I came out on the big bare hill, and began to walk among the wonderful rocks. I saw the terrible voor again on everything, for though the sky was brighter, the ring of wild hills all around was still dark, and the hanging woods looked dark and dreadful, and the strange rocks were as grey as ever; and when I looked down on them from the great mound, sitting on the stone, I saw all their amazing circles and rounds within rounds, and I had to sit quite still and watch them as they began to turn about me, and each stone danced in its place, and they seemed to go round and round in a great whirl, as if one were in the middle of all the stars and heard them rushing through the air. So

I went down among the rocks to dance with them and to sing extraordinary songs; and I went down through the other thicket, and drank from the bright stream in the close and secret valley, putting my lips down to the bubbling water; and then I went on till I came to the deep, brimming well among the glittering moss, and I sat down. I looked before me into the secret darkness of the valley, and behind me was the great high wall of grass, and all around me there were the hanging woods that made the valley such a secret place. I knew there was nobody here at all besides myself, and that no one could see me. So I took off my boots and stockings, and let my feet down into the water, saying the words that I knew. And it was not cold at all, as I expected, but warm and very pleasant, and when my feet were in it I felt as if they were in silk, or as if the nymph were kissing them. So when I had done, I said the other words and made the signs, and then I dried my feet with a towel I had brought on purpose, and put on my stockings and boots. Then I climbed up the steep wall, and went into the place where there are the hollows, and the two beautiful mounds, and the round ridges of land, and all the strange shapes. I did not go down into the hollow this time, but I turned at the end, and made out the figures quite plainly, as it was lighter, and I had remembered the story I had quite forgotten before, and in the story the two figures are called Adam and Eve, and only those who know the story understand what they mean. So I went on and on till I came to the secret wood which must not be described, and I crept into it by the way I had found. And when I had gone about halfway I stopped, and turned round, and got ready, and I bound the handkerchief tightly round my eyes, and made quite sure that I could not see at all, not a twig, nor the end of a leaf, nor the light of the sky, as it was an old red silk handkerchief with large yellow spots, that went round twice and covered my eyes, so that I could see nothing. Then I began to go on, step by step, very slowly. My heart beat faster and faster, and something rose in my throat that choked me and made me want to cry out, but I shut my lips, and went on. Boughs caught in my hair as I went, and great thorns tore me; but I went on to the end of the path. Then I stopped, and held out my arms and bowed, and I went round the first time, feeling with my hands, and there was nothing. I went round the second time, feeling with my hands and there was nothing. Then I went round the third time, feeling with my hands, and the story was all true, and I wished that the years were gone by, and that I had not so long a time to wait before I was happy for ever and ever.

Nurse must have been a prophet like those we read of in the Bible. Everything that she said began to come true, and since then other things that she told me of have happened. That was how I came to know that her stories were true and that I had not made up the secret myself out of my own head. But there was another thing that happened that day. I went a second time to the secret place. It was at the deep brimming well, and when I was standing on the moss I bent over and looked in, and then I knew who the white lady was that I had seen come out of the water in the wood long ago when I was quite little. And I trembled all over, because that told me other things. Then I remembered how sometime after I had seen the white people in the wood, nurse asked me more about them, and I told her all over again, and she listened, and said nothing for a long, long time, and at last she said, "You will see her again." So I understood what had happened and what was to happen. And I understood about the nymphs; how I might meet them in all kinds of places, and they would always help me, and I must always look for them, and find them in all sorts of strange shapes and appearances. And without the nymphs I could never have found the secret, and without them none of the other things could happen. Nurse had told me all about them long ago, but she called them by another name, and I did not know what she meant, or what her tales of them were about, only that they were very queer. And there were two kinds, the bright and the dark, and both were very lovely and very wonderful, and some people saw only one kind, and some only the other, but some saw them both. But usually the dark appeared first, and the bright ones came afterwards, and there were extraordinary tales about them. It was a day or two after I had come home from the secret place that I first really knew the nymphs. Nurse had shown me how to call them, and I had tried, but I did not know what she meant, and so I thought it was all nonsense. But I made up my mind I would try again, so I went to the wood where the pool was, where I saw the white people, and I tried again. The dark nymph, Alanna, came, and she turned the pool of water into a pool of fire. . . .

EPILOGUE

"That's a very queer story," said Cotgrave, handing back the green book to the recluse, Ambrose. "I see the drift of a good deal, but there are many things that I do not grasp at all. On the last page, for example, what does she mean by 'nymphs'?"

"Well, I think there are references throughout the manuscript to certain 'processes' which have been handed down by tradition from age to age. Some of these processes are just beginning to come within the purview of science, which has arrived at them—or rather at the steps which lead to them—by quite different paths. I have interpreted the reference to 'nymphs' as a reference to one of these processes."

"And you believe that there are such things?"

"Oh, I think so. Yes, I believe I could give you convincing evidence on that point. I am afraid you have neglected the study of alchemy. It is a pity, for the symbolism, at all events, is very beautiful, and moreover if you were acquainted with certain books on the subject, I could recall to your mind phrases which might explain a good deal in the manuscript that you have been reading."

"Yes; but I want to know whether you seriously think that there is any foundation of fact beneath these fancies. Is it not all a department of poetry; a curious dream which man has indulged himself?"

"I can only say that it is no doubt better for the great mass of people to dismiss it all as a dream. But if you ask my veritable belief—that goes quite the other way. No; I should not say belief, but rather knowledge. I may tell you that I have known cases in which men have stumbled quite by accident on certain of these 'processes,' and have been astonished by wholly unexpected results. In the cases I am thinking of there could have been no possibility of 'suggestion' or sub-conscious action of any kind. One might as well suppose a schoolboy 'suggesting' the existence of Æschylus to himself, while he plods mechanically through the declensions.

"But you have noticed the obscurity," Ambrose went on, "and in this particular case it must have been dictated by instinct, since the writer never thought that her manuscripts would fall into other hands. But the practice is universal, and for most excellent reasons. Powerful and sovereign medicines, which are, of necessity, virulent poisons also, are kept in a locked cabinet. The child may find the key by chance, and drink herself dead; but in most cases the search is educational, and the phials contain precious elixirs for him who has patiently fashioned the key for himself."

"You do not care to go into details?"

"No, frankly, I do not. No, you must remain unconvinced. But you saw how the manuscript illustrates the talk we had last week?"

"Is this girl still alive?"

"No. I was one of those who found her. I knew the father well; he was a lawyer, and had always left her very much to herself. He thought of nothing but deeds and leases, and the news came to him as an awful surprise. She was missing one morning; I suppose it was about a year after she had written what you have read. The servants were called, and they told things, and put the only natural interpretation on them—a perfectly erroneous one.

"They discovered that green book somewhere in her room, and I found her in the place that she described with so much dread, lying on the ground before the image."

"It was an image?"

"Yes; it was hidden by the thorns and the thick undergrowth that had surrounded it. It was a wild, lonely country; but you know what it was like by her description, though of course you will understand that the colours have been heightened. A child's imagination always makes the heights higher and the depths deeper than they really are; and she had, unfortunately for herself, something more than imagination. One might say, perhaps, that the picture in her mind which she succeeded in a measure in putting into words, was the scene as it would have appeared to an imaginative artist. But it is a strange, desolate land."

"And she was dead?"

"Yes. She had poisoned herself—in time. No; there was not a word to be said against her in the ordinary sense. You may recollect a story I told you the other night about a lady who saw her child's fingers crushed by a window?"

"And what was this statue?"

"Well, it was of Roman workmanship, of a stone that with the centuries had not blackened, but had become white and luminous. The thicket had grown up about it and concealed it, and in the Middle Ages the followers of a very old tradition had known how to use it for their own purposes. In fact it had been incorporated into the monstrous mythology of the Sabbath. You will have noted that those to whom a sight of that shining whiteness had been vouchsafed by chance, or rather, perhaps, by apparent chance, were required to blindfold themselves on their second approach. That is very significant."

"And is it there still?"

"I sent for tools, and we hammered it into dust and fragments."

"The persistence of tradition never surprises me," Ambrose went on after a pause. "I could name many an English parish where such traditions as that girl had listened to in her childhood are still existent in occult but unabated vigour. No, for me, it is the 'story' not the 'sequel,' which is strange and awful, for I have always believed that wonder is of the soul."

ALGERNON BLACKWOOD

THE WILLOWS

AFTER leaving Vienna, and long before you come to Buda-Pesth, the Danube enters a region of singular loneliness and desolation, where its waters spread away on all sides regardless of a main channel, and the country becomes a swamp for miles upon miles, covered by a vast sea of low willow-bushes. On the big maps this deserted area is painted in a fluffy blue, growing fainter in colour as it leaves the banks, and across it may be seen in large straggling letters the word *Sümpfe,* meaning marshes.

In high flood this great acreage of sand, shingle-beds, and willow-grown islands is almost topped by the water, but in normal seasons the bushes bend and rustle in the free winds, showing their silver leaves to the sunshine in an ever-moving plain of bewildering beauty. These willows never attain to the dignity of trees; they have no rigid trunks; they remain humble bushes, with rounded tops and soft outline, swaying on slender stems that answer to the least pressure of the wind; supple as grasses, and so continually shifting that they somehow give the impression that the entire plain is moving and *alive.* For the wind sends waves rising and falling over the whole surface, waves of leaves instead of waves of water, green swells like the sea, too, until the branches turn and lift, and then silvery white as their under-side turns to the sun.

Happy to slip beyond the control of the stern banks, the Danube here wanders about at will among the intricate network of channels intersecting the islands everywhere with broad avenues down which the waters pour with a shouting sound; making whirlpools, eddies, and foaming rapids; tearing at the sandy banks; carrying away masses of shore and willow-clumps; and forming new islands innumerable which shift daily in size and shape and possess at best an impermanent life, since the flood-time obliterates their very existence.

Properly speaking, this fascinating part of the river's life begins soon after leaving Pressburg, and we, in our Canadian canoe, with gipsy tent and frying-pan on board, reached it on the crest of a rising flood about mid-July. That very same morning, when the sky was reddening before sunrise, we had slipped swiftly through still-sleeping Vienna, leaving it a couple of hours later a mere patch of smoke against the blue hills of the Wienerwald on the horizon; we had breakfasted below Fischeramend under a grove of birch trees roaring in the wind; and had then swept on the tearing current past Orth, Hainburg, Petronell (the old Roman Carnuntum of Marcus Aurelius), and so under the frowning heights of Theben on a spur of the Carpathians, where the March steals in quietly from the left and the frontier is crossed between Austria and Hungary.

Racing along at twelve kilometres an hour soon took us well into Hungary, and the muddy waters—sure sign of flood—sent us aground on many a shingle-bed, and twisted us like a cork in many a sudden belching whirlpool before the towers of Pressburg (Hungarian, Poszóny) showed against the sky; and then the canoe, leaping like a spirited horse, flew at top speed under the grey walls, negotiated safely the sunken chain of the Fliegende Brücke ferry, turned the corner sharply to the left, and plunged on yellow foam into the wilderness of islands, sand-banks, and swamp-land beyond—the land of the willows.

The change came suddenly, as when a series of bioscope pictures snaps down on the streets of a town and shifts without warning into the scenery of lake and forest. We entered the land of desolation on wings, and in less than half an hour there was neither boat nor fishing-hut nor red roof, nor any single sign of human habitation and civilisation within sight. The sense of remoteness from the world of human kind, the utter isolation, the fascination of this singular world of willows, winds, and waters, instantly laid its spell upon us both, so that we allowed laughingly to one another that we ought by rights to have held some special kind of passport to admit us, and that we had, somewhat audaciously, come without asking leave into a separate little kingdom of wonder and magic—a kingdom that was reserved for the use of others who had a right to it, with everywhere unwritten warnings to trespassers for those who had the imagination to discover them.

Though still early in the afternoon, the ceaseless buffetings of a most tempestuous wind made us feel weary, and we at once began casting about for a suitable camping-ground for the night. But the bewildering character of the islands made landing difficult; the swirling flood carried us in-shore and then swept us out again; the willow branches tore our hands as we seized them to stop the canoe, and we pulled many a yard of sandy bank into the water before at length we shot with a great sideways blow from the wind into a backwater and managed to beach the bows in a cloud of spray. Then we lay panting and laughing after our exertions on hot yellow sand, sheltered from the wind, and in the full blaze of a scorching sun, a cloudless blue sky above, and an immense army of dancing, shouting willow bushes, closing in from all sides, shining with spray and clapping their thousand little hands as though to applaud the success of our efforts.

"What a river!" I said to my companion, thinking of all the way we had travelled from the source in the Black Forest, and how he had often been obliged to wade and push in the upper shallows at the beginning of June.

"Won't stand much nonsense now, will it?" he said, pulling the canoe a little farther into safety up the sand, and then composing himself for a nap.

I lay by his side, happy and peaceful in the bath of the elements—water, wind, sand, and the great fire of the sun—thinking of the long journey that lay behind us, and of the great stretch before us to the Black Sea, and how lucky I was to have such a delightful and charming travelling companion as my friend, the Swede.

We had made many similar journeys together, but the Danube, more than any other river I knew, impressed us from the very beginning with its *aliveness*. From its tiny bubbling entry into the world among the pinewood gardens of Donaueschingen, until this moment when it began to play the great river-game of losing itself among the deserted swamps, unobserved, unrestrained, it had seemed to us like following the growth of some living creature. Sleepy at first, but later developing violent desires as it became conscious of its deep soul, it rolled, like some huge fluid being, through all the countries we had passed, holding our little craft on its mighty shoulders, playing roughly with us sometimes, yet always friendly and well-meaning, till at length we had come inevitably to regard it as a Great Personage.

How, indeed, could it be otherwise, since it told us so much of its secret life? At night we heard it singing to the moon as we lay in our tent, uttering that odd sibilant note peculiar to itself and said to be caused by the rapid tearing of the pebbles along its bed, so great is its hurrying speed. We knew, too, the voice of its gurgling whirlpools, suddenly bubbling up on a surface previously quite calm; the roar of its shallows and swift rapids; its constant steady thundering below all mere surface sounds; and that ceaseless tearing of its icy waters at the banks. How it stood up and shouted when the rains fell flat upon its face! And how its laughter roared out when the wind blew upstream and tried to stop its growing speed! We knew all its sounds and voices, its tumblings and foamings, its unnecessary splashing against the bridges; that self-conscious chatter when there were hills to look on;

the affected dignity of its speech when it passed through the little towns, far too important to laugh; and all these faint, sweet whisperings when the sun caught it fairly in some slow curve and poured down upon it till the steam rose.

It was full of tricks, too, in its early life before the great world knew it. There were places in the upper reaches among the Swabian forests, when yet the first whispers of its destiny had not reached it, where it elected to disappear through holes in the ground, to appear again on the other side of the porous limestone hills and start a new river with another name; leaving, too, so little water in its own bed that we had to climb out and wade and push the canoe through miles of shallows.

And a chief pleasure, in those early days of its irresponsible youth, was to lie low, like Brer Fox, just before the little turbulent tributaries came to join it from the Alps, and to refuse to acknowledge them when in, but to run for miles side by side, the dividing line well marked, the very levels different, the Danube utterly declining to recognise the newcomer. Below Passau, however, it gave up this particular trick, for there the Inn comes in with a thundering power impossible to ignore, and so pushes and incommodes the parent river that there is hardly room for them in the long twisting gorge that follows, and the Danube is shoved this way and that against the cliffs, and forced to hurry itself with great waves and much dashing to and fro in order to get through in time. And during the fight our canoe slipped down from its shoulder to its breast, and had the time of its life among the struggling waves. But the Inn taught the old river a lesson, and after Passau it no longer pretended to ignore new arrivals.

This was many days back, of course, and since then we had come to know other aspects of the great creature, and across the Bavarian wheat plain of Straubing she wandered so slowly under the blazing June sun that we could well imagine only the surface inches were water, while below there moved, concealed as by a silken mantle, a whole army of Undines, passing silently and unseen down to the sea, and very leisurely too, lest they be discovered.

Much, too, we forgave her because of her friendliness to the birds and animals that haunted the shores. Cormorants lined the banks in lonely places in rows like short black palings; grey crows crowded the shingle-beds; storks stood fishing in the vistas of shallower water that opened up between the islands, and hawks, swans, and marsh birds of all sorts filled the air with glinting wings and singing, petulant cries. It was impossible to feel annoyed with the river's vagaries after seeing a deer leap with a splash into the water at sunrise and swim past the bows of the canoe; and often we saw fawns peering at us from the underbrush, or looked straight into the brown eyes of a stag as we charged full tilt round a corner and entered another reach of the river. Foxes, too, everywhere haunted the banks, tripping daintily among the driftwood and disappearing so suddenly that it was impossible to see how they managed it.

But now, after leaving Pressburg, everything changed a little, and the Danube became more serious. It ceased trifling. It was half-way to the Black Sea, within scenting distance almost of other, stranger countries where no tricks would be permitted or understood. It became suddenly grown-up, and claimed our respect and even our awe. It broke out into three arms, for one thing, that only met again a hundred kilometres farther down, and for a canoe there were no indications which one was intended to be followed.

"If you take a side channel," said the Hungarian officer we met in the Pressburg shop while buying provisions, "you may find yourselves, when the flood subsides, forty miles from anywhere, high and dry, and you may easily starve. There are no people, no farms, no fishermen. I warn you not to continue. The river, too, is still rising, and this wind will increase."

The rising river did not alarm us in the least, but the matter of being left high and dry by a sudden subsidence of the waters might be serious, and we had consequently laid in an extra stock of provisions. For the rest, the officer's prophecy held true, and the wind, blowing down a perfectly clear sky, increased steadily till it reached the dignity of a westerly gale.

It was earlier than usual when we camped, for the sun was a good hour or two from the horizon, and leaving my friend still asleep on the hot sand, I wandered about in desultory examination of our hotel. The island, I found, was less than an acre in extent, a mere sandy bank standing some two or three feet above the level of the river. The far end, pointing into the sunset, was covered with flying spray which the tremendous wind drove off the crests of the broken waves. It was triangular in shape, with the apex up-stream.

I stood there for several minutes, watching the impetuous crimson flood bearing down with a shouting roar, dashing in waves against the bank as though to sweep it bodily away, and then swirling by in two foaming streams on either side. The ground seemed to shake with the shock and rush, while the furious movement of the willow bushes as the wind poured over them increased the curious illusion that the island itself actually moved. Above, for a mile or two, I could see the great river descending upon me: it was like looking up the slope of a sliding hill, white with foam, and leaping up everywhere to show itself to the sun.

The rest of the island was too thickly grown with willows to make walking pleasant, but I made the tour, nevertheless. From the lower end the light, of course, changed, and the river looked dark and angry. Only the backs of the flying waves were visible, streaked with foam, and pushed forcibly by the great puffs of wind that fell upon them from behind. For a short mile it was visible, pouring in and out among the islands, and then disappearing with a huge sweep into the willows, which closed about it like a herd of monstrous antediluvian creatures crowding down to drink. They made me think of gigantic sponge-like growths that sucked the river up into themselves. They caused it to vanish from sight. They herded there together in such overpowering numbers.

Altogether it was an impressive scene, with its utter loneliness, its bizarre suggestion; and as I gazed, long and curiously, a singular emotion began to stir somewhere in the depths of me. Midway in my delight of the wild beauty, there crept, unbidden and unexplained, a curious feeling of disquietude, almost of alarm.

A rising river, perhaps, always suggests something of the ominous: many of the little islands I saw before me would probably have been swept away by the morning; this resistless, thundering flood of water touched the sense of awe. Yet I was aware that my uneasiness lay deeper far than the emotions of awe and wonder. It was not that I felt. Nor had it directly to do with the power of the driving wind—this shouting hurricane that might almost carry up a few acres of willows into the air and scatter them like so much chaff over the landscape. The wind was simply enjoying itself, for nothing rose out of the flat landscape to stop it, and I was conscious of sharing its great game with a kind of pleasurable excitement. Yet this novel emotion had nothing to do with the wind. Indeed, so vague was the sense of distress I experienced, that it was impossible to trace it to its source and deal with it accordingly, though I was aware somehow that it had to do with my realisation of our utter insignificance before this unrestrained power of the elements about me. The huge-grown river had something to do with it too—a vague, unpleasant idea that we had somehow trifled with these great elemental forces in whose power we lay helpless every hour of the day and night. For here, indeed, they were gigantically at play together, and the sight appealed to the imagination.

But my emotion, so far as I could understand it, seemed to attach itself more particularly to the willow bushes, to these acres and acres of willows, crowding, so thickly growing there, swarming everywhere the eye could reach, pressing upon the river as though to suffocate it, standing in dense array mile after mile beneath the sky, watching, waiting, listening. And, apart quite from the elements, the willows connected themselves subtly with my malaise, attacking the mind insidiously somehow by reason of their vast numbers, and contriving in some way or other to represent to the imagination a new and mighty power, a power, moreover, not altogether friendly to us.

Great revelations of nature, of course, never fail to impress in one way or another, and I was no stranger to moods of the kind. Mountains overawe and oceans terrify, while the mystery of great forests exercises a spell peculiarly its own. But all these, at one point or another, somewhere link on intimately with human life and human experience. They stir comprehensible, even if alarming, emotions. They tend on the whole to exalt.

With this multitude of willows, however, it was something far different, I felt. Some essence emanated from them that besieged the heart. A sense of awe awakened, true, but of awe touched somewhere by a vague terror. Their serried ranks, growing everywhere darker about me as the shadows deepened, moving furiously yet softly in the wind, woke in me the curious and unwelcome suggestion that we had trespassed here upon the borders of an alien world, a world where we were intruders, a world where we were not wanted or invited to remain—where we ran grave risks perhaps!

The feeling, however, though it refused to yield its meaning entirely to analysis, did not at the time trouble me by passing into menace. Yet it never left me quite, even during the very practical business of putting up the tent in a hurricane of wind and building a fire for the stew-pot. It remained, just enough to bother and perplex, and to rob a most delightful camping-ground of a good portion of its charm. To my companion, however, I said nothing, for he was a man I considered devoid of imagination. In the first place, I could never have explained to him what I meant, and in the second, he would have laughed stupidly at me if I had.

There was a slight depression in the centre of the island, and here we pitched the tent. The surrounding willows broke the wind a bit.

"A poor camp," observed the imperturbable Swede when at last the tent stood upright; "no stones and precious little firewood. I'm for moving on early to-morrow—eh? This sand won't hold anything."

But the experience of a collapsing tent at midnight had taught us many devices, and we made the cosy gipsy house as safe as possible, and then set about collecting a store of wood to last till bed-time. Willow bushes drop no branches, and driftwood was our only source of supply. We hunted the shores pretty thoroughly. Everywhere the banks were crumbling as the rising flood tore at them and carried away great portions with a splash and a gurgle.

"The island's much smaller than when we landed," said the accurate Swede. "It won't last long at this rate. We'd better drag the canoe close to the tent, and be ready to start at a moment's notice. *I* shall sleep in my clothes."

He was a little distance off, climbing along the bank, and I heard his rather jolly laugh as he spoke.

"By Jove!" I heard him call, a moment later, and turned to see what had caused his exclamation. But for the moment he was hidden by the willows, and I could not find him.

"What in the world's this?" I heard him cry again, and this time his voice had become serious.

I ran up quickly and joined him on the bank. He was looking over the river, pointing at something in the water.

"Good heavens, it's a man's body!" he cried excitedly. "Look!"

A black thing, turning over and over in the foaming waves, swept rapidly past. It kept disappearing and coming up to the surface again. It was about twenty feet from the shore, and just as it was opposite to where we stood it lurched round and looked straight at us. We saw its eyes reflecting the sunset, and gleaming an odd yellow as the body turned over. Then it gave a swift, gulping plunge, and dived out of sight in a flash.

"An otter, by gad!" we exclaimed in the same breath, laughing.

It *was* an otter, alive, and out on the hunt; yet it had looked exactly like the body of a drowned man turning helplessly in the current. Far below it came to the surface once again, and we saw its black skin, wet and shining in the sunlight.

Then, too, just as we turned back, our arms full of driftwood, another thing happened to recall us to the river bank. This time it really was a man, and what was more, a man in a boat. Now a small boat on the Danube was an unusual sight at any time, but here in this deserted region, and at flood time, it was so unexpected as to constitute a real event. We stood and stared.

Whether it was due to the slanting sunlight, or the refraction from the wonderfully illumined water, I cannot say, but, whatever the cause, I found it difficult to focus my sight properly upon the flying apparition. It seemed, however, to be a man standing upright in a sort of flat-bottomed boat, steering with a long oar, and being carried down the opposite shore at a tremendous pace. He apparently was looking across in our direction, but the distance was too great and the light too uncertain for us to make out very plainly what he was about. It seemed to me that he was gesticulating and making signs at us. His voice came across the water to us shouting something furiously, but the wind drowned it so that no single word was audible. There was something curious about the whole appearance—man, boat, signs, voice—that made an impression on me out of all proportion to its cause.

"He's crossing himself!" I cried. "Look, he's making the sign of the Cross!"

"I believe you're right," the Swede said, shading his eyes with his hand and watching the man out of sight. He seemed to be gone in a moment, melting away down there into the sea of willows where the sun caught them in the bend of the river and turned them into a great crimson wall of beauty. Mist, too, had begun to rise, so that the air was hazy.

"But what in the world is he doing at nightfall on this flooded river?" I said, half to myself. "Where is he going at such a time, and what did he mean by his signs and shouting? D'you think he wished to warn us about something?"

"He saw our smoke, and thought we were spirits probably," laughed my companion. "These Hungarians believe in all sorts of rubbish: you remember the shopwoman at Pressburg warning us that no one ever landed here because it belonged to some sort of beings outside man's world! I suppose they believe in fairies and elementals, possibly demons too. That peasant in the boat saw people on the islands for the first time in his life," he added, after a slight pause, "and it scared him, that's all."

The Swede's tone of voice was not convincing, and his manner lacked something that was usually there. I noted the change instantly while he talked, though without being able to label it precisely.

"If they had enough imagination," I laughed loudly—I remember trying to make as much *noise* as I could—"they might well people a place like this with the old gods of antiquity. The Romans must have haunted all this region more or less with their shrines and sacred groves and elemental deities."

The subject dropped and we returned to our stew-pot, for my friend was not given to imaginative conversation as a rule. Moreover, just then I remember feeling distinctly glad that he was not imaginative; his stolid, practical nature suddenly seemed to me welcome and comforting. It was an admirable temperament, I felt: he could steer down rapids like a red Indian, shoot dangerous bridges and whirlpools better than any white man I ever saw in a canoe. He was a grand fellow for an adventurous trip, a tower of strength when untoward things happened. I looked at his strong face and light curly hair as he staggered along under his pile of driftwood (twice the size of mine!), and I experienced a feeling of relief. Yes, I was distinctly glad just then that the Swede was—what he was, and that he never made remarks that suggested more than they said.

"The river's still rising, though," he added, as if following out some thoughts of his own, and dropping his load with a gasp. "This island will be under water in two days if it goes on."

"I wish the *wind* would go down," I said. "I don't care a fig for the river."

The flood, indeed, had no terrors for us; we could get off at ten minutes' notice, and the more water the better we liked it. It meant an increasing current and the obliteration of the treacherous shingle-beds that so often threatened to tear the bottom out of our canoe.

Contrary to our expectations, the wind did not go down with the sun. It seemed to increase with the darkness, howling overhead and shaking the willows round us like straws. Curious sounds accompanied it sometimes, like the explosion of heavy guns, and it fell upon the water and the island in great flat blows of immense power. It made me think of the sounds a planet must make, could we only hear it, driving along through space.

But the sky kept wholly clear of clouds, and soon after supper the full moon rose up in the east and covered the river and the plain of shouting willows with a light like the day.

We lay on the sandy patch beside the fire, smoking, listening to the noises of the night round us, and talking happily of the journey we had already made, and of our plans ahead. The map lay spread in the door of the tent, but the high wind made it hard to study, and presently we lowered the curtain and extinguished the lantern. The firelight was enough to smoke and see each other's faces by, and the sparks flew about overhead like fireworks. A few yards beyond, the river gurgled and hissed, and from time to time a heavy splash announced the falling away of further portions of the bank.

Our talk, I noticed, had to do with the far-away scenes and incidents of our first camps in the Black Forest, or of other subjects altogether remote from the present setting, for neither of us spoke of the actual moment more than was necessary—almost as though we had agreed tacitly to avoid discussion of the camp and its incidents. Neither the otter nor the boatman, for instance, received the honour of a single mention, though ordinarily these would have furnished discussion for the greater part of the evening. They were, of course, distinct events in such a place.

The scarcity of wood made it a business to keep the fire going, for the wind, that drove the smoke in our faces wherever we sat, helped at the same time to make a forced draught. We took it in turn to make foraging expeditions into the darkness, and the quantity the Swede brought back always made me feel that he took an absurdly long time finding it; for the fact was I did not care much about being left alone, and yet it always seemed to be my turn to grub about among the bushes or scramble along the slippery banks in the moonlight. The long day's battle with wind and water—such wind and such water!—had tired us both, and an early bed was the obvious programme. Yet neither of us made the move for the tent. We lay there, tending the fire, talking in desultory fashion, peering about us into the dense willow bushes, and listening to the thunder of wind and river. The loneliness of the place had entered our very bones, and silence seemed natural, for after a bit the sound of our voices became a trifle unreal and forced; whispering would have been the fitting mode of communication, I felt, and the human voice, always rather absurd amid the roar of the elements, now carried with it something almost illegitimate. It was like talking out loud in church, or in some place where it was not lawful, perhaps not quite *safe*, to be overheard.

The eeriness of this lonely island, set among a million willows, swept by a hurricane, and surrounded by hurrying deep waters, touched us both, I fancy. Untrodden by man, almost unknown to man, it lay there beneath the moon, remote from human influence, on the frontier of another world, an alien world, a world tenanted by willows only and the souls of willows. And we, in our rashness, had dared to invade it, even to make use of it! Something more than the power of its mystery stirred in me as I lay on the sand, feet to fire, and peered up through the leaves at the stars. For the last time I rose to get firewood.

"When this has burnt up," I said firmly, "I shall turn in," and my companion watched me lazily as I moved off into the surrounding shadows.

For an unimaginative man I thought he seemed unusually receptive that night, unusually open to suggestion of things other than sensory. He too was touched by the beauty and loneliness of the place. I was not altogether pleased, I remember, to recognise this slight change in him, and instead of immediately collecting sticks, I made my way to the far point of the island where the moonlight on plain and river could be seen to better advantage. The desire to be alone had come suddenly upon me; my former dread returned in force; there was a vague feeling in me I wished to face and probe to the bottom.

When I reached the point of sand jutting out among the waves, the spell of the place descended upon me with a positive shock. No mere "scenery" could have produced such an effect. There was something more here, something to alarm.

I gazed across the waste of wild waters; I watched the whispering willows; I heard the ceaseless beating of the tireless wind; and, one and all, each in its own way, stirred in me this sensation of a strange distress. But the *willows* especially: for ever they went on chattering and talking among themselves, laughing a little, shrilly crying out, sometimes sighing—but what it was they made so much to-do about belonged to the secret life of the great plain they inhabited. And it was utterly alien to the world I knew, or to that of the wild yet kindly elements. They made me think of a host of beings from another plane of life, another evolution altogether, perhaps, all discussing a mystery known only to themselves. I watched them moving busily together, oddly shaking their big bushy heads, twirling their myriad leaves even when there was no wind. They moved of their own will as though alive, and they touched, by some incalculable method, my own keen sense of the *horrible*.

There they stood in the moonlight, like a vast army surrounding our camp, shaking their innumerable silver spears defiantly, formed all ready for an attack.

The psychology of places, for some imaginations at least, is very vivid; for the wanderer, especially, camps have their "note" either of welcome or rejection. At first it may not always be apparent, because the busy preparations of tent and cooking prevent, but with the first pause—after supper usually—it comes and announces itself. And the note of this willow-camp now became unmistakably plain to me: we were interlopers, trespassers; we were not welcomed. The sense of unfamiliarity grew upon me as I stood there watching. We touched the frontier of a region where our presence was resented. For a night's lodging we might perhaps be tolerated; but for a prolonged and inquisitive stay—No! by all the gods of the trees and the wilderness, no! We were the first human influences upon this island, and we were not wanted. *The willows were against us.*

Strange thoughts like these, bizarre fancies, borne I know not whence, found lodgment in my mind as I stood listening.

What, I thought, if, after all, these crouching willows proved to be alive; if suddenly they should rise up, like a swarm of living creatures, marshalled by the gods whose territory we had invaded, sweep towards us off the vast swamps, booming overhead in the night—and then *settle down*! As I looked it was so easy to imagine they actually moved, crept nearer, retreated a little, huddled together in masses, hostile, waiting for the great wind that should finally start them a-running. I could have sworn their aspect changed a little, and their ranks deepened and pressed more closely together.

The melancholy shrill cry of a night-bird sounded overhead, and suddenly I nearly lost my balance as the piece of bank I stood upon fell with a great splash into the river, undermined by the flood. I stepped back just in time, and went on hunting for firewood again, half laughing at the odd fancies that crowded so thickly into my mind and cast their spell upon me. I recalled the Swede's remark about moving on next day, and I was just thinking that I fully agreed with him, when I turned with a start and saw the subject of my thoughts standing immediately in front of me. He was quite close. The roar of the elements had covered his approach.

"You've been gone so long," he shouted above the wind, "I thought something must have happened to you."

But there was that in his tone, and a certain look in his face as well, that conveyed to me more than his actual words, and in a flash I understood the real reason for his coming. It was because the spell of the place had entered his soul too, and he did not like being alone.

"River still rising," he cried, pointing to the flood in the moonlight, "and the wind's simply awful."

He always said the same things, but it was the cry for companionship that gave the real importance to his words.

"Lucky," I cried back, "our tent's in the hollow. I think it'll hold all right." I added something about the difficulty of finding wood, in order to explain my absence, but the wind caught my words and flung them across the river, so that he did not hear, but just looked at me through the branches, nodding his head.

"Lucky if we get away without disaster!" he shouted, or words to that effect; and I remember feeling half angry with him for putting the thought into words, for it was exactly what I felt myself. There was disaster impending somewhere, and the sense of presentiment lay unpleasantly upon me.

We went back to the fire and made a final blaze, poking it up with our feet. We took a last look round. But for the wind the heat would have been unpleasant. I put this thought into words, and I remember my friend's reply struck me oddly: that he would rather have the heat, the ordinary July weather, than this "diabolical wind."

Everything was snug for the night; the canoe lying turned over beside the tent, with both yellow paddles beneath her; the provision sack hanging from a willow-stem, and the washed-up dishes removed to a safe distance from the fire, all ready for the morning meal.

We smothered the embers of the fire with sand, and then turned in. The flap of the tent door was up, and I saw the branches and the stars and the white moonlight. The shaking willows and the heavy buffetings of the wind against our taut little house were the last things I remembered as sleep came down and covered all with its soft and delicious forgetfulness.

Suddenly I found myself lying awake, peering from my sandy mattress through the door of the tent. I looked at my watch pinned against the canvas, and saw by the bright moonlight that it was past twelve o'clock—the threshold of a new day—and I had therefore slept a couple of hours. The Swede was asleep still beside me; the wind howled as before; something plucked at my heart and made me feel afraid. There was a sense of disturbance in my immediate neighbourhood.

I sat up quickly and looked out. The trees were swaying violently to and fro as the gusts smote them, but our little bit of green canvas lay snugly safe in the hollow, for the wind passed over it without meeting enough resistance to make it vicious. The feeling of disquietude did not pass, however, and I crawled quietly out of the tent to see if our belongings were safe. I moved carefully so as not to waken my companion. A curious excitement was on me.

I was half-way out, kneeling on all fours, when my eye first took in that the tops of the bushes opposite, with their moving tracery of leaves, made shapes against the sky. I sat back on my haunches and stared. It was incredible, surely, but there, opposite and slightly above me, were shapes of some indeterminate sort among the willows, and as the branches swayed in the wind they seemed to group themselves about these shapes, forming a series of monstrous outlines that shifted rapidly beneath the moon. Close, about fifty feet in front of me, I saw these things.

My first instinct was to waken my companion, that he too might see them, but something made me hesitate—the sudden realisation, probably, that I should not welcome corroboration; and meanwhile I crouched there staring in amazement with smarting eyes. I was wide awake. I remember saying to myself that I was *not* dreaming.

They first became properly visible, these huge figures, just within the tops of the bushes—immense, bronze-coloured, moving, and wholly independent of the swaying of the branches. I saw them plainly and noted, now I came to examine them more calmly, that they were very much larger than human, and indeed that something in their appearance proclaimed them to be *not human* at all. Certainly they were not merely the moving tracery of the branches against the moonlight. They shifted independently. They rose upwards in a continuous stream from earth to sky, vanishing utterly as soon as they reached the dark of the sky. They were interlaced one with another, making a great column, and I saw their limbs and huge bodies melting in and out of each other, forming this serpentine line that bent and swayed and twisted spirally with the contortions of the wind-tossed trees. They were nude, fluid shapes, passing up the bushes, *within* the leaves almost—rising up in a living column into the heavens. Their faces I never could see. Unceasingly they poured upwards, swaying in great bending curves, with a hue of dull bronze upon their skins.

I stared, trying to force every atom of vision from my eyes. For a long time I thought they *must* every moment disappear and resolve themselves into the movements of the branches and prove to be an optical illusion. I searched everywhere for a proof of reality, when all the while I understood quite well that the standard of reality had changed. For the longer I looked the more certain I became that these figures were real and living, though perhaps not according to the standards that the camera and the biologist would insist upon.

Far from feeling fear, I was possessed with a sense of awe and wonder such as I have never known. I seemed to be gazing at the personified elemental forces of this haunted and primeval region. Our intrusion had stirred the powers of the place into activity. It was we who were the cause of the disturbance, and my brain filled to bursting with stories and legends of the spirits and deities of places that have been acknowledged and worshipped by men in all ages of the world's history. But, before I could arrive at any possible explanation, something impelled me to go farther out, and I crept forward on to the sand and stood upright. I felt the ground still warm under my bare feet; the wind tore at my hair and face; and the sound of the river burst upon my ears with a sudden roar. These things, I knew, were real, and proved that my senses were acting normally. Yet the figures still rose from earth to heaven, silent, majestically, in a great spiral of grace and strength that overwhelmed me at length with a genuine deep emotion of worship. I felt that I must fall down and worship—absolutely worship.

Perhaps in another minute I might have done so, when a gust of wind swept against me with such force that it blew me sideways, and I nearly stumbled and fell. It seemed to shake the dream violently out of me. At least it gave me another point of view somehow. The figures still remained, still ascended into heaven from the heart of the night, but my reason at last began to assert itself. It must be a subjective experience, I argued—none the less real for that, but still subjective. The moonlight and the branches combined to work out these pictures upon the mirror of my imagination, and for some reason I projected them outwards and made them appear objective. I knew this must be the case, of course. I was the subject of a vivid and interesting hallucination. I took courage, and began to move forward across the open patches of sand. By Jove, though, was it all hallucination? Was it merely subjective? Did not my reason argue in the old futile way from the little standard of the known?

I only know that great column of figures ascended darkly into the sky for what seemed a very long period of time, and with a very complete measure of reality as most men are accustomed to gauge reality. Then suddenly they were gone!

And, once they were gone and the immediate wonder of their great presence had passed, fear came down upon me with a cold rush. The esoteric meaning of this lonely and haunted region suddenly flamed up within me, and I began to tremble dreadfully. I took a quick look round—a look of horror that came near to panic—calculating vainly ways of escape; and then, realising how helpless I was to achieve anything really effective, I crept back silently into the tent and lay down again upon my sandy mattress, first lowering the door-curtain to shut out the sight of the willows in the moonlight, and then burying my head as deeply as possible beneath the blankets to deaden the sound of the terrifying wind.

As though further to convince me that I had not been dreaming, I remember that it was a long time before I fell again into a troubled and restless sleep; and even then only the upper crust of me slept, and underneath there was something that never quite lost consciousness, but lay alert and on the watch.

But this second time I jumped up with a genuine start of terror. It was neither the wind nor the river that woke me, but the slow approach of something that caused the sleeping portion of me to grow smaller and smaller till at last it vanished altogether, and I found myself sitting bolt upright—listening.

Outside there was a sound of multitudinous little patterings. They had been coming, I was aware, for a long time, and in my sleep they had first become audible. I sat there nervously wide awake as though I had not slept at all. It seemed to me that my breathing came with difficulty, and that there was a great weight upon the surface of my body. In spite of the hot night, I felt clammy with cold and shivered. Something surely was pressing steadily against the sides of the tent and weighing down upon it from above. Was it the body of the wind? Was this the pattering rain, the dripping of the leaves? The spray blown from the river by the wind and gathering in big drops? I thought quickly of a dozen things.

Then suddenly the explanation leaped into my mind: a bough from the poplar, the only large tree on the island, had fallen with the wind. Still half caught by the other branches, it would fall with the next gust and crush us, and meanwhile its leaves brushed and tapped upon the tight canvas surface of the tent. I raised the loose flap and rushed out, calling to the Swede to follow.

But when I got out and stood upright I saw that the tent was free. There was no hanging bough; there was no rain or spray; nothing approached.

A cold, grey light filtered down through the bushes and lay on the faintly gleaming sand. Stars still crowded the sky directly overhead, and the wind howled magnificently, but the fire no longer gave out any glow, and I saw the east reddening in streaks through the trees. Several hours must have passed since I stood there before watching the ascending figures, and the memory of it now came back to me horribly, like an evil dream. Oh, how tired it made me feel, that ceaseless raging wind! Yet, though the deep lassitude of a sleepless night was on me, my nerves were tingling with the activity of an equally tireless apprehension, and all idea of repose was out of the question. The river I saw had risen further. Its thunder filled the air, and a fine spray made itself felt through my thin sleeping shirt.

Yet nowhere did I discover the slightest evidences of anything to cause alarm. This deep, prolonged disturbance in my heart remained wholly unaccounted for.

My companion had not stirred when I called him, and there was no need to waken him now. I looked about me carefully, noting everything: the turned-over canoe; the yellow paddles—two of them, I'm certain; the provision sack and the extra lantern hanging together from the tree; and, crowding everywhere about me, enveloping all, the willows, those endless, shaking willows. A bird uttered its morning cry, and a string of duck passed with whirring flight overhead in the twilight. The sand whirled, dry and stinging, about my bare feet in the wind.

I walked round the tent and then went out a little way into the bush, so that I could see across the river to the farther landscape, and the same profound yet indefinable emotion of distress seized upon me again as I saw the interminable sea of bushes stretching to the horizon, looking ghostly and unreal in the wan light of dawn. I walked softly here and there, still puzzling over that odd sound of infinite pattering, and of that pressure upon the tent that had wakened me. It *must* have been the wind, I reflected—the wind beating upon the loose, hot sand, driving the dry particles smartly against the taut canvas—the wind dropping heavily upon our fragile roof.

Yet all the time my nervousness and malaise increased appreciably.

I crossed over to the farther shore and noted how the coastline had altered in the night, and what masses of sand the river had torn away. I dipped my hands and feet into the cool turrent, and bathed my forehead. Already there was a glow of sunrise in the sky and the exquisite freshness of coming day. On my way back I passed purposely beneath the very bushes where I had seen the column of figures rising into the air, and midway among the clumps I suddenly found myself overtaken by a sense of vast terror. From the shadows a large figure went swiftly by. Someone passed me, as sure as ever man did....

It was a great staggering blow from the wind that helped me forward again, and once out in the more open space, the sense of terror diminished strangely. The winds were about and walking, I remember saying to myself; for the winds often move like great presences under the trees. And altogether the fear that hovered about me was such an unknown and immense kind of fear, so unlike anything I had ever felt before, that it woke a sense of awe and wonder in me that did much to counteract its worst effects; and when I reached a high point in the middle of the island from which I could see the wide stretch of river, crimson in the sunrise, the whole magical beauty of it all was so overpowering that a sort of wild yearning woke in me and almost brought a cry up into the throat.

But this cry found no expression, for as my eyes wandered from the plain beyond to the island round me and noted our little tent half hidden among the willows, a dreadful discovery leaped out at me, compared to which my terror of the walking winds seemed as nothing at all.

For a change, I thought, had somehow come about in the arrangement of the landscape. It was not that my point of vantage gave me a different view, but that an alteration had apparently been effected in the relation of the tent to the willows, and of the willows to the tent. Surely the bushes now crowded much closer—unnecessarily, unpleasantly close. *They had moved nearer.*

Creeping with silent feet over the shifting sands, drawing imperceptibly nearer by soft, unhurried movements, the willows had come closer during the night. But had the wind moved them, or had they moved of themselves? I recalled the sound of infinite small patterings and the pressure upon the tent and upon my own heart that caused me to wake in terror. I swayed for a moment in the wind like a tree, finding it hard to keep my upright position on the sandy hillock. There was a suggestion here of personal agency, of deliberate intention, of aggressive hostility, and it terrified me into a sort of rigidity.

Then the reaction followed quickly. The idea was so bizarre, so absurd, that I felt inclined to laugh. But the laughter came no more readily than the cry, for the knowledge that my mind was so receptive to such dangerous imaginings brought the additional terror that it was through our minds and not through our physical bodies that the attack would come, and was coming.

The wind buffeted me about, and, very quickly it seemed, the sun came up over the horizon, for it was after four o'clock, and I must have stood on that little pinnacle of sand longer than I knew, afraid to come down to close quarters with the willows. I returned quietly, creepily, to the tent, first taking another exhaustive look round and—yes, I confess it—making a few measurements. I paced out on the warm sand the distances between the willows and the tent, making a note of the shortest distance particularly.

I crawled stealthily into my blankets. My companion, to

all appearances, still slept soundly, and I was glad that this was so. Provided my experiences were not corroborated, I could find strength somehow to deny them, perhaps. With the daylight I could persuade myself that it was all a subjective hallucination, a fantasy of the night, a projection of the excited imagination.

Nothing further came to disturb me, and I fell asleep almost at once, utterly exhausted, yet still in dread of hearing again that weird sound of multitudinous pattering, or of feeling the pressure upon my heart that had made it difficult to breathe.

The sun was high in the heavens when my companion woke me from a heavy sleep and announced that the porridge was cooked and there was just time to bathe. The grateful smell of frizzling bacon entered the tent door.

"River still rising," he said, "and several islands out in mid-stream have disappeared altogether. Our own island's much smaller."

"Any wood left?" I asked sleepily.

"The wood and the island will finish to-morrow in a dead heat," he laughed, "but there's enough to last us till then."

I plunged in from the point of the island, which had indeed altered a lot in size and shape during the night, and was swept down in a moment to the landing-place opposite the tent. The water was icy, and the banks flew by like the country from an express train. Bathing under such conditions was an exhilarating operation, and the terror of the night seemed cleansed out of me by a process of evaporation in the brain. The sun was blazing hot; not a cloud showed itself anywhere; the wind, however, had not abated one little jot.

Quite suddenly then the implied meaning of the Swede's words flashed across me, showing that he no longer wished to leave post-haste, and had changed his mind. "Enough to last till to-morrow"—he assumed we should stay on the island another night. It struck me as odd. The night before he was so positive the other way. How had the change come about?

Great crumblings of the banks occurred at breakfast, with heavy splashings and clouds of spray which the wind brought into our frying-pan, and my fellow-traveller talked incessantly about the difficulty the Vienna-Pesth steamers must have to find the channel in flood. But the state of his mind interested and impressed me far more than the state of the river or the difficulties of the steamers. He had changed somehow since the evening before. His manner was different—a trifle excited, a trifle shy, with a sort of suspicion about his voice and gestures. I hardly know how to describe it now in cold blood, but at the time I remember being quite certain of one thing—that he had become frightened?

He ate very little breakfast, and for once omitted to smoke his pipe. He had the map spread open beside him, and kept studying its markings.

"We'd better get off sharp in an hour," I said presently, feeling for an opening that must bring him indirectly to a partial confession at any rate. And his answer puzzled me uncomfortably: "Rather! If they'll let us."

"Who'll let us? The elements?" I asked quickly, with affected indifference.

"The powers of this awful place, whoever they are," he replied, keeping his eyes on the map. "The gods are here, if they are anywhere at all in the world."

"The elements are always the true immortals," I replied, laughing as naturally as I could manage, yet knowing quite well that my face reflected my true feelings when he looked up gravely at me and spoke across the smoke:

"We shall be fortunate if we get away without further disaster."

This was exactly what I had dreaded, and I screwed myself up to the point of the direct question. It was like agreeing to allow the dentist to extract the tooth; it *had* to come anyhow in the long run, and the rest was all pretence.

"Further disaster! Why, what's happened?"

"For one thing—the steering paddle's gone," he said quietly.

"The steering paddle gone!" I repeated, greatly excited, for this was our rudder, and the Danube in flood without a rudder was suicide. "But what——"

"And there's a tear in the bottom of the canoe," he added, with a genuine little tremor in his voice.

I continued staring at him, able only to repeat the words in his face somewhat foolishly. There, in the heat of the sun, and on this burning sand, I was aware of a freezing atmosphere descending round us. I got up to follow him, for he merely nodded his head gravely and led the way towards the tent a few yards on the other side of the fireplace. The canoe still lay there as I had last seen her in the night, ribs uppermost, the paddles, or rather, *the* paddle, on the sand beside her.

"There's only one," he said, stooping to pick it up. "And here's the rent in the base-board."

It was on the tip of my tongue to tell him that I had clearly noticed *two* paddles a few hours before, but a second impulse made me think better of it, and I said nothing. I approached to see.

There was a long, finely-made tear in the bottom of the canoe where a little slither of wood had been neatly taken clean out; it looked as if the tooth of a sharp rock or snag had eaten down her length, and investigation showed that the hole went through. Had we launched out in her without observing it we must inevitably have foundered. At first the water would have made the wood swell so as to close the hole, but once out in mid-stream the water must have poured in, and the canoe, never more than two inches above the surface, would have filled and sunk very rapidly.

"There, you see an attempt to prepare a victim for the sacrifice," I heard him saying, more to himself than to me, "two victims rather," he added as he bent over and ran his fingers along the slit.

I began to whistle—a thing I always do unconsciously when utterly nonplussed—and purposely paid no attention to his words. I was determined to consider them foolish.

"It wasn't there last night," he said presently, straightening up from his examination and looking anywhere but at me.

"We must have scratched her in landing, of course," I stopped whistling to say. "The stones are very sharp——"

I stopped abruptly, for at that moment he turned round and met my eye squarely. I knew just as well as he did how impossible my explanation was. There were no stones, to begin with.

"And then there's this to explain too," he added quietly, handing me the paddle and pointing to the blade.

A new and curious emotion spread freezingly over me as I took and examined it. The blade was scraped down all over, beautifully scraped, as though someone had sand-papered it with care, making it so thin that the first vigorous stroke must have snapped it off at the elbow.

"One of us walked in his sleep and did this thing," I said feebly, "or—or it has been filed by the constant stream of sand particles blown against it by the wind, perhaps."

"Ah," said the Swede, turning away, laughing a little, "you can explain everything!"

"The same wind that caught the steering paddle and flung it so near the bank that it fell in with the next lump that crumbled," I called out after him, absolutely determined to find an explanation for everything he showed me.

"I see," he shouted back, turning his head to look at me before disappearing among the willow bushes.

Once alone with these perplexing evidences of personal agency, I think my first thought took the form of "One of us must have done this thing, and it certainly was not I." But my second thought decided how impossible it was to suppose, under all the circumstances, that either of us had done it. That my companion, the trusted friend of a dozen similar expeditions, could have knowingly had a hand in it, was a suggestion not to be entertained for a moment. Equally absurd seemed the explanation that this imperturbable and densely practical nature had suddenly become insane and was busied with insane purposes.

Yet the fact remained that what disturbed me most, and kept my fear actively alive even in this blaze of sunshine and wild beauty, was the clear certainty that some curious alteration had come about in his *mind*—that he was nervous, timid, suspicious, aware of goings on he did not speak about, watching a series of secret and hitherto unmentionable events—waiting, in a word, for a climax that he expected, and, I thought, expected very soon. This grew up in my mind intuitively—I hardly knew how.

I made a hurried examination of the tent and its surroundings, but the measurements of the night remained the same. There were deep hollows formed in the sand I now noticed for the first time, basin-shaped and of various depths and sizes, varying from that of a tea-cup to a large bowl. The wind, no doubt, was responsible for these miniature craters, just as it was for lifting the paddle and tossing it towards the water. The rent in the canoe was the only thing that seemed quite inexplicable; and, after all, it *was* conceivable that a sharp point had caught it when we landed. The examination I made of the shore did not assist this theory, but all the same I clung to it with that diminishing portion of my intelligence which I called my "reason." An explanation of some kind was an absolute necessity, just as some working explanation of the universe is necessary—however absurd—to the happiness of every individual who seeks to do his duty in the world and face the problems of life. The simile seemed to me at the time an exact parallel.

I at once set the pitch melting, and presently the Swede joined me at the work, though under the best conditions in the world the canoe could not be safe for travelling till the following day. I drew his attention casually to the hollows in the sand.

"Yes," he said, "I know. They're all over the island. But *you* can explain them, no doubt!"

"Wind, of course," I answered without hesitation. "Have you never watched those little whirlwinds in the street that twist and twirl everything into a circle? This sand's loose enough to yield, that's all."

He made no reply, and we worked on in silence for a bit. I watched him surreptitiously all the time, and I had an idea he was watching me. He seemed, too, to be always listening attentively to something I could not hear, or perhaps for something that he expected to hear, for he kept turning about and staring into the bushes, and up into the sky, and out across the water where it was visible through the openings among the willows. Sometimes he even put his hand to his ear and held it there for several minutes. He said nothing to me, however, about it, and I asked no questions. And meanwhile, as he mended that torn canoe with the skill and address of a red Indian, I was glad to notice his absorption in the work, for there was a vague dread in my heart that he would speak of the changed aspect of the willows. And, if he had noticed *that*, my imagination could no longer be held a sufficient explanation of it.

At length, after a long pause, he began to talk.

"Queer thing," he added in a hurried sort of voice, as though he wanted to say something and get it over. "Queer thing, I mean, about that otter last night."

I had expected something so totally different that he caught me with surprise, and I looked up sharply.

"Shows how lonely this place is. Otters are awfully shy things——"

"I don't mean that, of course," he interrupted. "I mean—do you think—did you think it really *was* an otter?"

"What else, in the name of Heaven, what else?"

"You know, I saw it before you did, and at first it seemed—so *much* bigger than an otter."

"The sunset as you looked up-stream magnified it, or something," I replied.

He looked at me absently a moment, as though his mind were busy with other thoughts.

"It had such extraordinary yellow eyes," he went on half to himself.

"That was the sun too," I laughed, a trifle boisterously. "I suppose you'll wonder next if that fellow in the boat——"

I suddenly decided not to finish the sentence. He was in the act again of listening, turning his head to the wind, and something in the expression of his face made me halt. The subject dropped, and we went on with our caulking. Apparently he had not noticed my unfinished sentence. Five minutes, later, however, he looked at me across the canoe, the smoking pitch in his hand, his face exceedingly grave.

"I *did* rather wonder, if you want to know," he said slowly, "what that thing in the boat was. I remember thinking at the time it was not a man. The whole business seemed to rise quite suddenly out of the water."

I laughed again boisterously in his face, but this time there was impatience, and a strain of anger too, in my feeling.

"Look here now," I cried, "this place is quite queer enough without going out of our way to imagine things! That boat was an ordinary boat, and the man in it was an ordinary man, and they were both going down-stream as fast as they could lick. And that otter *was* an otter, so don't let's play the fool about it!"

He looked steadily at me with the same grave expression. He was not in the least annoyed. I took courage from his silence.

"And, for Heaven's sake," I went on, "don't keep pretending you hear things, because it only gives me the jumps, and there's nothing to hear but the river and this cursed old thundering wind."

"You *fool*!" he answered in a low, shocked voice, "you utter fool. That's just the way all victims talk. As if you didn't understand just as well as I do!" he sneered with scorn in his voice, and a sort of resignation. "The best thing you can do is to keep quiet and try to hold your mind as firm as possible. This feeble attempt at self-deception only makes the truth harder when you're forced to meet it."

My little effort was over, and I found nothing more to say, for I knew quite well his words were true, and that *I* was the fool, not *he*. Up to a certain stage in the adventure he kept ahead of me easily, and I think I felt annoyed to be out of it, to be thus proved less psychic, less sensitive than himself to these extraordinary happenings, and half ignorant all the time of what was going on under my very nose. *He knew* from the very beginning, apparently. But at the moment I wholly missed the point of his words about the necessity of there being a victim, and that we ourselves were destined to satisfy the want. I dropped all pretence thenceforward, but thenceforward likewise my fear increased steadily to the climax.

"But you're quite right about one thing," he added, before the subject passed, "and that is that we're wiser not to talk about it, or even to think about it, because what one *thinks* finds expression in words, and what one says, happens."

That afternoon, while the canoe dried and hardened, we spent trying to fish, testing the leak, collecting wood, and watching the enormous flood of rising water. Masses of driftwood swept near our shores sometimes, and we fished for them with long willow branches. The island grew perceptibly smaller as the banks were torn away with great gulps and splashes. The weather kept brilliantly fine till about four o'clock, and then for the first time for three days the wind showed signs of abating. Clouds began to gather in the southwest, spreading thence slowly over the sky.

This lessening of the wind came as a great relief, for the incessant roaring, banging, and thundering had irritated our nerves. Yet the silence that came about five o'clock with its sudden cessation was in a manner quite as oppressive. The booming of the river had everything in its own way then: it filled the air with deep murmurs, more musical than the wind noises, but infinitely more monotonous. The wind held many notes, rising, falling, always beating out some sort of great elemental tune; whereas the river's song lay between three notes at most—dull pedal notes, that held a lugubrious quality foreign to the wind, and somehow seemed to me, in my then nervous state, to sound wonderfully well the music of doom.

It was extraordinary, too, how the withdrawal suddenly of bright sunlight took everything out of the landscape that made for cheerfulness; and since this particular landscape had already managed to convey the suggestion of something sinister, the change of course was all the more unwelcome and noticeable. For me, I know, the darkening outlook became distinctly more alarming, and I found myself more than once calculating how soon after sunset the full moon would get up in the east, and whether the gathering clouds would greatly interfere with her lighting of the little island.

With this general hush of the wind—though it still indulged in occasional brief gusts—the river seemed to me to grow blacker, the willows to stand more densely together. The latter, too, kept up a sort of independent movement of their own, rustling among themselves when no wind stirred, and shaking oddly from the roots upwards. When common objects in this way become charged with the suggestion of horror, they stimulate the imagination far more than things of unusual appearance; and these bushes, crowding huddled about us, assumed for me in the darkness a bizarre *grotesque-*

rie of appearance that lent to them somehow the aspect of purposeful and living creatures. Their very ordinariness, I felt, masked what was malignant and hostile to us. The forces of the region drew nearer with the coming of night. They were focusing upon our island, and more particularly upon ourselves. For thus, somehow, in the terms of the imagination, did my really indescribable sensations in this extraordinary place present themselves.

I had slept a good deal in the early afternoon, and had thus recovered somewhat from the exhaustion of a disturbed night, but this only served apparently to render me more susceptible than before to the obsessing spell of the haunting. I fought against it, laughing at my feelings as absurd and childish, with very obvious physiological explanations, yet, in spite of every effort, they gained in strength upon me so that I dreaded the night as a child lost in a forest must dread the approach of darkness.

The canoe we had carefully covered with a waterproof sheet during the day, and the one remaining paddle had been securely tied by the Swede to the base of a tree, lest the wind should rob us of that too. From five o'clock onwards I busied myself with the stew-pot and preparations for dinner, it being my turn to cook that night. We had potatoes, onions, bits of bacon fat to add flavour, and a general thick residue from former stews at the bottom of the pot; with black bread broken up into it the result was most excellent, and it was followed by a stew of plums with sugar and a brew of strong tea with dried milk. A good pile of wood lay close at hand, and the absence of wind made my duties easy. My companion sat lazily watching me, dividing his attentions between cleaning his pipe and giving useless advice—an admitted privilege of the off-duty man. He had been very quiet all the afternoon, engaged in re-caulking the canoe, strengthening the tent ropes, and fishing for driftwood while I slept. No more talk about undesirable things had passed between us, and I think his only remarks had to do with the gradual destruction of the island, which he declared was now fully a third smaller than when we first landed.

The pot had just begun to bubble when I heard his voice calling to me from the bank, where he had wandered away without my noticing. I ran up.

"Come and listen," he said, "and see what you make of it." He held his hand cupwise to his ear, as so often before.

"*Now* do you hear anything?" he asked, watching me curiously.

We stood there, listening attentively together. At first I heard only the deep note of the water and the hissings rising from its turbulent surface. The willows, for once, were motionless and silent. Then a sound began to reach my ears faintly, a peculiar sound—something like the humming of a distant gong. It seemed to come across to us in the darkness from the waste of swamps and willows opposite. It was repeated at regular intervals, but it was certainly neither the sound of a bell nor the hooting of a distant steamer. I can liken it to nothing so much as to the sound of an immense gong, suspended far up in the sky, repeating incessantly its muffled metallic note, soft and musical, as it was repeatedly struck. My heart quickened as I listened.

"I've heard it all day," said my companion. "While you slept this afternoon it came all round the island. I hunted it down, but could never get near enough to see—to localise it correctly. Sometimes it was overhead, and sometimes it seemed under the water. Once or twice, too, I could have sworn it was not outside at all, but *within myself*—you know—the way a sound in the fourth dimension is supposed to come."

I was too much puzzled to pay much attention to his words. I listened carefully, striving to associate it with any known familiar sound I could think of, but without success. It changed in the direction, too, coming nearer, and then sinking utterly away into remote distance. I cannot say that it was ominous in quality, because to me it seemed distinctly musical, yet I must admit it set going a distressing feeling that made me wish I had never heard it.

"The wind blowing in those sand-funnels," I said determined to find an explanation, "or the bushes rubbing together after the storm perhaps."

"It comes off the whole swamp," my friend answered. "It comes from everywhere at once." He ignored my explanations. "It comes from the willow bushes somehow——"

"But now the wind has dropped," I objected. "The willows can hardly make a noise by themselves, can they?"

His answer frightened me, first because I had dreaded it, and secondly, because I knew intuitively it was true.

"It is *because* the wind has dropped we now hear it. It was drowned before. It is the cry, I believe, of the——"

I dashed back to my fire, warned by a sound of bubbling that the stew was in danger, but determined at the same time to escape further conversation. I was resolute, if possible, to avoid the exchanging of views. I dreaded, too, that he would begin about the gods, or the elemental forces, or something else disquieting, and I wanted to keep myself well in hand for what might happen later. There was another night to be faced before we escaped from this distressing place, and there was no knowing yet what it might bring forth.

"Come and cut up bread for the pot," I called to him, vigorously stirring the appetising mixture. That stew-pot held sanity for us both, and the thought made me laugh.

He came over slowly and took the provision sack from the tree, fumbling in its mysterious depths, and then emptying the entire contents upon the ground-sheet at his feet.

"Hurry up!" I cried; "it's boiling."

The Swede burst out into a roar of laughter that startled me. It was forced laughter, not artificial exactly, but mirthless.

"There's nothing here!" he shouted, holding his sides.

"Bread, I mean."

"It's gone. There is no bread. They've taken it!"

I dropped the long spoon and ran up. Everything the sack had contained lay upon the ground-sheet, but there was no loaf.

The whole dead weight of my growing fear fell upon me and shook me. Then I burst out laughing too. It was the only thing to do: and the sound of my laughter also made me understand his. The stain of psychical pressure caused it—this explosion of unnatural laughter in both of us; it was an effort of repressed forces to seek relief; it was a temporary safety-valve. And with both of us it ceased quite suddenly.

"How criminally stupid of me!" I cried, still determined to be consistent and find an explanation. "I clean forgot to buy a loaf at Pressburg. That chattering woman put everything out of my head, and I must have left it lying on the counter or——"

"The oatmeal, too, is much less than it was this morning," the Swede interrupted.

Why in the world need he draw attention to it? I thought angrily.

"There's enough for to-morrow," I said, stirring vigorously, "and we can get lots more at Komorn or Gran. In twenty-four hours we shall be miles from here."

"I hope so—to God," he muttered, putting the things back into the sack, "unless we're claimed first as victims for the sacrifice," he added with a foolish laugh. He dragged the sack into the tent, for safety's sake, I suppose, and I heard him mumbling on to himself, but so indistinctly that it seemed quite natural for me to ignore his words.

Our meal was beyond question a gloomy one, and we ate it almost in silence, avoiding one another's eyes, and keeping the fire bright. Then we washed up and prepared for the night, and, once smoking, our minds unoccupied with any definite duties, the apprehension I had felt all day long became more and more acute. It was not then active fear, I think, but the very vagueness of its origin distressed me far more than if I had been able to ticket and face it squarely. The curious sound I have likened to the note of a gong became now almost incessant, and filled the stillness of the night with a faint, continuous ringing rather than a series of distinct notes. At one time it was behind and at another time in front of us. Sometimes I fancied it came from the bushes on our left, and then again from the clumps on our right. More often it hovered directly overhead like the whirring of wings. It was really everywhere at once, behind, in front, at our sides and over our heads, completely surrounding us. The sound really defies description. But nothing within my knowledge is like that ceaseless muffled humming rising off the deserted world of swamps and willows.

We sat smoking in comparative silence, the strain growing every minute greater. The worst feature of the situation seemed to me that we did not know what to expect, and could therefore make no sort of preparation by way of defence. We could anticipate nothing. My explanations made in the sunshine, moreover, now came to haunt me with their foolish and wholly unsatisfactory nature, and it was more and more clear to us that some kind of plain talk with my companion was inevitable, whether I liked it or not. After all, we had to spend the night together, and to sleep in the same tent side by side. I saw that I could not get along much longer without the support of his mind, and for that, of course, plain talk was imperative. As long as possible, however, I postponed this little climax, and tried to ignore or laugh at the occasional sentences he flung into the emptiness.

Some of these sentences, moreover, were confoundedly disquieting to me, coming as they did to corroborate much that I felt myself: corroboration, too—which made it so much more convincing—from a totally different point of view. He composed such curious sentences, and hurled them at me in such an inconsequential sort of way, as though his main line of thought was secret to himself, and these fragments were bits he found it impossible to digest. He got rid of them by uttering them. Speech relieved him. It was like being sick.

"There are things about us, I'm sure, that make for disorder, disintegration, destruction, *our* destruction," he said once, while the fire blazed between us. "We've strayed out of a safe line somewhere."

And another time, when the gong sounds had come nearer, ringing much louder than before, and directly over our heads, he said as though talking to himself:

"I don't think a gramophone would show any record of that. The sound doesn't come to me by the ears at all. The vibrations reach me in another manner altogether, and seem to be within me, which is precisely how a fourth dimensional sound might be supposed to make itself heard."

I purposely made no reply to this, but I sat up a little closer to the fire and peered about me into the darkness. The clouds were massed all over the sky, and no trace of moonlight came through. Very still, too, everything was, so that the river and the frogs had things all their own way.

"It has that about it," he went on, "which is utterly out of common experience. It is *unknown*. Only one thing describes it really: it is a non-human sound; I mean a sound outside humanity."

Having rid himself of this indigestible morsel, he lay quiet for a time; but he had so admirably expressed my own feeling that it was a relief to have the thought out, and to have confined it by the limitation of words from dangerous wandering to and fro in the mind.

The solitude of that Danube camping-place, can I ever forget it? The feeling of being utterly alone on an empty planet! My thoughts ran incessantly upon cities and the haunts of men. I would have given my soul, as the saying is, for the "feel" of those Bavarian villages we had passed through by the score; for the normal, human commonplaces: peasants drinking beer, tables beneath the trees, hot sunshine, and a ruined castle on the rocks behind the red-roofed church. Even the tourists would have been welcome.

Yet what I felt of dread was no ordinary ghostly fear. It was infinitely greater, stranger, and seemed to arise from some dim ancestral sense of terror more profoundly disturbing than anything I had known or dreamed of. We had "strayed," as the Swede put it, into some region or some set of conditions where the risks were great, yet unintelligible to us; where the frontiers of some unknown world lay close about us. It was a spot held by the dwellers in some outer space, a sort of peep-hole whence they could spy upon the earth, themselves unseen, a point where the veil between had worn a little thin. As the final result of too long a sojourn here, we should be carried over the border and deprived of what we called "our lives," yet by mental, not physical, processes. In that sense, as he said, we should be the victims of our adventure—a sacrifice.

It took us in different fashion, each according to the measure of his sensitiveness and powers of resistance. I translated it vaguely into a personification of the mightily disturbed elements, investing them with the horror of a deliberate and malefic purpose, resentful of our audacious intrusion into their breeding-place; whereas my friend threw it into the unoriginal form at first of a trespass on some ancient shrine, some place where the old gods still held sway, where the emotional forces of former worshippers still clung, and the ancestral portion of him yielded to the old pagan spell.

At any rate, here was a place unpolluted by men, kept clean by the winds from coarsening human influences, a place where spiritual agencies were within reach and aggressive. Never, before or since, have I been so attacked by indescribable suggestions of a "beyond region," of another scheme of life, another revolution not parallel to the human. And in the end our minds would succumb under the weight of the awful spell, and we should be drawn across the frontier into *their* world.

Small things testified to the amazing influence of the place, and now in the silence round the fire they allowed themselves to be noted by the mind. The very atmosphere had proved itself a magnifying medium to distort every indication: the otter rolling in the current, the hurrying boatman making signs, the shifting willows, one and all had been robbed of its natural character, and revealed in something of its other aspect—as it existed across the border in that other region. And this changed aspect I felt was new not merely to me, but to the race. The whole experience whose verge we touched was unknown to humanity at all. It was a new order of experience, and in the true sense of the word *unearthly*.

"It's the deliberate, calculating purpose that reduces one's courage to zero," the Swede said suddenly, as if he had been actually following my thoughts. "Otherwise imagination might count for much. But the paddle, the canoe, the lessening food——"

"Haven't I explained all that once?" I interrupted viciously.

"You have," he answered dryly; "you have indeed."

He made other remarks too, as usual, about what he called the "plain determination to provide a victim"; but, having now arranged my thoughts better, I recognised that this was simply the cry of his frightened soul against the knowledge that he was being attacked in a vital part, and that he would be somehow taken or destroyed. The situation called for a courage and calmness of reasoning that neither of us could compass, and I have never before been so clearly conscious of two persons in me—the one that explained everything, and the other that laughed at such foolish explanations, yet was horribly afraid.

Meanwhile, in the pitchy night the fire died down and the wood pile grew small. Neither of us moved to replenish the stock, and the darkness consequently came up very close to our faces. A few feet beyond the circle of firelight it was inky black. Occasionally a stray puff of wind set the willows shivering about us, but apart from this not very welcome sound a deep and depressing silence reigned, broken only by the gurgling of the river and the humming in the air overhead.

We both missed, I think, the shouting company of the winds.

At length, at a moment when a stray puff prolonged itself as though the wind were about to rise again, I reached the point for me of saturation, the point where it was absolutely necessary to find relief in plain speech, or else to betray myself by some hysterical extravagance that must have been far worse in its effect upon both of us. I kicked the fire into a blaze, and turned to my companion abruptly. He looked up with a start.

"I can't disguise it any longer," I said; "I don't like this place, and the darkness, and the noises, and the awful feelings I get. There's something here that beats me utterly. I'm in a blue funk, and that's the plain truth. If the other shore was—different, I swear I'd be inclined to swim for it!"

The Swede's face turned very white beneath the deep tan of sun and wind. He stared straight at me and answered quietly, but his voice betrayed his huge excitement by its unnatural calmness. For the moment, at any rate, he was the strong man of the two. He was more phlegmatic, for one thing.

"It's not a physical condition we can escape from by running away," he replied, in the tone of a doctor diagnosing some grave disease; "we must sit tight and wait. There are forces close here that could kill a herd of elephants in a second as easily as you or I could squash a fly. Our only chance is to keep perfectly still. Our insignificance perhaps may save us."

I put a dozen questions into my expression of face, but found no words. It was precisely like listening to an accurate description of a disease whose symptoms had puzzled me.

"I mean that so far, although aware of our disturbing presence, they have not *found* us—not 'located' us, as the Americans say," he went on. "They're blundering about like men hunting for a leak of gas. The paddle and canoe and provisions prove that. I think they *feel* us, but cannot actually see us. We must keep our minds quiet—it's our minds they feel. We must control our thoughts, or it's all up with us."

"Death, you mean?" I stammered, icy with the horror of his suggestion.

"Worse—by far," he said. "Death, according to one's belief, means either annihilation or release from the limitations of the senses, but it involves no change of character. *You* don't suddenly alter just because the body's gone. But this means a radical alteration, a complete change, a horrible loss of oneself by substitution—far worse than death, and not even annihilation. We happen to have camped in a spot where their region touches ours, where the veil between has worn thin"—horrors! he was using my very own phrase, my actual words—"so that they are aware of our being in their neighbourhood."

"But *who* are aware?" I asked.

I forgot the shaking of the willows in the windless calm, the humming overhead, everything except that I was waiting for an answer that I dreaded more than I can possibly explain.

He lowered his voice at once to reply, leaning forward a little over the fire, an indefinable change in his face that made me avoid his eyes and look down upon the ground.

"All my life," he said, "I have been strangely, vividly conscious of another region—not far removed from our own world in one sense, yet wholly different in kind—where great things go on unceasingly, where immense and terrible personalities hurry by, intent on vast purposes compared to which earthly affairs, the rise and fall of nations, the destinies of empires, the fate of armies and continents, are all as dust in the balance; vast purposes, I mean, that deal directly with the soul, and not indirectly with mere expressions of the soul——"

"I suggest just now——" I began, seeking to stop him, feeling as though I was face to face with a madman. But he instantly overbore me with his torrent that *had* to come.

"You think," he said, "It is the spirits of the elements, and I thought perhaps it was the old gods. But I tell you now it is—*neither*. These would be comprehensible entities, for they have relations with men, depending upon them for worship or sacrifice, whereas these beings who are now about us have absolutely nothing to do with mankind, and it is mere chance that their space happens just at this spot to touch our own."

The mere conception, which his words somehow made so convincing, as I listened to them there in the dark stillness of that lonely island, set me shaking a little all over. I found it impossible to control my movements.

"And what do you propose?" I began again.

"A sacrifice, a victim, might save us by distracting them until we could get away," he went on, "just as the wolves stop to devour the dogs and give the sleigh another start. But—I see no chance of any other victim now."

I stared blankly at him. The gleam in his eyes was dreadful. Presently he continued.

"It's the willows, of course. The willows *mask* the others, but the others are feeling about for us. If we let our minds betray our fear, we're lost, lost utterly." He looked at me with an expression so calm, so determined, so sincere, that I no longer had any doubts as to his sanity. He was as sane as any man ever was. "If we can hold out through the night," he added, "we may get off in the daylight unnoticed, or rather, *undiscovered*."

"But you really think a sacrifice would——"

That gong-like humming came down very close over our heads as I spoke, but it was my friend's scared face that really stopped my mouth.

"Hush!" he whispered, holding up his hand. "Do not mention them more than you can help. Do not refer to them *by name*. To name is to reveal: it is the inevitable clue, and our only hope lies in ignoring them, in order that they may ignore us."

"Even in thought?" He was extraordinarily agitated.

"Especially in thought. Our thoughts make spirals in their world. We must keep them *out of our minds* at all costs if possible."

I raked the fire together to prevent the darkness having everything its own way. I never longed for the sun as I longed for it then in the awful blackness of that summer night.

"Were you awake all last night?" he went on suddenly.

"I slept badly a little after dawn," I replied evasively, trying to follow his instructions, which I knew instinctively were true, "but the wind, of course——"

"I know. But the wind won't account for all the noises."

"Then you heard it too?"

"The multiplying countless little footsteps I heard," he said, adding, after a moment's hesitation, "and that other sound——"

"You mean above the tent, and the pressing down upon us of something tremendous, gigantic?"

He nodded significantly.

"It was like the beginning of a sort of inner suffocation?" I said.

"Partly, yes. It seemed to me that the weight of the atmosphere had been altered—had increased enormously, so that we should be crushed."

"And *that*," I went on, determined to have it all out, pointing upwards where the gong-like note hummed ceaselessly, rising and falling like wind. "What do you make of that?"

"It's *their* sound," he whispered gravely. "It's the sound of their world, the humming in their region. The division here is so thin that it leaks through somehow. But, if you listen carefully, you'll find it's not above so much as around us. It's in the willows. It's the willows themselves humming, because here the willows have been made symbols of the forces that are against us."

I could not follow exactly what he meant by this, yet the thought and idea in my mind were beyond question the thought and idea in his. I realised what he realised, only with less power of analysis than his. It was on the tip of my tongue to tell him at last about my hallucination of the ascending figures and the moving bushes, when he suddenly thrust his face again close into mine across the firelight and began to speak in a very earnest whisper. He amazed me by his calmness and pluck, his apparent control of the situation. This man I had for years deemed unimaginative, stolid!

"Now listen," he said. "The only thing for us to do is to go on as though nothing had happened, follow our usual habits, go to bed, and so forth; pretend we feel nothing and notice nothing. It is a question wholly of the mind, and the less we think about them the better our chance of escape. Above all, don't *think*, for what you think happens!"

"All right," I managed to reply, simply breathless with his words and the strangeness of it all; "all right, I'll try, but tell me one thing more first. Tell me what you make of those hollows in the ground all about us, those sand-funnels?"

"No!" he cried, forgetting to whisper in his excitement. "I dare not, simply dare not, put the thought into words. If you have not guessed I am glad. Don't try to. *They* have put it into my mind; try your hardest to prevent their putting it into yours."

He sank his voice again to a whisper before he finished, and I did not press him to explain. There was already just about as much horror in me as I could hold. The conversation came to an end, and we smoked our pipes busily in silence.

Then something happened, something unimportant apparently, as the way is when the nerves are in a very great state of tension, and this small thing for a brief space gave me an entirely different point of view. I chanced to look down at my sand-shoe—the sort we used for the canoe—and something to do with the hole at the toe suddenly recalled to me the London shop where I had bought them, the difficulty the man had in fitting me, and other details of the uninteresting but practical operation. At once, in its train, followed a wholesome view of the modern sceptical world I was accustomed to move in at home. I thought of roast beef and ale, motor-cars, policemen, brass bands, and a dozen other things that proclaimed the soul of ordinariness or utility. The effect was immediate and astonishing even to myself. Psychologically, I suppose, it was simply a sudden and violent reaction after the strain of living in an atmosphere of things that to the normal consciousness must seem impossible and incredible. But, whatever the cause, it momentarily lifted the spell from my heart, and left me for the short space of a minute feeling free and utterly unafraid. I looked up at my friend opposite.

"You damned old pagan!" I cried, laughing aloud in his face. "You imaginative idiot! You superstitious idolator! You——"

I stopped in the middle, seized anew by the old horror. I tried to smother the sound of my voice as something sacrilegious. The Swede, of course, heard it too—the strange cry overhead in the darkness—and that sudden drop in the air as though something had come nearer.

He had turned ashen white under the tan. He stood bolt upright in front of the fire, stiff as a rod, staring at me.

"After that," he said in a sort of helpless, frantic way, "we must go! We can't stay now; we must strike camp this very instant and go on—down the river."

He was talking, I saw, quite wildly, his words dictated by abject terror—the terror he had resisted so long, but which had caught him at last.

"In the dark?" I exclaimed, shaking with fear after my hysterical outburst, but still realising our position better than he did. "Sheer madness! The river's in flood, and we've only got a single paddle. Besides, we only go deeper into their country! There's nothing ahead for fifty miles but willows, willows, willows!"

He sat down again in a state of semi-collapse. The positions, by one of those kaleidoscopic changes nature loves, were suddenly reversed, and the control of our forces passed over into my hands. His mind at last had reached the point where it was beginning to weaken.

"What on earth possessed you to do such a thing?" he whispered with the awe of genuine terror in his voice and face.

I crossed round to his side of the fire. I took both his hands in mine, kneeling down beside him and looking straight into his frightened eyes.

"We'll make one more blaze," I said firmly, "and then turn in for the night. At sunrise we'll be off full speed for Komorn. Now, pull yourself together a bit, and remember your own advice about *not thinking fear*!"

He said no more, and I saw that he would agree and obey. In some measure, too, it was a sort of relief to get up and make an excursion into the darkness for more wood. We kept close together, almost touching, groping among the bushes and along the bank. The humming overhead never ceased, but seemed to me to grow louder as we increased our distance from the fire. It was shivery work!

We were grubbing away in the middle of a thickish clump of willows where some driftwood from a former flood had caught high among the branches, when my body was seized in a grip that made me half drop upon the sand. It was the Swede. He had fallen against me, and was clutching me for support. I heard his breath coming and going in short gasps.

"Look! By my soul!" he whispered, and for the first time in my experience I knew what it was to hear tears of terror in a human voice. He was pointing to the fire, some fifty feet away. I followed the direction of his finger, and I swear my heart missed a beat.

There, in front of the dim glow, *something was moving.*

I saw it through a veil that hung before my eyes like the gauze drop-curtain used at the back of a theatre—hazily a little. It was neither a human figure nor an animal. To me it gave the strange impression of being as large as several animals grouped together, like horses, two or three, moving slowly. The Swede, too, got a similar result, though expressing it differently, for he thought it was shaped and sized like a clump of willow bushes, rounded at the top, and moving all over upon its surface—"coiling upon itself like smoke," he said afterwards.

"I watched it settle downwards through the bushes," he sobbed at me. "Look, by God! It's coming this way! Oh, oh!"—he gave a kind of whistling cry. *"They've found us."*

I gave one terrified glance, which just enabled me to see that the shadowy form was swinging towards us through the bushes, and then I collapsed backwards with a crash into the branches. These failed, of course, to support my weight, so that with the Swede on the top of me we fell in a struggling heap upon the sand. I really hardly knew what was happening. I was conscious only of a sort of enveloping sensation of icy fear that plucked the nerves out of their fleshly covering, twisted them this way and that, and replaced them quivering. My eyes were tightly shut; something in my throat choked me; a feeling that my consciousness was expanding, extending out into space, swiftly gave way to another feeling that I was losing it altogether, and about to die.

An acute spasm of pain passed through me, and I was aware that the Swede had hold of me in such a way that he hurt me abominably. It was the way he caught at me in falling.

But it was the pain, he declared afterwards, that saved me: it caused me to *forget them* and think of something else at the very instant when they were about to find me. It concealed my mind from them at the moment of discovery, yet just in time to evade their terrible seizing of me. He himself, he says, actually swooned at the same moment, and that was what saved him.

I only know that at a later date, how long or short is impossible to say, I found myself scrambling up out of the slippery network of willow branches, and saw my companion standing in front of me holding out a hand to assist me. I stared at him in a dazed way, rubbing the arm he had twisted for me. Nothing came to me to say, somehow.

"I lost consciousness for a moment or two," I heard him say. "That's what saved me. It made me stop thinking about them."

"You nearly broke my arm in two," I said, uttering my only connected thought at the moment. A numbness came over me.

"That's what saved *you*!" he replied. "Between us, we've managed to set them off on a false tack somewhere. The humming has ceased. It's gone—for the moment at any rate!"

A wave of hysterical laughter seized me again, and this time spread to my friend too—great healing gusts of shaking laughter that brought a tremendous sense of relief in their train. We made our way back to the fire and put the wood on so that it blazed at once. Then we saw that the tent had fallen over and lay in a tangled heap upon the ground.

We picked it up, and during the process tripped more than once and caught our feet in sand.

"It's those sand-funnels," exclaimed the Swede, when the tent was up again and the firelight lit up the ground for several yards about us. "And look at the size of them!"

All round the tent and about the fireplace where we had seen the moving shadows there were deep funnel-shaped hollows in the sand, exactly similar to the ones we had already found over the island, only far bigger and deeper, beautifully formed, and wide enough in some instances to admit the whole of my foot and leg.

Neither of us said a word. We both knew that sleep was the safest thing we could do, and to bed we went accordingly without further delay, having first thrown sand on the fire and taken the provision sack and the paddle inside the tent with us. The canoe, too, we propped in such a way at the end of the tent that our feet touched it, and the least motion would disturb and wake us.

In case of emergency, too, we again went to bed in our clothes, ready for a sudden start.

It was my firm intention to lie awake all night and watch, but the exhaustion of nerves and body decreed otherwise, and sleep after a while came over me with a welcome blanket of oblivion. The fact that my companion also slept quickened its approach. At first he fidgeted and constantly sat up, asking me if I "heard this" or "heard that." He tossed about on his cork mattress, and said the tent was moving and the river had risen over the point of the island; but each time I went out to look I returned with the report that all was well, and finally he grew calmer and lay still. Then at length his breathing became regular and I heard unmistakable sounds of snoring—the first and only time in my life when snoring has been a welcome and calming influence.

This, I remember, was the last thought in my mind before dozing off.

A difficulty in breathing woke me, and I found the blanket over my face. But something else besides the blanket was pressing upon me, and my first thought was that my companion had rolled off his mattress on to my own in his sleep. I called to him and sat up, and at the same moment it came to me that the tent was *surrounded*. That sound of multitudinous soft pattering was again audible outside, filling the night with horror.

I called again to him, louder than before. He did not answer, but I missed the sound of his snoring, and also noticed that the flap of the tent door was down. This was the unpardonable sin. I crawled out in the darkness to hook it back securely, and it was then for the first time I realised positively that the Swede was not there. He had gone.

I dashed out in a mad run, seized by a dreadful agitation, and the moment I was out I plunged into a sort of torrent of humming that surrounded me completely and came out of every quarter of the heavens at once. It was that same familiar humming—gone mad! A swarm of great invisible bees might have been about me in the air. The sound seemed to thicken the very atmosphere, and I felt that my lungs worked with difficulty.

But my friend was in danger, and I could not hesitate.

The dawn was just about to break, and a faint whitish light spread upwards over the clouds from a thin strip of clear horizon. No wind stirred. I could just make out the bushes and river beyond, and the pale sandy patches. In my excitement I ran frantically to and fro about the island, calling him by name, shouting at the top of my voice the first words that came into my head. But the willows smothered my voice, and the humming muffled it, so that the sound only travelled a few feet round me. I plunged among the bushes, tripping headlong, tumbling over roots, and scraping my face as I tore this way and that among the preventing branches.

Then, quite unexpectedly, I came out upon the island's point and saw a dark figure outlined between the water and the sky. It was the Swede. And already he had one foot in the river! A moment more and he would have taken the plunge.

I threw myself upon him, flinging my arms about his waist and dragging him shorewards with all my strength. Of course he struggled furiously, making a noise all the time just like that cursed humming, and using the most outlandish phrases in his anger about "going *inside* to Them," and "taking the way of the water and the wind," and God only knows what more besides, that I tried in vain to recall afterwards, but which turned me sick with horror and amazement as I listened. But in the end I managed to get him into the comparative safety of the tent, and flung him breathless and cursing upon the mattress where I held him until the fit had passed.

I think the suddenness with which it all went and he grew calm, coinciding as it did with the equally abrupt cessation of the humming and pattering outside—I think this was almost the strangest part of the whole business perhaps. For he just opened his eyes and turned his tired face up to me so that the dawn threw a pale light upon it through the doorway, and said, for all the world just like a frightened child:

"My life, old man—it's my life I owe you. But it's all over now anyhow. They've found a victim in our place!"

Then he dropped back upon his blankets and went to sleep literally under my eyes. He simply collapsed, and began to snore again as healthily as though nothing had happened and he had never tried to offer his own life as a sacrifice by drowning. And when the sunlight woke him three hours later—hours of ceaseless vigil for me—it became so clear to me that he remembered absolutely nothing of what he had attempted to do, that I deemed it wise to hold my peace and ask no dangerous questions.

He woke naturally and easily, as I have said, when the sun was already high in a windless hot sky, and he at once got up and set about the preparation of the fire for breakfast. I followed him anxiously at bathing, but he did not attempt to plunge in, merely dipping his head and making some remark about the extra coldness of the water.

"River's falling at last," he said, "and I'm glad of it."

"The humming has stopped too," I said.

He looked up at me quietly with his normal expression. Evidently he remembered everything except his own attempt at suicide.

"Everything has stopped," he said, "because——"

He hesitated. But I knew some reference to that remark he had made just before he fainted was in his mind, and I was determined to know it.

"Because 'They've found another victim'?" I said, forcing a little laugh.

"Exactly," he answered, "exactly! I feel as positive of it as though—as though—I feel quite safe again, I mean," he finished.

He began to look curiously about him. The sunlight lay in hot patches on the sand. There was no wind. The willows were motionless. He slowly rose to feet.

"Come," he said; "I think if we look, we shall find it."

He started off on a run, and I followed him. He kept to the banks, poking with a stick among the sandy bays and caves and little back-waters, myself always close on his heels.

"Ah!" he exclaimed presently, "ah!"

The tone of his voice somehow brought back to me a vivid sense of the horror of the last twenty-four hours, and I hurried up to join him. He was pointing with his stick at a large black object that lay half in the water and half on the sand. It appeared to be caught by some twisted willow roots so that the river could not sweep it away. A few hours before the spot must have been under water.

"See," he said quietly, "the victim that made our escape possible!"

And when I peered across his shoulder I saw that his stick rested on the body of a man. He turned it over. It was the corpse of a peasant, and the face was hidden in the sand. Clearly the man had been drowned, but a few hours before, and his body must have been swept down upon our island somewhere about the hour of the dawn—*at the very time the fit had passed.*

"We must give it a decent burial, you know."

"I suppose so," I replied. I shuddered a little in spite of

myself, for there was something about the appearance of that poor drowned man that turned me cold.

The Swede glanced up sharply at me, an undecipherable expression on his face, and began clambering down the bank. I followed him more leisurely. The current, I noticed, had torn away much of the clothing from the body, so that the neck and part of the chest lay bare.

Half-way down the bank my companion suddenly stopped and held up his hand in warning; but either my foot slipped, or I had gained too much momentum to bring myself quickly to a halt, for I bumped into him and sent him forward with a sort of leap to save himself. We tumbled together on to the hard sand so that our feet splashed into the water. And, before anything could be done, we had collided a little heavily against the corpse.

The Swede uttered a sharp cry. And I sprang back as if I had been shot.

At the moment we touched the body there rose from its surface the loud sound of humming—the sound of several hummings—which passed with a vast commotion as of winged things in the air about us and disappeared upwards into the sky, growing fainter and fainter till they finally ceased in the distance. It was exactly as though we had disturbed some living yet invisible creatures at work.

My companion clutched me, and I think I clutched him, but before either of us had time properly to recover from the unexpected shock, we saw that a movement of the current was turning the corpse round so that it became released from the grip of the willow roots. A moment later it had turned completely over, the dead face uppermost, staring at the sky. It lay on the edge of the main stream. In another moment it would be swept away.

The Swede started to save it, shouting again something I did not catch about a "proper burial"—and then abruptly dropped upon his knees on the sand and covered his eyes with his hands. I was beside him in an instant.

I saw what he had seen.

For just as the body swung round to the current the face and the exposed chest turned full towards us, and showed plainly how the skin and flesh were indented with small hollows, beautifully formed, and exactly similar in shape and kind to the sand-funnels that we had found all over the island.

"Their mark!" I heard my companion mutter under his breath. "Their awful mark!"

And when I turned my eyes again from his ghastly face to the river, the current had done its work, and the body had been swept away into mid-stream and was already beyond our reach and almost out of sight, turning over and over on the waves like an otter.

HENRY JAMES

THE JOLLY CORNER

1.

"EVERY one asks me what I 'think' of everything," said Spencer Brydon; "and I make answer as I can—begging or dodging the question, putting them off with any nonsense. It wouldn't matter to any of them really," he went on, "for, even were it possible to meet in that stand-and-deliver way so silly a demand on so big a subject, my 'thoughts' would still be almost altogether about something that concerns only myself." He was talking to Miss Staverton, with whom for a couple of months now he had availed himself of every possible occasion to talk; this disposition and this resource, this comfort and support, as the situation in fact presented itself, having promptly enough taken the first place in the considerable array of rather unattenuated surprises attending his so strangely belated return to America. Everything was somehow a surprise; and that might be natural when one had so long and so consistently neglected everything, taken pains to give surprises so much margin for play. He had given them more than thirty years—thirty-three, to be exact; and they now seemed to him to have organised their performance quite on the scale of that licence. He had been twenty-three on leaving New York—he was fifty-six today: unless indeed he were to reckon as he had sometimes, since his repatriation, found himself feeling; in which case he would have lived longer than is often allotted to man. It would have taken a century, he repeatedly said to himself, and said also to Alice Staverton, it would have taken a longer absence and a more averted mind than those even of which he had been guilty, to pile up the differences, the newnesses, the queernesses, above all the bignesses, for the better or the worse, that at present assaulted his vision wherever he looked.

The great fact all the while however had been the incalculability; since he *had* supposed himself, from decade to decade, to be allowing, and in the most liberal and intelligent manner, for brilliancy of change. He actually saw that he had allowed for nothing; he missed what he would have been sure of finding, he found what he would never have imagined. Proportions and values were upside-down; the ugly things he had expected, the ugly things of his far-away youth, when he had too promptly waked up to a sense of the ugly—these uncanny phenomena placed him rather, as it happened, under the charm; whereas the "swagger" things, the modern, the monstrous, the famous things, those he had more particularly, like thousands of ingenuous enquirers every year, come over to see, were exactly his sources of dismay. They were as so many set traps for displeasure, above all for reaction, of which his restless tread was constantly pressing the spring. It was interesting, doubtless, the whole show, but it would have been too disconcerting hadn't a certain finer truth saved the situation. He had distinctly not, in this steadier light, come over *all* for the monstrosities; he had come, not only in the last analysis but quite on the face of the act, under an impulse with which they had nothing to do. He had come—putting the thing pompously—to look at his "property," which he had thus for a third of a century not been within four thousand miles of; or, expressing it less sordidly, he had yielded to the humour of seeing again his house on the jolly corner, as he usually, and quite fondly, described it—the one in which he had first seen the light, in which various members of his family had lived and had died, in which the holidays of his over-schooled boyhood had been passed and the few social flowers of his chilled adolescence gathered, and which, alienated then for so long a period, had, through the successive deaths of his two brothers and the termination of old arrangements, come wholly into his hands. He was the owner of another, not quite so "good"—the jolly corner having been, from far back, superlatively extended and consecrated; and the value of the pair represented his main capital, with an income consisting, in these later years, of their respective rents which (thanks precisely to their original excellent type) had never been depressingly low. He could live in "Europe," as he had been in the habit of living, on the product of these flourishing New York leases, and all the better since, that of the second structure, the mere number in its long row, having within a twelvemonth fallen in, renovation at a high advance had proved beautifully possible.

These were items of property indeed, but he had found himself since his arrival distinguishing more than ever between them. The house within the street, two bristling blocks westward, was already in course of reconstruction as a tall mass of flats; he had acceded, some time before, to overtures for this conversion—in which, now that it was going forward, it had been not the least of his astonishments to find himself able, on the spot, and though without a previous ounce of such experience, to participate with a certain intelligence, almost with a certain authority. He had lived his life with his back so turned to such concerns and his face addressed to those of so different an order that he scarce knew what to make of this lively stir, in a compartment of his mind never yet penetrated, of a capacity for business and a sense for construction. These virtues, so common all round him now, had been dormant in his own organism—where it might be said of them perhaps that they had slept the sleep of the just. At present, in the splendid autumn weather—the autumn at least was a pure boon in the terrible place—he loafed about his "work" undeterred, secretly agitated; not in the least "minding" that the whole proposition, as they said, was vulgar and sordid, and ready to climb ladders, to walk the plank, to handle materials and look wise about them, to ask questions, in fine, and challenge explanations and really "go into" figures.

It amused, it verily quite charmed him; and, by the same stroke, it amused, and even more, Alice Staverton, though perhaps charming her perceptibly less. She wasn't however going to be better off for it, as *he* was—and so astonishingly much: nothing was now likely, he knew, ever to make her better off than she found herself, in the afternoon of life, as the delicately frugal possessor and tenant of the small house in Irving Place to which she had subtly managed to cling through her almost unbroken New York career. If he knew the way to it now better than to any other address among the dreadful multiplied numberings which seemed to him to reduce the whole place to some vast ledger-page, overgrown, fantastic, of ruled and criss-crossed lines and figures—if he had formed, for his consolation, that habit, it was really not a little because of the charm of his having encountered and recognised, in the vast wilderness of the wholesale, breaking through the mere gross generalisation of wealth and force and success, a small still scene where items and shades, all delicate things, kept the sharpness of the notes of a high voice perfectly trained, and where economy hung about like the scent of a garden. His old friend lived with one maid and herself dusted her relics and trimmed her lamps and polished her silver; she stood off, in the awful modern crush, when she could, but she sallied forth and did battle when the challenge was really to "spirit," the spirit she after all confessed to, proudly and a little shyly, as to that of the better time, that of *their* common, their quite far-away and antediluvian social period and order. She made use of the street-cars when need be, the terrible things that people scrambled for as the panic-stricken at sea scramble for the boats; she affronted, inscrutably, under stress, all the public concussions and ordeals; and yet, with that slim mystifying grace of her appearance, which defied you to say if she were a fair young woman who looked older through trouble, or a fine smooth older one who looked young through successful indifference; with her precious reference, above all, to memories and histories into which he could enter, she was as exquisite for him as some pale pressed flower (a rarity to begin with), and, failing other sweetnesses, she was a sufficient reward of his effort. They had communities of knowledge, "their" knowledge (this discriminating possessive was always on her lips) of presences of the other age, presences all over laid, in his case, by the experience of a man and the freedom of a wanderer, overlaid by pleasure, by infidelity, by passages of life that were strange and dim to her, just by "Europe" in short, but still unobscured, still exposed and cherished, under that pious visitation of the spirit from which she had never been diverted.

She had come with him one day to see how his "apartment-house" was rising; he had helped her over gaps and explained to her plans, and while they were there had happened to have, before her, a brief but lively discussion with the man in charge, the representative of the building-firm that had undertaken his work. He had found himself quite "standing-up" to this personage over a failure on the latter's part to observe some detail of one of their noted conditions, and had so lucidly urged his case that, besides ever so prettily flushing, at the time, for sympathy in his triumph, she had afterwards said to him (though to a slightly greater effect of irony) that he had clearly for too many years neglected a real gift. If he had but stayed at home he would have anticipated the inventor of the sky-scraper. If he had but stayed at home he would have discovered his genius in time really to start some new variety of awful architectural hare and run it till it burrowed in a gold-mine. He was to remember these words, while the weeks elapsed, for the small silver ring they had sounded over the queerest and deepest of his own lately most disguised and most muffled vibrations.

It had begun to be present to him after the first fortnight, it had broken out with the oddest abruptness, this particular wanton wonderment: it met him there—and this was the image under which he himself judged the matter, or at least, not a little, thrilled and flushed with it—very much as he might have been met by some strange figure, some unexpected occupant, at a turn of one of the dim passages of an empty house. The quaint analogy quite hauntingly remained with him, when he didn't indeed rather improve it by a still intenser form: that of his opening a door behind which he would have made sure of finding nothing, a door into a room shuttered and void, and yet so coming, with a great suppressed start, on some quite erect confronting presence, something planted in the middle of the place and facing him through the dusk. After that visit to the house in construction he walked with his companion to see the other and always so much the better one, which in the eastward direction formed one of the corners, the "jolly" one precisely, of the street now so generally dishonoured and disfigured in its westward reaches, and of the comparatively conservative Avenue. The Avenue still had pretensions, as Miss Staverton said, to decency; the old people had mostly gone, the old names were unknown, and here and there an old association seemed to stray, all vaguely, like some very aged person, out too late, whom you might meet and feel the impulse to watch or follow, in kindness, for safe restoration to shelter.

They went in together, our friends; he admitted himself with his key, as he kept no one there, he explained, preferring, for his reasons, to leave the place empty, under a simple arrangement with a good woman living in the neighbourhood and who came for a daily hour to open windows and dust and sweep. Spencer Brydon had his reasons and was growingly aware of them; they seemed to him better each time he was there, though he didn't name them all to his companion, any more than he told her as yet how often, how quite absurdly often, he himself came. He only let her see for the present, while they walked through the great blank rooms, that absolute vacancy reigned and that, from top to bottom, there was nothing but Mrs. Muldoon's broomstick, in a corner, to tempt the burglar. Mrs. Muldoon was then on the premises, and she loquaciously attended the visitors, preceding them from room to room and pushing back shutters and throwing up sashes—all to show them, as she remarked, how little there was to see. There was little indeed to see in the great gaunt shell where the main dispositions and the general apportionment of space, the style of an age of ampler allowances, had nevertheless for its master their honest pleading message, affecting him as some good old servant's, some lifelong retainer's appeal for a character, or even for a retiring-pension; yet it was also a remark of Mrs. Muldoon's that, glad as she was to oblige him by her noonday round, there was a request she greatly hoped he would never make of her. If he should wish her for any reason to come in after dark she would just tell him, if he "plased," that he must ask it of somebody else.

The fact that there was nothing to see didn't militate for the worthy woman against what one *might* see, and she put it frankly to Miss Staverton that no lady could be expected to like, could she? "craping up to thim top storeys in the ayvil hours." The gas and the electric light were off the house, and she fairly evoked a gruesome vision of her march through the great grey rooms—so many of them as there were too!—with her glimmering taper. Miss Staverton met her honest glare with a smile and the profession that she herself certainly would recoil from such an adventure. Spencer Brydon meanwhile held his peace—for the moment; the question of the "evil" hours in his old home had already become too grave for him. He had begun some time since to "crape," and he knew just why a packet of candles addressed to that pursuit had been stowed by his own hand, three weeks before, at the back of a drawer of the fine old sideboard that occupied, as a "fixture," the deep recess in the dining-room. Just now he laughed at his companions—quickly however changing the subject; for the reason that, in the first place, his laugh struck him even at that moment as starting the odd echo, the conscious human resonance (he scarce knew how to qualify it) that sounds made while he was there alone sent back to his ear or his fancy; and that, in the second, he imagined Alice Staverton for the instant on the point of asking him, with a divination, if he ever so prowled. There were divinations, he was unprepared for, and he had at all events averted enquiry by the time Mrs. Muldoon had left them, passing on to other parts.

There was happily enough to say, on so consecrated a spot, that could be said freely and fairly; so that a whole train of declarations was precipitated by his friend's having herself broken out, after a yearning look round: "But I hope you don't mean they want you to pull *this* to pieces!" His answer came, promptly, with his re-awakened wrath: it was of course exactly what they wanted, and what they were "at" him for, daily, with the iteration of people who couldn't for their life understand a man's liability to decent feelings. He had found the place, just as it stood and beyond what he could express, an interest and a joy. There were values other than the beastly rent-values, and in short, in short—! But it was thus Miss Staverton took him up. "In short you're to make so good a thing of your sky-scraper that, living in luxury on *those* ill-gotten gains, you can afford for a while to be sentimental here!" Her smile had for him, with the words, the particular mild irony with which he found half her talk suffused; an irony without bitterness and that came, exactly, from her having so much imagination—not, like the cheap sarcasms with which one heard most people, about the world of "society," bid for the reputation of cleverness, from nobody's really having any. It was agreeable to him at this very moment to be sure that when he had answered, after a brief demur,

"Well yes: so precisely, you may put it!" her imagination would still do him justice. He explained that even if never a dollar were to come to him from the other house he would nevertheless cherish this one; and he dwelt, further, while they lingered and wandered, on the fact of the stupefaction he was already exciting, the positive mystification he felt himself create.

He spoke of the value of all he read into it, into the mere sight of the walls, mere shapes of the rooms, mere sound of the floors, mere feel, in his hand, of the old silver-plated knobs of the several mahogany doors, which suggested the pressure of the palms of the dead; the seventy years of the past in fine that these things represented, the annals of nearly three generations, counting his grandfather's, the one that had ended there, and the impalpable ashes of his long-extinct youth, afloat in the very air like microscopic motes. She listened to everything; she was a woman who answered intimately but who utterly didn't chatter. She scattered abroad therefore no cloud of words; she could assent, she could agree, above all she could encourage, without doing that. Only at the last she went a little further than he had done himself. "And then how do you know? You may still, after all, want to live here." It rather indeed pulled him up, for it wasn't what he had been thinking, at least in her sense of the words. "You mean I may decide to stay on for the sake of it?"

"Well, *with* such a home—!" But, quite beautifully, she had too much tact to dot so monstrous an *i*, and it was precisely an illustration of the way she didn't rattle. How could any one—of any wit—insist on any one else's "wanting" to live in New York?

"Oh," he said, "I *might* have lived here (since I had my opportunity early in life); I might have put in here all these years. Then everything would have been different enough—and, I dare say, 'funny' enough. But that's another matter. And then the beauty of it—I mean of my perversity, of my refusal to agree to a 'deal'—is just in the total absence of a reason. Don't you see that if I had a reason about the matter at all it would *have* to be the other way, and would then be inevitably a reason of dollars? There are no reasons here *but* of dollars. Let us therefore have none whatever—not the ghost of one."

They were back in the hall then for departure, but from where they stood the vista was large, through an open door, into the great square main saloon, with its almost antique felicity of brave spaces between windows. Her eyes came back from that reach and met his own a moment. "Are you very sure the 'ghost' of one doesn't, much rather, serve—?"

He had a positive sense of turning pale. But it was as near as they were then to come. For he made answer, he believed, between a glare and a grin: "Oh ghosts—of course the place must swarm with them! I should be ashamed of it if it didn't. Poor Mrs. Muldoon's right, and it's why I haven't asked her to do more than look in."

Miss Staverton's gaze again lost itself, and things she didn't utter, it was clear, came and went in her mind. She might even for the minute, off there in the fine room, have imagined some element dimly gathering. Simplified like the death-mask of a handsome face, it perhaps produced for her just then an effect akin to the stir of an expression in the "set" commemorative plaster. Yet whatever her impression may have been she produced instead a vague platitude. "Well, if it were only furnished and lived in—!"

She appeared to imply that in case of its being still furnished he might have been a little less opposed to the idea of a return. But she passed straight into the vestibule, as if to leave her words behind her, and the next moment he had opened the house-door and was standing with her on the steps. He closed the door and, while he re-pocketed his key, looking up and down, they took in the comparatively harsh actuality of the Avenue, which reminded him of the assault of the outer light of the Desert on the traveller emerging from an Egyptian tomb. But he risked before they stepped into the street his gathered answer to her speech. "For me it *is* lived in. For me it *is* furnished." At which it was easy for her to sigh "Ah yes—!" all vaguely and discreetly; since his parents and his favourite sister, to say nothing of other kin, in numbers, had run their course and met their end there. That represented, within the walls, ineffaceable life.

It was a few days after this that, during an hour passed with her again, he had expressed his impatience of the too flattering curiosity—among the people he met—about his appreciation of New York. He had arrived at none at all that was socially producible, and as for that matter of his "thinking" (thinking the better or the worse of anything there) he was wholly taken up with one subject of thought. It was mere vain egoism, and it was moreover, if she liked, a morbid obsession. He found all things come back to the question of what he personally might have been, how he might have led his life and "turned out," if he had not so, at the outset, given it up. And confessing for the first time to the intensity within him of this absurd speculation—which but proved also, no doubt, the habit of too selfishly thinking—he affirmed the impotence there of any other source of interest, any other native appeal. "What would it have made of me, what would it have made of me? I keep for ever wondering, all idiotically; as if I could possibly know! I see what it has made of dozens of others, those I meet, and it positively aches within me, to the point of exasperation, that it would have made something of me as well. Only I can't make out *what*, and the worry of it, the small rage of curiosity never to be satisfied, brings back what I remember to have felt, once or twice, after judging best, for reasons, to burn some important letter unopened. I've been sorry, I've hated it—I've never known what was in the letter. You may of course say it's a trifle—!"

"I don't say it's a trifle," Miss Staverton gravely interrupted.

She was seated by her fire, and before her, on his feet and restless, he turned to and fro between this intensity of his idea and a fitful and unseeing inspection, through his single eye-glass, of the dear little old objects on her chimney-piece. Her interruption made him for an instant look at her harder. "I shouldn't care if you did!" he laughed, however; "and it's only a figure, at any rate, for the way I now feel. *Not* to have followed my perverse young course—and almost in the teeth of my father's curse, as I may say; not to have kept it up, so, 'over there,' from that day to this, without a doubt or a pang; not, above all, to have liked it, to have loved it, so much, loved it, no doubt, with such an abysmal conceit of my own preference: some variation from *that*, I say, must have produced some different effect for my life and for my 'form.' I should have stuck here—if it had been possible; and I was too young, at twenty-three, to judge, *pour deux sous*, whether it *were* possible. If I had waited I might have seen it was, and then I might have been, by staying here, something nearer to one of these types who have been hammered so hard and made so keen by their conditions. It isn't that I admire them so much—the question of any charm in them, or of any charm, beyond that of the rank money-passion, exerted by their conditions *for* them, has nothing to do with the matter: it's only a question of what fantastic, yet perfectly possible, development of my own nature I mayn't have missed. It comes over me that I had then a strange *alter ego* deep down somewhere within me, as the full-blown flower is in the small tight bud, and that I just took the course, I just transferred him to the climate, that blighted him for once and for ever."

"And you wonder about the flower," Miss Staverton said. "So do I, if you want to know; and so I've been wondering these several weeks. I believe in the flower," she continued, "I feel it would have been quite splendid, quite huge and monstrous."

"Monstrous above all!" her visitor echoed; "and I imagine, by the same stroke, quite hideous and offensive."

"You don't believe that," she returned; "if you did you wouldn't wonder. You'd know, and that would be enough for you. What you feel—and what I feel *for* you—is that you'd have had power."

"You'd have liked me that way?" he asked.

She barely hung fire. "How should I not have liked you?"

"I see. You'd have liked me, have preferred me, a billionaire!"

"How should I not have liked you?" she simply again asked.

He stood before her still—her question kept him motionless. He took it in, so much there was of it; and indeed his not otherwise meeting it testified to that. "I know at least what I am," he simply went on; "the other side of the medal's clear enough. I've not been edifying—I believe I'm thought in a hundred quarters to have been barely decent. I've followed strange paths and worshipped strange gods; it must have come to you again and again—in fact you've admitted to me as much—that I was leading, at any time these thirty years, a selfish frivolous scandalous life. And you see what it has made of me."

She just waited, smiling at him. "You see what it has made of *me*."

"Oh you're a person whom nothing can have altered. You were born to be what you are, anywhere, anyway: you've the perfection nothing else could have blighted. And don't you see how, without my exile, I shouldn't have been waiting till now—?" But he pulled up for the strange pang.

"The great thing to see," she presently said, "seems to me to be that it has spoiled nothing. It hasn't spoiled your being here at last. It hasn't spoiled this. It hasn't spoiled your speaking—" She also however faltered.

He wondered at everything her controlled emotion might

mean. "Do you believe then—too dreadfully!—that I *am* as good as I might ever have been?"

"Oh no! Far from it!" With which she got up from her chair and was nearer to him. "But I don't care," she smiled.

"You mean I'm good enough?"

She considered a little. "Will you believe it if I say so? I mean will you let that settle your question for you?" And then as if making out in his face that he drew back from this, that he had some idea which, however absurd, he couldn't yet bargain away: "Oh you don't care either—but very differently: you don't care for anything but yourself."

Spencer Brydon recognised it—it was in fact what he had absolutely professed. Yet he importantly qualified. "*He* isn't myself. He's the just so totally other person. But I do want to see him," he added. "And I can. And I shall."

Their eyes met for a minute while he guessed from something in hers that she divined his strange sense. But neither of them otherwise expressed it, and her apparent understanding, with no protesting shock, no easy derision, touched him more deeply than anything yet, constituting for his stifled perversity, on the spot, an element that was like breathable air. What she said however was unexpected. "Well, *I've* seen him."

"You—?"

"I've seen him in a dream."

"Oh a 'dream'—!" It let him down.

"But twice over," she continued. "I saw him as I see you now."

"You've dreamed the same dream—?"

"Twice over," she repeated. "The very same."

This did somehow a little speak to him, as it also gratified him. "You dream about me at that rate?"

"Ah about *him*!" she smiled.

His eyes again sounded her. "Then you know all about him." And as she said nothing more: "What's the wretch like?"

She hesitated, and it was as if he were pressing her so hard that, resisting for reasons of her own, she had to turn away. "I'll tell you some other time!"

2.

It was after this that there was most of a virtue for him, most of a cultivated charm, most of a preposterous secret thrill, in the particular form of surrender to his obsession and of address to what he more and more believed to be his privilege. It was what in these weeks he was living for—since he really felt life to begin but after Mrs. Muldoon had retired from the scene and, visiting the ample house from attic to cellar, making sure he was alone, he knew himself in safe possession and, as he tacitly expressed it, let himself go. He sometimes came twice in the twenty-four hours; the moments he liked best were those of gathering dusk, of the short autumn twilight; this was the time of which, again and again, he found himself hoping most. Then he could, as seemed to him, most intimately wander and wait, linger and listen, feel his fine attention, never in his life before so fine, on the pulse of the great vague place: he preferred the lampless hour and only wished he might have prolonged each day the deep crepuscular spell. Later—rarely much before midnight, but then for a considerable vigil—he watched with his glimmering light; moving slowly, holding it high, playing it far, rejoicing above all, as much as he might, in open vistas, reaches of communication between rooms and by passages; the long straight chance or show, as he would have called it, for the revelation he pretended to invite. It was practice he found he could perfectly "work" without exciting remark; no one was in the least the wiser for it; even Alice Staverton, who was moreover a well of discretion, didn't quite fully imagine.

He let himself in and let himself out with the assurance of calm proprietorship; and accident so far favoured him that, if a fat Avenue "officer" had happened on occasion to see him entering at eleven-thirty, he had never yet, to the best of his belief, been noticed as emerging at two. He walked there on the crisp November nights, arrived regularly at the evening's end; it was as easy to do this after dining out as to take his way to a club or to his hotel. When he left his club, if he hadn't been dining out, it was ostensibly to go to his hotel; and when he left his hotel, if he had spent a part of the evening there, it was ostensibly to go to his club. Everything was easy in fine; everything conspired and promoted: there was truly even in the strain of his experience something that glossed over, something that salved and simplified, all the rest of consciousness. He circulated, talked, renewed, loosely and pleasantly, old relations—met indeed, so far as he could, new expectations and seemed to make out on the whole that in spite of the career, of such different contacts, which he had spoken of to Miss Staverton as ministering so little, for those who might have watched it, to edification, he was positively rather liked than not. He was a dim secondary social success—and all with people who had truly not an idea of him. It was all mere surface sound, this murmur of their welcome, this popping of their corks—just as his gestures of response were the extravagant shadows, emphatic in proportion as they meant little, of some game of *ombres chinoises*. He projected himself all day, in thought, straight over the bristling line of hard unconscious heads and into the other, the real, the waiting life; the life that, as soon as he had heard behind him the click of his great house-door, began for him, on the jolly corner, as beguilingly as the slow opening bars of some rich music follows the tap of the conductor's wand.

He always caught the first effect of the steel point of his stick on the old marble of the hall pavement, large black-and-white squares that he remembered as the admiration of his childhood and that had then made in him, as he now saw, for the growth of an early conception of style. This effect was the dim reverberating tinkle as of some far-off bell hung who should say where?—in the depths of the house, of the past, of that mystical other world that might have flourished for him had he not, for weal or woe, abandoned it. On this impression he did ever the same thing; he put his stick noiselessly away in a corner—feeling the place once more in the likeness of some great glass bowl, all precious concave crystal, set delicately humming by the play of a moist finger round its edge. The concave crystal held, as it were, this mystical other world, and the indescribably fine murmur of its rim was the sigh there, the scarce audible pathetic wail to his strained ear, of all the old baffled forsworn possibilities. What he did therefore by this appeal of his hushed presence was to wake them into such measure of ghostly life as they might still enjoy. They were shy, all but unappeasably shy, but they weren't really sinister; at least they weren't as he had hitherto felt them—before they had taken the Form he so yearned to make them take, the Form he at moments saw himself in the light of fairly hunting on tiptoe, the points of his evening-shoes, from room to room and from storey to storey.

That was the essence of his vision—which was all rank folly, if one would, while he was out of the house and otherwise occupied, but which took on the last verisimilitude as soon as he was placed and posted. He knew what he meant and what he wanted; it was as clear as the figure on a cheque presented in demand for cash. His *alter ego* "walked"—that was the note of his image of him, while his image of his motive for his own odd pastime was the desire to waylay him and meet him. He roamed, slowly, warily, but all restlessly, he himself did—Mrs. Muldoon had been right, absolutely, with her figure of their "craping"; and the presence he watched for would roam restlessly too. But it would be as cautious and as shifty; the conviction of its probable, in fact its already quite sensible, quite audible evasion of pursuit grew for him from night to night, laying on him finally a rigour to which nothing in his life had been comparable. It had been the theory of many superficially-judging persons, he knew, that he was wasting that life in a surrender to sensations, but he had tasted of no pleasure so fine as his actual tension, had been introduced to no sport that demanded at once the patience and the nerve of this stalking of a creature more subtle, yet at bay perhaps more formidable, than any beast of the forest. The terms, the comparisons, the very practices of the chase positively came again into play; there were even moments when passages of his occasional experience as a sportsman, stirred memories, from his younger time, of moor and mountain and desert, revived for him—and to the increase of his keenness—by the tremendous force of analogy. He found himself at moments—once he had placed his single light on some mantel-shelf or in some recess—stepping back into shelter or shade, effacing himself behind a door or in an embrasure, as he had sought of old the vantage of rock and tree; he found himself holding his breath and living in the joy of the instant, the supreme suspense created by big game alone.

He wasn't afraid (though putting himself the question as he believed gentlemen on Bengal tiger-shoots or in close quarters with the great bear of the Rockies had been known to confess to having put it); and this indeed—since here at least he might be frank!—because of the impression, so intimate and so strange, that he himself produced as yet a dread, produced certainly a strain, beyond the liveliest he was likely to feel. They fell for him into categories, they fairly became familiar, the signs, for his own perception, of the alarm his presence and his vigilance created; though leaving him always to remark, portentously, on his probably having formed a relation, his probably enjoying a consciousness, unique in the experience of man. People enough, first and last, had been in terror of apparitions, but who had ever before so turned the tables and become himself, in the apparitional world, an incalculable terror? He might have found this sublime had he quite dared to think of it; but he didn't too much insist, truly, on that side of his privilege. With habit and repetition he gained to an extraordinary degree the power to penetrate the dusk of distances and the darkness of corners, to resolve back into their innocence the treacheries of uncertain light, the evil-looking forms taken in the gloom by mere shadows, by accidents of the air, by shifting effects of perspective; putting down his dim luminary he could still wander on without it, pass into other rooms and, only knowing it was there behind him in case of need, see his way about, visually project for his purpose a comparative clearness. It made him feel, this acquired faculty, like some monstrous stealthy cat; he wondered if he would have glared at these moments with large shining yellow eyes, and what it mightn't verily be, for the poor hard-pressed *alter ego*, to be confronted with such a type.

He liked however the open shutters; he opened everywhere those Mrs. Muldoon had closed, closing them as carefully afterwards, so that she shouldn't notice: he liked—oh this he did like, and above all in the upper rooms!—the sense of the hard silver of the autumn stars through the window-panes, and scarcely less the flare of the street-lamps below, the white electric lustre which it would have taken curtains to keep out. This was human actual social; this was of the world he had lived in, and he was more at his ease certainly for the countenance, coldly general and impersonal, that all the while and in spite of his detachment it seemed to give him. He had support of course mostly in the rooms at the wide front and the prolonged side; it failed him considerably in the central shades and the parts at the back. But if he sometimes, on his rounds, was glad of his optical reach, so none the less often the rear of the house affected him as the very jungle of his prey. The place was there more subdivided; a large "extension" in particular, where small rooms for servants had been multiplied, abounded in nooks and corners, in closets and passages, in the ramifications especially of an ample back staircase over which he leaned, many a time, to look far down—not deterred from his gravity even while aware that he might, for a spectator, have figured some solemn simpleton playing at hide-and-seek. Outside in fact he might himself make that ironic *rapprochement*; but within the walls, and in spite of the clear windows, his consistency was proof against the cynical light of New York.

It had belonged to that idea of the exasperated consciousness of his victim to become a real test for him; since he had quite put it to himself from the first that, oh distinctly! he could "cultivate" his whole perception. He had felt it as above all open to cultivation—which indeed was but another name for his manner of spending his time. He was bringing it on, bringing it to perfection, by practice; in consequence of which it had grown so fine that he was now aware of impressions, attestations of his general postulate, that couldn't have broken upon him at once. This was the case more specifically with a phenomenon at last quite frequent for him in the upper rooms, the recognition—absolutely unmistakeable, and by a turn dating from a particular hour, his resumption of his campaign after a diplomatic drop, a calculated absence of three nights—of his being definitely followed, tracked at a distance carefully taken and to the express end that he should the less confidently, less arrogantly, appear to himself merely to pursue. It worried, it finally quite broke him up, for it proved, of all the conceivable impressions, the one least suited to his book. He was kept in sight while remaining himself—as regards the essence of his position—sightless, and his only recourse then was in abrupt turns, rapid recoveries of ground. He wheeled about, retracing his steps, as if he might so catch in his face at least the stirred air of some other quick revolution. It was indeed true that his fully dislocalised thought of these manœuvres recalled to him Pantaloon, at the Christmas farce, buffeted and tricked from behind by ubiquitous Harlequin; but it left intact the influence of the conditions themselves each time he was re-exposed to them, so that in fact this association, had he suffered it to become constant, would on a certain side have but ministered to his intenser gravity. He had made, as I have said, to create on the premises the baseless sense of a reprieve, his three absences; and the result of the third was to confirm the after-effect of the second.

On his return, that night—the night succeeding his last intermission—he stood in the hall and looked up the staircase with a certainty more intimate than any he had yet known. "He's *there*, at the top, and waiting—not, as in general, falling back for disappearance. He's holding his ground, and it's the first time—which is a proof, isn't it? that something has happened for him." So Brydon argued with his hand on the banister and his foot on the lowest stair; in which position he felt as never before the air chilled by his logic. He himself turned cold in it, for he seemed of a sudden to know what now was involved. "Harder pressed?—yes, he takes it in, with its thus making clear to him that I've come, as they say, 'to stay.' He finally doesn't like and can't bear it, in the sense, I mean, that his wrath, his menaced interest, now balances with his dread. I've hunted him till he has 'turned': that, up there, is what has happened—he's the fanged or the antlered animal brought at last to bay." There came to him, as I say—but determined by an influence beyond my notation!—the acuteness of this certainty; under which however the next moment he had broken into a sweat that he would as little have consented to attribute to fear as he would have dared immediately to act upon it for enterprise. It marked none the less a prodigious thrill, a thrill that represented sudden dismay, no doubt, but also represented, and with the self-same throb, the strangest, the most joyous, possibly the next minute almost the proudest, duplication of consciousness.

"He has been dodging, retreating, hiding, but now, worked up to anger, he'll fight!"—this intense impression made a single mouthful, as it were, of terror and applause. But what was wondrous was that the applause, for the felt fact, was so eager, since, if it was his other self he was running to earth, this ineffable identity was thus in the last resort not unworthy of him. It bristled there—somewhere near at hand, however unseen still—as the hunted thing, even as the trodden worm of the adage *must* at last bristle; and Brydon at this instant tasted probably of a sensation more complex than had ever before found itself consistent with sanity. It was as if it would have shamed him that a character so associated with his own should triumphantly succeed in just skulking, should to the end not risk the open, so that the drop of this danger was, on the spot, a great lift of the whole situation. Yet with another rare shift of the same subtlety he was already trying to measure by how much more he himself might now be in peril of fear; so rejoicing that he could, in another form, actively inspire that fear, and simultaneously quaking for the form in which he might passively know it.

The apprehension of knowing it must after a little have grown in him, and the strangest moment of his adventure perhaps, the most memorable or really most interesting, afterwards, of his crisis, was the lapse of certain instants of concentrated conscious *combat*, the sense of a need to hold on to something, even after the manner of a man slipping and slipping on some awful incline; the vivid impulse, above all, to move, to act, to charge, somehow and upon something—to show himself, in a word, that he wasn't afraid. The state of "holding-on" was thus the state to which he was momentarily reduced; if there had been anything, in the great vacancy, to seize, he would presently have been aware of having clutched it as he might under a shock at home have clutched the nearest chair-back. He had been surprised at any rate—of this he *was* aware—into something unprecedented since his original appropriation of the place; he had closed his eyes, held them tight, for a long minute, as with that instinct of dismay and that terror of vision. When he opened them the room, the other contiguous rooms, extraordinarily, seemed lighter—so light, almost, that at first he took the change for day. He stood firm, however that might be, just where he had paused; his resistance had helped him—it was as if there were something he had tided over. He knew after a little what this was—it had been in the imminent danger of flight. He had stiffened his will against going; without this he would have made for the stairs, and it seemed to him that, still with his eyes closed, he would have descended them, would have known how, straight and swiftly, to the bottom.

Well, as he had held out, here he was—still at the top, among the more intricate upper rooms and with the gauntlet of the others, of all the rest of the house, still to run when it should be his time to go. He would go at his time—only at his time: didn't he go every night very much at the same hour? He took out his watch—there was light for that: it was scarcely a quarter past one, and he had never withdrawn so soon. He reached his lodgings for the most part at two—with his walk of a quarter of an hour. He would wait for the last quarter—he wouldn't stir till then; and he kept his watch there with his eyes on it, reflecting while he held it that this deliberate wait, a wait with an effort, which he recognised, would serve perfectly for the attestation he desired to make. It would prove his courage—unless indeed the latter might most be proved by his budging at last from his place. What he mainly felt now was that, since he hadn't originally scuttled, he had his dignities—which had never in his life seemed so many—all to preserve and to carry aloft. This was before him in truth as a physical image, an image almost worthy of an age of greater romance. That remark indeed glimmered for him only to glow the next instant with a finer light; since what age of romance, after all, could have matched either the state of his mind or, "objectively," as they said, the wonder of his situation? The only difference would have been that, brandishing his dignities over his head as in a parchment scroll, he might then—that is in the heroic time—have proceeded downstairs with a drawn sword in his other grasp.

At present, really, the light he had set down on the mantel of the next room would have to figure his sword; which utensil, in the course of a minute, he had taken the requisite number of steps to possess himself of. The door between the rooms was open, and from the second another door opened to a third. These rooms, as he remembered, gave all three upon a common corridor as well, but there was a fourth, beyond them, without issue save through the preceding. To have moved, to have heard his step again, was appreciably a help; though even in recognising this he lingered once more a little by the chimney-piece on which his light had rested. When he next moved, just hesitating where to turn, he found himself considering a circumstance that, after his first and comparatively vague apprehension of it, produced in him the start that often attends some pang of recollection, the violent shock of having ceased happily to forget. He had come into sight of the door in which the brief chain of communication ended and which he now surveyed from the nearer threshold, the one not directly facing it. Placed at some distance to the left of this point, it would have admitted him to the last room of the four, the room without other approach or egress, had it not, to his intimate conviction, been closed *since* his former visitation, the matter probably of a quarter of an hour before. He stared with all his eyes at the wonder of the fact, arrested again where he stood and again holding his breath while he sounded its sense. Surely it had been *subsequently* closed—that is it had been on his previous passage indubitably open!

He took it full in the face that something had happened between—that he couldn't not have noticed before (by which he meant on his original tour of all the rooms that evening) that such a barrier had exceptionally presented itself. He had indeed since that moment undergone an agitation so extraordinary that it might have muddled for him any earlier view; and he tried to convince himself that he might perhaps then have gone into the room and, inadvertently, automatically, on coming out, have drawn the door after him. The difficulty was that this exactly was what he never did; it was against his whole policy, as he might have said, the essence of which was to keep vistas clear. He had them from the first, as he was well aware, quite on the brain: the strange apparition, at the far end of one of them, of his baffled "prey" (which had become by so sharp an irony so little the term now to apply!) was the form of success his imagination had most cherished, projecting into it always a refinement of beauty. He had known fifty times the start of perception that had afterwards dropped; had fifty times gasped to himself "There!" under some fond brief hallucination. The house, as the case stood, admirably lent itself; he might wonder at the taste, the native architecture of the particular time, which could rejoice so in the multiplication of doors—the opposite extreme to the modern, the actual almost complete proscription of them; but it had fairly contributed to provoke this obsession of the presence encountered telescopically, as he might say, focussed and studied in diminishing perspective and as by a rest for the elbow.

It was with these considerations that his present attention was charged—they perfectly availed to make what he saw portentous. He *couldn't,* by any lapse, have blocked that aperture; and if he hadn't, if it was unthinkable, why what else was clear but that there had been another agent? Another agent?—he had been catching, as he felt, a moment back, the very breath of him; but when had he been so close as in this simple, this logical, this completely personal act? It was so logical, that is, that one might have *taken* it for personal; yet for what did Brydon take it, he asked himself, while, softly panting, he felt his eyes almost leave their sockets. Ah this time at last they *were,* the two, the opposed projections of him, in presence; and this time, as much as one would, the question of danger loomed. With it rose, as not before, the question of courage—for what he knew the blank face of the door to say to him was "Show us how much you have!" It stared, it glared back at him with that challenge; it put to him the two alternatives: should he just push it open or not? Oh to have this consciousness was to *think*—and to think, Brydon knew, as he stood there, was, with the lapsing moments, not to have acted! Not to have acted—that was the misery and the pang—was even still not to act; was in fact *all* to feel the thing in another, in a new and terrible way. How long did he pause and how long did he debate? There was presently nothing to measure it; for his vibration had already changed—as just by the effect of its intensity. Shut up there, at bay, defiant, and with the prodigy of the thing palpably proveably *done*, thus giving notice like some stark signboard—under that accession of accent the situation itself had turned; and Brydon at last remarkably made up his mind on what it had turned to.

It had turned altogether to a different admonition; to a supreme hint, for him, of the value of Discretion! This slowly dawned, no doubt—for it could take its time; so perfectly, on his threshold, had he been stayed, so little as yet had he either advanced or retreated. It was the strangest of all things that now when, by his taking ten steps and applying his hand to a latch, or even his shoulder and his knee, if necessary, to a panel, all the hunger of his prime need might have been met, his high curiosity crowned, his unrest assuaged—it was amazing, but it was also exquisite and rare, that insistence should have, at a touch, quite dropped from him. Discretion—he jumped at that; and yet not, verily, at such a pitch, because it saved his nerves or his skin, but because, much more valuably, it saved the situation. When I say he "jumped" at it I feel the consonance of this term with the fact that—at the end indeed of I know not how long—he did move again, he crossed straight to the door. He wouldn't touch it—it seemed now that he might *if* he would: he would only just wait there a little, to show, to prove, that he wouldn't. He had thus another station, close to the thin partition by which revelation was denied him; but with his eyes bent and his hands held off in a mere intensity of stillness. He listened as if there had been something to hear, but this attitude, while it lasted, was his own communication. "If you won't then—good: I spare you and I give up. You affect me as by the appeal positively for pity: you convince me that for reasons rigid and sublime—what do I know?—we both of us should have suffered. I respect them then, and, though moved and privileged as, I believe, it has never been given to man, I retire, I renounce—never, on my honour, to try again. So rest for ever—and let *me*!"

That, for Brydon was the deep sense of this last demonstration—solemn, measured, directed, as he felt it to be. He brought it to a close, he turned away; and now verily he knew how deeply he had been stirred. He retraced his steps, taking up his candle, burnt, he observed, well-nigh to the socket, and marking again, lighten it as he would, the distinctness of his footfall; after which, in a moment, he knew himself at the other side of the house. He did here what he had not yet done at these hours—he opened half a casement, one of those in the front, and let in the air of the night; a thing he would have taken at any time previous for a sharp rupture of his spell. His spell was broken now, and it didn't matter—broken by his concession and his surrender, which made it idle henceforth that he should ever come back. The empty street—its other life so marked even by the great lamplit vacancy—was within call, within touch; he stayed there as to be in it again, high above it though he was still perched; he watched as for some comforting common fact, some vulgar human note, the passage of a scavenger or a thief, some night-bird however base. He would have blessed that sign of life; he would have welcomed positively the slow approach of his friend the policeman, whom he had hitherto only sought to avoid, and was not sure that if the patrol had come into sight he mightn't have felt the impulse to get into relation with it, to hail it, on some pretext, from his fourth floor.

The pretext that wouldn't have been too silly or too compromising, the explanation that would have saved his dignity and kept his name, in such a case, out of the papers, was not definite to him: he was so occupied with the thought of recording his Discretion—as an effect of the vow he had just uttered to his intimate adversary—that the importance of this loomed large and something had overtaken all ironically his sense of proportion. If there had been a ladder applied to the front of the house, even one of the vertiginous perpendiculars employed by painters and roofers and sometimes left standing overnight, he would have managed somehow, astride of the window-sill, to compass by outstretched leg and arm that mode of descent. If there had been some such uncanny thing as he had found in his room at hotels, a workable fire-escape in the form of notched cable or a canvas shoot, he would have availed himself of it as a proof—well, of his present delicacy. He nursed that sentiment, as the question stood, a little in vain, and even—at the end of he scarce knew, once more, how long—found it, as by the action on his mind of the failure of response of the outer world, sinking back to vague anguish. It seemed to him he had waited an age for some stir of the great grim hush; the life of the town was itself under a spell—so unnaturally, up and down the whole prospect of known and rather ugly objects, the blankness and the silence lasted. Had they ever, he asked himself, the hard-faced houses, which had begun to look livid in the dim dawn, had they ever spoken so little to any need of his spirit? Great builded voids, great crowded stillnesses put on, often, in the heart of cities, for the small hours, a sort of sinister mask, and it was of this large collective negation that Brydon presently became conscious—all the more that the break of day was, almost incredibly, now at hand, proving to him what a night he had made of it.

He looked again at his watch, saw what had become of his time-values (he had taken hours for minutes—not, as in other tense situations, minutes for hours) and the strange air of the streets was but the weak, the sullen flush of a dawn in which everything was still locked up. His choked appeal from his own open window had been the sole note of life, and he could but break off at last as for a worse despair. Yet while so deeply demoralised he was capable again of an impulse denoting—at least by his present measure—extraordinary resolution; of retracing his steps to the spot where he had turned cold with the extinction of his last pulse of doubt as to there being in the place another presence than his own. This required an effort strong enough to sicken him; but he had his reason, which over-mastered for the moment everything else. There was the whole of the rest of the house to traverse, and how should he screw himself to that if the door he had seen closed were at present open? He could hold to the idea that the closing had practically been for him an act of mercy, a chance offered him to descend, depart, get off the ground and never again profane it. This conception held together, it worked; but what it meant for him depended now clearly on the amount of forbearance his recent action, or rather his recent inaction, had engendered. The image of the "presence," whatever it was, waiting there for him to go—this image had not yet been so concrete for his nerves as when he stopped short of the point at which certainty would have come to him. For, with all his resolution, or more exactly with all his dread, he did stop short—he hung back from really seeing. The risk was too great and his fear too definite: it took at this moment an awful specific form.

He knew—yes, as he had never known anything—that, *should* he see the door open, it would all too abjectly be the end of him. It would mean that the agent of his shame—for his shame was the deep abjection—was once more at large and in general possession; and what glared him thus in the face was the act that this would determine for him. It would send him straight about to the window he had left open, and by that window, be long ladder and dangling rope as absent as they would, he saw himself uncontrollably insanely fatally take his way to the street. The hideous chance of this he at least could avert; but he could only avert it by recoiling in time from assurance. He had the whole house to deal with, this fact was still there; only he now knew that uncertainty alone could start him. He stole back from where he had checked himself—merely to do so was suddenly like safety—and, making blindly for the greater staircase, left gaping rooms and sounding passages behind. Here was the top of the stairs, with a fine large dim descent and three spacious landings to mark off. His instinct was all for mildness, but his feet were harsh on the floors, and, strangely, when he had in a couple of minutes become aware of this, it counted somehow for help. He couldn't have spoken, the tone of his voice would have scared him, and the common conceit or resource of "whistling in the dark" (whether literally or figuratively) have appeared basely vulgar; yet he liked none the less to hear himself go, and when he had reached his first landing—taking it all with no rush, but quite steadily—that stage of success drew from him a gasp of relief.

The house, withal, seemed immense, the scale of space again inordinate; the open rooms to no one of which his eyes deflected, gloomed in their shuttered state like mouths of caverns; only the high skylight that formed the crown of the deep well created for him a medium in which he could advance, but which might have been, for queerness of colour, some watery under-world. He tried to think of something noble, as that his property was really grand, a splendid possession; but this nobleness took the form too of the clear delight with which he was finally to sacrifice it. They might come in now, the builders, the destroyers—they might come as soon as they would. At the end of two flights he had dropped to another zone, and from the middle of the third, with only one more left, he recognised the influence of the lower windows, of half-drawn blinds, of the occasional gleam of street-lamps, of the glazed spaces of the vestibule. This was the bottom of the sea, which showed an illumination of its own and which he even saw paved—when at a given moment he drew up to sink a long look over the banisters—with the marble squares of his childhood. By that time indubitably he felt, as he might have said in a commoner cause, better; it had allowed him to stop and draw breath, and the ease increased with the sight of the old black-and-white slabs. But what he most felt was that now surely, with the element of impunity pulling him as by hard firm hands, the case was settled for what he might have seen above had he dared that last look. The closed door, blessedly remote now, was still closed—and he had only in short to reach that of the house.

He came down further, he crossed the passage forming the access to the last flight; and if here again he stopped an instant it was almost for the sharpness of the thrill of assured escape. It made him shut his eyes—which opened again to the straight slope of the remainder of the stairs. Here was impunity still, but impunity almost excessive; inasmuch as the side-lights and the high fan-tracery of the entrance were glimmering straight into the hall; an appearance produced, he the next instant saw, by the fact that the vestibule gaped wide, that the hinged halves of the inner door had been thrown far back. Out of that again the *question* sprang at him, making his eyes, as he felt, half-start from his head, as they had done, at the top of the house, before the sign of the other door. If he had left that one open, hadn't he left this one closed, and wasn't he now in *most* immediate presence of some inconceivable occult activity? It was as sharp, the question, as a knife in his side, but the answer hung fire still and seemed to lose itself in the vague darkness to which the thin admitted dawn, glimmering archwise over the whole outer door, made a semicircular margin, a cold silvery nimbus that seemed to play a little as he looked—to shift and expand and contract.

It was as if there had been something within it, protected by indistinctness and corresponding in extent with the opaque surface behind, the painted panels of the last barrier to his escape, of which the key was in his pocket. The indistinctness mocked him even while he stared, affected him as somehow shrouding or challenging certitude, so that after faltering an instant on his step he let himself go with the sense that here *was* at last something to meet, to touch, to take, to know—something all unnatural and dreadful, but to advance upon which was the condition for him either of liberation or of supreme defeat. The penumbra, dense and dark, was the virtual screen of a figure which stood in it as still as some image erect in a niche or as some black-vizored sentinel guarding a treasure. Brydon was to know afterwards, was to recall and make out, the particular thing he had believed during the rest of his descent. He saw, in its great grey glimmering margin, the central vagueness diminish, and he felt it to be taking the very form toward which, for so many days, the passion of his curiosity had yearned. It gloomed, it loomed, it was something, it was somebody, the prodigy of a personal presence.

Rigid and conscious, spectral yet human, a man of his own substance and stature waited there to measure himself with his power to dismay. This only could it be—this only till he recognised, with his advance, that what made the face dim was the pair of raised hands that covered it and in which, so far from being offered in defiance, it was buried as for dark deprecation. So Brydon, before him, took him in; with every fact of him now, in the higher light, hard and acute—his planted stillness, his vivid truth, his grizzled bent head and white masking hands, his queer actuality of evening-dress, of dangling double eye-glass, of gleaming silk lappet and white linen, of pearl button and gold watch-guard and polished shoe. No portrait by a great modern master could have presented him with more intensity, thrust him out of his frame with more art, as if there had been "treatment," of the consummate sort, in his every shade and salience. The revulsion, for our friend, had become, before he knew it, immense—this drop, in the act of apprehension, to the sense of his adversary's inscrutable manœuvre. That meaning at least, while he gaped, it offered him; for he could but gape at his other self in this other anguish, gape as a proof that *he*, standing there for the achieved, the enjoyed, the triumphant life, couldn't be faced in his triumph. Wasn't the proof in the splendid covering hands, strong and completely spread?—so spread and so intentional that, in spite of a special verity that surpassed every other, the fact that one of these hands had lost two fingers, which were reduced to stumps, as if accidentally shot away, the face was effectually guarded and saved.

"Saved," though, *would* it be?—Brydon breathed his wonder till the very impunity of his attitude and the very insistence of his eyes produced, as he felt, a sudden stir which showed the next instant as a deeper portent, while the head raised itself, the betrayal of a braver purpose. The hands, as he looked, began to move, to open; then, as if deciding in a flash, dropped from the face and left it uncovered and presented. Horror, with the sight, had leaped into Brydon's throat, gasping there in a sound he couldn't utter; for the bared identity was too hideous as *his*, and his glare was the passion of his protest. The face, *that* face, Spencer Brydon's?—he searched it still, but looking away from it in dismay and denial, falling straight from his height and sublimity. It was unknown, inconceivable, awful, disconnected from any possibility—! He had been "sold," he inwardly moaned, stalking such game as this: the presence before him was a presence, the horror within him a horror, but the waste of his nights had been only grotesque and the success of his adventure an irony. Such an identity fitted his at *no* point, made its alternative monstrous. A thousand times yes, as it came upon him nearer now—the face was the face of a stranger. It came upon him nearer now, quite as one of those expanding fantastic images projected by the magic lantern of childhood; for the stranger, whoever he might be, evil, odious, blatant, vulgar, had advanced as for aggression, and he knew himself give ground. Then harder pressed still, sick with the force of his shock, and falling back as under the hot breath and the roused passion of a life larger than his own, a rage of personality before which his own collapsed, he felt the whole vision turn to darkness and his very feet give way. His head went round; he was going; he had gone.

3.

What had next brought him back, clearly—though after how long?—was Mrs. Muldoon's voice, coming to him from quite near, from so near that he seemed presently to see her as kneeling on the ground before him while he lay looking up at her; himself not wholly on the ground, but half-raised and upheld—conscious, yes, of tenderness of support and, more particularly, of a head pillowed in extraordinary softness and faintly refreshing fragrance. He considered, he wondered, his wit but half at his service; then another face intervened, bending more directly over him, and he finally knew that Alice Staverton had made her lap an ample and perfect cushion to him, and that she had to this end seated herself on the lowest degree of the staircase, the rest of his long person remaining stretched on his old black-and-white slabs. They were cold, these marble squares of his youth; but *he* somehow was not, in this rich return of consciousness—the most wonderful hour, little by little, that he had ever known, leaving him, as it did, so gratefully, so abysmally passive, and yet as with a treasure of intelligence waiting all round him for quiet appropriation; dissolved, he might call it, in the air of the place and producing the golden glow of a late autumn afternoon. He had come back, yes—come back from further away than any man but himself had ever travelled; but it was strange how with this sense what he had come back *to* seemed really the great thing, and as if his prodigious journey had been all for the sake of it. Slowly but surely his consciousness grew, his vision of his state thus completing itself; he had been miraculously *carried* back—lifted and carefully borne as from where he had been picked up, the uttermost end of an interminable grey passage. Even with this he was suffered to rest, and what had now brought him to knowledge was the break in the long mild motion.

It had brought him to knowledge, to knowledge—yes, this was the beauty of his state; which came to resemble more and more that of a man who has gone to sleep on some news of a great inheritance, and then, after dreaming it away, after profaning it with matters strange to it, has waked up again to serenity of certitude and has only to lie and watch it grow. This was the drift of his patience—that he had only to let it shine on him. He must moreover, with intermissions, still have been lifted and borne; since why and how else should he have known himself, later on, with the afternoon glow intenser, no longer at the foot of his stairs—situated as these now seemed at that dark other end of his tunnel—but on a deep window-bench of his high saloon, over which had been spread, couch-fashion, a mantle of soft stuff lined with grey fur that was familiar to his eyes and that one of his hands kept fondly feeling as for its pledge of truth. Mrs. Muldoon's face had gone, but the other, the second he had recognised, hung over him in a way that showed how he was still propped and pillowed. He took it all in, and the more he took it the more it seemed to suffice: he was as much at peace as if he had had food and drink. It was the two women who had found him, on Mrs. Muldoon's having plied, at her usual hour, her latch-key—and on her having above all arrived while Miss Staverton still lingered near the house. She had been turning away, all anxiety, from worrying the vain bell-handle—her calculation having been of the hour of the good woman's visit; but the latter, blessedly, had come up while she was still there, and they had entered together. He had then lain, beyond the vestibule, very much as he was lying now—quite, that is, as he appeared to have fallen, but all so wondrously without bruise or gash; only in a depth of stupor. What he most took in, however, at present, with the steadier clearance, was that Alice Staverton had for a long unspeakable moment not doubted he was dead.

"It must have been that I *was*." He made it out as she held him. "Yes—I can only have died. You brought me literally to life. Only," he wondered, his eyes rising to her, "only, in the name of all the benedictions, how?"

It took her but an instant to bend her face and kiss him, and something in the manner of it, and in the way her hands clasped and locked his head while he felt the cool charity and virtue of her lips, something in all this beatitude somehow answered everything.

"And now I keep you," she said.

"Oh keep me, keep me!" he pleaded while her face still hung over him: in response to which it dropped again and stayed close, clingingly close. It was the seal of their situation—of which he tasted the impress for a long blissful moment in silence. But he came back. "Yet how did you know—?"

"I was uneasy. You were to have come, you remember—and you had sent no word."

"Yes, I remember—I was to have gone to you at one today." It caught on to their "old" life and relation—which were so near and so far. "I was still out there in my strange darkness—where was it, what was it? I must have stayed there so long." He could but wonder at the depth and the duration of his swoon.

"Since last night?" she asked with a shade of fear for her possible indiscretion.

"Since this morning—it must have been: the cold dim dawn of to-day. Where have I been," he vaguely wailed, "where have I been?" He felt her hold him close, and it was as if this helped him now to make in all security his mild moan. "What a long dark day!"

All in her tenderness she had waited a moment. "In the cold dim dawn?" she quavered.

But he had already gone on piecing together the parts of the whole prodigy. "As I didn't turn up you came straight—?"

She barely cast about. "I went first to your hotel—where they told me of your absence. You had dined out last evening and hadn't been back since. But they appeared to know you had been at your club."

"So you had the idea of *this*—?"

"Of what?" she asked in a moment.

"Well—of what has happened."

"I believed at least you'd have been here. I've known, all along," she said, "that you've been coming."

"'Known' it—?"

"Well, I've believed it. I said nothing to you after that talk we had a month ago—but I felt sure. I knew you *would*," she declared.

"That I'd persist, you mean?"

"That you'd see him."

"Ah but I didn't!" cried Brydon with his long wail. "There's somebody—an awful beast; whom I brought, too horribly, to bay. But it's not me."

At this she bent over him again, and her eyes were in his eyes. "No—it's not you." And it was as if, while her face hovered, he might have made out in it, hadn't it been so near, some particular meaning blurred by a smile. "No, thank heaven," she repeated, "it's not you! Of course it wasn't to have been."

"Ah but it *was*," he gently insisted. And he stared before him now as he had been staring for so many weeks. "I was to have known myself."

"You couldn't!" she returned consolingly. And then reverting, and as if to account further for what she had herself done, "But it wasn't only *that*, that you hadn't been at home," she went on. "I waited till the hour at which we had found Mrs. Muldoon that day of my going with you; and she arrived, as I've told you, while, failing to bring any one to the door, I lingered in my despair on the steps. After a little, if she hadn't come, by such a mercy, I should have found means to hunt her up. But it wasn't," said Alice Staverton, as if once more with her fine intentions—"it wasn't only that."

His eyes, as he lay, turned back to her. "What more then?"

She met it, the wonder she had stirred. "In the cold dim dawn, you say? Well, in the cold dim dawn of this morning I too saw you."

"Saw *me*—?"

"Saw *him*," said Alice Staverton. "It must have been at the same moment."

He lay an instant taking it in—as if he wished to be quite reasonable. "At the same moment?"

"Yes—in my dream again, the same one I've named to you. He came back to me. Then I knew it for a sign. He had come to you."

At this Brydon raised himself; he had to see her better. She helped him when she understood his movement, and he sat up, steadying himself beside her there on the window-bench and with his right hand grasping her left. "*He* didn't come to me."

"You came to yourself," she beautifully smiled.

"Ah I've come to myself now—thanks to you, dearest. But this brute, with his awful face—this brute's a black stranger.

He's none of *me*, even as I *might* have been," Brydon sturdily declared.

But she kept the clearness that was like the breath of infallibility. "Isn't the whole point that you'd have been different?"

He almost scowled for it. "As different as *that*—?"

Her look again was more beautiful to him than the things of this world. "Haven't you exactly wanted to know *how* different? So this morning," she said, "you appeared to me."

"Like *him*?"

"A black stranger!"

"Then how did you know it was I?"

"Because, as I told you weeks ago, my mind, my imagination, has worked so over what you might, what you mightn't have been—to show you, you see, how I've thought of you. In the midst of that you came to me—that my wonder might be answered. So I knew," she went on; "and believed that, since the question held you too so fast, as you told me that day, you too would see for yourself. And when this morning I again saw I knew it would be because you had—and also then, from the first moment, because you somehow wanted me. *He* seemed to tell me of that. So why," she strangely smiled, "shouldn't I like him?"

It brought Spencer Brydon to his feet. "You 'like' that horror—?"

"I *could* have liked him. And to me," she said, "he was no horror. I had accepted him."

"'Accepted'—?" Brydon oddly sounded.

"Before, for the interest of his difference—yes. And as *I* didn't disown him, as *I* knew him—which you at last, confronted with him in his difference, so cruelly didn't, my dear,—well, he must have been, you see, less dreadful to me. And it may have pleased him that I pitied him."

She was beside him on her feet, but still holding his hand—still with her arm supporting him. But though it all brought for him thus a dim light, "You 'pitied' him?" he grudgingly, resentfully asked.

"He has been unhappy, he has been ravaged," she said.

"And haven't I been unhappy? Am not I—you've only to look at me!—ravaged?"

"Ah I don't say I like him *better*," she granted after a thought. "But he's grim, he's worn—and things have happened to him. He doesn't make shift, for sight, with your charming monocle."

"No"—it struck Brydon; "I couldn't have sported mine 'down-town.' They'd have guyed me there."

"His great convex pince-nez—I saw it, I recognised the kind—is for his poor ruined sight. And his poor right hand—!"

"Ah!" Brydon winced—whether for his proved identity or for his lost fingers. Then, "He has a million a year," he lucidly added. "But he hasn't you."

"And he isn't—no, he isn't—*you*!" she murmured, as he drew her to his breast.

WALTER DE LA MARE

SEATON'S AUNT

I HAD HEARD rumours of Seaton's Aunt long before I actually encountered her. Seaton, in the hush of confidence, or at any little show of toleration in our part would remark, "My aunt," or "My old aunt, you know," as if his relative might be a kind of cement to an *entente cordiale*.

He had an unusual quantity of pocket-money; or, at any rate, it was bestowed on him in unusually large amounts; and he spent it freely, though none of us would have described him as an "awfully generous chap." "Hullo, Seaton," we would say, "the old Begum?" At the beginning of term, too, he used to bring back surprising and exotic dainties in a box with a trick padlock that accompanied him from his first appearance at Gummidge's in a billy-cock hat to the rather abrupt conclusion of his schooldays.

From a boy's point of view he looked distastefully foreign, with his yellow skin, and slow chocolate-coloured eyes, and lean weak figure. Merely for his looks he was treated by most of us true-blue Englishmen with condescension, hostility, or contempt. We used to call him "Pongo," but without any much better excuse for the nickname than his skin. He was, that is, in one sense of the term what he assuredly was not in the other sense, a sport.

Seaton and I, I may say, were never in any sense intimate at school; our orbits only intersected in class. I kept deliberately aloof from him. I felt vaguely he was a sneak, and remained quite unmollified by advances on his side, which, in a boy's barbarous fashion, unless it suited me to be magnanimous, I haughtily ignored.

We were both of us quick-footed, and at Prisoner's Base used occasionally to hide together. And so I best remember Seaton—his narrow watchful face in the dusk of a summer evening; his peculiar crouch, and his inarticulate whisperings and mumblings. Otherwise he played all games slackly and limply; used to stand and feed at his locker with a crony or two until his "tuck" gave out; or waste his money on some outlandish fancy or other. He bought, for instance, a silver bangle, which he wore above his left elbow, until some of the fellows showed their masterly contempt of the practice by dropping it nearly red-hot down his neck.

It needed, therefore, a rather peculiar taste, a rather rare kind of schoolboy courage and indifference to criticism, to be much associated with him. And I had neither the taste nor, perhaps, the courage. None the less, he did make advances, and on one memorable occasion went to the length of bestowing on me a whole pot of some outlandish mulberry-coloured jelly that had been duplicated in his term's supplies. In the exuberance of my gratitude I promised to spend the next half-term holiday with him at his aunt's house.

I had clean forgotten my promise when, two or three days before the holiday, he came up and triumphantly reminded me of it.

"Well, to tell you the honest truth, Seaton, old chap—" I began graciously: but he cut me short.

"My aunt expects you," he said; "she is very glad you are coming. She's sure to be quite decent to *you*, Withers."

I looked at him in sheer astonishment; the emphasis was so uncalled for. It seemed to suggest an aunt not hitherto hinted at, and a friendly feeling on Seaton's side that was far more disconcerting than welcome.

We reached his home partly by train, partly by a lift in an empty farm-cart, and partly by walking. It was a whole-day holiday, and we were to sleep the night; he lent me extraordinary night-gear, I remember. The village street was unusually wide, and was fed from a green by two converging roads, with an inn, and a high green sign at the corner. About a hundred yards down the street was a chemist's shop—a Mr. Tanner's. We descended the two steps into his dusky and odorous interior to buy, I remember, some rat poison. A little beyond the chemist's was the forge. You then walked along a very narrow path, under a fairly high wall, nodding here and there with weeds and tufts of grass, and so came to the iron garden-gates, and saw the high flat house behind its huge sycamore. A coach-house stood on the left of the house, and on the right a gate led into a kind of rambling orchard. The lawn lay away over to the left again, and at the bottom (for the whole garden sloped gently to a sluggish and rushy pond-like stream) was a meadow.

We arrived at noon, and entered the gates out of the hot dust beneath the glitter of the dark-curtained windows. Seaton led me at once through the little garden-gate to show me his tadpole pond, swarming with what (being myself not in the least interested in low life) I considered the most horrible creatures—of all shapes, consistencies, and sizes, but with whom Seaton seemed to be on the most intimate of terms. I can see his absorbed face now as he sat on his heels and fished the slimy things out in his sallow palms. Wearying at last of these pets, we loitered about awhile in an aimless fashion. Seaton seemed to be listening, or at any rate waiting, for something to happen or for someone to come. But nothing did happen and no one came.

That was just like Seaton. Anyhow, the first view I got of his aunt was when, at the summons of a distant gong, we turned from the garden, very hungry and thirsty, to go into luncheon. We were approaching the house when Seaton suddenly came to a standstill. Indeed, I have always had the impression that he plucked at my sleeve. Something, at least, seemed to catch me back, as it were, as he cried, "Look out, there she is!"

She was standing at an upper window which opened wide on a hinge, and at first sight she looked an excessively tall and overwhelming figure. This, however, was mainly because the window reached all but to the floor of her bedroom. She was in reality rather an undersized woman, in spite of her long face and big head. She must have stood, I think, unusually still, with eyes fixed on us, though this impression may be due to Seaton's sudden warning and to my consciousness of the cautious and subdued air that had fallen on him at sight of her. I know that without the least reason in the world I felt a kind of guiltiness, as if I had been "caught." There was a silvery star pattern sprinkled on her black silk dress, and even from the ground I could see the immense coils of her hair and the rings on her left hand which was held fingering the small jet buttons of her bodice. She watched our united advance without stirring, until, imperceptibly, her eyes raised and lost themselves in the distance, so that it was out of an assumed reverie that she appeared suddenly to awaken to our presence beneath her when we drew close to the house.

"So this is your friend, Mr. Smithers, I suppose?" she said, bobbing to me.

"Withers, Aunt," said Seaton.

"It's much the same," she said, with eyes fixed on me. "Come in, Mr. Withers, and bring him along with you."

She continued to gaze at me—at least, I think she did so. I know that the fixity of her scrutiny and her ironical "Mr." made me feel peculiarly uncomfortable. None the less she was extremely kind and attentive to me, though, no doubt, her kindness and attention showed up more vividly against her complete neglect of Seaton. Only one remark that I have any recollection of she made to him: "When I look on my nephew, Mr. Smithers, I realize that dust we are, and dust shall become. You are hot, dirty, and incorrigible, Arthur."

She sat at the head of the table, Seaton at the foot, and I, before a wide waste of damask tablecloth, between them. It was an old and rather close dining-room, with windows thrown wide to the green garden and a wonderful cascade of fading roses. Miss Seaton's great chair faced this window, so that its rose-reflected light shone full on her yellowish face, and on just such chocolate eyes as my schoolfellow's, except that hers were more than half-covered by unusually long and heavy lids.

There she sat, steadily eating, with those sluggish eyes fixed for the most part on my face; above them stood the deep-lined fork between her eyebrows; and above that the wide expanse of a remarkable brow beneath its strange steep bank of hair. The lunch was copious, and consisted, I remember, of all such dishes as are generally considered too rich and too good for the schoolboy digestion—lobster mayonnaise, cold game sausages, an immense veal and ham pie farced with eggs, truffles and numberless delicious flavours; besides kickshaws, creams and sweetmeats. We even had wine, a half-glass of old darkish sherry each.

Miss Seaton enjoyed and indulged an enormous appetite. Her example and a natural schoolboy voracity soon overcame my nervousness of her, even to the extent of allowing me to enjoy to the best of my bent so rare a spread. Seaton was singularly modest; the greater part of his meal consisted of almonds and raisins which he nibbled surreptitiously and as if he found difficulty in swallowing them.

I don't mean that Miss Seaton "conversed" with me. She merely scattered trenchant remarks and now and then twinkled a baited question over my head. But her face was like a dense and involved accompaniment to her talk. She presently dropped the "Mr.," to my intense relief, and called me now Withers, or Wither, now Smithers, and even once towards the close of the meal distinctly Johnson, though how on earth my name suggested it, or whose face mine had reanimated in memory, I cannot conceive.

"And is Arthur a good boy at school, Mr. Wither?" was one of her many questions. "Does he please his masters? Is he first in his class? What does the reverend Dr. Gummidge think of him, eh?"

I knew she was jeering at him, but her face was adamant against the least flicker of sarcasm or facetiousness. I gazed fixedly at a blushing crescent of lobster.

"I think you're eighth, aren't you, Seaton?"

Seaton moved his small pupils towards his aunt. But she continued to gaze with a kind of concentrated detachment at me.

"Arthur will never make a brilliant scholar, I fear," she said, lifting a dexterously-burdened fork to her wide mouth. . . .

After luncheon she preceded me up to my bedroom. It was a jolly little bedroom, with a brass fender and rugs and a polished floor, on which it was possible, I afterwards found, to play "snow-shoes." Over the washstand was a little black-framed water-colour drawing, depicting a large eye with an extremely fish-like intensity in the spark of light on the dark pupil; and in "illuminated" lettering beneath was printed very minutely, "Thou God Seest ME," followed by a long looped monogram, "S. S.," in the corner. The other pictures were all of the sea: brigs on blue water; a schooner overtopping chalk cliffs; a rocky island of prodigious steepness, with two tiny sailors dragging a monstrous boat up a shelf of beach.

"This is the room, Withers, my brother William died in when a boy. Admire the view!"

I looked out of the window across the tree-tops. It was a day hot with sunshine over the green fields, and the cattle were standing swishing their tails in the shallow water. But the view at the moment was only exaggeratedly vivid because I was horribly dreading that she would presently enquire after my luggage, and I had not brought even a toothbrush. I need have had no fear. Hers was not that highly-civilised type of mind that is stuffed with sharp, material details. Nor could her ample presence be described as in the least motherly.

"I would never consent to question a schoolfellow behind my nephew's back," she said, standing in the middle of the room, "but tell me, Smithers, why is Arthur so unpopular? You, I understand, are his only close friend." She stood in a dazzle of sun, and out of it her eyes regarded me with such leaden penetration beneath their thick lids that I doubt if my face concealed the least thought from her. "But there, there," she added very suavely, stooping her head a little, "don't trouble to answer me. I never extort an answer. Boys are queer fish. Brains might perhaps have suggested his washing his hands before luncheon; but—not my choice, Smithers. God forbid! And now, perhaps, you would like to go into the garden again. I cannot actually see from here, but I should not be surprised if Arthur is now skulking behind that hedge."

He was. I saw his head come out and take a rapid glance at the windows.

"Join him, Mr. Smithers; we shall meet again, I hope, at the tea-table. The afternoon I spend in retirement."

Whether or not, Seaton and I had not been long engaged with the aid of two green switches in riding round and round a lumbering old grey horse we found in the meadow, before a rather bunched-up figure appeared, walking along the field-path on the other side of the water, with a magenta parasol studiously lowered in our direction throughout her slow progress, as if that were the magnetic needle and we the fixed Pole. Seaton at once lost all nerve in his riding. At the next lurch of the old mare's heels he toppled over into the grass, and I slid off the sleek broad back to join him where he stood, rubbing his shoulder and sourly watching the rather pompous figure till it was out of sight.

"Was that your aunt, Seaton?" I enquired; but not till then.

He nodded.

"Why didn't she take any notice of us, then?"

"She never does."

"Why not?"

"Oh, she knows all right, without; that's the damn awful part of it." Seaton was about the only fellow at Gummidge's who ever had the ostentation to use bad language. He had suffered for it too. But it wasn't, I think, bravado. I believe he really felt certain things more intensely than most of the other fellows, and they were generally things that fortunate and average people do not feel at all—the peculiar quality, for instance, of the British schoolboy's imagination.

"I tell you, Withers," he went on moodily, slinking across the meadow with his hands covered up in his pockets, "she sees everything. And what she doesn't see she knows without."

"But how?" I said, not because I was much interested, but because the afternoon was so hot and tiresome and purposeless, and it seemed more of a bore to remain silent. Seaton turned gloomily and spoke in a very low voice.

"Don't appear to be talking of her, if you wouldn't mind. It's—because she's in league with the devil." He nodded his head and stooped to pick up a round flat pebble. "I tell you," he said, still stooping, "you fellows don't realise what it is. I know I'm a bit close and all that. But so would you be if you had that old hag listening to every thought you think."

I looked at him, then turned and surveyed one by one the windows of the house.

"Where's your *pater*?" I said awkwardly.

"Dead, ages and ages ago, and my mother too. She's not my aunt by rights."

"What is she, then?"

"I mean she's not my mother's sister, because my grandmother married twice; and she's one of the first lot. I don't know what you call her, but anyhow she's not my real aunt."

"She gives you plenty of pocket-money."

Seaton looked steadfastly at me out of his flat eyes. "She can't give me what's mine. When I come of age half of the whole lot will be mine; and what's more"—he turned his back on the house—"I'll make her hand over every blessed shilling of it."

I put my hands in my pockets and stared at Seaton.

"Is it much?"

He nodded.

"Who told you?" He got suddenly very angry; a darkish red came into his cheeks, his eyes glistened, but he made no answer, and we loitered listlessly about the garden until it was time for tea. . . .

Seaton's aunt was wearing an extraordinary kind of lace jacket when we sidled sheepishly into the drawing-room together. She greeted me with a heavy and protracted smile, and bade me bring a chair close to the little table.

"I hope Arthur has made you feel at home," she said as she handed me my cup in her crooked hand. "He don't talk much to me; but then I'm an old woman. You must come again, Wither, and draw him out of his shell. You old snail!" She wagged her head at Seaton, who sat munching cake and watching her intently.

"And we must correspond, perhaps." She nearly shut her eyes at me. "You must write and tell me everything behind the creature's back." I confess I found her rather disquieting company. The evening drew on. Lamps were brought in by a man with a nondescript face and very quiet footsteps. Seaton was told to bring out the chess-men. And we played a game, she and I, with her big chin thrust over the board at every move as she gloated over the pieces and occasionally croaked "Check!"—after which she would sit back inscrutably staring at me. But the game was never finished. She simply hemmed me defencelessly in with a cloud of men that held me impotent, and yet one and all refused to administer to my poor flustered old king a merciful *coup de grâce*.

"There," she said, as the clock struck ten—"a drawn game, Withers. We are very evenly matched. A very creditable defence, Withers. You know your room. There's supper on a tray in the dining-room. Don't let the creature over-eat himself. The gong will sound three-quarters of an hour *before* a punctual breakfast." She held out her cheek to Seaton, and he kissed it with obvious perfunctoriness. With me she shook hands.

"An excellent game," she said cordially, "but my memory is poor, and"—she swept the pieces helter-skelter into the box—"the result will never be known." She raised her great head far back. "Eh?"

It was a kind of challenge, and I could only murmur: "Oh, I was absolutely in a hole, you know!" when she burst out laughing and waved us both out of the room.

Seaton and I stood and ate our supper, with one candlestick to light us, in a corner of the dining-room. "Well, and how would you like it?" he said very softly after cautiously poking his head round the doorway.

"Like what?"

"Being spied on—every blessed thing you do and think?"

"I shouldn't like it at all," I said, "if she does."

"And yet you let her smash you up at chess!"

"I didn't let her!" I said, indignantly.

"Well, you funked it, then."

"And I didn't funk it either," I said; "she's so jolly clever with her knights." Seaton stared fixedly at the candle. "You wait, that's all," he said slowly. And we went upstairs to bed.

I had not been long in bed, I think, when I was cautiously awakened by a touch on my shoulder. And there was Seaton's face in the candlelight and his eyes looking into mine.

"What's up?" I said, rising quickly to my elbow.

"Don't scurry," he whispered, "or she'll hear. I'm sorry for waking you, but I didn't think you'd be asleep so soon."

"Why, what's the time, then?" Seaton wore, what was

then rather unusual, a night-suit, and he hauled his big silver watch out of the pocket in his jacket.

"It's a quarter to twelve. I never get to sleep before twelve—not here."

"What do you do, then?"

"Oh, I read and listen."

"Listen?"

Seaton stared into his candleflame as if he were listening even then. "You can't guess what it is. All you read in ghost stories, that's all rot. You can't see much, Withers, but you know all the same."

"Know what?"

"Why, that they're there."

"Who's there?" I asked fretfully, glancing at the door.

"Why, in the house. It swarms with 'em. Just you stand still and listen outside my bedroom door in the middle of the night. I have, dozens of times; they're all over the place."

"Look here, Seaton," I said, "you asked me to come here, and I didn't mind chucking up a leave just to oblige you and because I'd promised; but don't get talking a lot of rot, that's all, or you'll know the difference when we get back."

"Don't fret," he said coldly, turning away. "I shan't be at school long. And what's more, you're here now, and there isn't anybody else to talk to. I'll chance the other."

"Look here, Seaton," I said, "you may think you're going to scare me with a lot of stuff about voices and all that. But I'll just thank you to clear out; and you may please yourself about pottering about all night."

He made no answer; he was standing by the dressing-table looking across his candle into the looking-glass; he turned and stared slowly round the walls.

"Even this room's nothing more than a coffin. I suppose she told you—'It's all exactly the same as when my brother William died'—trust her for that! And good luck to him, say I. Look at that." He raised his candle close to the little water-colour I have mentioned. "There's hundreds of eyes like that in this house; and even if God does see you, He takes precious good care you don't see Him. And it's just the same with them. I tell you what, Withers, I'm getting sick of all this. I shan't stand it much longer."

The house was silent within and without, and even in the yellowish radiance of the candle a faint silver showed through the open window on my blind. I slipped off the bed-clothes, wide awake, and sat irresolute on the bed-side.

"I know you're only guying me," I said angrily, "but why is the house full of—what you say? Why do you hear—what you *do* hear? Tell me that, you silly fool!"

Seaton sat down on a chair and rested his candlestick on his knee. He blinked at me calmly. "She brings them," he said with lifted eyebrows.

"Who? Your aunt?"

He nodded.

"How?"

"I told you" he answered pettishly. "She's in league. You don't know. She as good as killed my mother; I know that. But it's not only her by a long chalk. She just sucks you dry. I know. And that's what she'll do for me; because I'm like her—like my mother, I mean. She simply hates to see me alive. I wouldn't be like that old she-wolf for a million pounds. And so"—he broke off, with a comprehensive wave of his candlestick—"they're always here. Ah, my boy, wait till she's dead! She'll hear something then, I can tell you. It's all very well now, but wait till then! I wouldn't be in her shoes when she has to clear out—for something. Don't you go and believe I care for ghosts, or whatever you like to call them. We're all in the same box. We're all under her thumb."

He was looking almost nonchalantly at the ceiling at the moment, when I saw his face change, saw his eyes suddenly drop like shot birds and fix themselves on the cranny of the door he had just left ajar. Even from where I sat I could see his colour change; he went greenish. He crouched without stirring, simply fixed. And I, scarcely daring to breathe, sat with creeping skin, simply watching him. His hands relaxed, and he gave a kind of sigh.

"Was that one?" I whispered, with a timid show of jauntiness. He looked round, opened his mouth, and nodded. "What?" I said. He jerked his thumb with meaningful eyes, and I knew that he meant that his aunt had been there listening at our door cranny.

"Look here, Seaton," I said once more, wriggling to my feet. "You may think I'm a jolly noodle; just as you please. But your aunt has been civil to me and all that, and I don't believe a word you say about her, that's all, and never did. Every fellow's a bit off his pluck at night, and you may think it a fine sport to try your rubbish on me. I heard your aunt come upstairs before I fell asleep. And I'll bet you a level tanner she's in bed now. What's more, you can keep your blessed ghosts to yourself. It's a guilty conscience, I should think."

Seaton looked at me curiously, without answering for a moment. "I'm not a liar, Withers; but I'm not going to quarrel either. You're the only chap I care a button for; or, at any rate, you're the only chap that's ever come here; and it's something to tell a fellow what you feel. I don't care a fig for fifty thousand ghosts, although I swear on my solemn oath that I know they're here. But she"—he turned deliberately—"you laid a tanner she's in bed, Withers; well, I know different. She's never in bed much of the night, and I'll prove it, too, just to show you I'm not such a nolly as you think I am. Come on!"

"Come on where?"

"Why to see."

I hesitated. He opened a large cupboard and took out a small dark dressing-gown and a kind of shawl-jacket. He threw the jacket on the bed and put on the gown. His dusky face was colourless, and I could see by the way he fumbled at the sleeves he was shivering. But it was no good showing the white feather now. So I threw the tasselled shawl over my shoulders and, leaving our candle brightly burning on the chair, we went out together and stood in the corridor.

"Now then, listen!" Seaton whispered.

We stood leaning over the staircase. It was like leaning over a well, so still and chill the air was all around us. But presently, as I suppose happens in most old houses, began to echo and answer in my ears a medley of small stirrings and whisperings. Now out of the distance an old timber would relax its fibres, or a scurry die away behind the perishing wainscot. But amid and behind such sounds as these I seemed to begin to be conscious, as it were, of the lightest of footfalls, sounds as faint as the vanishing remembrance of voices in a dream. Seaton was all in obscurity except his face; out of that his eyes gleamed darkly, watching me.

"You'd hear, too, in time, my fine soldier," he muttered. "Come on!"

He descended the stairs, slipping his lean fingers lightly along the balusters. He turned to the right at the loop, and I followed him barefooted along a thickly-carpeted corridor. At the end stood a door ajar. And from here we very stealthily and in complete blackness ascended five narrow stairs. Seaton, with immense caution, slowly pushed open a door, and we stood together looking into a great pool of duskiness, out of which, lit by the feeble clearness of a night-light, rose a vast bed. A heap of clothes lay on the floor; beside them two slippers dozed, with noses each to each, two yards apart. Somewhere a little clock ticked huskily. There was a rather close smell of lavender and *eau de cologne*, mingled with the fragrance of ancient sachets, soaps, and drugs. Yet it was a scent even more peculiarly commingled than that.

And the bed! I stared warily in; it was mounded gigantically, and it was empty.

Seaton turned a vague pale face, all shadows. "What did I say?" he muttered. "Who's—who's the fool now, I say? How are we going to get back without meeting her, I say? Answer me that! Oh, I wish to goodness you hadn't come here, Withers."

He stood visibly shivering in his skimpy gown, and could hardly speak for his teeth chattering. And very distinctly, in the hush that followed his whisper, I heard approaching a faint unhurried voluminous rustle. Seaton clutched my arm, dragged me to the right across the room to a large cupboard, and drew the door close to on us. And, presently, as with bursting lungs I peeped out into the long, low, curtained bedroom, waddled in that wonderful great head and body. I can see her now, all patched and lined with shadow, her tied-up hair (she must have had enormous quantities of it for so old a woman), her heavy lids above those flat, slow, vigilant eyes. She just passed across my ken in the vague dusk; but the bed was out of sight.

We waited on and on, listening to the clock's muffled ticking. Not the ghost of a sound rose up from the great bed. Either she lay archly listening or slept a sleep serener than an infant's. And when, it seemed, we had been hours in hiding and were cramped, chilled, and half suffocated, we crept out on all fours, with terror knocking at our ribs, and so down the five narrow stairs and back to the little candle-lit blue-and-gold bedroom.

Once there, Seaton gave in. He sat livid on a chair with closed eyes.

"Here," I said, shaking his arm, "I'm going to bed; I've had enough of this foolery; I'm going to bed." His lips quivered, but he made no answer. I poured out some water into my basin and, with that cold pictured azure eye fixed on us, bespattered Seaton's sallow face and forehead and dabbled his hair. He presently sighed and opened fish-like eyes.

"Come on!" I said. "Don't get shamming, there's a good chap. Get on my back, if you like, and I'll carry you into your bedroom."

He waved me away and stood up. So, with my candle in one hand, I took him under the arm and walked him along according to his direction down the corridor. His was a much dingier room than mine, and littered with boxes, paper, cages, and clothes. I huddled him into bed and turned to go. And suddenly, I can hardly explain it now, a kind of cold and deadly terror swept over me. I almost ran out of the room, with eyes fixed rigidly in front of me, blew out my candle, and buried my head under the bedclothes.

When I awoke, roused not by a gong, but by a long-continued tapping at my door, sunlight was raying in on cornice and bedpost, and birds were singing in the garden. I got up, ashamed of the night's folly, dressed quickly, and went downstairs. The breakfast room was sweet with flowers and fruit and honey. Seaton's aunt was standing in the garden beside the open French window, feeding a great flutter of birds. I watched her for a moment, unseen. Her face was set in a deep reverie beneath the shadow of a big loose sunhat. It was deeply lined, crooked, and, in a way I can't describe, fixedly vacant and strange. I coughed, and she turned at once with a prodigious smile to enquire how I had slept. And in that mysterious way by which we learn each other's secret thoughts without a sentence spoken I knew that she had followed every word and movement of the night before, and was triumphing over my affected innocence and ridiculing my friendly and too easy advances.

We returned to school, Seaton and I, lavishly laden, and by rail all the way. I made no reference to the obscure talk we had had, and resolutely refused to meet his eyes or to take up the hints he let fall. I was relieved—and yet I was sorry—to be going back, and strode on as fast as I could from the station, with Seaton almost trotting at my heels. But he insisted on buying more fruits and sweets—my share of which I accepted with a very bad grace. It was uncomfortably like a bribe; and, after all, I had no quarrel with his rum old aunt, and hadn't really believed half the stuff he had told me.

I saw as little of him as I could after that. He never referred to our visit or resumed his confidences, though in class I would sometimes catch his eye fixed on mine, full of a mute understanding, which I easily affected not to understand. He left Gummidge's, as I have said, rather abruptly, though I never heard of anything to his discredit. And I did not see him or have any news of him again till by chance we met one summer afternoon in the Strand.

He was dressed rather oddly in a coat too large for him and a bright silky tie. But we instantly recognized one another under the awning of a cheap jeweller's shop. He immediately attached himself to me and dragged me off, not too cheerfully, to lunch with him at an Italian restaurant near by. He chattered about our old school, which he remembered only with dislike and disgust; told me cold-bloodedly of the disastrous fate of one or two of the old fellows who had been among his chief tormentors; insisted on an expensive wine and the whole gamut of the foreign menu; and finally informed me, with a good deal of niggling, that he had come up to town to buy an engagement-ring.

And of course: "How is your aunt?" I enquired at last.

He seemed to have been awaiting the question. It fell like a stone into a deep pool, so many expressions flitted across his long un-English face.

"She's aged a good deal," he said softly, and broke off.

"She's been very decent," he continued presently after, and paused again. "In a way." He eyed me fleetingly. "I dare say you heard that—she—that is, that we—had lost a good deal of money."

"No," I said.

"Oh, yes!" said Seaton, and paused again.

And somehow, poor fellow, I knew, in the clink and clatter

of glass and voices that he had lied to me; that he did not possess, and never had possessed, a penny beyond what his aunt had squandered on his too ample allowance of pocket-money.

"And the ghosts?" I enquired quizzically.

He grew instantly solemn, and, though it may have been my fancy, slightly yellowed. But "You are making game of me. Withers," was all he said.

He asked for my address, and I rather reluctantly gave him my card.

"Look here, Withers," he said, as we stood together in the sunlight on the kerb, saying good-bye, "here I am, and—and it's all very well. I'm not perhaps as fanciful as I was. But you are practically the only friend I have on earth—except Alice.... And there—to make a clean breast of it, I'm not sure that my aunt cares much about my getting married. She doesn't say so, of course. You know her well enough for that." He looked sidelong at the rattling gaudy traffic.

"What I was going to say is this: Would you mind coming down? You needn't stay the night unless you please, though, of course, you know you would be awfully welcome. But I should like you to meet my—to meet Alice; and then, perhaps, you might tell me your honest opinion of—of the other too."

I vaguely demurred. He pressed me. And we parted with a half promise that I would come. He waved his ball-topped cane at me and ran off in his long jacket after a bus.

A letter arrived soon after, in his small weak handwriting, giving me full particulars regarding route and trains. And without the least curiosity, even, perhaps with some little annoyance that chance should have thrown us together again, I accepted his invitation and arrived one hazy midday at his out-of-the-way station to find him sitting on a low seat under a clump of double hollyhocks, awaiting me.

His face looked absent and singularly listless; but he seemed, none the less, pleased to see me.

We walked up the village street, past the little dingy apothecary's and the empty forge, and, as on my first visit, skirted the house together, and, instead of entering by the front door, made our way down the green path into the garden at the back. A pale haze of cloud muffled the sun; the garden lay in a grey shimmer—its old trees, its snap-dragoned faintly glittering walls. But now on them was an air of slovenliness where before all had been neat and methodical. In a patch of shallowly-dug soil stood a worndown spade leaning against a tree. There was an old broken wheelbarrow. The roses had run to leaf and briar; the fruit-trees were unpruned. The goddess of neglect brooded in secret.

"You ain't much of a gardener, Seaton," I said, with a sigh of ease.

"I think, do you know, I like it best like this," said Seaton. "We haven't any man now, of course. Can't afford it." He stood staring at his little dark square of freshly-turned earth. "And it always seems to me," he went on ruminatingly, "that, after all, we are nothing better than interlopers on the earth, disfiguring and staining wherever we go. I know it's shocking blasphemy to say so, but then it's different here, you see. We are farther away."

"To tell you the truth, Seaton, I *don't* quite see," I said; "but it isn't a new philosophy, is it? Anyhow, it's a precious beastly one."

"It's only what I think," he replied, with all his odd old stubborn meekness.

We wandered on together, talking little, and still with that expression of uneasy vigilance on Seaton's face. He pulled out his watch as we stood gazing idly over the green meadows and the dark motionless bulrushes.

"I think, perhaps, it's nearly time for lunch," he said. "Would you like to come in?"

We turned and walked slowly towards the house, across whose windows I confess my own eyes, too, went restlessly wandering in search of its rather disconcerting inmate. There was a pathetic look of draggledness, of want of means and care, rust and overgrowth and faded paint. Seaton's aunt, a little to my relief, did not share our meal. Seaton carved the cold meat, and dispatched a heaped-up plate by an elderly servant for his aunt's private consumption. We talked little and in half-suppressed tones, and sipped a bottle of Madeira which Seaton had rather heedfully fetched out of the great mahogany sideboard.

I played him a dull and effortless game of chess, yawning between the moves he himself made almost at haphazard, and with attention elsewhere engaged. About five o'clock came the sound of a distant ring, and Seaton jumped up, overturning the board, and so ending a game that else might have fatuously continued to this day. He effusively excused himself, and after some little while returned with a slim, dark, rather sallow girl of about nineteen, in a white gown and hat, to whom I was presented with some little nervousness as his "dear old friend and schoolfellow."

We talked on in the pale afternoon light, still, as it seemed to me, and even in spite of a real effort to be clear and gay, in a half-suppressed, lack-lustre fashion. We all seemed, if it were not my fancy, to be expectant, to be rather anxiously awaiting an arrival, the appearance of someone who all but filled our collective consciousness. Seaton talked least of all, and in a restless interjectory way, as he continually fidgeted from chair to chair. At last he proposed a stroll in the garden before the sun should have quite gone down.

Alice walked between us. Her hair and eyes were conspicuously dark against the whiteness of her gown. She carried herself not ungracefully, and yet without the least movement of her arms and body, and answered us both without turning her head. There was a curious provocative reserve in that impassive and rather long face, a half-unconscious strength of character.

And yet somehow I knew—I believe we all knew—that this walk, this discussion of their future plans was a futility. I had nothing to base such a cynicism on, except only a vague sense of oppression, the foreboding remembrance of the inert invincible power in the background, to whom optimistic plans and love-making and youth are as chaff and thistle-down. We came back, silent, in the last light. Seaton's aunt was there—under an old brass lamp. Her hair was as barbarously massed and curled as ever. Her eyelids, I think, hung even a little heavier in age over their slow-moving inscrutable pupils. We filed in softly out of the evening, and I made my bow.

"In this short interval, Mr. Withers," she remarked amiably, "you have put off youth, put on the man. Dear me, how sad it is to see the young days vanishing! Sit down. My nephew tells me you met by chance—or act of Providence, shall we call it?—and in my beloved Strand! You, I understand, are to be best man—yes, best man, or am I divulging secrets?" She surveyed Arthur and Alice with overwhelming graciousness. They sat apart on two low chairs and smiled in return.

"And Arthur—how do you think Arthur is looking?"

"I think he looks very much in need of a change," I said deliberately.

"A change! Indeed?" She all but shut her eyes at me and with an exaggerated sentimentality shook her head. "My dear Mr. Withers! Are we not *all* in need of a change in this fleeting, fleeting world?" She mused over the remark like a connoisseur. "And you," she continued, turning abruptly to Alice, "I hope you pointed out to Mr. Withers all my pretty bits?"

"We walked round the garden," said Alice, looking out of the window. "It's a very beautiful evening."

"*Is* it?" said the old lady, starting up violently. "Then on this very beautiful evening we will go in to supper. Mr. Withers, your arm; Arthur, bring your bride."

I can scarcely describe with what curious ruminations I

led the way into the faded, heavy-aired dining-room, with this indefinable old creature leaning weightily on my arm—the large flat bracelet on the yellow-laced wrist. She fumed a little, breathed rather heavily, as if with an effort of mind rather than of body; for she had grown much stouter and yet little more proportionate. And to talk into the great white face, so close to mine, was a queer experience in the dim light of the corridor, and even in the twinkling crystal of the candles. She was naïve—appallingly naïve; she was sudden and superficial; she was even arch; and all these in the brief, rather puffy passage from one room to the other, with these two tongue-tied children bringing up the rear. The meal was tremendous. I have never seen such a monstrous salad. But the dishes were greasy and over-spiced, and were indifferently cooked. One thing only was quite unchanged—my hostess's appetite was as Gargantuan as ever. The old solid candelabra that lighted us stood before her high-backed chair. Seaton sat a little removed, with his plate almost in darkness.

And throughout this prodigious meal his aunt talked, mainly to me, mainly at Seaton, with an occasional satirical courtesy to Alice and muttered explosions of directions to the servant. She had aged, and yet, if it be not nonsense to say so, seemed no older. I suppose to the Pyramids a decade is but as the rustling down of a handful of dust. And she reminded me of some such unshakable prehistoricism. She certainly was an amazing talker—racy, extravagant, with a delivery that was perfectly overwhelming. As for Seaton—her flashes of silence were for him. On her enormous volubility would suddenly fall a hush: acid sarcasm would be left implied; and she would sit softly moving her great head, with eyes fixed full in a dreamy smile; but with her whole attention, one could see, slowly, joyously absorbing his mute discomfiture.

She confided in us her views on a theme vaguely occupying at the moment, I suppose, all our minds. "We have barbarous institutions, and so must put up, I suppose, with a never-ending procession of fools—of fools *ad infinitum*. Marriage, Mr. Withers, was instituted in the privacy of a garden; *sub rosa*, as it were. Civilization flaunts it in the glare of day. The dull marry the poor; the rich the effete; and so our New Jerusalem is peopled with naturals, plain and coloured, at either end. I detest folly; I detest still more (if I must be frank, dear Arthur) mere cleverness. Mankind has simply become a tailless host of uninstinctive animals. We should never have taken to Evolution, Mr. Withers. 'Natural Selection!'—little gods and fishes!—the deaf for the dumb. We should have used our brains—intellectual pride, the ecclesiastics call it. And by brains I mean—what do I mean, Alice?—I mean, my dear child," and she laid two gross fingers on Alice's narrow sleeve, "I mean courage. Consider it, Arthur. I read that the scientific world is once more beginning to be afraid of spiritual agencies. Spiritual agencies that tap, and actually float, bless their hearts! I think just one more of those mulberries—thank you.

"They talk about 'blind Love,' " she ran inconsequently on as she helped herself, with eyes roving the dish, "but why blind? I think, do you know, from weeping over its rickets. After all, it is we plain women that triumph, Mr. Withers, beyond the mockery of time. Alice, now! Fleeting, fleeting is youth, my child. What's that you were confiding to your plate, Arthur? Satirical boy. He laughs at his old aunt: nay, but thou didst laugh. He detests all sentiment. He whispers the most acid asides. Come, my love, we will leave these cynics; we will go and commiserate with each other on our sex. The choice of two evils, Mr. Smithers!" I opened the door, and she swept out as if borne on a torrent of unintelligible indignation; and Arthur and I were left in the clear four-flamed light alone.

For a while we sat in silence. He shook his head at my cigarette-case, and I lit a cigarette. Presently he fidgeted in his chair and poked his head forward into the light. He paused to rise and shut again the shut door.

"How long will you be?" he said, standing by the table.

I laughed.

"Oh, it's not that!" he said, in some confusion. "Of course, I like to be with her. But it's not that. The truth is, Withers, I don't care about leaving her too long with my aunt."

I hesitated. He looked at me questioningly.

"Look here, Seaton," I said, "you know well enough that I don't want to interfere in your affairs, or to offer advice where it is not wanted. But don't you think perhaps you may not treat your aunt quite in the right way? It's all simply a matter of give and take. I have an old godmother, or something. She talks, too. . . . A little allowance: it does no harm. But hang it all, I'm no talker."

He sat down with his hands in his pockets and still with his eyes fixed almost incredulously on mine. "How?" he said.

"Well, my dear fellow, if I'm any judge—mind, I don't say that I am—but I can't help thinking she thinks you don't care for her; and perhaps takes your silence for—for bad temper. She has been very decent to you, hasn't she?"

" 'Decent'? My God!" said Seaton.

I smoked on in silence; but he continued to look at me with that peculiar concentration I remembered of old.

"I don't think, perhaps, Withers," he began presently, "I don't think you quite understand. Perhaps you are not quite our kind. You always did, just like the other fellows, guy me at school. You laughed at me that night you came to stay here—about the voices and all that. But I don't mind being laughed at—because I know."

"Know what?" It was the same old system of dull question and evasive answer.

"I mean I know that what we see and hear is only the smallest fraction of what is. I know she lives quite out of this. She *talks* to you; but it's all make-believe. It's all a 'parlour game.' She's not really with you; only pitting her outside wits against yours and enjoying the fooling. She's living on inside, on what you're rotten without. That's what it is—a cannibal feast. She's a spider. It doesn't much matter what you call it. It means the same kind of thing. I tell you, Withers, she hates me; and you can scarcely dream what that hatred means. I used to think I had an inkling of the reason. It's oceans deeper than that. It just lies behind: herself against myself. Why, after all, how much do we really understand of anything? We don't even know our own histories, and not a tenth, not a tenth of the reasons. What has life been to me?—nothing but a trap. And when one is set free, it only begins again. I thought you might understand; but you are on a different level: that's all."

"What on earth are you talking about?" I said, contemptuously, in spite of myself.

"I mean what I say," he said gutturally. "All this outside's only make-believe—but there! what's the good of talking? So far as this is concerned I'm as good as done. You wait."

Seaton blew out three of the candles and, leaving the vacant room in semi-darkness, we groped our way along the corridor to the drawing-room. There a full moon stood shining in at the long garden windows. Alice sat stooping at the door, with her hands clasped, looking out, alone.

"Where is she?" Seaton asked in a low tone.

Alice looked up; their eyes met in a kind of instantaneous understanding, and the door immediately afterwards opened behind us.

"*Such* a moon!" said a voice that, once heard, remained unforgettably on the ear. "A night for lovers, Mr. Withers, if ever there was one. Get a shawl, my dear Arthur, and take Alice for a little promenade. I dare say we old cronies will manage to keep awake. Hasten, hasten, Romeo! My poor, poor Alice, how laggard a lover!"

Seaton returned with a shawl. They drifted out into the moonlight. My companion gazed after them till they were out of hearing, turned to me gravely, and suddenly twisted her white face into such a convulsion of contemptuous amusement that I could only stare blankly in reply.

"Dear innocent children!" she said, with inimitable unctuousness. "Well, well, Mr. Withers, we poor seasoned old creatures must move with the times. Do you sing?"

I scouted the idea.

"Then you must listen to my playing. Chess"—she clasped her forehead with both cramped hands—"chess is now completely beyond my poor wits."

She sat down at the piano and ran her fingers in a flourish over the keys. "What shall it be? How shall we capture them, those passionate hearts? That first fine careless rapture? Poetry itself." She gazed softly into the garden a moment, and presently, with a shake of her body, began to play the opening bars of Beethoven's "Moonlight" Sonata. The piano was old and woolly. She played without music. The lamplight was rather dim. The moonbeams from the window lay across the keys. Her head was in shadow. And whether it was simply due to her personality or to some really occult skill in her playing I cannot say: I only know that she gravely and deliberately set herself to satirize the beautiful music. It brooded on the air, disillusioned, charged with mockery and bitterness. I stood at the window; far down the path I could see the white figure glimmering in that pool of colourless light. A few faint stars shone, and still that amazing woman behind me dragged out of the unwilling keys her wonderful grotesquerie of youth and love and beauty. It came to an end. I knew the player was watching me. "Please, please, go on!" I murmured, without turning. "Please go on playing, Miss Seaton."

No answer was returned to my rather fluttering sarcasm, but I knew in some indefinite way that I was being acutely scrutinized, when suddenly there followed a procession of quiet, plaintive chords which broke at last softly into the hymn, *A Few More Years Shall Roll.*

I confess it held me spellbound. There is a wistful, strained, plangent pathos in the tune; but beneath those masterly old hands it cried softly and bitterly the solitude and desperate estrangement of the world. Arthur and his lady-love vanished from my thoughts. No one could put into a rather hackneyed old hymn-tune such an appeal who had never known the meaning of the words. Their meaning, anyhow, isn't commonplace. I turned very cautiously and glanced at the musician. She was leaning forward a little over the keys, so that at the approach of my cautious glance she had but to turn her face into the thin flood of moonlight for every feature to become distinctly visible. And so, with the tune abruptly terminated, we steadfastly regarded one another, and she broke into a chuckle of laughter.

"Not quite so seasoned as I supposed, Mr. Withers. I see you are a real lover of music. To me it is too painful. It evokes too much thought. . . ."

I could scarcely see her little glittering eyes under their penthouse lids.

"And now," she broke off crisply, "tell me, as a man of the world, what do you think of my new niece?"

I was not a man of the world, nor was I much flattered in my stiff and dullish way of looking at things by being called one; and I could answer her without the least hesitation.

"I don't think, Miss Seaton, I'm much of a judge of character. She's very charming."

"A brunette?"

"I think I prefer dark women."

"And why? Consider, Mr. Withers; dark hair, dark eyes, dark cloud, dark night, dark vision, dark death, dark grave, dark DARK!"

Perhaps the climax would have rather thrilled Seaton, but I was too thick-skinned. "I don't know much about all that," I answered rather pompously. "Broad daylight's difficult enough for most of us."

"Ah," she said, with a sly inward burst of satirical laughter.

"And I suppose," I went on, perhaps a little nettled, "it isn't the actual darkness one admires, it's the contrast of the skin, and the colour of the eyes, and—and their shining. Just as," I went blundering on, too late to turn back, "just as you only see the stars in the dark. It would be a long day without any evening. As for death and the grave, I don't suppose we shall much notice that." Arthur and his sweetheart were slowly returning along the dewy path. "I believe in making the best of things."

"How very interesting!" came the smooth answer. "I see you are a philosopher, Mr. Withers. H'm! 'As for death and the grave, I don't suppose we shall much notice that.' Very interesting.... And I'm sure," she added in a particularly suave voice, "I profoundly hope so." She rose slowly from her stool. "You will take pity on me again, I hope. You and I would get on famously—kindred spirits—elective affinities. And, of course, now that my nephew's going to leave me, now that his affections are centred on another, I shall be a very lonely old woman.... Shall I not, Arthur?"

Seaton blinked stupidly. "I didn't hear what you said, Aunt."

"I was telling our old friend, Arthur, that when you are gone I shall be a very lonely old woman."

"Oh, I don't think so," he said in a strange voice.

"He means, Mr. Withers, he means, my dear child," she said, sweeping her eyes over Alice, "he means that I shall have memory for company—heavenly memory—the ghosts of other days. Sentimental boy! And did you enjoy our music, Alice? Did I really stir that youthful heart?... O, O, O," continued the horrible old creature, "you billers and cooers, I have been listening to such flatteries, such confessions! Beware, beware, Arthur, there's many a slip." She rolled her little eyes at me, she shrugged her shoulders at Alice, and gazed an instant stonily into her nephew's face.

I held out my hand. "Good-night, good-night!" she cried. "'He that fights and runs away.' Ah, good-night. Mr. Withers; come again soon!" She thrust out her cheek at Alice, and we all three filed slowly out of the room.

Black shadow darkened the porch and half the spreading sycamore. We walked without speaking up the dusty village street. Here and there a crimson window glowed. At the fork of the high-road I said good-bye. But I had taken hardly more than a dozen paces when a sudden impulse seized me.

"Seaton!" I called.

He turned in the moonlight.

"You have my address; if by any chance, you know, you should care to spend a week or two in town between this and the—the Day, we should be delighted to see you."

"Thank you, Withers, thank you," he said in a low voice.

"I dare say"—I waved my stick gallantly to Alice—"I dare say you will be doing some shopping; we could all meet," I added, laughing.

"Thank you, thank you, Withers—immensely," he repeated.

And so we parted.

But they were out of the jog-trot of my prosaic life. And being of a stolid and incurious nature, I left Seaton and his marriage, and even his aunt, to themselves in my memory, and scarcely gave a thought to them until one day I was walking in the Strand again, and passed the flashing gloaming of the covered-in jeweller's shop where I had accidentally encountered my old schoolfellow in the summer. It was one of those still, close autumnal days after a rainy night. I cannot say why, but a vivid recollection returned to my mind of our meeting and of how suppressed Seaton had seemed, and of how vainly he had endeavoured to appear assured and eager. He must be married by now, and had doubtless returned from his honeymoon. And I had clean forgotten my manners, had sent not a word of congratulation, nor—as I might very well have done, and as I knew he would have been immensely pleased at my doing—the ghost of a wedding-present.

On the other hand, I pleaded with myself, I had had no invitation. I paused at the corner of Trafalgar Square, and at the bidding of one of those caprices that seize occasionally on even an unimaginative mind, I suddenly ran after a green 'bus that was passing, and found myself bound on a visit I had not in the least foreseen.

The colours of autumn were over the village when I arrived. A beautiful late afternoon sunlight bathed thatch and meadow. But it was close and hot. A child, two dogs, a very old woman with a heavy basket I encountered. One or two incurious tradesmen looked idly up as I passed by. It was all so rural and so still, my whimsical impulse had so much flagged, that for a while I hesitated to venture under the shadow of the sycamore tree to enquire after the happy pair. I deliberately passed by the faint-blue gates and continued my walk under the high green and tufted wall. Hollyhocks had attained their topmost bud and seeded in the little cottage gardens beyond; the Michaelmas daisies were in flower; a sweet warm aromatic smell of fading leaves was in the air. Beyond the cottages lay a field where cattle were grazing, and beyond that I came to a little churchyard. Then the road wound on, pathless and houseless, among gorse and bracken. I turned impatiently and walked quickly back to the house and rang the bell.

The rather colourless elderly woman who answered my enquiry informed me that Miss Seaton was at home, as if only taciturnity forbade her adding, "But she doesn't want to see *you*."

"Might I, do you think, have Mr. Arthur's address?" I said.

She looked at me with quiet astonishment, as if waiting for an explanation. Not the faintest of smiles came into her thin face.

"I will tell Miss Seaton," she said after a pause. "Please walk in."

She showed me into the dingy, undusted drawing-room, filled with evening sunshine and with the green-dyed light that penetrated the leaves overhanging the long French windows. I sat down and waited on and on, occasionally aware of a creaking footfall overhead. At last the door opened a little, and the great face I had once known peered round at me. For it was enormously changed; mainly, I think, because the old eyes had rather suddenly failed, and so a kind of stillness and darkness lay over its calm and wrinkled pallor.

"Who is it?" she asked.

I explained myself and told her the occasion of my visit.

She came in and shut the door carefully after her and, though the fumbling was scarcely perceptible, groped her way to a chair. She had on an old dressing-gown, like a cassock, of a patterned cinnamon colour.

"What is it you want?" she said, seating herself and lifting her blank face to mine.

"Might I just have Arthur's address?" I said deferentially. "I am so sorry to have disturbed you."

"H'm. You have come to see my nephew?"

"Not necessarily to see him, only to hear how he is, and, of course, Mrs. Seaton, too. I am afraid my silence must have appeared . . ."

"He hasn't noticed your silence," croaked the old voice out of the great mask; "besides, there isn't any Mrs. Seaton."

"Ah, then," I answered, after a momentary pause, "I have not seemed so black as I painted myself! And how is Miss Outram?"

"She's gone into Yorkshire," answered Seaton's aunt.

"And Arthur too?"

She did not reply, but simply sat blinking at me with lifted chin, as if listening, but certainly not for what I might have to say. I began to feel rather at a loss.

"You were no close friend of my nephew's, Mr. Smithers?" she said presently.

"No," I answered, welcoming the cue, "and yet, do you know, Miss Seaton, he is one of the very few of my old schoolfellows I have come across in the last few years, and I suppose as one gets older one begins to value old associations. . . ." My voice seemed to trail off into a vacuum. "I thought Miss Outram," I hastily began again, "a particularly charming girl. I hope they are both quite well."

Still the old face solemnly blinked at me in silence.

"You must find it very lonely, Miss Seaton, with Arthur away?"

"I was never lonely in my life," she said sourly. "I don't look to flesh and blood for my company. When you've got to be my age, Mr. Smithers (which God forbid), you'll find life a very different affair from what you seem to think it is now. You won't seek company then, I'll be bound. It's thrust on you." Her face edged round into the clear green light, and her eyes groped, as it were, over my vacant, disconcerted face. "I dare say, now," she said, composing her mouth, "I dare say my nephew told you a good many tarradiddles in his time. Oh, yes, a good many, eh? He was always a liar. What, now, did he say of me? Tell me, now." She leant forward as far as she could, trembling, with an ingratiating smile.

"I think he is rather superstitious," I said coldly, "but, honestly, I have a very poor memory, Miss Seaton."

"Why?" she said. "*I* haven't."

"The engagement hasn't been broken off, I hope."

"Well, between you and me," she said, shrinking up and with an immensely confidential grimace, "it has."

"I'm sure I'm very sorry to hear it. And where is Arthur?"

"Eh?"

"Where is Arthur?"

We faced each other mutely among the dead old by-gone furniture. Past all my scrutiny was that large, flat, grey, cryptic countenance. And then, suddenly, our eyes for the first time really met. In some indescribable way out of that thick-lidded obscurity a far small something stooped and looked out at me for a mere instant of time that seemed of almost intolerable protraction. Involuntarily I blinked and shook my head. She muttered something with great rapidity, but quite inarticulately; rose and hobbled to the door. I thought I heard, mingled in broken mutterings, something about tea.

"Please, please, don't trouble," I began, but could say no more, for the door was already shut between us. I stood and looked out on the long-neglected garden. I could just see the bright greenness of Seaton's old tadpole pond. I wandered about the room. Dusk began to gather, the last birds in that dense shadowiness of trees had ceased to sing. And not a sound was to be heard in the house. I waited on and on, vainly speculating. I even attempted to ring the bell; but the wire was broken, and only jangled loosely at my efforts.

I hesitated, unwilling to call or to venture out, and yet more unwilling to linger on, waiting for a tea that promised to be an exceedingly comfortless supper. And as darkness drew down, a feeling of the utmost unease and disquietude came over me. All my talks with Seaton returned on me with a suddenly enriched meaning. I recalled again his face as we had stood hanging over the staircase, listening in the small hours to the inexplicable stirrings of the night. There were no candles in the room; every minute the autumnal darkness deepened. I cautiously opened the door and listened, and with some little dismay withdrew, for I was uncertain of my way out. I even tried the garden, but was confronted under a veritable thicket of foliage by a padlocked gate. It would be a little too ignominious to be caught scaling a friend's garden fence!

Cautiously returning into the still and musty drawing-room, I took out my watch, and gave the incredible old woman ten minutes in which to reappear. And when that tedious ten minutes had ticked by I could scarcely distinguish its hands. I determined to wait no longer, drew open the door, and trusting to my sense of direction, groped my way through the corridor that I vaguely remembered led to the front of the house.

I mounted three or four stairs and, lifting a heavy curtain, found myself facing the starry fanlight of the porch. Hence I glanced into the gloom of the dining-room. My fingers were on the latch of the outer door when I heard a faint stirring in the darkness above the hall. I looked up and became conscious of, rather than saw, the huddled old figure looking down on me.

There was an immense hushed pause. Then, "Arthur, Arthur," whispered an inexpressibly peevish rasping voice, "is that you? Is that you, Arthur?"

I can scarcely say why, but the question horribly startled me. No conceivable answer occurred to me. With head craned back, hand clenched on my umbrella, I continued to stare up into the gloom, in this fatuous confrontation.

"Oh, oh," the voice croaked. "It is you, is it? *That* disgusting man! . . . Go away out. Go away out."

Hesitating no longer, I caught open the door and, slamming it behind me, ran out into the garden, under the gigantic old sycamore, and so out at the open gate.

I found myself half up the village street before I stopped running. The local butcher was sitting in his shop reading a piece of newspaper by the light of a small oil-lamp. I crossed the road and enquired the way to the station. And after he had with minute and needless care directed me, I asked casually if Mr. Arthur Seaton still lived with his aunt at the big house just beyond the village. He poked his head in at the little parlour door.

"Here's a gentleman enquiring after young Mr. Seaton, Millie," he said. "He's dead, ain't he?"

"Why, yes, bless you," replied a cheerful voice from within. "Dead and buried these three months or more—young Mr.

Seaton. And just before he was to be married, don't you remember, Bob?"

I saw a fair young woman's face peer over the muslin of the little door at me.

"Thank you," I replied, "then I go straight on?"

"That's it, sir; past the pond, bear up the hill a bit to the left, and then there's the station lights before your eyes."

We looked intelligently into each other's faces in the beam of the smoky lamp. But not one of the many questions in my mind could I put into words.

And again I paused irresolutely a few paces further on. It was not, I fancy, merely a foolish apprehension of what the raw-boned butcher might "think" that prevented my going back to see if I could find Seaton's grave in the benighted churchyard. There was precious little use in pottering about in the muddy dark merely to discover where he was buried. And yet I felt a little uneasy. My rather horrible thought was that, so far as I was concerned—one of his extremely few friends—he had never been much better than "buried" in my mind.

H.P. LOVECRAFT

THE COLOUR OUT OF SPACE

WEST OF Arkham the hills rise wild, and there are valleys with deep woods that no axe has ever cut. There are dark narrow glens where the trees slope fantastically, and where thin brooklets trickle without ever having caught the glint of sunlight. On the gentler slopes there are farms, ancient and rocky, with squat, moss-coated cottages brooding eternally over old New England secrets in the lee of great ledges; but these are all vacant now, the wide chimneys crumbling and the shingled sides bulging perilously beneath low gambrel roofs.

The old folk have gone away, and foreigners do not like to live there. French-Canadians have tried it, Italians have tried it, and the Poles have come and departed. It is not because of anything that can be seen or heard or handled, but because of something that is imagined. The place is not good for the imagination, and does not bring restful dreams at night. It must be this which keeps the foreigners away, for old Ammi Pierce has never told them of anything he recalls from the strange days. Ammi, whose head has been a little queer for years, is the only one who still remains, or who ever talks of the strange days; and he dares to do this because his house is so near the open fields and the travelled roads around Arkham.

There was once a road over the hills and through the valleys, that ran straight where the blasted heath is now; but people ceased to use it and a new road was laid curving far toward the south. Traces of the old one can still be found amidst the weeds of a returning wilderness, and some of them will doubtless linger even when half the hollows are flooded for the new reservoir. Then the dark woods will be cut down and the blasted heath will slumber far below blue waters whose surface will mirror the sky and ripple in the sun. And the secrets of the strange days will be one with the deep's secrets; one with the hidden lore of old ocean, and all the mystery of primal earth.

When I went into the hills and vales to survey for the new reservoir they told me the place was evil. They told me this in Arkham, and because that is a very old town full of witch legends I thought the evil must be something which grandams had whispered to children through centuries. The name "blasted heath" seemed to me very odd and theatrical, and I wondered how it had come into the folklore of a Puritan people. Then I saw that dark westward tangle of glens and slopes for myself, and ceased to wonder at anything besides its own elder mystery. It was morning when I saw it, but shadow lurked always there. The trees grew too thickly, and their trunks were too big for any healthy New England wood. There was too much silence in the dim alleys between them, and the floor was too soft with the dank moss and mattings of infinite years of decay.

In the open spaces, mostly along the line of the old road, there were little hillside farms; sometimes with all the buildings standing, sometimes with only one or two, and sometimes with only a lone chimney or fast-filling cellar. Weeds and briers reigned, and furtive wild things rustled in the undergrowth. Upon everything was a haze of restlessness and oppression; a touch of the unreal and the grotesque, as if some vital element of perspective or chiaroscuro were awry. I did not wonder that the foreigners would not stay, for this was no region to sleep in. It was too much like a landscape of Salvator Rosa; too much like some forbidden woodcut in a tale of terror.

But even all this was not so bad as the blasted heath. I knew it the moment I came upon it at the bottom of a spacious valley; for no other name could fit such a thing, or any other thing fit such a name. It was as if the poet had coined the phrase from having seen this one particular region. It must, I thought as I viewed it, be the outcome of a fire; but why had nothing new ever grown over those five acres of grey desolation that sprawled open to the sky like a great spot eaten by acid in the woods and fields? It lay largely to the north of the ancient road line, but encroached a little on the other side. I felt an odd reluctance about approaching, and did so at last only because my business took me through and past it. There was no vegetation of any kind on that broad expanse, but only a fine grey dust or ash which no wind seemed ever to blow about. The trees near it were sickly and stunted, and many dead trunks stood or lay rotting at the rim. As I walked hurriedly by I saw the tumbled bricks and stones of an old chimney and cellar on my right, and the yawning black maw of an abandoned well whose stagnant vapours played strange tricks with the hues of the sunlight. Even the long, dark woodland climb beyond seemed welcome in contrast, and I marvelled no more at the frightened whispers of Arkham people. There had been no house or ruin near; even in the old days the place must have been lonely and remote. And at twilight, dreading to repass that ominous spot, I walked circuitously back to the town by the curving road on the south. I vaguely wished some clouds would gather, for an odd timidity about the deep skyey voids above had crept into my soul.

In the evening I asked old people in Arkham about the blasted heath, and what was meant by that phrase "strange days" which so many evasively muttered. I could not, however, get any good answers, except that all the mystery was much more recent than I had dreamed. It was not a matter of old legendry at all, but something within the lifetime of those who spoke. It had happened in the 'eighties, and a family had disappeared or was killed. Speakers would not be exact; and because they all told me to pay no attention to old Ammi Pierce's crazy tales, I sought him out the next morning, having heard that he lived alone in the ancient tottering cottage where the trees first begin to get thick. It was a fearsomely archaic place, and had begun to exude the faint miasmal odour which clings about houses that have stood too long. Only with persistent knocking could I rouse the aged man, and when he shuffled timidly to the door I could tell he was not glad to see me. He was not so feeble as I had expected; but his eyes drooped in a curious way, and his unkempt clothing and white beard made him seem very worn and dismal. Not knowing just how he could best be launched on his tales, I feigned a matter of business; told him of my surveying, and asked vague questions about the district. He was far brighter and more educated than I had been led to think, and before I knew it had grasped quite as much of the subject as any man I had talked with in Arkham. He was not like other rustics I had known in the sections where reservoirs were to be. From him there were no protests at the miles of old wood and farmland to be blotted out, though perhaps there would have been had not his home lain outside the bounds of the future lake. Relief was all that he shewed; relief at the doom of the dark ancient valleys through which he had roamed all his life. They were better under water now—better under water since the strange days. And with this opening his husky voice sank low, while his body leaned forward and his right forefinger began to point shakily and impressively.

It was then that I heard the story, and as the rambling voice scraped and whispered on I shivered again and again despite the summer day. Often I had to recall the speaker from ramblings, piece out scientific points which he knew only by a fading parrot memory of professors' talk, or bridge over gaps where his sense of logic and continuity broke down. When he was done I did not wonder that his mind had snapped a trifle, or that the folk of Arkham would not speak much of the blasted heath. I hurried back before sunset to my hotel, unwilling to have the stars come out above me in the open; and the next day returned to Boston to give up my position. I could not go into that dim chaos of old forest and slope again, or face another time that grey blasted heath where the black well yawned deep beside the tumbled bricks and stones. The reservoir will soon be built now, and all those elder secrets will be safe forever under watery fathoms. But even then I do not believe I would like to visit that country by night—at least, not when the sinister stars are out; and nothing could bribe me to drink the new city water of Arkham.

It all began, old Ammi said, with the meteorite. Before that time there had been no wild legends at all since the witch trials, and even then these western woods were not feared half so much as the small island in the Miskatonic where the devil held court beside a curious stone altar older than the Indians. These were not haunted woods, and their fantastic dusk was never terrible till the strange days. Then there had come that white noontide cloud, that string of explosions in the air, and that pillar of smoke from the valley far in the wood. And by night all Arkham had heard of the great rock that fell out of the sky and bedded itself in the ground beside the well at the Nahum Gardner place. That was the house which had stood where the blasted heath was to come—the trim white Nahum Gardner house amidst its fertile gardens and orchards.

Nahum had come to town to tell people about the stone, and had dropped in at Ammi Pierce's on the way. Ammi was forty then, and all the queer things were fixed very strongly in his mind. He and his wife had gone with the three professors from Miskatonic University who hastened out the next morning to see the weird visitor from unknown stellar space, and had wondered why Nahum had called it so large the day before. It had shrunk, Nahum said as he pointed out the big brownish mound above the ripped earth and charred grass near the archaic well-sweep in his front yard; but the wise men answered that stones do not shrink. Its heat lingered persistently, and Nahum declared it had glowed faintly in the night. The professors tried it with a geologist's hammer and found it was oddly soft. It was, in truth, so soft as to be almost plastic; and they gouged rather than chipped a specimen to take back to the college for testing. They took it in an old pail borrowed from Nahum's kitchen, for even the small piece refused to grow cool. On the trip back they stopped at Ammi's to rest, and seemed thoughtful when Mrs. Pierce remarked that the fragment was growing smaller and burning the bottom of the pail. Truly, it was not large, but perhaps they had taken less than they thought.

The day after that—all this was in June of '82—the professors had trooped out again in a great excitement. As they passed Ammi's they told him what queer things the specimen had done, and how it had faded wholly away when they put it in a glass beaker. The beaker had gone, too, and the wise men talked of the strange stone's affinity for silicon. It had acted quite unbelievably in that well-ordered laboratory; doing nothing at all and shewing no occluded gases when heated on charcoal, being wholly negative in the borax bead, and soon proving itself absolutely non-volatile at any producible temperature, including that of the oxy-hydrogen blowpipe. On an anvil it appeared highly malleable, and in the dark its luminosity was very marked. Stubbornly refusing to grow cool, it soon had the college in a state of real excitement; and when upon heating before the spectroscope it displayed shining bands unlike any known colours of the normal spectrum there was much breathless talk of new elements, bizarre optical properties, and other things which puzzled men of science are wont to say when faced by the unknown.

Hot as it was, they tested it in a crucible with all the proper reagents. Water did nothing. Hydrochloric acid was the same. Nitric acid and even aqua regia merely hissed and spattered against its torrid invulnerability. Ammi had difficulty in recalling all these things, but recognised some solvents as I mentioned them in the usual order of use. There were ammonia and caustic soda, alcohol and ether, nauseous carbon disulphide and a dozen others; but although the weight grew steadily less as time passed, and the fragment seemed to be slightly cooling, there was no change in the solvents to shew that they had attacked the substance at all. It was a metal, though, beyond a doubt. It was magnetic, for one thing; and after its immersion in the acid solvents there seemed to be faint traces of the Widmannstätten figures found on meteoric iron. When the cooling had grown very considerable, the testing was carried on in glass; and it was in a glass beaker that they left all the chips made of the original fragment during the work. The next morning both chips and beaker were gone without trace, and only a charred spot marked the place on the wooden shelf where they had been.

All this the professors told Ammi as they paused at his door, and once more he went with them to see the stony messenger from the stars, though this time his wife did not accompany him. It had now most certainly shrunk, and even the sober professors could not doubt the truth of what they saw. All around the dwindling brown lump near the well was a vacant space, except where the earth had caved in; and whereas it had been a good seven feet across the day before, it was now scarcely five. It was still hot, and the sages studied its surface curiously as they detached another and larger piece with hammer and chisel. They gouged deeply this time, and as they pried away the smaller mass they saw that the core of the thing was not quite homogeneous.

They had uncovered what seemed to be the side of a large coloured globule imbedded in the substance. The colour, which resembled some of the bands in the meteor's strange spectrum, was almost impossible to describe; and it was only by analogy that they called it colour at all. Its texture was glossy, and upon tapping it appeared to promise both brittleness and hollowness. One of the professors gave it a smart blow with a hammer, and it burst with a nervous little pop. Nothing was emitted, and all trace of the thing vanished with the puncturing. If left behind a hollow spherical space about three inches across, and all thought it probable that others would be discovered as the enclosing substance wasted away.

Conjecture was vain; so after a futile attempt to find additional globules by drilling, the seekers left again with their new specimen—which proved, however, as baffling in the laboratory as its predecessor had been. Aside from being almost plastic, having heat, magnetism, and slight luminosity, cooling slightly in powerful acids, possessing an unknown spectrum, wasting away in air, and attacking silicon compounds with mutual destruction as a result, it presented no identifying features whatsoever; and at the end of the tests the college scientists were forced to own that they could not place it. It was nothing of this earth, but a piece of the great outside; and as such dowered with outside properties and obedient to outside laws.

That night there was a thunderstorm, and when the professors went out to Nahum's the next day they met with a bitter disappointment. The stone, magnetic as it had been, must have had some peculiar electrical property; for it had "drawn the lightning," as Nahum said, with a singular persistence. Six times within an hour the farmer saw the lightning strike the furrow in the front yard, and when the storm was over nothing remained but a ragged pit by the ancient well-sweep, half-choked with caved-in earth. Digging had borne no fruit, and the scientists verified the fact of the utter vanishment. The failure was total; so that nothing was left to do but go back to the laboratory and test again the disappearing fragment left carefully cased in lead. That fragment lasted a week, at the end of which nothing of value had been learned of it. When it had gone, no residue was left behind, and in time the professors felt scarcely sure they had indeed seen with waking eyes that cryptic vestige of the fathomless gulfs outside; that lone, weird message from other universes and other realms of matter, force, and entity.

As was natural, the Arkham papers made much of the incident with its collegiate sponsoring, and sent reporters to talk with Nahum Gardner and his family. At least one Boston daily also sent a scribe, and Nahum quickly became a kind of local celebrity. He was a lean, genial person of about fifty, living with his wife and three sons on the pleasant farmstead in the valley. He and Ammi exchanged visits frequently, as did their wives; and Ammi had nothing but praise for him after all these years. He seemed slightly proud of the notice his place had attracted, and talked often of the meteorite in the succeeding weeks. That July and August were hot, and Nahum worked hard at his haying in the ten-acre pasture across Chapman's Brook; his rattling wain wearing deep ruts in the shadowy lanes between. The labour tired him more than it had in other years, and he felt that age was beginning to tell on him.

Then fell the time of fruit and harvest. The pears and apples slowly ripened, and Nahum vowed that his orchards were prospering as never before. The fruit was growing to phenomenal size and unwonted gloss, and in such abundance that extra barrels were ordered to handle the future crop. But with the ripening came sore disappointment; for of all that gorgeous array of specious lusciousness not one single jot was fit to eat. Into the fine flavour of the pears and apples had crept a stealthy bitterness and sickishness, so that even the smallest of bites induced a lasting disgust. It was the same with the melons and tomatoes, and Nahum sadly saw that his entire crop was lost. Quick to connect events, he declared that the meteorite had poisoned the soil, and thanked heaven that most of the other crops were in the upland lot along the road.

Winter came early, and was very cold. Ammi saw Nahum less often than usual, and observed that he had begun to look worried. The rest of his family, too, seemed to have grown taciturn; and were far from steady in their churchgoing or their attendance at the various social events of the countryside. For this reserve or melancholy no cause could be found, though all the household confessed now and then to poorer health and a feeling of vague disquiet. Nahum himself gave the most definite statement of anyone when he said he was disturbed about certain footprints in the snow. They were the usual winter prints of red squirrels, white rabbits, and foxes, but the brooding farmer professed to see something not quite right about their nature and arrangement. He was never specific, but appeared to think that they were not as characteristic of the anatomy and habit of squirrels and rabbits and foxes as they ought to be. Ammi listened without interest to this talk until one night when he drove past Nahum's house in his sleigh on the way back from Clark's Corners. There had been a moon, and a rabbit had run across the road, and the leaps of the rabbit were longer than either Ammi or his horse liked. The latter, indeed, had almost run away when brought up by a firm rein. Thereafter Ammi gave Nahum's tales more respect, and wondered why the Gardner dogs seemed so cowed and quivering every morning. They had, it developed, nearly lost the spirit to bark.

In February the McGregor boys from Meadow Hill were out shooting woodchucks, and not far from the Gardner place bagged a very peculiar specimen. The proportions of its body seemed slightly altered in a queer way impossible to describe, while its face had taken on an expression which no one ever saw in a woodchuck before. The boys were genuinely frightened, and threw the thing away at once, so that only their grotesque tales of it ever reached the people of the countryside. But the shying of the horses near Nahum's house had now become an acknowledged thing, and all the basis for a cycle of whispered legend was fast taking form.

People vowed that the snow melted faster around Nahum's than it did anywhere else, and early in March there was an awed discussion in Potter's general store in Clark's Corners. Stephen Rice had driven past Gardner's in the morning, and had noticed the skunk-cabbages coming up through the mud by the woods across the road. Never were things of such size seen before, and they had held strange colours that could not be put into any words. Their shapes were monstrous, and the horse had snorted at an odour which struck Stephen as wholly unprecedented. That afternoon several persons drove past to see the abnormal growth, and all agreed that plants of that kind ought never to sprout in a healthy world. The bad fruit of the fall before was freely mentioned, and it went from mouth to mouth that there was poison in Nahum's ground. Of course it was the meteorite; and remembering how strange the men from the college had found that stone to be, several farmers spoke about the matter to them.

One day they paid Nahum a visit; but having no love of wild tales and folklore were very conservative in what they inferred. The plants were certainly odd, but all skunk-cabbages are more or less odd in shape and odour and hue. Perhaps some mineral element from the stone had entered the soil, but it would soon be washed away. And as for the footprints and frightened horses—of course this was mere country talk which such a phenomenon as the aërolite would be certain to start. There was really nothing for serious men to do in cases of wild gossip, for superstitious rustics will say and believe anything. And so all through the strange days the professors stayed away in contempt. Only one of them, when given two phials of dust for analysis in a police job over a year and a half later, recalled that the queer colour of that skunk-cabbage had been very like one of the anomalous bands of light shewn by the meteor fragment in the college spectroscope, and like the brittle globule found imbedded in the stone from the abyss. The samples in this analysis case gave the same odd bands at first, though later they lost the property.

The trees budded prematurely around Nahum's, and at night they swayed ominously in the wind. Nahum's second son Thaddeus, a lad of fifteen, swore that they swayed also when there was no wind; but even the gossips would not credit this. Certainly, however, restlessness was in the air. The entire Gardner family developed the habit of stealthy listening, though not for any sound which they could consciously name. The listening was, indeed, rather a product of moments when consciousness seemed half to slip away. Unfortunately such moments increased week by week, till it became common speech that "something was wrong with all Nahum's folks." When the early saxifrage came out it had another strange colour; not quite like that of the skunk-cabbage, but plainly related and equally unknown to anyone who saw it. Nahum took some blossoms to Arkham and shewed them to the editor of the *Gazette*, but that dignitary did no more than write a humorous article about them, in which the dark fears of rustics were held up to polite ridicule. It was a mistake of Nahum's to tell a stolid city man about the way the great, overgrown mourning-cloak butterflies behaved in connexion with these saxifrages.

April brought a kind of madness to the country folk, and began that disuse of the road past Nahum's which led to its ultimate abandonment. It was the vegetation. All the orchard trees blossomed forth in strange colours, and through the stony soil of the yard and adjacent pasturage there sprang up a bizarre growth which only a botanist could connect with the proper flora of the region. No sane wholesome colours were anywhere to be seen except in the green grass and leafage; but everywhere those hectic and prismatic variants of some diseased, underlying primary tone without a place among the known tints of earth. The Dutchman's breeches became a thing of sinister menace, and the bloodroots grew insolent in their chromatic perversion. Ammi and the Gardners thought that most of the colours had a sort of haunting familiarity, and decided that they reminded one of the brittle globule in the meteor. Nahum ploughed and sowed the ten-acre pasture and the upland lot, but did nothing with the land around the house. He knew it would be of no use, and hoped that the summer's strange growths would draw all the poison from the soil. He was prepared for almost anything now, and had grown used to the sense of something near him waiting to be heard. The shunning of his house by neighbours told on him, of course; but it told on his wife more. The boys were better off, being at school each day; but they could not help being frightened by the gossip. Thaddeus, an especially sensitive youth, suffered the most.

In May the insects came, and Nahum's place became a nightmare of buzzing and crawling. Most of the creatures seemed not quite usual in their aspects and motions, and their nocturnal habits contradicted all former experience. The Gardners took to watching at night—watching in all directions at random for something... they could not tell what. It was then that they all owned that Thaddeus had been right about the trees. Mrs. Gardner was the next to see it from the window as she watched the swollen boughs of a maple against a moonlit sky. The boughs surely moved, and there was no wind. It must be the sap. Strangeness had come into everything growing now. Yet it was none of Nahum's family at all who made the next discovery. Familiarity had dulled them, and what they could not see was glimpsed by a timid woodmill salesman from Bolton who drove by one night in ignorance of the country legends. What he told in Arkham was given a short paragraph in the *Gazette*; and it was there that all the farmers, Nahum included, saw it first.

The night had been dark and the buggy-lamps faint, but around a farm in the valley which everyone knew from the account must be Nahum's the darkness had been less thick. A dim though distinct luminosity seemed to inhere in all the vegetation, grass, leaves, and blossoms alike, while at one moment a detached piece of the phosphorescence appeared to stir furtively in the yard near the barn.

The grass had so far seemed untouched, and the cows were freely pastured in the lot near the house, but toward the end of May the milk began to be bad. Then Nahum had the cows driven to the uplands, after which the trouble ceased. Not long after this the change in grass and leaves became apparent to the eye. All the verdure was going grey, and was developing a highly singular quality of brittleness. Ammi was now the only person who ever visited the place, and his visits were becoming fewer and fewer. When school closed the Gardners were virtually cut off from the world, and sometimes let Ammi do their errands in town. They were failing curiously both physically and mentally, and no one was surprised when the news of Mrs. Gardner's madness stole around.

It happened in June, about the anniversary of the meteor's fall, and the poor woman screamed about things in the air which she could not describe. In her raving there was not a single specific noun, but only verbs and pronouns. Things moved and changed and fluttered, and ears tingled to impulses which were not wholly sounds. Something was taken away—she was being drained of something—something was fastening itself on her that ought not to be—someone must make it keep off—nothing was ever still in the night—the walls and windows shifted. Nahum did not send her to the county asylum, but let her wander about the house as long as she was harmless to herself and others. Even when her expression changed he did nothing. But when the boys grew afraid of her, and Thaddeus nearly fainted at the way she made faces at him, he decided to keep her locked up in the attic. By July she had ceased to speak and crawled on all fours, and before that month was over Nahum got the mad notion that she was slightly luminous in the dark, as he now clearly saw was the case with the nearby vegetation.

It was a little before this that the horses had stampeded. Something had aroused them in the night, and their neighing and kicking in the stalls had been terrible. There seemed virtually nothing to do to calm them, and when Nahum opened the stable door they all bolted out like frightened woodland deer. It took a week to track all four, and when found they were seen to be quite useless and unmanageable. Something had snapped in their brains, and each one had to be shot for its own good. Nahum borrowed a horse from Ammi for his haying, but found it would not approach the barn. It shied, balked, and whinnied, and in the end he could do nothing but drive it into the yard while the men used their own strength to get the heavy wagon near enough the hayloft for convenient pitching. And all the while the vegetation was turning grey and brittle. Even the flowers whose hues had been so strange were greying now, and the fruit was coming out grey and dwarfed and tasteless. The asters and goldenrod bloomed grey and distorted, and the roses and zinneas and hollyhocks in the front yard were such blasphemous-looking things that Nahum's oldest boy Zenas cut them down. The strangely puffed insects died about that time, even the bees that had left their hives and taken to the woods.

By September all the vegetation was fast crumbling to a greyish powder, and Nahum feared that the trees would die before the poison was out of the soil. His wife now had spells of terrific screaming, and he and the boys were in a constant state of nervous tension. They shunned people now, and when school opened the boys did not go. But it was Ammi, on one of his rare visits, who first realised that the well water was no longer good. It had an evil taste that was not exactly foetid nor exactly salty, and Ammi advised his friend to dig another well on higher ground to use till the soil was good again. Nahum, however, ignored the warning, for he had by that time become calloused to strange and unpleasant things. He and the boys continued to use the tainted supply, drinking it as listlessly and mechanically as they ate their meagre and ill-cooked meals and did their thankless and monotonous chores through the aimless days. There was something of stolid resignation about them all, as if they walked half in another world between lines of nameless guards to a certain and familiar doom.

Thaddeus went mad in September after a visit to the well. He had gone with a pail and had come back empty-handed, shrieking and waving his arms, and sometimes lapsing into an inane titter or a whisper about "the moving colours down there." Two in one family was pretty bad, but Nahum was very brave about it. He let the boy run about for a week until he began stumbling and hurting himself, and then he shut him in an attic room across the hall from his mother's. The way they screamed at each other from behind their locked doors was very terrible, especially to little Merwin, who fancied they talked in some terrible language that was not of earth. Merwin was getting frightfully imaginative, and his restlessness was worse after the shutting away of the brother who had been his greatest playmate.

Almost at the same time the mortality among the livestock commenced. Poultry turned greyish and died very quickly, their meat being found dry and noisome upon cutting. Hogs grew inordinately fat, then suddenly began to undergo loathsome changes which no one could explain. Their meat was of course useless, and Nahum was at his wit's end. No rural veterinary would approach his place, and the city veterinary from Arkham was openly baffled. The swine began growing grey and brittle and falling to pieces before they died, and their eyes and muzzles developed singular alterations. It was very inexplicable, for they had never been fed from the tainted vegetation. Then something struck the cows. Certain areas or sometimes the whole body would be uncannily shrivelled or compressed, and atrocious collapses or disintegrations were common. In the last stages—and death was always the result—there would be a greying and turning brittle like that which beset the hogs. There could be no question of poison, for all the cases occurred in a locked and undisturbed barn. No bites of prowling things could have brought the virus, for what live beast of earth can pass through solid obstacles? It must only be natural disease—yet what disease could wreak such results was beyond any mind's guessing. When the harvest came there was not an animal surviving on the place, for the stock and poultry were dead and the dogs had run away. These dogs, three in number, had all vanished one night and were never heard of again. The five cats had left some time before, but their going was scarcely noticed since there now seemed to be no mice, and only Mrs. Gardner had made pets of the graceful felines.

On the nineteenth of October Nahum staggered into Ammi's house with hideous news. The death had come to poor Thaddeus in his attic room, and it had come in a way which could not be told. Nahum had dug a grave in the railed family plot behind the farm, and had put therein what he found. There could have been nothing from outside, for the small barred window and locked door were intact; but it was much as it had been in the barn. Ammi and his wife consoled the stricken man as best they could, but shuddered as they did so. Stark terror seemed to cling around the Gardners and all they touched, and the very presence of one in the house was a breath from regions unnamed and unnamable. Ammi accompanied Nahum home with the greatest reluctance, and did what he might to calm the hysterical sobbing of little Merwin. Zenas needed no calming. He had come of late to do nothing but stare into space and obey what his father told him; and Ammi thought that his fate was very merciful. Now and then Merwin's screams were answered faintly from the attic, and in response to an inquiring look Nahum said that his wife was getting very feeble. When night approached, Ammi managed to get away; for not even friendship could make him stay in that spot when the faint glow of the vegetation began and the trees may or may not have swayed without wind. It was really lucky for Ammi that he was not more imaginative. Even as things were, his mind was bent ever so slightly; but had he been able to connect and reflect upon all the portents around him he must inevitably have turned a total maniac. In the twilight he hastened home, the screams of the mad woman and the nervous child ringing horribly in his ears.

Three days later Nahum lurched into Ammi's kitchen in the early morning, and in the absence of his host stammered out a desperate tale once more, while Mrs. Pierce listened in a clutching fright. It was little Merwin this time. He was gone. He had gone out late at night with a lantern and pail for water, and had never come back. He'd been going to pieces for days, and hardly knew what he was about. Screamed at everything. There had been a frantic shriek from the yard then, but before the father could get to the door, the boy was gone. There was no glow from the lantern he had taken, and of the child himself no trace. At the time Nahum thought the lantern and pail were gone too; but when dawn came, and the man had plodded back from his all-night search of the woods and fields, he had found some very curious things near the well. There was a crushed and apparently somewhat melted mass of iron which had certainly been the lantern; while a bent bail and twisted iron hoops beside it, both half-fused, seemed to hint at the remnants of the pail. That was all. Nahum was past imagining, Mrs. Pierce was blank, and Ammi, when he had reached home and heard the tale, could give no guess. Merwin was gone, and there would be no use in telling the people around, who shunned all Gardners now.

No use, either, in telling the city people at Arkham who laughed at everything. Thad had gone, and now Mernie was gone. Something was creeping and creeping and waiting to be seen and felt and heard. Nahum would go soon, and he wanted Ammi to look after his wife and Zenas if they survived him. It must all be a judgment of some sort; though he could not fancy what for, since he had always walked uprightly in the Lord's ways so far as he knew.

For over two weeks Ammi saw nothing of Nahum; and then, worried about what might have happened, he overcame his fears and paid the Gardner place a visit. There was no smoke from the great chimney, and for a moment the visitor was apprehensive of the worst. The aspect of the whole farm was shocking—greyish withered grass and leaves on the ground, vines falling in brittle wreckage from archaic walls and gables, and great bare trees clawing up at the grey November sky with a studied malevolence which Ammi could not but feel had come from some subtle change in the tilt of the branches. But Nahum was alive, after all. He was weak, and lying on a couch in the low-ceiled kitchen, but perfectly conscious and able to give simple orders to Zenas. The room was deadly cold; and as Ammi visibly shivered, the host shouted huskily to Zenas for more wood. Wood, indeed, was sorely needed; since the cavernous fireplace was unlit and empty, with a cloud of soot blowing about in the chill wind that came down the chimney. Presently Nahum asked him if the extra wood had made him any more comfortable, and then Ammi saw what had happened. The stoutest cord had broken at last, and the hapless farmer's mind was proof against more sorrow.

Questioning tactfully, Ammi could get no clear data at all about the missing Zenas. "In the well—he lives in the well—" was all that the clouded father would say. Then there flashed across the visitor's mind a sudden thought of the mad wife, and he changed his line of inquiry. "Nabby? Why, here she is!" was the surprised response of poor Nahum, and Ammi soon saw that he must search for himself. Leaving the harmless babbler on the couch, he took the keys from their nail beside the door and climbed the creaking stairs to the attic. It was very close and noisome up there, and no sound could be heard from any direction. Of the four doors in sight, only one was locked, and on this he tried various keys on the ring he had taken. The third key proved the right one, and after some fumbling Ammi threw open the low white door.

It was quite dark inside, for the window was small and half-obscured by the crude wooden bars; and Ammi could see nothing at all on the wide-planked floor. The stench was beyond enduring, and before proceeding further he had to retreat to another room and return with his lungs filled with breathable air. When he did enter he saw something dark in the corner, and upon seeing it more clearly he screamed outright. While he screamed he thought a momentary cloud eclipsed the window, and a second later he felt himself brushed as if by some hateful current of vapour. Strange colours danced before his eyes; and had not a present horror numbed him he would have thought of the globule in the meteor that the geologists' hammer had shattered, and of the morbid vegetation that had sprouted in the spring. As it was he thought only of the blasphemous monstrosity which confronted him, and which all too clearly had shared the nameless fate of young Thaddeus and the livestock. But the terrible thing about this horror was that it very slowly and perceptibly moved as it continued to crumble.

Ammi would give me no added particulars to this scene, but the shape in the corner does not reappear in his tale as a moving object. There are things which cannot be mentioned, and what is done in common humanity is sometimes cruelly judged by the law. I gathered that no moving thing was left in that attic room, and that to leave anything capable of motion there would have been a deed so monstrous as to damn any accountable being to eternal torment. Anyone but a stolid farmer would have fainted or gone mad, but Ammi walked conscious through that low doorway and locked the accursed secret behind him. There would be Nahum to deal with now; he must be fed and tended, and removed to some place where he could be cared for.

Commencing his descent of the dark stairs, Ammi heard a thud below him. He even thought a scream had been suddenly choked off, and recalled nervously the clammy vapour which had brushed by him in that frightful room above. What presence had his cry and entry started up? Halted by some vague fear, he heard still further sounds below. Indubitably there was a sort of heavy dragging, and a most detestably sticky noise as of some fiendish and unclean species of suction. With an associative sense goaded to feverish heights, he thought unaccountably of what he had seen upstairs. Good God! What eldritch dream-world was this into which he had blundered? He dared move neither backward nor forward, but stood there trembling at the black curve of the boxed-in staircase. Every trifle of the scene burned itself into his brain. The sounds, the sense of dread expectancy, the darkness, the steepness of the narrow steps—and merciful heaven! . . . the faint but unmistakable luminosity of all the woodwork in sight; steps, sides, exposed laths, and beams alike!

Then there burst forth a frantic whinny from Ammi's horse outside, followed at once by a clatter which told of a frenzied runaway. In another moment horse and buggy had gone beyond earshot, leaving the frightened man on the dark stairs to guess what had sent them. But that was not all. There had been another sound out there. A sort of liquid splash—water—it must have been the well. He had left Hero untied near it, and a buggy-wheel must have brushed the coping and knocked in a stone. And still the pale phosphorescence glowed in that detestably ancient woodwork. God! how old the house was! Most of it built before 1670, and the gambrel roof not later than 1730.

A feeble scratching on the floor downstairs now sounded distinctly, and Ammi's grip tightened on a heavy stick he had picked up in the attic for some purpose. Slowly nerving himself, he finished his descent and walked boldly toward the kitchen. But he did not complete the walk, because what he sought was no longer there. It had come to meet him, and it was still alive after a fashion. Whether it had crawled or whether it had been dragged by any external force, Ammi could not say; but the death had been at it. Everything had happened in the last half-hour, but collapse, greying, and disintegration were already far advanced. There was a horrible brittleness, and dry fragments were scaling off. Ammi could not touch it, but looked horrifiedly into the distorted parody that had been a face. "What was it, Nahum—what was it?" He whispered, and the cleft, bulging lips were just able to crackle out a final answer.

"Nothin' . . . nothin' . . . the colour . . . it burns . . . cold an' wet . . . but it burns . . . it lived in the well . . . I seen it . . . a kind o' smoke . . . jest like the flowers last spring . . . the well shone at night . . . Thad an' Mernie an' Zenas . . . everything alive . . . suckin' the life out of everthing . . . in that stone . . . it must a' come in that stone . . . pizened the whole place . . . dun't know what it wants . . . that round thing them men from the college dug outen the stone . . . they smashed it . . . it was that same colour . . . jest the same, like the flowers an' plants . . . must a' ben more of 'em . . . seeds . . . seeds . . . they growed . . . I seen it the fust time this week . . . must a' got strong on Zenas . . . he was a big boy, full o' life . . . it beats down your mind an' then gits ye . . . burns ye up . . . in the well water . . . you was right about that . . . evil water . . . Zenas never come back from the well . . . can't git away . . . draws ye . . . ye know summ'at's comin', but 'tain't no use . . . I seen it time an' agin senct Zenas was took . . . whar's Nabby, Ammi? . . . my head's no good . . . dun't know how long senct I fed her . . . it'll git her ef we ain't keerful . . . jest a colour . . . her face is gettin' to hev that colour sometimes towards night . . . an' it burns an' sucks . . . it come from some place whar things ain't as they is here . . . one o' them professors said so . . . he was right . . . look out, Ammi, it'll do suthin' more . . . sucks the life out . . ."

But that was all. That which spoke could speak no more because it had completely caved in. Ammi laid a red-checked tablecloth over what was left and reeled out the back door into the fields. He climbed the slope to the ten-acre pasture and stumbled home by the north road and the woods. He could not pass that well from which his horse had run away. He had looked at it through the window, and had seen that no stone was missing from the rim. Then the lurching buggy had not dislodged anything after all—the splash had been something else—something which went into the well after it had done with poor Nahum . . . .

When Ammi reached his house the horse and buggy had arrived before him and thrown his wife into fits of anxiety. Reassuring her without explanations, he set out at once for Arkham and notified the authorities that the Gardner family was no more. He indulged in no details, but merely told of the deaths of Nahum and Nabby, that of Thaddeus already being known, and mentioned that the cause seemed to be the same strange ailment which had killed the livestock. He also stated that Merwin and Zenas had disappeared. There was considerable questioning at the police station, and in the end Ammi was compelled to take three officers to the Gardner farm, together with the coroner, the medical examiner, and the veterinary who had treated the diseased animals. He went much against his will, for the afternoon was advancing and he feared the fall of night over that accursed place, but it was some comfort to have so many people with him.

The six men drove out in a democrat-wagon, following Ammi's buggy, and arrived at the pest-ridden farmhouse about four o'clock. Used as the officers were to gruesome experiences, not one remained unmoved at what was found in the attic and under the red-checked tablecloth on the floor below. The whole aspect of the farm with its grey desolation was terrible enough, but those two crumbling objects were beyond all bounds. No one could look long at them, and even the medical examiner admitted that there was very little to examine. Specimens could be analysed, of course, so he busied himself in obtaining them—and here it develops that a very puzzling aftermath occurred at the college laboratory where the two phials of dust were finally taken. Under the spectroscope both samples gave off an unknown spectrum, in which many of the baffling bands were precisely like those which the strange meteor had yielded in the previous year. The property of emitting this spectrum vanished in a month, the dust thereafter consisting mainly of alkaline phosphates and carbonates.

Ammi would not have told the men about the well if he had thought they meant to do anything then and there. It was getting toward sunset, and he was anxious to be away. But he could not help glancing nervously at the stony curb by the great sweep, and when a detective questioned him he admitted that Nahum had feared something down there—so much so that he had never even thought of searching it for Merwin or Zenas. After that nothing would do but that they empty and explore the well immediately, so Ammi had to wait trembling while pail after pail of rank water was hauled up and splashed on the soaking ground outside. The men sniffed in disgust at the fluid, and toward the last held their noses against the foetor they were uncovering. It was not so long a job as they had feared it would be, since the water was phenomenally low. There is no need to speak too exactly of what they found. Merwin and Zenas were both there, in part, though the vestiges were mainly skeletal. There were also a small deer and a large dog in about the same state, and a number of bones of smaller animals. The ooze and slime at the bottom seemed inexplicably porous and bubbling, and a man who descended on hand-holds with a long pole found that he could sink the wooden shaft to any depth in the mud of the floor without meeting any solid obstruction.

Twilight had now fallen, and lanterns were brought from the house. Then, when it was seen that nothing further could be gained from the well, everyone went indoors and conferred in the ancient sitting-room while the intermittent light of a spectral half-moon played wanly on the grey desolation outside. The men were frankly nonplussed by the entire case, and could find no convincing common element to link the strange vegetable conditions, the unknown disease of livestock and humans, and the unaccountable deaths of Merwin and Zenas in the tainted well. They had heard the common country talk, it is true; but could not believe that anything contrary to natural law had occurred. No doubt the meteor had poisoned the soil, but the illness of persons and animals who had eaten nothing grown in that soil was another matter. Was it the well water? Very possibly. It might be a good idea to analyse it. But what peculiar madness could have made both boys jump into the well? Their deeds were so similar—and the fragments shewed that they had both suffered from the grey brittle death. Why was everything so grey and brittle?

It was the coroner, seated near a window overlooking the yard, who first noticed the glow about the well. Night had fully set in, and all the abhorrent grounds seemed faintly luminous with more than the fitful moonbeams; but this new glow was something definite and distinct, and appeared to shoot up from the black pit like a softened ray from a searchlight, giving dull reflections in the little ground pools where the water had been emptied. It had a very queer colour, and as all the men clustered round the window Ammi gave a violent start. For this strange beam of ghastly miasma was to him of no unfamiliar hue. He had seen that colour before, and feared to think what it might mean. He had seen it in the nasty brittle globule in the aërolite two summers ago, had seen it in the crazy vegetation of the springtime, and had thought he had seen it for an instant that very morning against the small barred window of that terrible attic room where nameless things had happened. It had flashed there a second, and a clammy and hateful current of vapour had brushed past him—and then poor Nahum had been taken by something of that colour. He had said so at the last—said it was like the globule and the plants. After that had come the runaway in the yard and the splash in the well—and now that well was belching forth to the night a pale insidious beam of the same daemoniac tint.

It does credit to the alertness of Ammi's mind that he puzzled even at that tense moment over a point which was essentially scientific. He could not but wonder at his gleaning of the same impression from a vapour glimpsed in the daytime, against a window opening on the morning sky, and from a nocturnal exhalation seen as a phosphorescent mist against the black and blasted landscape. It wasn't right—it was against Nature—and he thought of those terrible last words of his stricken friend, "It come from some place whar things ain't as they is here . . . one o' them professors said so . . . ."

All three horses outside, tied to a pair of shrivelled saplings by the road, were now neighing and pawing frantically. The wagon driver started for the door to do something, but Ammi laid a shaky hand on his shoulder. "Dun't go out thar," he whispered. "They's more to this nor what we know. Nahum said somethin' lived in the well that sucks your life out. He said it must be some'at growed from a round ball like one we all seen in the meteor stone that fell a year ago June. Sucks an' burns, he said, an' is jest a cloud of colour like that light out thar now, that ye can hardly see an' can't tell what it is.

Nahum thought it feeds on everything livin' an' gits stronger all the time. He said he seen it this last week. It must be somethin' from away off in the sky like the men from the college last year says the meteor stone was. The way it's made an' the way it works ain't like no way o' God's world. It's some'at from beyond."

So the men paused indecisively as the light from the well grew stronger and the hitched horses pawed and whinnied in increasing frenzy. It was truly an awful moment; with terror in that ancient and accursed house itself, four monstrous sets of fragments—two from the house and two from the well—in the woodshed behind, and that shaft of unknown and unholy iridescence from the slimy depths in front. Ammi had restrained the driver on impulse, forgetting how uninjured he himself was after the clammy brushing of that coloured vapour in the attic room, but perhaps it is just as well that he acted as he did. No one will ever know what was abroad that night; and though the blasphemy from beyond had not so far hurt any human of unweakened mind, there is no telling what it might not have done at that last moment, and with its seemingly increased strength and the special signs of purpose it was soon to display beneath the half-clouded moonlit sky.

All at once one of the detectives at the window gave a short, sharp gasp. The others looked at him, and then quickly followed his own gaze upward to the point at which its idle straying had been suddenly arrested. There was no need for words. What had been disputed in country gossip was disputable no longer, and it is because of the thing which every man of that party agreed in whispering later on that the strange days are never talked about in Arkham. It is necessary to premise that there was no wind at that hour of the evening. One did arise not long afterward, but there was absolutely none then. Even the dry tips of the lingering hedge-mustard, grey and blighted, and the fringe on the roof of the standing democrat-wagon were unstirred. And yet amid that tense, godless calm the high bare boughs of all the trees in the yard were moving. They were twitching morbidly and spasmodically, clawing in convulsive and epileptic madness at the moonlit clouds; scratching impotently in the noxious air as if jerked by some alien and bodiless line of linkage with subterrene horrors writhing and struggling below the black roots.

Not a man breathed for several seconds. Then a cloud of darker depth passed over the moon, and the silhouette of clutching branches faded out momentarily. At this there was a general cry; muffled with awe, but husky and almost identical from every throat. For the terror had not faded with the silhouette, and in a fearsome instant of deeper darkness the watchers saw wriggling at that treetop height a thousand tiny points of faint and unhallowed radiance, tipping each bough like the fire of St. Elmo or the flames that came down on the apostles' heads at Pentecost. It was a monstrous constellation of unnatural light, like a glutted swarm of corpse-fed fireflies dancing hellish sarabands over an accursed marsh; and its colour was that same nameless intrusion which Ammi had come to recognise and dread. All the while the shaft of phosphorescence from the well was getting brighter and brighter, bringing to the minds of the huddled men a sense of doom and abnormality which far outraced any image their conscious minds could form. It was no longer *shining* out, it was *pouring* out; and as the shapeless stream of unplaceable colour left the well it seemed to flow directly into the sky.

The veterinary shivered, and walked to the front door to drop the heavy extra bar across it. Ammi shook no less, and had to tug and point for lack of a controllable voice when he wished to draw notice to the growing luminosity of the trees. The neighing and stamping of the horses had become utterly frightful, but not a soul of that group in the old house would have ventured forth for any earthly reward. With the moments the shining of the trees increased, while their restless branches seemed to strain more and more toward verticality. The wood of the well-sweep was shining now, and presently a policeman dumbly pointed to some wooden sheds and beehives near the stone wall on the west. They were commencing to shine, too, though the tethered vehicles of the visitors seemed so far unaffected. Then there was a wild commotion and clopping in the road, and as Ammi quenched the lamp for better seeing they realised that the span of frantic greys had broke their sapling and run off with the democrat-wagon.

The shock served to loosen several tongues, and embarrassed whispers were exchanged. "It spreads on everything organic that's been around here," muttered the medical examiner. No one replied, but the man who had been in the well gave a hint that his long pole must have stirred up something intangible. "It was awful," he added. "There was no bottom at all. Just ooze and bubbles and the feeling of something lurking under there." Ammi's horse still pawed and screamed deafeningly in the road outside, and nearly drowned its owner's faint quaver as he mumbled his formless reflections. "It come from that stone . . . it growed down thar . . . it got everything livin' . . . it fed itself on 'em, mind and body . . . Thad an' Mernie, Zenas an' Nabby . . . Nahum was the last . . . they all drunk the water . . . it got strong on 'em . . . it come from beyond, whar things ain't like they be here . . . now it's goin' home . . . ."

At this point, as the column of unknown colour flared suddenly stronger and began to weave itself into fantastic suggestions of shape which each spectator later described differently, there came from poor Hero such a sound as no man before or since ever heard from a horse. Every person in that low-pitched sitting room stopped his ears, and Ammi turned away from the window in horror and nausea. Words could not convey it—when Ammi looked out again the hapless beast lay huddled inert on the moonlit ground between the splintered shafts of the buggy. That was the last of Hero till they buried him next day. But the present was no time to mourn, for almost at this instant a detective silently called attention to something terrible in the very room with them. In the absence of the lamplight it was clear that a faint phosphorescence had begun to pervade the entire apartment. It glowed on the broad-planked floor and the fragment of rag carpet, and shimmered over the sashes of the small-paned windows. It ran up and down the exposed corner-posts, coruscated about the shelf and mantel, and infected the very doors and furniture. Each minute saw it strengthen, and at last it was very plain that healthy living things must leave that house.

Ammi shewed them the back door and the path up through the fields to the ten-acre pasture. They walked and stumbled as in a dream, and did not dare look back till they were far away on the high ground. They were glad of the path, for they could not have gone the front way, by that well. It was bad enough passing the glowing barn and sheds, and those shining orchard trees with the gnarled, fiendish contours; but thank heaven the branches did their worst twisting high up. The moon went under some very black clouds as they crossed the rustic bridge over Chapman's Brook, and it was blind groping from there to the open meadows.

When they looked back toward the valley and the distant Gardner place at the bottom they saw a fearsome sight. All the farm was shining with the hideous unknown blend of colour; trees, buildings, and even such grass and herbage as had not been wholly changed to lethal grey brittleness. The boughs were all straining skyward, tipped with tongues of foul flame, and lambent tricklings of the same monstrous fire were creeping about the ridgepoles of the house, barn, and sheds. It was a scene from a vision of Fuseli, and over all the rest reigned that riot of luminous amorphousness, that alien and undimensioned rainbow of cryptic poison from the well—seething, feeling, lapping, reaching, scintillating, straining, and malignly bubbling in its cosmic and unrecognisable chromaticism.

Then without warning the hideous thing shot vertically up toward the sky like a rocket or meteor, leaving behind no trail and disappearing though a round and curiously regular hole in the clouds before any man could gasp or cry out. No watcher can ever forget that sight, and Ammi stared blankly at the stars of Cygnus, Deneb twinkling above the others, where the unknown colour had melted into the Milky Way. But his gaze was the next moment called swiftly to earth by the crackling in the valley. It was just that. Only a wooden ripping and crackling, not an explosion, as so many others of the party vowed. Yet the outcome was the same, for in one feverish, kaleidoscopic instant there burst up from that doomed and accursed farm a gleamingly eruptive cataclysm of unnatural sparks and substance; blurring the glance of the few who saw it, and sending forth to the zenith a bombarding cloudburst of such coloured and fantastic fragments as our universe must needs disown. Through quickly reclosing vapours they followed the great morbidity that had vanished, and in another second they had vanished too. Behind and below was only a darkness to which the men dared not return, and all about was a mounting wind which seemed to sweep down in black, frore gusts from interstellar space. It shrieked and howled, and lashed the fields and distorted woods in a mad cosmic frenzy, till soon the trembling party realised it would be no use waiting for the moon to shew what was left down there at Nahum's.

Too awed even to hint theories, the seven shaking men trudged back toward Arkham by the north road. Ammi was worse than his fellows, and begged them to see him inside his own kitchen, instead of keeping straight on to town. He did not wish to cross the nighted, wind-whipped woods alone to his home on the main road. For he had had an added shock that the others were spared, and was crushed forever with a brooding fear he dared not even mention for many years to come. As the rest of the watchers on that tempestuous hill had stolidly set their faces toward the road, Ammi had looked back an instant at the shadowed valley of desolation so lately sheltering his ill-starred friend. And from that stricken, far-away spot he had seen something feebly rise, only to sink down again upon the place from which the great shapeless horror had shot into the sky. It was just a colour—but not any colour of our earth or heavens. And because Ammi recognised that colour, and knew that this last faint remnant must still lurk down there in the well, he has never been quite right since.

Ammi would never go near the place again. It is over half a century now since the horror happened, but he has never been there, and will be glad when the new reservoir blots it out. I shall be glad, too, for I do not like the way the sunlight changed colour around the mouth of that abandoned well I passed. I hope the water will always be very deep—but even so, I shall never drink it. I do not think I shall visit the Arkham country hereafter. Three of the men who had been with Ammi returned the next morning to see the ruins by daylight, but there were not any real ruins. Only the bricks of the chimney, the stones of the cellar, some mineral and metallic litter here and there, and the rim of that nefandous well. Save for Ammi's dead horse, which they towed away and buried, and the buggy which they shortly returned to him, everything that had ever been living had gone. Five eldritch acres of dusty grey desert remained, nor has anything ever grown there since. To this day it sprawls open to the sky like a great spot eaten by acid in the woods and fields, and the few who have ever dared glimpse it in spite of the rural tales have named it "the blasted heath."

The rural tales are queer. They might be even queerer if city men and college chemists could be interested enough to analyse the water from that disused well, or the grey dust that no wind seems ever to disperse. Botanists, too, ought to study the stunted flora on the borders of that spot, for they might shed light on the country notion that the blight is spreading—little by little, perhaps an inch a year. People say the colour of the neighbouring herbage is not quite right in the spring, and that wild things leave queer prints in the light winter snow. Snow never seems quite so heavy on the blasted heath as it is elsewhere. Horses—the few that are left in this motor age—grow skittish in the silent valley; and hunters cannot depend on their dogs too near the splotch of greyish dust.

They say the mental influences are very bad, too. Numbers went queer in the years after Nahum's taking, and always they lacked the power to get away. Then the stronger-minded folk all left the region, and only the foreigners tried to live in the crumbling old homesteads. They could not stay, though; and one sometimes wonders what insight beyond ours their wild, weird stores of whispered magic have given them. Their dreams at night, they protest, are very horrible in that grotesque country; and surely the very look of the dark realm is enough to stir a morbid fancy. No traveller has ever escaped a sense of strangeness in those deep ravines, and artists shiver as they paint thick woods whose mystery is as much of the spirit as of the eye. I myself am curious about the sensation I derived from my one lone walk before Ammi told me his tale. When twilight came I had vaguely wished some clouds would gather, for an odd timidity about the deep skyey voids above had crept into my soul.

Do not ask me for my opinion. I do not know—that is all. There was no one but Ammi to question; for Arkham people will not talk about the strange days, and all three professors who saw the aërolite and its coloured globule are dead. There were other globules—depend upon that. One must have fed itself and escaped, and probably there was another which was too late. No doubt it is still down the well—I know there was something wrong with the sunlight I saw above that miasmal brink. The rustics say the blight creeps an inch a year, so perhaps there is a kind of growth or nourishment even now. But whatever daemon hatchling is there, it must be tethered to something or else it would quickly spread. Is it fastened to the roots of those trees that claw the air? One of the current Arkham tales is about fat oaks that shine and move as they ought not to do at night.

What it is, only God knows. In terms of matter I suppose the thing Ammi described would be called a gas, but this gas obeyed laws that are not of our cosmos. This was no fruit of such worlds and suns as shine on the telescopes and photographic plates of our observatories. This was no breath from the skies whose motions and dimensions our astronomers measure or deem too vast to measure. It was just a colour out of space—a frightful messenger from unformed realms of infinity beyond all Nature as we know it; from realms whose mere existence stuns the brain and numbs us with the black extra-cosmic gulfs it throws open before our frenzied eyes.

I doubt very much if Ammi consciously lied to me, and I do not think his tale was all a freak of madness as the townfolk had forewarned. Something terrible came to the hills and valleys on that meteor, and something terrible—though I know not in what proportion—still remains. I shall be glad to see the water come. Meanwhile I hope nothing will happen to Ammi. He saw so much of the thing—and its influence was so insidious. Why has he never been able to move away? How clearly he recalled those dying words of Nahum's—"can't git away . . . draws ye . . . ye know summ'at's comin', but 'tain't no use. . . ." Ammi is such a good old man—when the reservoir gang gets to work I must write the chief engineer to keep a sharp watch on him. I would hate to think of him as the grey, twisted, brittle monstrosity which persists more and more in troubling my sleep.

A NOTE ON THE SELECTION

"THE OLDEST and strongest emotion of mankind is fear," H. P. Lovecraft writes at the opening of his seminal study "Supernatural Horror in Literature."[1] Lovecraft's essay was first published in 1927 in the only issue ever to appear of a little magazine called *The Recluse*, though he continued intermittently to rework and add to the piece for much of his life. "Supernatural Horror in Literature" is a complicated and ambitious work. It is in large part an exercise in historical scholarship: Lovecraft sets out to establish a distinguished pedigree for a branch of literature too often viewed with easy condescension and he finds one that stretches back via Emily Brontë and Dickens through *Doctor Faustus* and the *Morte d'Arthur* to real classic classics like Apuleius and finally (that is, to begin with) to such pseudepigraphical biblical texts as The Book of Enoch (but why not the Bible itself? Job? Or Genesis?) and beyond into the realm of "earliest folklore." But it is also the tribute of a younger writer to his masters—Poe, Bierce, Blackwood, Dunsany prominent among them—as well as a characteristically bravura piece of prose in which favorite words like "horrible" and "hideous" and "noxious" are flaunted with determined abandon. Most importantly, however, from his essay's stark initial proposition on, Lovecraft is

1. See S.T. Joshi's indispensable *The Annotated Supernatural Horror in Literature* (New York: Hippocampus Press, 2000), as well as his critical study *The Weird Tale* (Austin: University of Texas Press, 1990). The author would like to acknowledge his indebtedness to Joshi's unequaled erudition and expertise in all weird things.

working to discern in the shape of the past a way forward for himself. At once apologia and manifesto, the study offers a new understanding of supernatural fiction, or, as he calls it, the "weird tale." In place of the high camp of the Gothic (as it had come to seem as early as *Northanger Abbey*) or the Hallowe'en trappings of the proverbial campfire story, Lovecraft presents himself as the prophet of a new literature born of and suffused with an ancient aura of insuperable and pervasive foundational fear.

Cosmic horror. "The true weird tale," Lovecraft writes, "has something more than a secret murder, bloody bones, or a sheeted form clanking chains according to rule. A certain atmosphere of breathless and unexplainable dread of outer, unknown forces must be present; and there must be a hint, expressed with a seriousness and portentousness becoming its subject, of that most terrible conception of the human brain—a malign and particular suspension or defeat of those fixed laws of Nature which are our only safeguard against the assaults of chaos and daemons of unplumbed space." The familiar scenes of daily life fall away to reveal an unthinkable, encompassing alien dimension that threatens to engulf and destroy everything. It may break out of space or out of time, a pastness or futurity suddenly erupting within or descending upon the present. It may break out of the supposed sanctum of the self—the familiar figure in the mirror abruptly proving itself a stranger, a ghost, a mere host to an entity of some unimagined sort. Or it may emerge in the body like a disease, corrupting its tissues and disorganizing its structures, so that it turns pestilent and repugnant, oozing or crumbling away before our eyes.

The tale of cosmic horror reveals the appalling unnatural essence of nature, something positively indifferent or actively inimical to humanity, which, from the vertiginous perspective thus disclosed, find itself everywhere set apart, outside, undone. There is, as has often been noted, a distinctly gnostic component to Lovecraft's way of thinking, not least in his conception of the writer as an inhuman agent, in communication and possibly in sympathy with those alien dimensions others fear to face. To that extent, the tale of cosmic terror represents a threat, disclosing an unthinkable reality more real than that we know, and its writer is a kind of terrorist, calling the reader to account—an account, however, that can never properly be made, since what we are answerable for and to is, precisely, the unaccountable.

Or so in theory. But of course "we cannot expect all weird tales to conform absolutely to any theoretical model," as Lovecraft sensibly avers. And he recognizes, too, that "much of the choicest weird work is unconscious; appearing in memorable fragments scattered through material whose massed effect may be of a very different cast." (It is curious in this regard that the fascination today with "outsider art" has not been accompanied by a parallel interest in "outsider writing," though a few such texts, most famously Daniel Paul Schreber's *Memoirs of My Nervous Illness*, composed contemporaneously with many of the tales here, have succeeded in imposing themselves on the public consciousness.) For all that, Lovecraft was adamant in his insistence that the best tales of cosmic horror manifest a particular art, a particularly difficult one indeed since the trick is to describe the indescribable, even the unbearable (something which at times threatens to reduce even the most careful examples of the genre to hysterics). "Atmosphere is the all important thing," Lovecraft declares. Not plot. The story will not proceed to a single horrifying revelation, but instead cultivate a state of ongoing suspense that, even when the story is told, should prove next to impossible to dispel. The story prolongs itself as near as it can to the point of the unendurable. Here again one thinks of the images of deliquescence and decay so dear to Lovecraft—images of substances literally fallen, slow-motion pictures of dissolution indistinguishable from the stirrings of some hideous new breed of life.

This collection begins with Poe's "MS. Found in a Bottle" and ends with Lovecraft's "The Colour Out of Space," presenting a selection of weird tales that have established themselves as classics of the genre. In making it I have been guided to a large degree by the recommendations of Lovecraft himself. Thus one finds Algernon Blackwood's "The Willows," Arthur Machen's "The White People," M.P. Shiel's "The House of Sounds," all of which Lovecraft discusses in "Supernatural Horror" and which later he included in a list of favorite weird tales assembled for the magazine *Fantasy Fan*. Walter de la Mare's "Seaton's Aunt" was also a particular favorite. I should say, though, that among the three stories by Ambrose Bierce included here the one Lovecraft liked above all, "The Death of Halpin Frayser," is not to be found. I have chosen instead of that longish story several shorter ones, hoping to represent something of this toughminded, yet elusive writer's unusual range, as well as the influence he exercised on other writers. Thus "The Damned Thing" lurks behind Lovecraft's "The Colour Out of Space," while "An Inhabitant of Carcosa" helped to stimulate Robert Chambers's short story sequence *The King in Yellow* (notable for featuring a range of characters reduced to madness after reading an addictive book entitled—*The King in Yellow*), which is the source of "The Repairer of Reputations." Bierce's story would seem to be a send-up of a communication transmitted in a séance, but, as is often the case in his work, the satirical, the far-fetched, assumes an unlikely life of its own, leaving the reader in doubt as to how to take it, though of course the frantic narrator of the Chambers story takes it very much to heart.

Two of the stories may be thought to have a more tenuous

relation to the central argument of "Supernatural Horror in Literature." Everybody knows of Bram Stoker's *Dracula*, and Lovecraft joins the chorus singing its praises. He doesn't however mention "The Squaw," and it might well be argued that this story is not an example of cosmic horror at all but rather a piece of grisly grand guignol acted out on a historical stage, one that improbably yokes together the Middle Ages, the Wild West, and a couple of—as it turns out quite justifiably—antsy American tourists. But then who is to say that this irruption of inhuman savagery within a historical context that seems almost Disneyfied isn't as cosmic—and telling—an example of horror as any extraterrestrial invasion? Finally there is Henry James, not much admired by Lovecraft, who scolds him for his "prolixity and pomposity," though condescending to praise *The Turn of the Screw*. I have chosen, however, the less-familiar later work "The Jolly Corner," for there James pushes the psychological currency of his fiction to a very weird place indeed.[2]

Lovecraft's disdain for James may in part reflect the antagonism, rapidly widening when he wrote, between writers for popular markets and so-called literary writers. But if there is

2. There are also of course important omissions. Lovecraft writes of William Hope Hodgson's *The Night Land*:

> The picture of a night-black, dead planet, with the remains of the human race concentrated in a stupendously vast metal pyramid and besieged by monstrous, hybrid, and altogether unknown forces of the darkness, is something that no reader can ever forget. Shapes and entities of an altogether non-human and inconceivable sort—the prowlers of the black, man-forsaken, and unexplored world outside the pyramid—are *suggested* and *partly* described with ineffable potency; while the night-bound landscape with its chasms and slopes and dying volcanism takes on an almost sentient terror beneath the author's touch.

Midway through the book the central figure ventures outside the pyramid on a quest through death-haunted realms untrod by man for millions of years—and in his slow, minutely described day-by-day progress over unthinkable leagues of immemorial blackness there is a sense of cosmic alienage, breathless mystery, and terrified expectancy unrivalled in the whole range of literature.

an occasion for issuing this gathering of stories under this cover, it is in hope of contributing somewhat to the subversion of such a distinction. For the works here, long rightly prized by afficionados of horror literature and devotees of Lovecraft, alter our perception of literature and its possibilities. They provide a context, for example, in which James's hypertrophically subtle style may appear to be an efflorescence of the uncanny, and the compulsive, as much as it is an exercise in the high style. Lovecraft duly notes the connection between the weird tale and such varied literary productions as the French *conte cruel* and German *Hausmärchen*, while an affinity may also be seen to exist with Lautréamont and Rimbaud, as well as the surrealists. Or what about a link to Conrad's *Heart of Darkness* or Stephen Crane's *The Black Riders*? Looking further forward yet, one may find a surprising something of Bierce in Borges (who admired Machen), of Chambers in William Burroughs, and of Shiel in Beckett.

The point of such comparisons is not to justify the writers included here by comparison to others anointed, however reluctantly in some cases, by literary powers-that-be, but simply to suggest that the weird story provides a vantage, certainly as central as any, from which to view the landscape, literary and otherwise, of our time. And as well as satisfying the appetite, the work here does raise some interesting critical issues. In the dark corridors and church basements of the Gothic, one discovers not only specters of primal fear, but the dressed-up, artificially stimulated corpse of feudalism capering in the arms of dubiously enlightened young ladies; here, in a variety of stories spanning the divide between the nineteenth and twentieth centuries, stories of exploration, tourism, and invention, one sees a wavering reflection of the Victorian ethos of relentless expansion in that first era of globalization which Karl Polanyi dubbed "the great transformation" (itself a possible title for a further—or ongoing—tale of cosmic horror). Then, too, the sense that there is a secret at the heart of things, as in "Seaton's Aunt," one that is the particular property of an inscrutably malign elite, continues to enjoy an actual relevance even as it feeds the nightmares of paranoids. For that matter "The Colour Out of Space" might be read as foretelling the poisoned environment of the contemporary world. Which is not to detect there, or anywhere in these pages, some agenda of *bien pensant* rectification and amelioration. One of the things that sets the tale of cosmic terror off from run-of-the-mill literary fiction is that, unnerving though it may be, it is happily devoid of moral reflection, much less a moral.

But no doubt the most important achievement of the weird tale is to have kept something, however mutant, of the mythological, in all its awestruck uncertainty and willful speculative farfetchedness, alive. And yet it is not just the strange doings recorded here that capture and hold the attention. In these stories of, among other things, impossible explorations, treacherous inventions, abortive communications, and inscrutable signs, language itself may be pushed towards a kind of impasse—in, for example, the blurtings and babblings of Machen's possessed girl or the maddening echo chamber of Shiel's "House of Sounds," in the way Lovecraft resorts to the barest, most abstract of nouns, "shape" or "thing," to evoke horror at its most inescapably imposing. The effect of both the mythmaking and the verbal invention may at times seem as nearly clumsy as wildly inspired, and yet that variability, and vulnerability, is crucial to the stories' character and art. Certainly it contributes to what must be the strangest and most memorable of their qualities: their weird compassion. Fear may be our "oldest and strongest emotion," but it emerges from these writers' tellings as something more than that, something bigger than us, and something that puts us in touch with bigger—unimaginably bigger—things. Fear is the cement and solvent of this and every world. Even the gods tremble. One thinks of

Melville's oddly tender aside in *Moby-Dick*, another extraordinary exploration of the depths:

> Though in many of its aspects this visible world seems formed in love, the invisible spheres were formed in fright.

—D. THIN

ABOUT THE AUTHORS

AMBROSE BIERCE (1842–1914) was born in Ohio and served in the Civil War. A lifelong journalist, he disappeared mysteriously in Mexico in 1913 while on his way to meet Pancho Villa's army. Among his works are two collections of stories, *Tales of Soldiers and Civilians* and *Can Such Things Be?*, and a brilliant satire, *The Devil's Dictionary*.

ALGERNON BLACKWOOD (1869–1951) was born into an upper-class British family. He emigrated to America at the age of twenty and stayed there some ten years, during which time he worked as a reporter for *The New York Evening Sun* and *The New York Times*. When he returned to England he turned to writing fiction and soon made a name for himself with the John Silence stories, which relate the exploits of a psychic detective. Blackwood became famous in later years for playing "the Ghost Man" on BBC radio.

R.W. CHAMBERS (1865–1933) was born in Brooklyn and studied at the Art Students League and the Ecole des Beaux-Arts, exhibiting in the Salon in 1889. He sold illustrations to fashion magazines in New York City before taking up writing and finding success with his collection of stories *The King in Yellow,* which includes "The Repairer of Reputations." In later life Chambers published a number of highly successful popular novels, including *The Restless Sex* and *Police!!!*, the proceeds from which allowed him to settle in a mansion in upstate New York, where he devoted himself to hunting and fishing.

WALTER DE LA MARE (1876–1956) was one of seven children of an official at the Bank of England. He did not attend university, but worked as a bookkeeper for an oil company for some eighteen years, in the course of which he published the poems and stories that secured his literary reputation. In 1908 a grant from the Civil List allowed him to write full time. De la Mare's fiction includes the novels *The Return* and *The Memoirs of a Midget*, as well as many stories. His poems for children and adults and his brilliantly inventive anthologies were much admired by T. S. Eliot, who became his publisher, and by W. H. Auden.

HENRY JAMES (1843–1916) was born in New York City. His father was a distinguished theologian and a follower of Emanuel Swedenborg; his older brother William James became one of America's finest philosophers. James attended Harvard Law School and, with the encouragement of William Dean Howells, took to writing criticism and fiction. After 1866 he lived largely in Europe. His many works include the novels *A Portrait of a Lady*, *The Wings of the Dove*, *The Ambassadors*, and *The Golden Bowl*, as well as many short stories.

H. P. LOVECRAFT (1890–1937) was born and died in Providence, Rhode Island. His father died of syphilis when he was eight years old; his mother was later institutionalized for mental illness; and Lovecraft himself was a sickly child. In 1913 he joined the United Amateur Press Association, beginning a career as a writer in the course of which he published poems, journalism, and stories. Increasingly drawn to horror fiction, Lovecraft was a regular contributor to the Chicago pulp magazine *Weird Tales*. His first book-length collection of stories, *The Outsider*, did not appear until 1939, two years after his death.

ARTHUR MACHEN (1863–1947) was born in Wales. After failing to gain admission to the Royal College of Surgeons, he worked, not very successfully, as a journalist and translator (most famously of Casanova's memoirs). A friend of the mystic A. E. Waite and a member of the Order of Golden Dawn, Machen was deeply interested in the occult. His fiction includes *The Great God Pan*, *The Three Impostors*, and *The Hill of Dreams*.

EDGAR ALLAN POE (1809–1849) was the son of two traveling actors. Born in Boston, he was orphaned early and adopted by a tobacco exporter in Richmond, Virginia. Poe attended the University of Virginia, which he left because of gambling debts, and West Point, from which he was dishonorably discharged. "MS. Found in a Bottle" was Poe's first significant success, and it helped him to obtain an editorial position on *The Southern Literary Messenger* in Baltimore, though he was soon fired for drinking. Poe married his thirteen-year-old cousin, Virginia, and moved north, where he lived in New York City and Philadelphia while continuing to produce poems, criticism, and stories at a prodigious rate. After his wife's death from tuberculosis, Poe's behavior became increasingly erratic. In 1849 he was found drunk and delirious in a bar in Baltimore, the apparent victim of a political gang that had kept him inebriated while escorting him from ballot station to ballot station to cast repeat votes. He died four days later.

M. P. SHIEL (1865–1947) was born in the West Indies, the son of a Methodist minister of Irish and African descent. Shiel studied classics at King's College London, flirted with medicine, then took up journalism. His most popular work in his lifetime was his novel *The Yellow Danger*, and Shiel, who became increasingly xenophobic over the course of his life, is said to have invented the term "the yellow peril." His best-known work today is the remarkable apocalyptic fantasy *The Purple Cloud*. Described by contemporaries as "gorgeously mad," Shiel had become a reclusive religious maniac by the time of his death. His last book, *Jesus*, remains unpublished.

BRAM STOKER (1847–1912) was born in Dublin and studied mathematics at Trinity College, by which time he was already composing horror stories. He published *Dracula* in 1897. Among Stoker's other books are *The Jewel of Seven Stars* and *The Lair of the White Worm*.

D. THIN was born in Grand Island, Nebraska, and studied in Paris.

OTHER NEW YORK REVIEW CLASSICS

For a complete list of titles, visit www.nyrb.com or write to:
Catalog Requests, NYRB, 435 Hudson Street, New York, NY 10014

J.R. ACKERLEY My Dog Tulip*
J.R. ACKERLEY We Think the World of You*
RENATA ADLER Pitch Dark*
RENATA ADLE R Speedboat*
AESCHYLUS Prometheus Bound; translated by Joel Agee*
DANTE ALIGHIERI The Inferno
KINGSLEY AMIS The Alteration*
KINGSLEY AMIS Dear Illusion: Collected Stories*
KINGSLEY AMIS The Green Man*
KINGSLEY AMIS Lucky Jim*
W.H. AUDEN W.H. Auden's Book of Light Verse
ERICH AUERBACH Dante: Poet of the Secular World
DOROTHY BAKER Cassandra at the Wedding*
DOROTHY BAKER Young Man with a Horn*
J.A. BAKER The Peregrine
S. JOSEPHINE BAKER Fighting for Life*
HONORÉ DE BALZAC The Human Comedy: Selected Stories*
SYBILLE BEDFORD A Legacy*
MAX BEERBOHM The Prince of Minor Writers: The Selected Essays of Max Beerbohm
STEPHEN BENATAR Wish Her Safe at Home*
FRANS G. BENGTSSON The Long Ships*
ADOLFO BIOY CASARES Asleep in the Sun
ADOLFO BIOY CASARES The Invention of Morel
EVE BABITZ Eve's Hollywood*
CAROLINE BLACKWOOD Great Granny Webster*
RONALD BLYTHE Akenfield: Portrait of an English Village*
NICOLAS BOUVIER The Way of the World
EMMANUEL BOVE Henri Duchemin and His Shadows*
MALCOLM BRALY On the Yard*
SIR THOMAS BROWNE Religio Medici and Urne-Buriall*
JOHN HORNE BURNS The Gallery
ROBERT BURTON The Anatomy of Melancholy
CAMARA LAYE The Radiance of the King
GIROLAMO CARDANO The Book of My Life
DON CARPENTER Hard Rain Falling*
BLAISE CENDRARS Moravagine
EILEEN CHANG Love in a Fallen City
EILEEN CHANG Naked Earth
UPAMANYU CHATTERJEE English, August: An Indian Story
NIRAD C. CHAUDHURI The Autobiography of an Unknown Indian
ANTON CHEKHOV The Prank: The Best of Young Chekhov
GABRIEL CHEVALLIER Fear: A Novel of World War I*
JOHN COLLIER Fancies and Goodnights
CARLO COLLODI The Adventures of Pinocchio*
BARBARA COMYNS The Vet's Daughter
ALBERT COSSERY Proud Beggars*

* *Also available as an electronic book.*

HAROLD CRUSE The Crisis of the Negro Intellectual
ASTOLPHE DE CUSTINE Letters from Russia*
LORENZO DA PONTE Memoirs
ELIZABETH DAVID Summer Cooking
L.J. DAVIS A Meaningful Life*
MARIA DERMOÛT The Ten Thousand Things
DER NISTER The Family Mashber
TIBOR DÉRY Niki: The Story of a Dog
ARTHUR CONAN DOYLE The Exploits and Adventures of Brigadier Gerard
CHARLES DUFF A Handbook on Hanging
BRUCE DUFFY The World As I Found It*
DAPHNE DU MAURIER Don't Look Now: Stories
ELAINE DUNDY The Dud Avocado*
G.B. EDWARDS The Book of Ebenezer Le Page
JOHN EHLE The Land Breakers*
MARCELLUS EMANTS A Posthumous Confession
EURIPIDES Grief Lessons: Four Plays; translated by Anne Carson
J.G. FARRELL Troubles*
J.G. FARRELL The Siege of Krishnapur*
J.G. FARRELL The Singapore Grip*
KENNETH FEARING The Big Clock
KENNETH FEARING Clark Gifford's Body
FÉLIX FÉNÉON Novels in Three Lines*
M.I. FINLEY The World of Odysseus
THOMAS FLANAGAN The Year of the French*
SANFORD FRIEDMAN Conversations with Beethoven*
MASANOBU FUKUOKA The One-Straw Revolution*
MARC FUMAROLI When the World Spoke French
CARLO EMILIO GADDA That Awful Mess on the Via Merulana
BENITO PÉREZ GÁLDOS Tristana*
MAVIS GALLANT The Cost of Living: Early and Uncollected Stories*
MAVIS GALLANT Paris Stories*
GABRIEL GARCÍA MÁRQUEZ Clandestine in Chile: The Adventures of Miguel Littín
LEONARD GARDNER Fat City*
ALAN GARNER Red Shift*
WILLIAM H. GASS In the Heart of the Heart of the Country: And Other Stories*
WILLIAM H. GASS On Being Blue: A Philosophical Inquiry*
THÉOPHILE GAUTIER My Fantoms
JEAN GENET Prisoner of Love
ÉLISABETH GILLE The Mirador: Dreamed Memories of Irène Némirovsky by Her Daughter*
JOHN GLASSCO Memoirs of Montparnasse*
P.V. GLOB The Bog People: Iron-Age Man Preserved
NIKOLAI GOGOL Dead Souls*
PAUL GOODMAN Growing Up Absurd: Problems of Youth in the Organized Society*
EDWARD GOREY (EDITOR) The Haunted Looking Glass
JEREMIAS GOTTHELF The Black Spider*
WILLIAM LINDSAY GRESHAM Nightmare Alley*
EMMETT GROGAN Ringolevio: A Life Played for Keeps
VASILY GROSSMAN An Armenian Sketchbook*
VASILY GROSSMAN Life and Fate*
VASILY GROSSMAN The Road*
OAKLEY HALL Warlock

PATRICK HAMILTON The Slaves of Solitude
PATRICK HAMILTON Twenty Thousand Streets Under the Sky
PETER HANDKE Slow Homecoming
ELIZABETH HARDWICK The New York Stories of Elizabeth Hardwick*
ELIZABETH HARDWICK Sleepless Nights*
L.P. HARTLEY The Go-Between*
NATHANIEL HAWTHORNE Twenty Days with Julian & Little Bunny by Papa
ALFRED HAYES In Love*
ALFRED HAYES My Face for the World to See*
PAUL HAZARD The Crisis of the European Mind: 1680–1715*
RUSSELL HOBAN Turtle Diary*
JANET HOBHOUSE The Furies
HUGO VON HOFMANNSTHAL The Lord Chandos Letter*
JAMES HOGG The Private Memoirs and Confessions of a Justified Sinner
RICHARD HOLMES Shelley: The Pursuit*
ALISTAIR HORNE A Savage War of Peace: Algeria 1954–1962*
GEOFFREY HOUSEHOLD Rogue Male*
BOHUMIL HRABAL Dancing Lessons for the Advanced in Age*
BOHUMIL HRABAL The Little Town Where Time Stood Still*
DOROTHY B. HUGHES The Expendable Man*
RICHARD HUGHES A High Wind in Jamaica*
RICHARD HUGHES In Hazard*
INTIZAR HUSAIN Basti*
MAUDE HUTCHINS Victorine
YASUSHI INOUE Tun-huang*
HENRY JAMES The New York Stories of Henry James*
HENRY JAMES The Other House
HENRY JAMES The Outcry
TOVE JANSSON Fair Play *
TOVE JANSSON The Summer Book*
TOVE JANSSON The True Deceiver*
TOVE JANSSON The Woman Who Borrowed Memories: Selected Stories*
RANDALL JARRELL (EDITOR) Randall Jarrell's Book of Stories
DAVID JONES In Parenthesis
JOSEPH JOUBERT The Notebooks of Joseph Joubert; translated by Paul Auster
KABIR Songs of Kabir; translated by Arvind Krishna Mehrotra*
FRIGYES KARINTHY A Journey Round My Skull
ERICH KÄSTNER Going to the Dogs: The Story of a Moralist*
HELEN KELLER The World I Live In
YASHAR KEMAL Memed, My Hawk
RAYMOND KENNEDY Ride a Cockhorse*
DAVID KIDD Peking Story*
ROBERT KIRK The Secret Commonwealth of Elves, Fauns, and Fairies
DEZSŐ KOSZTOLÁNYI Skylark*
TÉTÉ-MICHEL KPOMASSIE An African in Greenland
GYULA KRÚDY The Adventures of Sindbad*
GYULA KRÚDY Sunflower*
SIGIZMUND KRZHIZHANOVSKY Autobiography of a Corpse*
SIGIZMUND KRZHIZHANOVSKY The Letter Killers Club*
SIGIZMUND KRZHIZHANOVSKY Memories of the Future
K'UNG SHANG-JEN The Peach Blossom Fan*
GERT LEDIG The Stalin Front*

PATRICK LEIGH FERMOR Between the Woods and the Water*
PATRICK LEIGH FERMOR The Broken Road*
PATRICK LEIGH FERMOR A Time of Gifts*
PATRICK LEIGH FERMOR A Time to Keep Silence*
PATRICK LEIGH FERMOR The Traveller's Tree*
D.B. WYNDHAM LEWIS AND CHARLES LEE (EDITORS) The Stuffed Owl
SIMON LEYS The Death of Napoleon*
GEORG CHRISTOPH LICHTENBERG The Waste Books
JAKOV LIND Soul of Wood and Other Stories
DWIGHT MACDONALD Masscult and Midcult: Essays Against the American Grain*
NORMAN MAILER Miami and the Siege of Chicago*
CURZIO MALAPARTE Kaputt
CURZIO MALAPARTE The Skin
JANET MALCOLM In the Freud Archives
JEAN-PATRICK MANCHETTE Fatale*
JEAN-PATRICK MANCHETTE The Mad and the Bad*
OLIVIA MANNING Fortunes of War: The Balkan Trilogy*
OLIVIA MANNING Fortunes of War: The Levant Trilogy*
JAMES VANCE MARSHALL Walkabout*
GUY DE MAUPASSANT Afloat
GUY DE MAUPASSANT Alien Hearts*
JAMES McCOURT Mawrdew Czgowchwz*
WILLIAM McPHERSON Testing the Current*
DAVID MENDEL Proper Doctoring: A Book for Patients and Their Doctors*
HENRI MICHAUX Miserable Miracle
JESSICA MITFORD Hons and Rebels
JESSICA MITFORD Poison Penmanship*
NANCY MITFORD The Sun King*
NANCY MITFORD Voltaire in Love*
MICHEL DE MONTAIGNE Shakespeare's Montaigne; translated by John Florio*
HENRY DE MONTHERLANT Chaos and Night
BRIAN MOORE The Lonely Passion of Judith Hearne*
BRIAN MOORE The Mangan Inheritance*
ALBERTO MORAVIA Agostino*
ALBERTO MORAVIA Contempt*
JAN MORRIS Conundrum*
JAN MORRIS Hav*
PENELOPE MORTIMER The Pumpkin Eater*
ÁLVARO MUTIS The Adventures and Misadventures of Maqroll
L.H. MYERS The Root and the Flower*
NESCIO Amsterdam Stories*
DARCY O'BRIEN A Way of Life, Like Any Other
SILVINA OCAMPO Thus Were Their Faces*
RUSSELL PAGE The Education of a Gardener
ALEXANDROS PAPADIAMANTIS The Murderess
BORIS PASTERNAK, MARINA TSVETAYEVA, AND RAINER MARIA RILKE Letters, Summer 1926
CESARE PAVESE The Selected Works of Cesare Pavese
LUIGI PIRANDELLO The Late Mattia Pascal
JOSEP PLA The Gray Notebook
ANDREY PLATONOV The Foundation Pit
ANDREY PLATONOV Happy Moscow
ANDREY PLATONOV Soul and Other Stories